CAPTIVE QUEEN

CROWN OF ELLOVA VOL: 2

SIENNA HARLOW

CONTENTS

What to expect for Captive Queen
May contain minor spoilers

- Sex
- Grief
- Language
- Kidnapping
- Physical violence
- Attempted murder
- Threats of violence
- Near drowning, eels
- Death (ON-page gore)
- Alcohol consumption
- Mentions of past parental deaths
- Sexual harassment (NOT by MMC)
- Verbally abusive brother (on page)
- FMC is slapped across the face (NOT by MMC)
- Pet in a dangerous situation (no animals are harmed)
- Brief mention of pregnancy (NOT the main characters)
- Non-consensual touching under threat of harm (NOT by MMC)
- Child with life-threatening illness receiving experimental magical medical treatment

NOTE: This author and the medical community at large strongly advise against using *anything* other than water-based lubrication for your sexy, fun times. This is a work of magical fiction, and no attempt at recreation should be pursued.

THE MORTAL REALM
KALVORN PALACE
KALVORN
AIRVELL RIVER
LAVENCIA PALACE
TREE PORTAL
THE IRON CASTLE
VENNEEM MOUNTAINS
THE MERAWOOD FOREST
BEGGARS' ROW
THE VERGE
ARANELLE ORPHANAGE
THE FORGE
IZADELLA'S COTTAGE
ADREANIA
THE DIVIDE
ELBASAN SEA

THE FAE REALM
MAP ICONS
THE INK COURT
THE GEM COURT
COURT OF SHELLS
AIRVELL SPRING
AIRVELL LAKE
ALTINIA MOUNTAINS
THE GEM COURT
QUARTZRIDGE
THE INK COURT
ELLOVA
BARDHANA LIBRARY
LAVENCIA
THE HIGH COURT OF ELLOVA
MERIDIA COVE
COURT OF SWORDS
LARISSIAN FORTRESS
CALANTHA MEADOWS
COURT OF SHELLS
COURT OF GREEN
COURT OF GREEN
COURT OF SWORDS
NUEENA'S SHIP

Characters
Izadella: Iz-ah-dell-ah
Leon: Lee-on
Nueena: New-ee-nah
Tavien: Tay-vee-en
Viella: Vie-elle-ah
Lillian: Lil-ee-an
Jedrick: Jed-ricc
Grayden: Grey-din
Zilas: Z-eye-lis
Lyrora: La-roar-ah
Erenia: Ee-re-nee-uh
Hiliyah: Hi-lee-ah
Alachite: Al-luh-kite
Nyvenah: Nye-ven-nah
Camarra: Ka-marr-ah
Kole: Kohl
Everett: Ever-ret
Cyanna: Sigh-anna
Lazalai: Laz-ah-lie
Vaylin: Vay-lynn
Kaylena: Kay-lee-na
Zarella: Zaa-rell-ah
Alvina: Al-vee-nah
Drystan: Dry-stan

Ellova: Ello-vaa
Adreania: Ah-dree-knee-ah
Versairen: Ver-sair-renn
Kalvorn: Cal-vorn
Venneem Mountains: Ven-nee-m
Altinia Mountains: Al-ti-niaa
Bardhana: Bard-ha-na
Lavencia: La-ven-sia
Elbasan Sea: El-bass-ce-nn
Zemra: Zem-rah
Navlue: Nah-vloo
Shyrell: Shai-rell
Lochkiss: Lock-kiss
Vedesdron: Ve-dez-d-ron
Ellovians: Ell-oh-vee-ans

<u>*The High Court of Ellova*</u>
The high fae court
Guardian: Nyvenah, Realm Keeper
Court Color: Purple Capital City: Lavencia
Governs, guides, and oversees all six courts to ensure the safety, wellbeing, and happiness of all Ellovians.
<u>**The Gem Court**</u>
The fae court of artisans
Guardian: Lazalai, Artistry Keeper
Court Color: Yellow Capital City: Quartzridge
Artists, jewelers, perfumers, beaders, leatherworkers, metalwork, painters, potters, carpenters, and sculptors.
<u>**The Ink Court**</u>
The fae court of knowledge
Guardian: Reyna, Scroll Keeper
Court Color: Black Capital City: Bardhana Library
Educators, scholars, healers, scribes, writers, poets, and temple workers.
<u>*Court of Shells*</u>
The fae court of the sea
Guardian: Koray, Wave Keeper
Court Color: Blue Capital City: Meridia Cove
Sea crews, dock workers, fishers, shipowners, sea sentinels, and water guards.
<u>*Court of Green*</u>
The fae court of provisions
Guardian: Camarra, Seed Keeper
Court Color: Green Capital City: Calantha Meadows
Farm keepers, livestock guardians, garden tenders, bakers, chefs, cloudkeepers, and provisions providers.
<u>*Court of Swords*</u>
The fae court of protection
Guardian: Bria, Sword Keeper
Court Color: Red Capital City: Larissian Fortress
Guards, sentinels, blacksmiths, and sentries.

Glossary

Fae: A magical being with powerful qualities. They look similar to mortals but tend to be taller with pointed ears. All fae possess magic and have a lifespan of a thousand years or more, but with enough magic, they can be nearly immortal. How powerful a fae is depends on their bloodline; magic is passed down through birth. Iron will burn to the touch and can kill them.

Mortal: Mortals (also known as humans) possess no magic and have a lifespan of 70–80 years.

Dewling: In Ellova, fae children are considered dewlings until they are 50 years old. A 50-year-old fae would look the same age as a 25-year-old mortal.

Mates: The term used for a committed fae relationship and meant to be a permanent union. A title of respect and claiming, couples must be together for decades before one can state someone is their mate. Matehood doesn't always last forever because fae lives are long, but it's mourned when it ends.

Zemras: Soulbonded mates. This merging of souls exists solely to connect two fae souls on an eternally deeper level for paramount emotional, spiritual, and physical intimacy. Zemras share pain, pleasure, and power.

Zemra Stones: A magic crystal set that can only be found in the Zemra Temple. The physical symbol of their soulbonded matehood, each crystal holds a small part of each other's magic. Through the connection they share with the stones, they can sense each other's emotions and needs. The Zemra magic connects them by soul, magic, and mind.

Zemra Temple: A hidden temple. Veiled in secrecy, but if mates truly believe that they are Zemras, they will attempt to enter the temple. Zemra guides are required to find the temple, and acceptance into the temple is followed by a Zemra ceremony with friends and family. It has age restrictions and laws regarding a visit. Consequences are harsh for even attempting to find it without the blessings of the faes' court Guardians. Unsanctioned visits to the temple resulting in a bond are punished with complete separation for one month.

Zemra Temple Rejection: A fae only has one chance to attempt to access the temple with their mate. If their mate is not their Zemra, the temple will not allow them to enter. A temple rejection is mourned and typically the couple's relationship will end due to the emotional pain of choosing wrong and never being able to find their Zemra.

The Divide: The invisible barrier between the mortal and fae realms, where the Merawood Forest ends and the kingdom of Adreania begins. The Divide was created to stop the stolen fae crown from siphoning all the magic in Ellova.

Merawood Forest: An enchanted forest that protects Ellova. The forest stands between Ellova in the east and the mortal kingdoms to the west.

The Verge: Protective enchantments between the Merawood Forest and Ellova. A vow of no harm to Ellova is needed to enter. It is the only way it will allow anyone to pass through. If a traveler is lying, the Verge rejects their oath.

Realm Keeper: Governs, guides, and oversees all six courts to ensure the safety, well-being, and happiness of all Ellovians. Only the fae with the most power will be accepted by the Ellovian throne.

Lochkiss: If eaten, it grants the ability to speak and hear underwater. It has a gummy texture but no taste. The lochkiss turns water into air. It also gives the ability to control buoyancy. The effects last for weeks.

An enervation death: A fae death by a broken heart. If a fae experiences great heartache like the loss of a child, mate, or Zemra, it can result in shattered magic, which leads to death. Bright white scars spread out over the skin as their magic slowly seeps out of them. There is no healing or recovering from a broken heart. How long the death takes depends on age and how much magic they were born with.

Anafaea flower: Fae flora. The anafaea flower has not been seen in centuries. In the fae history scrolls, it is said it could cure almost anything and force even death to yield to it.

Anafaea Elixir: A healing mixture containing water blutells, anafaea flowers, the salvidah herb, and healing water from the Airvell River as well as other ingredients.

Shyrell: Resting during bloodline bleeding. Magic is passed down through birth. Since any fae bleeding typically displays the possibility of fertility to carry on the magical bloodline, it is a sacred tradition for the heads of the family to bring tea and sweets. The suffering one experiences to one day continue the family's magic is met with gratitude. Bleeding is treated with great care and rest. Fae bloodline bleeding happens once a year.

Jewelsmith: A fae who can manipulate metals.

Sharing shades: A type of claiming through fashion at public events. One way to show others that the couple is spoken for. Formalwear is cut from the same fabrics so the couple will match.

<u>Family Bloodlines</u>

Zarella Verrelia's Family Line
Great-Great-Grandmother: Zarella, First Realm Keeper of Ellova
Great-Grandmother: Lilac
Grandmother: Rose
Mother: Nyvenah - Mated - Father: Alachite
Daughter: Nueena - Zemra: Tavien

Alvina Vanabalt's Family Line

Great-Great-Grandmother: Alvina Vanabalt, the Forger
Great-Grandmother: Naewyn
Grandmother: Voelle
Mother: Ambra - Father: Nolan Aranelle
Daughter: Izadella Aranelle

Fae Queen Inara's Family Line

Mother: Inara, queen of the mortal realm
Married - Drystan Fasaile
Daughter: Arelia

The Broken Royal Mortal Line

Brother to the King: Kalden Fasaile
Past King: Drystan Fasaile - Married - Unknown Queen

Current King of Adreania: King Jedrick
4 deceased sons
Son: Prince Grayden - Married -
Daughter-in-Law: Princess Erenia
Daughter: Princess Lyrora

CROWN OF ELLOVA
VOL: 1 SUMMARY

Izadella is a half-fae/half-mortal jewelry maker who sneaks into the dreary mortal realm of Adreania to sell her jewelry for her last mortal relative, Cyanna, who runs an orphanage there.

Working for King Jedrick is Leon, his healer. Leon and Della have had crushes on each other for years. They see each other once every month at the King's Bazaar but can only speak briefly. The stolen crown Jedrick wears is sucking the life out of the land and making all the mortals sick.

Prince Grayden, Jedrick's son, says he's going to restore the magic to Adreania and plans to go to war with Kalvorn, the neighboring kingdom. Prince Grayden is secretly working with someone from Ellova.

A traitor to the fae realm.

Leon tries to send Della away for her safety, but she refuses, expecting to never see him again. When she is heading home that night, she runs into Jedrick, who has been kidnapped.

The king dies, and Della is forced to wear the crown.

Leon is there, having gone after Jedrick, and Della takes him to her cottage. They share her bed for one night. Della tries to get rid of Leon in the morning, but he refuses to be separated from her.

She also learns she is queen of Adreania because she has the crown.

Della must take Leon to Ellova after they are attacked by Grayden's men. Della uses the crown's magic to save them.

Leon meets Nueena, Della's best friend, and her Zemra, Tavien. Nueena is about to become Ellova's Realm Keeper. Leon also meets Lillian, who is the commander of Ellova's armies. Her mate is Viella, Ellova's spy guardian.

Mortals are forbidden but Leon is allowed to stay.

While he is there, he helps to create the elixir, which they hope will save those who are sick in Adreania. He cannot stay long, though; the magic will drive him to madness.

They also find out the crown is going to kill Izadella.

Izadella, Nueena, Tavien, and Leon go to the market and meet Hiliyah, the royal gown designer. They also meet Kole and his co-captain, Everett. Kole shows romantic interest in Della, but Leon makes it clear Kole's advances are unwelcome.

Della and Leon have deep feelings for each other. She has liked him for so long, but he cannot stay in Ellova so they have nowhere they can be together. Fae can also die of broken hearts and she is scared that when he dies in a few decades it will kill her too, as it did her mother.

Nueena grows the long-lost anafaea flowers, a key ingredient to the elixir, in her magical garden. Camarra, the Court of Green Guardian, has confirmed the rumors of soil not yielding as much as in previous years. They believe the crown may be behind it.

Izadella, Nueena, Tavien, and Leon get the Forger's Journal from the library. The Forger is Della's ancestor who made the crown. Della hopes it has the answer to taking off the crown as it is making her weak.

In the journal they learn that thousands of years ago Zarella, Nueena's ancestor, had forbidden Alvina from making the crown for Inara. Inara fell in love with the evil mortal king Drystan, Grayden's ancestor, and she needed to take magic with her to be his queen. Alvina made her a crown anyway and a glamour ring to hide her fae nature, making her look mortal.

Fae Queen Inara had a child and was killed by her husband. Her daughter was hidden away by Drystan's brother, Prince Kalden, and they were never seen again.

Inside the journal they find the healing salvidah leaves, another ingredient needed for the elixir. Nueena grows it in her greenhouse. Leon and Tavien start making the elixir.

They also learn the crown is a keyed item. That means that an item was created and can only be used/touched by whoever it was keyed to. After the original owner or bloodline dies, the items will choose who can control it.

Della and Leon grow closer and closer, finding it hard to keep their feelings to themselves. They yearn to be together. Leon is fully committed to her but Della is scared.

They go to the Gem Court for one of Nueena's coronation celebrations. They stay in the same room together and are tasked with going to the Airvell Spring. Della and Leon ride on horseback to the spring to collect blutells, the last ingredient for the elixir. To be able to stay underwater for a long time they eat lochkiss, which turns water into air so they can breathe.

Della shows Leon the underwater cave she went to when she was sad as a dewling after the loss of her parents. She tells Leon about how her parents died. Her mom experienced an enervation death, which is death by a broken heart.

Leon pretends to chase her, but the crown takes that as a threat and attacks him. Leon and Della hook up at the bottom of the spring.

Nueena has her celebration.

Della and Leon fight about their relationship. Leon thinks they are Zemras, but mortals cannot withstand the magic.

One week later, Kaylena, Nueena's youngest sister, asks to go to the chocolate shop. Everett is their guard. He protects them when he discovers someone is following Della, which leads them to believe someone knows she has the crown.

Della finds Leon in the garden, they hook up again, and afterwards they are attacked by firefae.

To Sierra, who would go to Mordor with me.
Thank you for the years of effort you put into these books.

CHAPTER 1

*T*he ancient fae garden of Ellova burns.

The firefae who attacked Leon and me, seek the crown, willing to kill for it, die for it.

I choke on the clouds of ash and smoke swirling upward, pulling on the iron net I am trapped in. My jewelsmith blood leaves me untouched by the crimson flames that lap at my arms and legs, but the heat from the blaze strangles me, the fire searing the fabric of my dress.

My burning throat is raw from screaming for Leon through the embers of all the work we have done to create the elixir.

Alarm bells alert everyone of danger, drowning out my agony, but it's going to be too late.

Every precious petal of the lifesaving anafaea flower has been reduced to nothing, and with it, our quest to save the mortals. How many of them will die because of these firefae?

The children of Beggars' Row will be orphaned after the illness takes their parents and Cyanna will not be there to protect them.

This is all my fault.

Ellova was supposed to be safe, as it always has been. How could we have a traitor in our midst willing to help Grayden? What could that terrible king offer an Ellovian to betray us like this?

Leon, bloody and bruised, lies unmoving near the male he killed, flames reflecting off the pools of blood that surround them.

Is he even breathing?

Hot tears stream down my face while I yell his name over and over again.

It *cannot* end like this. We haven't had enough time together, even for what little this life offered to us.

My soul shatters as one of the firefae drags me through the flames away from the only man I've ever loved.

The remaining firefae's fists burn brightly. He laughs, raising his sword, lighting it on fire with his fingers as he walks towards Leon, who is nearly lifeless between us. Dirt flies at my feet, kicked up as I thrash. I beg my powers to rise so I can protect Leon, but the iron net imprisoning me blocks even the crown's magic.

The fire wielder stands above Leon, flaming blade raised. I cannot tear my eyes away, even knowing whatever is about to happen will haunt me forever. I never should have allowed Leon to come to Ellova.

Pure agony erupts in me as the flaming sword swings down.

Leon's eyes open and he rolls sharply towards his attacker, the sword piercing the ground Leon had just been lying on.

Relief knocks the breath out of me. *Please, let us survive this. He needs to know I love him. I will spend any amount of time we have left with him. If death is to take me, it cannot be here, not like this.*

The attacker strikes again but this time he does not miss. He stabs Leon in the abdomen with the burning blade, my wails echoing off the burned garden walls.

Leon stands, clutches his middle for only a moment before he lunges forward and slices his dagger deep across the fire wielder's thighs, blood spraying and drenching the attacker's knees and boots. He curses Leon and falls to the ground, trying to stop the outpour. Before he can cauterize the wound, Leon lands three brutal punches. He grabs the terrified fae by the hair to expose his bobbing throat.

Leon slices it open with my golden dagger.

Light leaves the attacker's eyes as a river of crimson pours over his collar, and Leon shoves the body to the burning floor.

For the first time since the three firefae arrived, hope swirls up within me, but I need to get Leon to a healer. There is only one attacker left! I try to claw at him through the net, scratching and kicking. I imagine vines springing up to strangle him, but the crown's magic is as bound by the iron as my magic is by the crown.

The one dragging me away from my love curses loudly, dropping the locked net I'm ensnared in. My attacker rips off the leather gloves he needed to touch the iron net and stalks away from me, pulling his bow and arrow off his back.

The male's fists burst with flames, and he aims the burning arrow at Leon.

I dig my fingers into the soil, screaming, begging the crown to help, to fight for me, to stop the attack. The world is spinning, but I refuse to faint, painful pressure is building. The flames have spread, and the garden disappears into ash, leaving me choking on the smoke. My eyes sting as if they are on fire.

I will not leave Leon alone to fight. We protect each other. 'Til the end. He may be able to dodge a sword but with his wounded mortal form, he cannot escape a speeding arrow.

Still tangled with the net in the burning soil, and with no magic to answer my call, I launch myself at the back of our attacker's knees with all the force I have in me. The slam knocks him off balance.

The arrow sails beyond Leon, just missing his throat.

Staggering, the male frantically tries to light another arrow, but Leon flies at him, taking him down to the ground with a quickness I've never known my kind mortal to possess. My love wraps his bloodied hands around the fae's neck. The attacker claws at Leon's wounded arm, gasping for air. Leon's beautifully enraged face will be the last thing he sees.

Good.

Leon and I have so few precious moments left, and they tried to take them from us. I turn my head, not needing to witness Leon's revenge.

How did these bastards get in?

Shouts reverberate around the garden's archway before Lillian and Everett burst through. A wave of the High Court protectors, honeyguards, follow them, weapons ready. Lillian runs straight towards Leon, her sword ready. "STOP! WE NEED HIM ALIVE!"

Leon hesitates, getting in one last squeeze, the male's eyes bulging, but he lets go. The firefae coughs, sputtering for breath. Leon pushes off his chest, barely able to stand, holding his bloody and burned arm to his stomach. Archers surround us.

The attacker closes his eyes.

I grapple with the iron net, desperate to reach Leon. Touch him, hold him. Just one touch to prove to my racing heart he is truly all right.

Everett waves his hands in the air and water appears, swirling before him. He moves his arms around in a circle over the garden, releasing it. The water flows like a twisted river, extinguishing the flames as its snakes around the garden, flooding it. Honeyguards search for any other traitors, and the ones who can wield water help to put out the flames all around us.

Tendrils of smoke rise towards the starry night sky that seemed so beautiful minutes ago.

One of the honeyguards pulls at the chainmail net's locked clasp to attempt to release me before I can warn her of what type of metal it is made of, and she yelps in pain when the iron burns her.

Leon is covered in gore but hobbles to me. With his wounded hands, Leon undoes the lock's release, and I am finally free. The crown's magic returns, starting to crush me with its rising wave of unending pressure. Darkness clouds my vision, and I sway. Leon hauls me up, slamming me to his chest.

"You're alive!" I sob all over again, clinging to him with my ear pressed against his rapid heartbeat. His soft lips graze the top of my head, just above the crown. My scalp throbs from when my attacker dragged me down by my hair. The icy fear in my chest melts in his strong, warm arms.

Alive. Alive. Alive.

The sweet relief is overwhelming. If he hadn't been here, they would have taken me. We stare at each other, twin expressions of horror and surprise that we survived. He brushes a thumb across my cheek, smearing the spattered blood there, but I cannot bring myself to care. My vision clears from the tears, and I take in his handsome face, wounded as it is. *He's alive.*

He's alive and I love him.

"Leon, I—"

"Please tell me you're all right." he says, his breathing labored, before his guttural gasp cuts off my confession. Honeyguards shout behind us. Leon spins us and shoves me to the ground as a fireball slams into his side.

I frantically pull away from him only to be met with a new horror as he lies next me, bleeding everywhere. Part of his shirt has been burned away, revealing a new blistering wound on most of his torso. *No!*

I press my hands into the arm the sword sliced open to try to stop the rush of blood, wishing to scream and never stop. "Leon, it's gonna be okay. We have healers!" It can't possibly be comforting to him, as it comes out in a broken sob.

His eyes flutter shut. *No, no, no!*

"LILLIAN, I NEED A HEALER!" I wail, but she cannot help me.

The firefae has escaped the honeyguards. Engulfed in his flames, he lifts his arm to send another fireball at me, but a wave of water from Everett extinguishes the attacker. Lillian blasts her magic at him and tackles him, shoving him into the wet soil. Another honey-guard rips off our attacker's mask and grabs his collar, pulling him towards her. "Who are you?"

He opens his mouth to speak, but blood spills from it in dark rivulets, his head falling backward. She screams in frustration as his body goes limp, the last male who attacked us silenced forever.

Now we will never know who sent them.

She turns to Everett. "Get her out of here! There could be more of them!"

No!

Everett lunges towards me, grabs me around the waist, and tears me away from Leon. The crown's magic is weakened from the iron collar but still reacts to my fear, sending a blast of magic into Everett, who grunts in pain. He stumbles but maintains his footing.

I do not wish to harm my friend. It's clear that he is trying to help me, that I need to be removed for my own safety, but if Leon dies, I need to be there with him! He cannot die alone like this.

My bitter screams of agony turn to rage. "Put me down! Leon! LEON!"

The crushing pain in my chest makes it hard to breathe but still I scream for him. Over and over again.

The archers surrounding us part to let Everett through. When we pass, they close the circle again, blocking Leon and Lillian from my view. He half carries, half drags me away from Leon, who lies unresponsive on the burned soil. I thrash in his arms, my nails dig into his forearms, but it's no use. He is so much stronger and taller than I am.

"There could be more attackers. I have to get you to safety!" Everett says through clenched teeth. "Lillian gave me an order!"

My heel collides with his shin. "Please, please, put me down! *Please*, Everett."

"I'm sorry, Della!" His voice sounds just as broken as mine. *"I'm sorry."*

He races past the scorched statues of Inara, Zarella, and Alvina, continuing past the stone entryway towards the palace. I refuse to stop fighting him. I don't care that he's trying to protect me. I don't care if there are more firefae about to descend on the garden. I need to get back to Leon.

My elbow connects with Everett's nose, and he yelps in pain. Guilt can wait for tomorrow. Right now, he is the only thing keeping me from Leon. I attempt to knock my head back into his nose, but he manages to avoid me.

We collide with something solid and warm, but I don't stop fighting Everett.

"What the fuck is going on!" Tavien towers over us, taking in the sight of my nails marking up Everett's arms around my waist, my torn gown smeared with red. "Is that *your* blood?"

I shake my head, still struggling to break free. "Leon and I were ambushed in the garden. He's still there! I have to get back to him."

Everett is quick to follow my words and tries to move past Tavien. "Lillian gave me an order to get her to safety! Their attackers are dead but there may be more."

Fast as lightning, Tavien waves his arm, magic bursting from him. A glowing sphere of cobalt flames swirl around us like shadows. "Put. Her. Down!" Venom drips from his voice.

Everett growls, "Damn it, Tavien! There could be more attackers! Let me do my job!"

Tavien does not repeat himself, only glaring at Everett 'til he lets out a frustrated breath but slowly releases me. When I touch the ground, my legs give out and I stumble forward, Tavien catching me.

I attempt to flee again but he stops me with an arm around my shoulders, pulling me back against him, holding me up. "Lillian knows what is best. We need to wait for her. She knows how important Leon is to you. She's going to do everything she can for him."

I gasp at the air, but my lungs refuse to cooperate, the anguish of the evening stealing breaths.

Lillian's voice rings out in this distance. "LET'S GO! Healer's Hall, now!"

I sag with relief against Tavien.

Leon is alive. For now.

"The garden." My voice breaks. "It's all destroyed. I'm so sorry." I turn to look up at him.

His gaze softens. "As long as you are all right, that's what matters."

A commotion turns my head towards the small path leading away from the palace, and heels reverberate off the stone. Nueena rushes out, bounding towards us, her eyes never leaving mine. Tavien releases me and my vision goes black for a moment. The shield opens, allowing her to enter, and I nearly collapse into her.

Nueena takes in my blood-covered gown, searching for nonexistent wounds. Her eyes shine furiously. "Who did this to you?"

CHAPTER 2

I shake my head. "All we know about the attackers is that they were firefae. Three of them. Leon was hurt." New torture fractures me. "I'm so, so sorry, Nueena. The garden. It's gone. They destroyed everything."

Nueena blinks away tears and straightens her shoulders. "We will find a way to restore it." She looks past me. "The honeyguards have Leon. Let's follow them."

I spin around, nearly tripping again, and take off running towards the group leaving the garden. The honeyguards are on high alert, surrounding a floating Leon, Lillian running next to him, her magic keeping him suspended. A healer races after them towards the palace, her white healing magic circling him.

"Lillian!" My vision blurs with more tears, but the devastation to his body is clear.

"He's alive! Della, have you been wounded in *any* way?"

"No, no, Leon saved me." I grip his hand. He lies there, frozen by magic, unmoving. Our group moves as one. With a brief blessing from the goddess Ellova, the healer's chambers are not far, just inside the palace back entrance. The fae lights flashing in the hallway let the healers know they are needed immediately.

We are ushered into the first room, Leon's body floating gently to a soft bed. Our escort leaves, and Lillian seals Nueena and Tavien inside with me.

Blood stains tarnish the white marble as Leon's wounds drip into a puddle at my feet.

Every crimson droplet is a reminder he would have died protecting me.

Ashlea, the palace's head healer, rushes towards Leon, cuts open his ruined shirt with her jeweled dagger, and places her tan, tattooed palms on him. Her hands glow as she fills his body with her magic. Light shines out of every wound, highlighting his injuries. His bleeding slows, the wounds knitting back together.

The shine of the healing magic dims, and the angry red blisters of his burned skin slowly fade to pink.

The cerulean-haired healer lowers her glowing hands, glancing around at us. "If I am not mistaken, this man is mortal."

Oh no.

"He is," Nueena says calmly. "I would appreciate your discretion. He poses no harm to Ellova and is here with the High Court's blessing."

Ashlea bows slightly. "Of course. Healing magic works quickly to stop any life-threatening injuries, but severe wounds take more time. I am unfamiliar with mortal anatomy so I cannot offer any promises of a complete recovery, he has lost a staggering amount of blood. Rest is what he needs now."

Leon's shallow breaths slowly even out and that is enough for now, my shoulders drop with relief. "Thank you, Ash."

She pulls up a cushioned stool with the Ink Court's symbol embroidered on it and motions for me to sit next to Leon, reaching out to squeeze my shoulder after I'm seated.

Ashlea waves her hand, and the blood vanishes from Leon and me, our clothing torn but clean. She bows to Nueena before exiting, leaving Lillian, Tavien, Nueena, and me alone with Leon.

What if he doesn't survive this dreadful night? He's mortal. Even fae healing magic might not be enough.

Nueena leans down and wraps her arms around me from

behind. "I need to speak with my parents, but I will be back as soon as I can. They need to know what happened."

I hate to wake them up, to ruin anyone else's night, but I nod.

"Del, I'm incredibly relieved you are safe, that you *both* are."

I place my hands over hers, pulling her tighter. "Thank Ellova you were not there. You could have been hurt."

Nueena lets out a little laugh, "I would have loved to see them try." She kisses the top of my head.

Tavien peers down at Leon. "The two of you found something rare and precious. The time you have together is already not enough. He would not have any of it stolen for something as trivial as death."

I cannot help but smile at his kind words for a moment. "I feel so guilty, Tav. If he hadn't—"

"He and I have not been friends long, but I know what he would say, and I'd tell Nueena the same thing: it was worth it. Leon would not want your guilt. He has fought to stay with you at every turn for this exact reason."

I know he is right, but the guilt eats at me, swallowing me whole. Nueena holds out her hand, and he takes it. They leave together, arm in arm.

Lillian walks over to me with glossy eyes. "This never should have happened. I was a fool for placing too much trust in the safety of the palace." My friend of many years gazes down at Leon. "He has my eternal gratitude for saving you." Her throat bobs.

"Oh, Lil." I stand so I can embrace her. Her arms slowly wrap around me. I've known her for over a hundred years and I have never seen her hold back tears. She is always so stoic and strong, an unbreakable shield, showing softness only to her mate. "You do a wonderful job of protecting Ellova. I have no doubt we will find whoever was responsible for this and make them pay."

She pulls back first. "I will give you time alone with him. I need to go to Viella. I'm sure she's still awake at this hour and will need to be updated on tonight's events." She pats my cheek affectionately. "Try and get some sleep."

I let out a little laugh. "I make no promises."

The door closes with a soft click, and Leon and I are alone. I return to my place beside him.

The peaceful chamber is decorated with soft blue walls and shelves lined with herbs and remedies. A small marble fountain bubbles in the corner, creating a soothing sound. The crystal window outside the door reveals multiple honeyguards standing on alert, amid chairs for visitors lining the wall.

How I wish Farren were here instead of exploring the forest around my cottage. My sweet fox has always been such a comfort when I needed him. Stroking his soft black fur is more calming than any tonic.

I lay my head on Leon's chest and my tears glisten on his skin. *He is going to be all right.* I tell myself this over and over again, but it does nothing to calm my racing heart.

I love Leon, but how can I tell him now?

He deserves to know how deeply I care for him, but if I say it, I cannot take the words back. I know he feels what I do, that he patiently holds back, waiting for me to confess it first. If he knows I love him, if I say those words, he will never leave. No amount of begging or bargaining would convince him to abandon me here.

Just the way my father couldn't—*wouldn't*—stay away from my mother and me. Not even when he forgot who we were, becoming angry, confused, and lost in the Merawood Forest. Or when we were reduced to picnics on the Divide, my mother and me on one side, him on the other.

Leon would rather die—by the burning hands of masked firefae or his own madness consuming his mind—than be parted from me. The guilt of his constant sacrifice is a knife to my gut.

He risked himself, as if my life is more important than his.

He shouldn't have to choose.

No, I cannot tell him what he truly means to me. It will only lead him to destruction.

The sight of him in this room causes my chest to tighten painfully. Eventually, I fall asleep, tears still falling, comforted by his slow, rhythmic heartbeats.

~

*M*ovement startles me awake. "Leon?" I whisper into the darkness.

The dim lights slowly brighten the room, and blinding joy erupts in me when Leon's green eyes flicker open.

"Not exactly the ending to the evening I hoped for." His joke turns into a cough. I find no humor in it, but I try to smile at him. I'm sure it comes out more of a grimace.

"Leon, I cannot express how mournful I am."

He watches me with concerned eyes and pulls my wrist to his mouth. "It's over. You are safe and that is all that matters," he whispers into my skin before pressing a soft kiss there and pulling me into the bed with him. I curl up into his side. It's not all that matters, but arguing with this selfless man is hopeless. Still trembling, I cling to him; his soft strokes down my back are blissful.

I turn my head to rest my chin on his chest, watching him.

The firefae who attacked us could have taken me and the crown. Unless whoever is hunting me knows how to remove this blasted thing, they'd find a way to kill me just to get it off my head. Leon would have died attempting to stop them. If they are working with Grayden, they will use the magic to destroy Kalvorn and possibly Ellova. I shove down the urge to scream and cry and beg Leon to leave here, return to the mortal realm, and find safety away from the affairs of the fae.

"Izadella, stop."

My brows pull together. "Stop what?"

Leon reaches up and rubs my cheek with his thumb. "I know what you're thinking. It's written all over your beautiful face. You want me to leave, don't you?"

He knows me too well.

"Of course, I don't *want* you to but tonight proved you're not safe here."

He shakes his head. "No, tonight proved I was right. You are not as protected in Ellova as you swore you were. Even more reason for me to stay. The only thing that will separate us is time, and even then, I will fight for every last divine second."

I close my eyes and bury my face into him, our bodies pressed together. The emotions that swell within me pour out, and the traitorous tears leave a small splash on his chest as evidence of my breaking heart.

Leon's lips graze my temple and linger there, whispering comfort into my skin. "Oh, strawberries." He pets my head in soft, sweeping motions. "There will always be danger. No place is truly safe, but our futures are entwined. I am meant to be beside you. I am yours, always."

I do not speak, only focusing on his calming touch.

Always.

With his arms wrapped tightly around me, we stay like that for a long while. The terrors of today are seared so deeply within me, only Leon can heal it, parts of me only he can soothe. The words *I love you* balance on the tip of my tongue, but I keep my feelings close to my heart.

CHAPTER 3

The shields lower and a honeyguard pulls open the door to our room.

Leon and I break away from each other, our private moment over. Parting with him leaves an ache, not just from my body, but one deep within my soul that rages to leave Leon's touch. That indescribable sensation demands I keep him close. The same feeling had been drawing us towards each other for years.

Lillian and Viella are the first to arrive. Eyes red-rimmed, Vi throws herself over Leon and me. "I cannot believe this happened, Leon. We are forever grateful you protected Izzy the way you did."

Leon awkwardly pats her on the arm.

Alachite and Nyvenah are not far behind. They rush towards me; their hair still wrapped in silks at the late hour. Tavien and Nueena are close behind.

It brings me such immense solace to be surrounded by so many that I love here.

Nueena places glittering protective wards that flare up around the room, the falling sparkles fading as they touch the floor. I slip from the bed to stand and embrace Nyvenah. She holds me tightly, rocking us with a gentle rhythm. Alachite moves to comfort me, a heavy hand on my shoulders.

"Dewdrop, are you all right?"

"Physically, yes. Leon stopped them from taking me."

Alachite looks from me to Leon. "And you?"

"I'm well enough." With pride in his voice, Leon says, "She helped a great deal, knocked the last attacker over so I could stop him."

I slip from Nyvenah's concerned embrace and sit back on the stool next to Leon. He and I stare at each other for a moment.

Lillian solemnly addresses the room. "We've searched the grounds, and there's no sign of anyone else. We do not yet know who was involved, but guessing from their ability to wield fire, we could assume they're from the Court of Swords."

"Someone knows Izadella has the crown," Leon offers in explanation, rubbing his arm where the magic is healing. "They tried to take it, saying they needed her alive when they were shooting those blasted fireballs at us."

Viella moves up behind me. She hums a soothing song, her fingers heating while she rubs my neck and shoulders. I lean into her tenderness, thankful for her.

"Please tell us everything you remember," Nyvenah asks gently.

Everyone stares at me with varying expressions of concern or anger as I retell all that happened during the attack, and the powers the males used. I do leave out the details of Leon devouring me like a delicacy in the gardens just prior to the firefae descending upon us though.

Lillian sends me an apologetic frown. "You may need to be removed from the palace and brought to a safer location. Somewhere hidden."

"No!" Nueena and I say it at the same time.

They cannot hide me away, not now. The coronation ball is in a few days, and missing Nueena's coronation ceremony would devastate both of us. We've been dreaming about the day she would be crowned Realm Keeper since we were dewlings.

"I know we can all protect her," said Lillian, "especially Nueena, but with the coronation coming up, the attackers will know they are never far from each other. Plus, the entire realm knows

Nueena's schedule for the upcoming events. They could plan another attack at any one of them, knowing Della would be there."

"Whoever attacked them now understands neither Izadella nor the crown are easily stolen," Tavien counters. "More protection should be added, but removal is not the answer. The metal net they used to trap Della was made of iron. It could not have come from Ellova. Whoever is working with King Grayden in the mortal realm, whoever gave him the sacred navlue fruit, must know you have the crown."

"How could anyone have known I have the crown?" I ask. "Nueena glamoured me and I've kept it hidden. The only mortals who have seen me wear it are Grayden's guards, who no longer have memories, if they survived at all. We are missing something."

Grayden will stop at nothing to get back the crown. If he is determined to drag me back to Adreania, maybe I am putting everyone I love in danger.

Whoever Ellova's traitor is, they could use anyone in this room against me. Nausea pulsates in my gut at the thought. Maybe it's safer if I leave, telling no one where I am.

Then everyone will be protected.

"This is the safest place for you, for now," Nyvenah agrees, "but if there is another attack, we must consider hiding you somewhere far away."

Nueena looks at me. "You are *not* allowed to be alone. Tavien or I need to be with you, or you are to be with Lillian or Viella. Lillian, if you have any honeyguards you completely trust, assign them to protection duty."

"Of course."

"Leon did a wonderful job of protecting me," I interject.

Alachite speaks this time. "He did, but this puts him in danger, too. Leon is mortal, and mortality is far more fragile. The head healer told us his injuries should have been life-ending. The palace is safest for Della, but perhaps it's time to have another conversation whether Ellova is the best place for you, Leon. Mortals are not meant to be here and that is just one reason." He gives me a regretful expression.

My shoulders slump from his honesty. A war rises in me—to agree that Leon needs to leave or beg Alachite to take it back—but I cannot argue when his words hold so much truth.

What our attacker said back in the garden swirls in my mind. *"Step away from her and she will not be subjected to the view of your head being removed from your body."*

"No, but she may watch your death if she wishes."

Leon threw himself in front of those evil firefae for me. He killed for me, and he nearly died for me as well.

He softly taps the top of my hand, and I realize I'm squeezing his fingers so hard my knuckles are white. When I try to pull my hand away, he interlaces our fingers and softly sweeps his thumb against my skin to soothe my fraying nerves.

My heart twists at the sight of our joined hands, how he seeks to comfort me as if he is not the one wounded.

"I say this with great respect for all of you," Leon speaks with determination, "but I am not leaving here no matter what risks to my own safety that decision brings. I will not abandon my work on the elixir, nor will I leave Izadella's side."

Alachite looks unconvinced. "You are wounded, Leon. You will not be any good to the mortals, or Della, if you are dead."

"That is *my* decision to make, *my* life. I choose to protect those I care about," Leon says, his jaw tight. "Izadella was adamant I knew all the dangers when I demanded she stay under my protection, wherever she was going. I was the last person to be seen with Adreania's late King Jedrick. There are certainly wanted posters all over the mortal realm with my likeness on them. My life is in no more danger here than it is there. At least in Ellova I can still do some good."

I'm torn apart, wishing him near one moment and gone the next. I know Leon is right; he may not be safe anywhere, but a cold sweat breaks out over my skin at the thought of him risking his life for mine again.

"How soon can the elixir be ready?" Lillian asks Tavien.

Tavien gives me a sympathetic nod before explaining. "We have one small batch that will be ready in a day or so. We will not be able to see what, if any, is salvageable from the gardens 'til morning. Since it was the work of firefae, depending on what type of fire they used, the soil may be ruined as well."

I sigh deeply at Tavien's words, visions of burning flora seared into my soul.

Tavien continues, "If that is the case, we will need to regrow somewhere else if we can, but that garden held great magic from Zarella. It's possible the flowers cannot be grown elsewhere. The batch Leon and I have been developing still needs to be tested. If it is unsuccessful, there will be no need to even try and grow the anafaea again."

"What do you propose?" Nyvenah asks him, but the way she purses her lips tells me she already thinks she won't like his answer.

"We have to ensure the elixir is distributed and is successful. Someone needs to return to the mortal realm."

"We do not need to go further than Beggars' Row," I interject, "and no one needs to stay there."

Nyvenah spins towards her daughter, knowing Nueena too well. "You are *not* going."

"Fine, but we will not abandon the elixir when those who need it can still be saved. Della cannot go; she must be protected from Grayden at all costs. Leon is a wanted man. Tavien is too tall; no one would believe he is mortal were he found. I believe it is safe, but we need to take precautions." She turns to Viella. "Have any of our spies said anything that would lead us to believe they are looking for the fae or planning on bringing one back to Adreania?"

"No. Grayden is planning a disastrous war with Kalvorn, but no mention of any fae or Ellova."

"So, it should be safe for someone to slip in and out?" Nueena says.

"Yes, in theory. That is why I am going," Viella announces casually.

Lillian practically vibrates with irritation at the idea, fists balling at her side, her voice low. "Viella, *please*. Send someone else."

Viella holds up her hand to Lillian, whose face is reddening. "No one knows who I am in Adreania. If anyone spots me, I will appear mortal; I'm shorter than Izzy. You know I've been there before without any trouble. Most importantly, you are forgetting the reason I am Ellova's Spy Guardian, a position, I will remind you, that *you* recommended me for. Yes, my magic will be taken but you know I have spent decades ensuring I know how to defend myself. Most of that training came directly from you. Now, do you think I am incapable of this?"

Lillian is quiet for a long moment before she grits out a low "No. Of course not, but you have other spies. It does not have to be you."

Viella's cheerful disposition fades away. "Anyone else I send will need to be briefed on the situation. Questions will arise. Most of my spies, like many in Ellova, see Adreania as the enemy, not a place filled with oppressed and starving mortals. To them it is the birthplace of Drystan's vile line. Many lost family in the war or they disappeared when Ellova was sealed off to the fae who refused to go to battle. We have a bloody history with the mortals, but innocent lives worth saving are still there. They cannot fight back against Grayden if they are dead, and if we have any hope of getting Izzy on the throne that is rightfully hers, we need allies."

My stomach drops.

I want to be brave, to charge into Adreania and make everything right. To be the ruler they need, but the thought makes me want to run into the forest and never return.

Lillian's tone borders on begging. "Elle, it's dangerous."

She rarely uses Viella's shortened name in front of us. Maybe this conversation is best to happen between the two of them.

"Are you forbidding me from going?" Viella asks, raising one beautiful, sculpted eyebrow.

Lillian turns with a wave of her hand and strides away from her mate. A small drink cart has appeared in the corner, filled with wine, teapots, finger sandwiches, and frosted bottles. She grabs a glass, pours the liquor, and drinks in one long gulp. "No."

"Then unless anyone else has a better idea, we can discuss this in the morning. The coronation is drawing nearer. Let us use this time wisely—figure out who was behind this attack and how they knew about the crown."

Lillian pours another splash of the golden liquor and sits down, defeated. "I'll go with you."

"No, I cannot have my commander and spy guardian both in danger," Nyvenah says, her tone final.

Lillian opens her mouth to argue but takes a long swig instead.

Tavien turns to look at me. "Fire magic may be a Court of Swords trait, but we need to start asking which court stands to gain the most. We know it's not the Gem Court. After Reyna, Lazalai is the Guardian I would trust the most. She loves you like a daughter. She would have come to you first instead of putting you in danger."

Lazalai is not one for power. Most of my court are exceedingly happy in the jeweled temples, creating and crafting, spending time with fellow artisans. We are poets and writers, painters and sculptors.

We are the court of lovers; warriors we are not.

Alachite nods. "If they were all masked, and none here knew the dead, then all Guardians would need to be alerted. Camarra is already here for the coronation. I will send a message to the Court of Swords and Court of Shells. Bria and Koray will need to arrive earlier than expected to be spoken with on the matter."

"I agree." Nyvenah paces around the room. "They should be updated. They need not know the details but should be aware of a hostile new mortal ruler and the potential threat if the two other kingdoms go to war."

"They may not wish for Ellova to involve themselves in the affairs of mortals," Viella says, making two cups of almond tea.

Nyvenah laughs. "That is not for them to decide. They have a sworn duty to protect Ellova. A mortal war would spill into the Merawood Forest, and we risk being discovered once more. Their involvement is not needed if they refuse the call of their Realm Keeper, but the High Court of Ellova has a long memory."

Leon sits up and gingerly gets out of bed, addressing the room. "It's been a long night, and I wish to return to the west wing. Izadella has not slept well, and I am in desperate need of a bath."

I gently place my hand on his arm. "We should wait for a healer."

"No need. Whatever magic she used worked wonders. Any recovery needed can be done in our rooms. You will sleep better in your own bed."

Lillian nods. "I will assign a trusted honeyguard first thing in the morning."

I resign myself to being followed around for the foreseeable future, but I would rather it not be a stranger entangled in my life, even if my anger at Everett has not dissipated. "Can you see if Everett is available?"

"I will ask Koray. If they approve and Everett accepts, he will be at your door tomorrow."

Well, at least I will have a friend nearby.

Nyvenah gives me one last hug and embraces Leon. "Thank you for keeping her safe."

"It is my honor."

CHAPTER 4

*T*avien and Leon walk ahead of us, discussing the elixir, as we leave the Healer's Hall and head to our rooms. Nueena and I trail behind them, our arms tightly locked together, passing by rows of windows in silence.

The stars are fading, the purple sky peeking out in greeting.

After wishing Nueena and Tavien a few hours of rest, Leon and I head straight to my bathing chamber, where I fill the tub with steaming water and soap. Bubbles rise merrily, resistant to our somber mood. "Get in."

He disrobes and I tear off my ruined gown. Hand in hand, we descend into the small steaming pool. A few small balls of dim light illuminate us.

Naked before me, his bruised body on full display, I can see everything he endured. Burn marks are healing but the fresh pink takes up most of his torso. The closed slash on his arm is a reminder of how much he cares for me, but the worst is his stomach, where the burning sword gutted him, leaving behind a twisted, crimson scar. An ache in my throat builds and tightens. He quickly sits on the underwater ledge, pulling me onto his lap.

We face each other but we don't speak, and his palms slide up my waist, touching as much skin as possible before coming up to cup my face.

Our time in the garden before the attack was perfect. *He* was perfect. The memory of his mouth on mine comes rushing back, paired with his strong hands on my hips and his ravenous tongue. I will need to give him a proper thank-you for that mind-blowing orgasm.

And thank him for saving my life.

Our lips meet, his soft and gentle, slowly tasting. Evidence we are both here, safe and whole.

I wrap my arms around his neck, pressing into him, needing skin to skin to remind myself this is real, and he wasn't taken from me.

His touch fills me with a warm lightness and finally allows my heart to stop beating like it's trying to take flight inside my rib cage.

When we break apart, we rest our foreheads together, breathing deeply of each other. Leon's hand goes to the back of my head to bring my lips back to his, but I hiss in pain. My scalp aches.

Leon's eyes go cold. "He hurt you. Why didn't you tell the healer?"

"I will be fine by morning. Please do not fret. It's *you* I'm worried about."

He takes a shuddering breath. "They are all dead." His green eyes go unfocused, his words likely a reminder for himself more so than for me.

"Thank you," I whisper.

His attention returns to me, his hands wandering back to my waist. "Whatever for?"

"You didn't let them take me."

"I would *never* let them take you from me. You have my blood and my blade. Remember? To heal you when you need it, to protect and defend, to care for and serve you in *all* ways. Izadella, you are *my queen,* and I am yours to command. Forever."

"I do not wish for your servitude. I only want you."

"Oh, it is so much more than servitude. It is my utter surrender." His lips brush my cheek. "My only desire." He moves his head and repeats the kiss on the other cheek. "It would *ruin me* if harm ever came to you."

Leon lifts me off him, turns my body away, and draws me back into his lap. He grabs some cleansing oil, and I sigh deeply as he pours the fragrant mixture into my hair. With the gentlest of care, his hands coax away the pain of the evening and melt the tension that had made a dwelling there, all of it dissolving under his tender touch.

I submerge myself to rinse, the pain gone, and then it is his turn. I return to his lap, Leon tugging me closer to him. Bubbles trailing my touch, I move my hands up to his shoulders and through his hair, careful of his newly healed arm.

The ephemeral nature of a mortal existence mocks me with every rhythmic beat of his heart beneath mine.

His stubble is rough against my palms when I cup his face. "You fought so hard to keep me alive tonight but think of what your death would do to me. I know you want to protect me, but you *cannot* die to do so. It would destroy me. You could go through all the trouble of dying to keep me safe just to be the one who lands the final blow when I die of a broken heart. Don't die just to kill me, Leon."

He gapes at me, his beautiful face frozen. I should tell him I love him, to be honest, the way he has always been with me, but tonight does not feel right. So much has been lost.

Whoever seeks the crown knows who I am and whom I love. What lengths will they go to get it back?

We may have no way to save the mortals without the anafaea flower. Without the elixir, without the healing it would bring, the mortals are too weak to stand up to Grayden, too weak to fight.

Grayden will get them all killed in his useless war with Kalvorn.

His quest for revenge and power.

And Leon. Tonight proved how much I need him, but I need him *alive*. He was lucky tonight; he might not be next time.

Mortals are breakable, their lives over in a flash.

There is no path for us that leads to a happy ending.

His death might come from trying to protect me or from the

madness his stubbornness will bring. We may find a way to be happy for a time, but then I would be forced to watch age and decay ravage his body, robbing me of a lifetime with the man I love.

"Well," he says, breaking the silence, "it is a very good thing I have no plans to die. I promise you this: you will have a long and beautiful life ahead of you. I just wish to be a part of it for as long as you will have me."

Our lips meet again, slow and sweet. I can only hope he tastes all the love I have for him even if I cannot speak it. May he know with every touch and taste that I say it in the only way I can right now.

Once we are both clean, we leave the small pool. The water drains, and with it, my hope for the mortals washes away.

He drapes us in plush towels and draws me near again. I cling to him, and he chuckles, leaning down to place a delicate kiss on my forehead.

Leon leads me to my bed, my limbs heavy with exhaustion. He goes to my wardrobe and pulls out a soft sleep dress with two high slits, the color of a summer sunset. Its bright colors are so at odds with the hopelessness that has taken up residence within me.

Ellova has always been safe; it's my home.

Maybe I'm being selfish by staying here, grasping on to the shattered belief in the palace's safety. What if it had been Nueena with me instead of Leon? Would they have tried to kill their future Realm Keeper?

They would have lost that battle, but she still could have gotten hurt.

Leon stands before me. "Lift your arms for me. You need rest."

I do what he asks, overwhelmed with gratitude for him, and he slips the vibrant fabric over me. He pulls back the covers, and I crawl in. The sheets still smell like strawberry and herbs. Leon leaves for the briefest of moments before returning in his own night attire.

Neither of us speaks. He simply pulls back the bedding, gently fanning them out over us.

The crystal lights dim and then fade out, leaving us in darkness.

Before I am able to move to him, demanding his warmth and comfort, one arm reaches around my back and the other hooks a hand under my thigh, pulling me to drape over his naked chest. Callused fingers slowly trace the back of my exposed thigh, his other hand tangles gently in my hair.

A flash of the male who attacked us invades my memory, my tiredness dissolving. *The lifeless body jerks once as Leon pulls my dagger from the ghastly remnants of his eye socket.*

The strands of my hair slip through Leon's fingers as I lift my head, my fae sight revealing the outline of his features painted in shadows. His breaths are easy, body relaxed, a man not about to lose a moment of sleep over the horrors of today.

I will a crystal light to return and he blinks at the sudden glow. "You killed tonight. As a man of medicine, do you have complicated feelings on the matter? Healers are sworn to protect life." I lean my head back in surprise at the sudden smirk that pulls on his lips in the dim light of the single crystal that floats in the corner.

"Did you think my vows to protect and defend you were just pretty words? That the blood seeping into the soil tonight was a vow so easily broken? If I hadn't killed them, they would have taken you, hurt you, maybe worse." He pushes a lock of hair behind my ear. "There is no amount of blood I would not spill to keep you near me."

"I know you think death is a fair price to protect me, but—"

His response is to pull me back down to him, returning me to his chest. "Turn the light back off, Izadella."

He is as infuriating as he is honorable, and I cannot resist him. Once I am nestled against him again, the crystal restores us into darkness, and his hand continues its gentle caress on my body.

"*You* are all I care about. Those men deserved death because they came to harm you. Their deaths were kind. Swift. Full of mercy compared to what they offered me. Had there been time, I would have had them experience pain only a healer's hand can cause. I have studied every detail of the body, spent decades of research on every tendon and ligament, vein and bone. Healers have dark knowledge of the precise ways to slice and break and stitch back together for an *agonizingly* slow death. I know how to keep a soul on the brink of leisurely execution but never granting it the sweet relief of eternal rest."

The violence in what he says, the *truth* in it, steals the breath from my lungs. He means every word. There is nothing he won't do for me, no one he won't kill. I cannot decide if this terrifies me or thrills me. Perhaps both?

I do not have any words in response to that, but we do not need them tonight. My lips find his in the dark and I am met with his mouth, hungry for mine. Leon's arms move around my waist. The bloodshed of the evening fades with each moment in his arms, my sense of safety slowly returning.

We lie there together, limbs and tongues entwined, 'til the press of our lips becomes lazy, and I pull back.

"I—" It almost slips past, that I love him. The words desperate to be let out. In answer, he kisses me one last time before I lay my cheek down on his skin, ready to end the pleasure and pain of today.

His soothing touch and warm body bring me closer to sleep as his hands move over my back in comforting circles, reassuring me I am gifted one more day with him.

I cannot escape the crushing weight that he has my whole heart in his mortal hands. No matter what he does, his death will shatter it, whether it is tomorrow or in fifty years.

Only time will tell if I will survive it.

CHAPTER 5

hen morning finally arrives, I lie in bed for a few minutes longer, wishing I could pretend last night was just a horrible dream, but the scent of burning flora and blood haunts me, my own screams for Leon echoing in my mind.

No matter how warm and safe I am with him, I need to check on Nueena.

Leon still holds me in his sleep, his eyebrows furrowing as I slide out of the soft bed.

Most of his wounds have healed but his skin is still marred with scarring. In the early glow of a new day, my heavy heart weighs me down. Dressing in a simple black dress is a slow task after the events of yesterday. Yellows and golds seem too bright for such a sorrowful morning.

I sit at my vanity; our crumpled sheets reflected in the large mirror. The crown sits atop me, a reminder that safety here is not the promise I once believed. The pain in my head eased during the night. Sections of my hair are braided so it can be wrapped around the circlet, the golden morning sun glinting off it.

If it can only be removed in death, would Grayden wait for the magic to destroy me, or would he kill me the same way his twisted ancestor King Drystan murdered his fae queen, Inara?

Did Drystan pass down the knowledge of how to kill a fae?

Once the crown is hidden with braids and citrine hair pins, I leave my dark thoughts in my rooms, closing the door softly behind me.

Nueena sits alone at the driftwood table in the middle of our living space, her untouched breakfast before her. She's absorbed in Inara's diary and scribbles notes in her perfect calligraphy. She gives me a soft, tired smile when I stand before her. Her attire is curated with a simplistic sadness: a black gown like mine with no embellishments or jewels, and her many braids twisted on the top of her head.

"How are you feeling?" we ask at the same time, laughing lightly at our shared thoughts.

I sigh. "Physically fine. Soul-wise? Like I spent yesterday training in one of Lillian's defense classes and lost every attack. Have you been to the gardens yet?"

Nueena shakes her head, despair in her eyes. "No, no. I was waiting for you. Everyone else is finishing the last of the elixir. My emotions are a pendulum of thinking we can regrow the garden, make it new, but then misery takes over, and I wonder if we have failed before we truly started. It's been quite a morning." She lets out a shaky sigh, and sips her steaming teacup, pushing her plate towards me.

I take two bites of a large flaky pastry filled with savory herb sausages and crispy red potatoes and wrap the rest in cloth for the walk. "Come on; let's go. Dwelling on the what-ifs can hurt more than the truth."

She hesitates for a moment, lips pursed together, eyes drawn downward towards her notes, but she nods.

Halfway to the gardens, I tear the pastry in two and hand her half. We eat in silence, preparing for the morning that awaits us on burnt soil. As we approach, the high wall blocks our view, but the honeyguards' pitiful looks paint a clear picture of destruction. They have been stationed outside all night and report that all has been quiet.

At our presence, the door of thick ivy glides away and the

twisted thorns release from the stone archway. Nueena and I slip our fingers together and hold our breath as the entrance reveals itself.

Soot blankets the statues of our ancestors like a dark tapestry, their enchanted flower crowns consumed by the fire. Rows of scorched soil is all that is left of this divine sanctuary. Even the ivy that climbed up the stone wall has burned away.

The historic scrolls cite this as the birthplace of the fae, and now it is nothing but ash at our feet.

All of the work to supply Adreania with the life-saving elixir is gone. The firefae have cost us the lives of countless mortals. We put weeks of labor into that garden. The hope we had found just burned away, and for what?

A crown that cannot be removed anyway.

The bodies of those who attacked us have been moved, but death lingers in the air. The birds' cheerful songs are missing. The city center sounds of the Lavencia market bring forth a sliver of proof that there is still life and joy in the capital city of Ellova, but here in this once-sacred garden, grief prevails.

I take Nueena's hand and pull her towards the center of the largest garden plot and we sit side by side in the dirt and ashes, knees touching.

We have no words for each other, simply sitting with our sorrow over what has been lost and what was almost taken.

Nueena and I have been friends for over a century, closer than sisters with every passing decade. I've seen every emotion she has, been there for triumphs and failures. She is the other part of my heart, the twin of my soul; her pain is my pain. The evidence of her grief slides down her cheeks in a river of anguish with no way for me to take the hurt from her.

I've rarely seen Nueena cry. One of the last times was when her Zemra ceremony ended and she and Tavien were pulled apart after their last dance. It is a sacred decree that mates must be at least seventy years old to even speak with the temple guardians for the opportunity to prove that they are truly Zemras.

Though it broke Nyvenah's heart, her role as Realm Keeper

demanded by law that she dole out the punishment: any fae found guilty of miraculously completing the Zemra voyage to find the temple before seventy years must be kept apart for one month, isolated from each other.

It was agony to watch. Zemras are never meant to be separated, especially not when the Zemra bond is so new, but Nyvenah is a fair and just ruler whose laws apply to her own dewlings.

Tavien and Nueena knew the cost. They believed in their love so much that they accepted their punishment, but it did not stop her from weeping as they took her from him.

Hopelessness seizes my heart at the sight of her crying again.

This garden and the memories it once held are now tainted and destroyed.

"Let us try to regrow." I attempt to sound encouraging, but we both know firefae magic can have lasting destruction.

Those who are born with the ability to wield it have many different types and shades of flame. Just like Tavien's protective fire, it can be wielded to help and protect, heat homes, and cook meals, but there is also a type of magic that devastates.

A dark ruination that other magic cannot fix.

Nueena nods, and with the clasp of our hands together, we dig our fingers below the ash and dirt in an attempt at what was so wonderful the first time. I call to the crown's magic, and I beg for it to come forward. The crown hums, but the magic cannot. It hits what I can only describe as a wall within me as it attempts to flow into the soil tainted with embers of ruin and the blood of the dead.

Nueena collapses into me, tears turning into sobs as she curls herself into a ball, leaning her head on my thigh. I rub her back but do not offer pretty lies that it will all be right. She deserves my honesty.

When the shaking of her body slows, she finally speaks.

"What if this is a sign that I'm going to be a terrible Realm Keeper?" she whispers.

I stop the rhythmic circles, shocked by her words. "You're going to be an *amazing* Keeper. You were born for this."

"But what if all we did for the elixir was for nothing and we failed? What if the mortals don't want liberation from Grayden? What if the elixir works and they still choose him?"

"I have seen with my own eyes the suffering of the mortals. We will try to give them everything they didn't know they deserved and find a way to see their children thrive, to see communities rebuilt."

My hand returns to soft circles on her back, and she is quiet for a long time.

Nueena sits up, wiping another tear. "It's not just that. I'll be Realm Keeper soon. The entire fae realm will be upon my shoulders, the responsibility of so many. Their lives, their businesses, their well-being. Six courts and countless fae. What if I fail them in ways I didn't even know that I could?"

I see something rare in her golden eyes as she twists her Zemra stone necklace around her finger. Fear.

"Nueena, you could never fail. You are a true leader, and you know the needs of others are just as important as your own. You have led and will continue to lead with kindness and unwavering grace with a heart for justice."

She nods slowly, lost in thought.

"How did we meet?" I ask softly.

She gives me an odd look. "Umm…at the cottage."

I let out a small laugh. "Yes, but why were you, a small dewling, running through a storm in a forest in the middle of night?"

A small smile appears on her full lips. "I went looking for that." She nods towards the crown hidden in my hair.

"Yes, you did. As this tiny dewling, you put the needs of your mother before your own safety. With no thought of the danger, you truly believed you could sneak into a forbidden realm to retrieve a crown your mother needed. It was absolutely foolish to try, but that's who you are."

She remains quiet, so I keep going, needing her to see what I see in this rare moment of doubt. "The Realm of Ellova will thrive with your passion, integrity, and sacrifice."

"So much could go wrong."

"You are never alone. Not everything will be solely on you. You have your family, counselors, advisors, guardians, a literal army, and—" I gently knock my shoulder into hers. "—one very supportive jewelry maker."

A real smile spreads across her beautiful face. "I know. I will never walk this path alone."

"No, you won't. Of that, I am sure." I yank her into my arms, and we hold each other for a long time before we pull apart.

"First task," Nueena says, straightening her back, "we need to clear this cursed soil. Tavien can research ways to purify the garden, if it can be saved at all. The plants will need another month to mature on the vine under moonlight, so this delays the creation of more elixir. Tomorrow, Viella will hand out as many doses as she can to the mortals but cannot give them hope that more is coming. We will need more time for research, time we don't have." She closes her eyes and tilts her head towards the sunlight, basking in the rays. "The elixir will not be enough. Grayden cannot be allowed to stay on that throne. He is going to send his people into a war with Kalvorn to be slaughtered over a crown Kalvorn can neither find nor wield. Princess Lyrora would be next in line to inherit, right?"

"Yes. Grayden and Erenia have no children." I think of all the times we have met, however brief. "Lyrora is kind, beloved by those at court, though I'm not sure how much of her education would be applicable to ruling. I'm sure her brother shoved her away to learn embroidery and proper etiquette."

"And Erenia? What's she like? Anyone is better than Grayden, but I'm curious about his wife and if she shares his values."

"Queen Erenia is just as much of a victim of him as his people are. She may wish to return home to Versairen and rid herself of Adreania entirely. If she stayed, I believe she would offer valuable counsel. I may be Adreania's queen by right of the crown, but it should be Lyrora who takes the throne. It is her birthright."

"If you think she's the best choice, Ellova will support her claim."

"If I reveal myself to have the crown, a bounty of elixirs, and as many fae weapons as Ellova can spare, we may be able to remove him. I would never ask any Ellovian to risk their lives."

"I will not allow you to go unguarded."

Tavien appears with a wave at the gates. Nueena stands and offers her hands to me to pull me up with ease. We dust the ash from our dresses and walk arm in arm to him.

"Good morning, my lovelies," Tavien greets us. "Leon is in the apothecary, finishing up one of the last parts of the elixir." Tavien takes Nueena's face in his hands for a long, tender kiss. Their Zemra stones glow softly at the nearness. I turn my head and watch the doves fly over, small rolls of paper attached to their legs, as they carry letters around the realm.

When they break apart, Tavien keeps his arm wrapped around Nueena and pulls me into them. I lean into his comforting familiar warmth, wrapped in the scent of leather-bound books and Nueena's sweet perfume.

"Are you both all right?" he asks.

Nueena looks at me, determination burning bright in her eyes. "We will be."

CHAPTER 6

ueena, Tavien, and I round the corner that leads to the royal west wing. Everett leans against our front door, waiting.

His nose is bruised where my elbow collided with his face and my stomach sours with guilt. I know he was trying to protect me last night, following a direct order from Lillian and honoring our years of friendship, but all of that logic cannot take away the phantom sensation of panic as he dragged me away from a dying Leon.

He straightens when we reach him, eyebrows pulled down in concern. "I would say good morning, but I don't know how much goodness we will find after last night. Della, how are you feeling?"

"I'm all right. Alive, at least, which is more than I can say for our attackers," I say with a forced smile, jesting to liven the mood.

Everett laughs, but Nueena and Tavien find no humor in it.

"I know Lillian has assigned you as personal guard to Della, but we are returning to our rooms," Tavien says flatly.

Everett smiles brightly. "Nyvenah wishes to speak with her." He turns to me. "I am to escort you there."

I try not to let my face fall. I enjoy Everett's company, always have. If I must have a guard by my side, I'm thankful it's him, but he stands as a reminder that I'm not safe here. That *Leon* is not safe. It will also be harder to hide the crown with him hovering around me, but all I can do is plaster on another smile that doesn't reach my eyes. "Oh, all right. One moment, please."

Their quiet conversation about last night's horrors fades as I walk swiftly into my room. I grab the gift I made for Nyvenah to wear at the coronation off my worktable and wrap it in silk, sending up a quick gratitude prayer to Ellova that I finished it before my magic was taken from me.

Before I can leave, Nueena takes my hand. "Come find me when you return. We have much to discuss."

I nod, and by the subtle smile she gives me, I can only guess she wishes to speak about Leon.

She is probably eager to know if anything has happened between us after last night.

I have much to tell her.

The hallway's marble floors sparkle in the early-morning sunrays through the dome-shaped window, leading to the center of the palace. The top of the market is just in view, the sounds of busy shoppers filtering in with the scent of baking bread and roasting meat. The Realm Keeper's apartments are a few floors above us.

"Everett, I appreciate your willingness to watch over me, but I know you have more important duties."

"What could be more important than your safety?" He tosses back his light brown hair, his sapphire-studded sword swaying at his hip. "The Court of Shells has plenty of other sea sentinels ready for duty. They won't miss me." Everett puts his arm around my shoulders in a friendly gesture, squeezing gently in comfort that I appreciate, but it only makes me miss Leon more. His scent of bergamot and ocean breeze is pleasant, but I long for Leon's tantalizing sweet strawberry and herb that always soothes.

I step away as we reach a spiral staircase, and he removes his arm so we can ascend. He offers me his hand in a gentlemanly gesture, which I accept as I reach the first step, and he follows me up.

"How is your friend? Still with the infirmary's healers?"

Friend.

Leon *is* my friend, but that word no longer fits him. Friendship could no longer encompass the depth of what I feel for him. How much I love him, long for him. What is etched on my soul is exquisite delirium of desire.

"He is well." There is nothing about Leon he needs to know.

Everett is sincere when he says, "Please accept my apologies about last night. I know my obedience to Lillian caused you great distress. That was never my intention. I was terrified seeing you in that burning garden and I just wished to keep you safe."

"I understand. I do." How would I have felt if I arrived only to find my friend in danger? Of course they would be my priority, too. I look back briefly. "Sorry about your nose."

"Oh, that's all right. Do you have any idea why you were attacked?"

His curiosity is warranted but I need to lie. Fast. "Someone is unhappy with the High Court. We believe they were trying to send a message with the garden. It was unfortunate I was there for a late-night stroll."

"Well, I am very glad you are both safe."

When we reach the top of the stairs, Nyvenah's two honey-guards allow me to pass as they always have but quickly cross their spears when Everett attempts to follow me.

"Only family past this point," one of them says with a hint of annoyance.

Everett takes a large step back; his hands raised in front of him in jest. "Of course. I'll wait here." He winks at me, leaning against the railing.

I send Everett a small wave and make my way down the hallway to Nyvenah's rooms. The castle below is buzzing with anticipation for the upcoming coronation ball, but the top floor is peaceful.

I knock, but when no one answers, I enter Nyvenah's and Alachite's personal living space, my heels echoing over the moon-stone floor. Remnants of lunch that have yet to be cleared away, remain on the large dining room table. Wisteria hangs outside over the floor-length oval windows that I pass. The door to their chambers open, a neatly made bed corner peeking into view.

Family portraits and commissioned paintings from the Gem Court cover most of the wall space, with plush cream couches in one corner and a door leading to a large library with vibrant texts just behind it.

"Hello?" I call out from the doorway to her bedroom.

"Here," Nyvenah's kind voice calls out, and I follow it, finding her deep in her closet. Her white hair is down, curls cascading to her knees. She wears the Realm Keepers crown as she always does, made of braided gold with six points of striking craftsmanship. One for each court.

She is looking between two stunningly crafted gowns hanging off the beautiful oak that grows in the middle of the space. One branch displays a light lavender gown, its long sleeves encrusted with crystals swirling down, a heavy skirt at the bottom. The next one is deep purple with a high neckline and short straps that hang off the shoulders with sheer material over the green underdress. The skirt has enchanted green leaves that fan out at the bottom.

"Can't decide?" I ask, taking a seat on a cushioned footstool a few inches from her.

She shakes her head, frowning at the dresses, but focuses on me. "You had quite a terrible night. How are you feeling?"

"I'm all right," I say, placing my head on her hip, her hand quickly coming up to lightly stroke my hair in an affectionate touch that I lean into.

"Leon was very brave, protecting you the way he did. I'm sure it was without hesitation. He truly cares deeply for you."

"He does." My throat tightens but I refuse to cry. Wishing to give her the gift I made for the coronation ball, I change the topic. "Have you decided on jewelry?" I ask, looking at the two dresses. The one with long sleeves is elegant, exactly what one would expect the ruler of a realm to wear to celebrate her daughter's ascension to the throne, but the lighter gown would make dancing easier, leaving room for movement and rhythm in Alachite's arms.

"Not yet. Reyna found a lovely pair of earrings in one of the archives and brought them over this morning." She holds up the jewel-encrusted set.

"It's beautiful! I made you something." I straighten and hold out my gift, which she gingerly unwraps. "I completed it weeks ago, thankfully, before all of this." I wave a hand at the crown on my head and its unwelcome residence.

I try to keep the sadness out of my voice, but her eyes soften at me, so I know she heard it.

Within the silk is a necklace with five purple stones: two dark-purple, pear-shaped ones on the end with two round, smaller, paler gems, one each side. Four stones for her three daughters and me hang down, and in the center, another is so light in color it looks closer to a diamond than an amethyst.

Nyvenah's face brightens with genuine surprise and delight, one hand over her heart. "Oh, Della, this is stunning. Thank you. Help me put it on?"

I stand as she pulls her hair to the side so I can clasp the two ends of the necklace together. She stands in front of a giant mirror and admires it.

"Nueena is blessed to have such a friend."

I laugh a little at that. "No, it's *my* honor to have *her*. She was born for this and is going to make us all very proud."

"That she is." The gloss of Nyvenah's eyes and the pride in her voice brings tears rushing back.

"Nueena's rule in Ellova will be one of honesty, strength, and passionate stewardship of the fae here. You raised a daughter we can believe in." My vision blurs as we smile at each other.

"I have something for you as well." Nyvenah goes into her study and returns to me, holding out a scroll of paper.

Her Realm Keeper seal is pressed deep into the rich gold-and-purple wax that keeps the paper neatly rolled. Unraveling it, I scan the contents, which appear to be some decree.

Henceforth, Leon, healer from Adreania, is now a recognized citizen of Ellova and an honored member of the Ellovian High Court.

"Oh, Nyvenah," I whisper, reading the words over and over again.

"Leon has worked tirelessly to assist with the elixir, and his affections are clear. While I still have many concerns and fear this will end in heartache for you, I do not wish to add to your reluctance with him. I know if Alachite were mortal, I would have taken any time I could with him and gladly mourned for a thousand years for that treasured time." She takes my hand. "You have much to consider: the possibility of a broken heart that leads to an enervation death, the madness, and the dagger of time. Love is not always easy, but it is worth it. I wish to see you happy, like all my dewlings."

I nod, overwhelmed with the decree in my hand. *"Thank you."* It's a broken whisper wrapped in gratitude.

"Nueena knows, but you do not have to mention it to anyone besides her just yet. If you wish to continue to tell him that mortals are still forbidden as a way to protect your heart, I will not say anything, and he can continue believing that. This is your gift to give him, if and when *you* are ready."

We are quiet together for a long time as I reread the words before I throw my arms around her. "Thank you."

She pulls me into a mother's hug, her body swaying back and forth with me cradled against her. "I have a meeting but go find Nueena. The two of you have a long day ahead of you."

~

*E*verett escorts me back to my rooms, but before I can release him from his protection duties, he asks to come in. "Could I get the next book in the series you lent me?"

I know exactly where the book is. It will take no time to pass it over and make up a reason for him to leave so I can find Leon. "Of course. Come on in."

"Thank you."

The main living area is empty, and he follows me inside. "I'll be right back." I'm halfway through the library when his own footsteps follow mine and I wish he stayed in the main entrance.

It feels too intimate for even a friend I care deeply about.

This is Leon's space. A place for soft touches and sweet, stolen moments. *Our space.* Our sanctuary from impending madness and murderous crowns.

I quickly move to the small bookshelf in my room and find the next book in the series. It's one of my favorites, plenty of action and adventure. I grab the worn leather book, and when I turn around, I find him standing before me, surprisingly close.

His eyes are brimming with soft concern. "Della, sleep abandoned me last night. I kept thinking of the garden on fire and you in the flames. You could've been seriously hurt or—" He doesn't manage to finish the sentence.

Killed.

I open my mouth to speak, but he rushes to finish.

"I know this is your home, but after what happened in the market and then the garden and now Lillian assigning me as your protector...maybe this isn't the place for you anymore." He takes my hand, his thumb caressing my knuckle. "I can keep you safe."

It's sweet that he cares, but I slip my hand out of his. "I may not be safe here, but there is nowhere else I would rather be." He cannot offer me any more protection than I have now, but it is a kind offer from a trusted friend. "I will not leave my home so close to the coronation unless Nueena thinks it is necessary." I press the book into his chest and leave the room, knowing he will follow.

"I can take you to the Court of Shells' seaside manor. I know a village nearby we can hide away in. Please. We can take Farren too. He will love chasing those little blue crabs."

My heart clenches at the mention of Farren. He would adore a new place to explore.

I hesitate. Maybe it would be for the best. I could be putting everyone in danger. Some of Grayden's traitorous firefae allies may be dead, but he will find more, if he hasn't already. They are willing to kill to get me, no matter who I am with.

Am I selfish for staying?

My stomach sinks. I cannot ask anyone else this question or they will rush to reassure me I am not, even if it is a lie.

"I will leave that decision up to Nueena and Nyvenah. If they say it's best I leave, I will consider it. Lillian has already made that suggestion and it was rejected."

Everett purses his lips and nods. "If you change your mind, let me know. Lillian said you are safe in your room, but I will be near should you need me."

He leaves but his words bring new dismay.

The elixir is nearly complete and so is Leon's role in it. He has proven he would rather go mad than be parted from me. Maybe I need to make a choice for the both of us to keep us alive, even if it means not being able to say goodbye.

CHAPTER 7

As the day goes on, my eyes wander to the front door increasingly wondering when Leon will be back. Tavien had spent the past few hours with him as they finished the last of the elixir for Viella to take tonight and Leon did not return to our rooms with him.

I give up on waiting and head towards the temporary apothecary. The early-afternoon sunbeams illuminate the hallway in golden yellows.

A dull throb starts at the back of my head, crawling up towards the crown, and I rub the back of my neck to try and ease the discomfort.

I knock lightly, a little worried he might not want company or a distraction, but unable to stay away. A piece of me was missing even though he was only down the hall, an emptiness sitting within me whenever he wasn't near. All the warnings to keep him at a distance had failed—not to fall for a mortal who would be leaving soon, whom there was no future with; and we needed to discuss what we did in the garden, and how it needs to not happen again.

The attack only showed me how dangerous this place is for him.

The wooden door opens wide, and Leon is there with a smile on his face. I can't help returning it, my heart skipping at his stare.

"Hi," I whisper.

"Well, hello. How are you?" he asks. His black and gray hair is ruffled, and his first few buttons undone to reveal a dusting of dark hair over a smooth chest. His sleeves are rolled up too, with a few ink stains on his hands.

Gods, he is so beautiful. And kind and patient and protective. Everything that he is just makes me want him more, pulling me deeper into this unexpected bond.

"Good, good, yeah, great, great." My face heats and I know my traitorous cheeks are turning pink.

His smile widens at my flustered response. I know he can tell I'm staring at his lips.

"Would you like to come in? An attendant brought some breakfast and tea a while ago. I'm sure it's cold by now, but probably still good."

I shake my head. "All the teapots are enchanted. They will stay hot forever if left alone. Never a cold teacup in Ellova."

"Now that is delightfully helpful. I do not know how I'm expected to leave a place where the tea is never cold. This is truly paradise." He means it in jest, but the joke hurts my heart. My attempt to step into the room is blocked when he doesn't move away from the door, so I end up close to him. I should take a step back, but oh, Ellova's grave, I both dread and wish for him to brush his lips against mine again, taste me.

He must see the longing on my face; his knowing smile is wide as he leans forward to kiss me. My breath hitching at that overwhelming strawberry and herb scent, memories of him soaked in blood. He'd been willing to die to protect me and had nearly succeeded.

I stumble back.

Whenever he is near, I feel I am being torn apart. To chase after him on this road of destruction that ends in heartache or put up a fortress around my soul to protect us both.

He must be infuriated by my inability to choose.

For a brief moment, hurt and confusion flash in his eyes and he backs away, shoulders sinking. "My apologies, Izadella, I—"

Fuck it.

His words stumble as I wrap my arms around his neck, pulling him to me. His strong hands reverently circle my soft waist and around my back. The dress I wear is backless, so when his rough hands slide over bare skin, I shiver at the touch, only feeling whole in his arms.

A whimpering moan escapes my lips as his tongue meets mine. Demanding more, he tugs me even tighter against him.

Leon spins us, kicks the door shut, and walks us past the elixir to the long workbench he has set up, the desk covered with his papers, glass measuring jars, and ingredients. Without separating us, he hauls me up to the table and sits me in front of him, knocking over a few of the closed glass vials he was studying, sending papers flying.

The silky threads of his hair slide through my fingers. His mouth leaves mine, and I groan in protest before he starts to chart sensual kisses along my jaw. One hand is still on my lower back, pressing me closer, but his other hand has made its way up to my throat. His hand has me in a loose hold. I tip my head to the side to give him better access, which he eagerly accepts, his tongue trailing up. Leon moans low against my skin, pulling and sucking the delicate flesh of my neck.

My breaths come out unevenly at his attention. His hands don't move from my lower back or the side of my face, and his mouth returns to mine in a rough, capturing kiss.

I'm greedy for him.

My hands caress at the dark shadow on his face. The moan he elicits from me sounds closer to a sob, and tears swell. Flashes of last night's gore as he lies nearly dead, how I almost lost him over my selfless desire to have him near, replays in my mind.

His hand is on my face when a single tear makes its way to his finger, and he pulls back without removing his hand. His gaze is full of concern, and it makes me want to cry harder.

"Leon."

"Did you want to stop?" he asks softly, and he kisses away the new tears.

"No! Yes? I don't know." It comes out breathless and all at once.

He takes a step back, pulling the chair out from the desk, and sits down. Looking up at me with a gentle expression of understanding, waiting for me to process my emotions.

"Leon, I have…" I pause while I search for the words, but none of them truly can express the depths of my adoration. *Don't say love; don't say love.* "…strong…feelings for you." If I say *love*, there will be no turning back.

"As do I. I'm glad we've cleared that up." His smile is endearing, and I try to smile in return but fail. He takes both of his hands in mine. "Run away with me?"

I gawk at him. "Leon, we have nowhere to go. You have known this from the start! Mortals aren't meant to be here! Fae need magic, something the mortal realm is severely lacking."

Whatever we feel for each other we are as incompatible as the sun and the moon.

"We will find a way." He says it with some calmness, like one speaks of the weather and not the reason my soul is snapping in two.

He squeezes my hands before he brings them up to his soft lips, pressing them to my knuckles, his gold ring glinting from the crystal light above us.

"You can exist in the mortal realm with the crown. Inara did it. The crown holds all the magic you need. We could try. Maybe not forever, nothing truly is, but I would rather have a short time together than nothing at all." He says it, but his words don't have much hope in them.

"Leon. The crown is going to kill me."

He ignores that. "You keep saying it's not safe for me here, and last night proved *you* are not safe here. We can leave, go where no one can find us."

I now have two men insisting on stealing me away, but only one tempts me.

"Ellova is my home and Nueena is about to be Realm Keeper. I…I can't just leave…"

"We meet in the middle of our realms. I'll build you a damn castle on the Divide."

I take a deep breath, pulling my hands from his. "I need to tell you about my parents."

"If it will not pain you too much to do so." He sits back in his chair, ready for the miserable tale.

"My mother, Ambra, and the women before her were all fae. Alvina had been pregnant when she was exiled, and later my grandmother would visit Ellova in secret, eventually getting pregnant one of the few times she was here. My mother lived alone for hundreds of years after my grandmother and great-grandmother passed. The lower amounts of magic near the Divide gave them shorter lifespans, so she was left on her own. One day a young mortal woman appeared. She was a swordsmith, and the horrible king of Adreania at the time accused her of treason for sabotaging his sword when he lost a royal sword fight in front of his court."

"Bastard."

I wholeheartedly agree. "Her punishment was being sent into the forest to die. She was terrified and said the forest led her here. My mother was happy for the company, and they spent part of the winter making weapons. Her brothers were desperate to save their sister, so they built a tunnel to find her. The same one I traveled through each month."

"They sound like they were very good brothers indeed," Leon says.

"The forest means death for those who wish to harm, or seek Ellova for sinister reasons, but for grieving brothers seeking a lost sister, they were allowed to pass and found the cottage. The eldest brother was my father, Nolan, and my mother fell in love with him despite the hundreds of years between their ages. He was the best swordsmith in all of Adreania. I do not believe they knew about the madness. How could they have when my mother had been completely cut off from Ellova? Soon she was pregnant; whether by purpose or accident, I never asked."

"How often could he see you?" Leon's hands have found their

way to my calves, where he rubs the back of them in a comforting gesture while I speak.

"Since my mother couldn't survive on the other side of the Divide, he visited as often as he could, traveling back and forth regularly for years, but the longer he stayed with us, the more he seemed confused. When he crossed back over the Divide, the confusion would eventually ease. He said that when he was in Adreania, he was perfectly fine, but when he was here, on fae soil, he would forget who my mother and I were and why he was with us or believe that the fae were out to destroy the mortals as they had in the war long ago."

"It breaks my heart you went through this, love."

I shake my head. "I was too young for this, but it devastated my mother. He would beg to see me, but within a few hours would forget who I was, and as a child I couldn't understand why. One day my mother had just gone into the garden to pull some vegetables for dinner, and he had forgotten who she was to him, thinking she was a deceiving fae who had taken me because I looked like his sister when she was young. He must have assumed I was mortal. He tried to take me to the mortal realm, but the Merawood Forest stopped him, tangled me in branches 'til my mother arrived. She was enraged he would try to take me across the Divide. By nightfall he remembered everything and was beyond remorseful. She wouldn't allow him near the cottage again. After that, we met in the forest at the barrier between realms, him on one side and my mother and me on the other side, daily, for a long time. We had picnics together in the afternoons. He would read to me while my mother made jewelry, and he even taught me how to wield a blade. Then one day he didn't show; his sister did. Cyanna's ancestor. There had been a fire at his forge. He didn't make it."

Leon stands, sliding between my legs, and draws me into a long and soothing hug.

"I'm so sorry, Izadella," he whispers into my hair.

My forehead is peppered with soft presses of his lips, which only makes me squeeze him tighter.

For this part I do not want to hold eye contact, so when he tries to pull back, I cling to him.

"Fae can die from broken hearts. My mother was alone for centuries and finally found love. It broke her when he forgot who she was, and it destroyed her when he died. So, forgive my heart that demands I withdraw from you, only for it to find itself in agony if you are not near."

The room grows warmer by the second, my voice rising with panic, chest tightening with every breath I take. The air is disappearing, suddenly out of my grasp.

I finally let him pull back from me, my fingers clutching the front of his tunic, and he places a hand over my chest, near my neck. His other hand is still on my back, keeping us close together.

"Can you take a deep breath for me?" he asks in the soothing tone of a skilled healer. We do not break eye contact and Leon takes deep, exaggerated breaths that I imitate over and over again 'til the panic fades away.

"Izadella, we do not have to have this figured out today. You said it yourself: few mortals have been here, so we don't fully know how the magic will affect me or you, or how long that might take to become noticeable. If you say magic affects mortals differently, I believe you, and when I start to feel a bit mad or start thinking trees are singing to me, I will seek refuge in Versairen, all right?"

He reaches up and presses a long kiss to my forehead.

"It's been a long day. We can continue this lively discussion at a later time. You should go find Viella. I need to finish here."

"You don't seem worried." It comes out more accusatory than I mean it to, but I need to know I am not alone in this panic.

His answering smile is soft and kind. "That's because I'm not. I will have whatever part of your life you wish to give me. If that is 'til next week or 'til I am a wrinkled old man, that is for you to decide. I will not be part of your regrets." With that, he pulls me to my feet. My heels click on the floor as he walks me to the door and holds it open for me. Before I pass, he leans down and kisses my cheek.

"Thank you, Leon. For everything." It is just a whisper, but I can feel his smile pressed to my skin when he kisses it one last time.

"Anything for you, Strawberries."

CHAPTER 8

$\mathcal{I}$'ve barely made it ten steps into the west wing before a knock rings out in the main living space. Hoping it's Leon, I'm slightly disappointed when it's Viella who comes bounding in.

"May we discuss tonight?" She beams at me, holding up a wig of long dark locks.

"Sure, I can find the others, and we can—"

She loops her arm with mine and leads me into the library. "We will speak with them later too. I would just like to go over it a few times. I'm feeling..." She searches for the right word, "...nervous about it." Her bright smile dims to reveal a sliver of apprehension.

Nervous? That's not something I would ever associate with her. I debate asking where Lillian is, as she would want to be briefed on this as well, but Viella sought me out alone and I have to assume it was on purpose. If she needs to review the plan a hundred times to feel comfortable, I'm willing to do it. "Of course. Anything for you."

Her shoulders drop with relief. "Thank you, Izzy."

I find some blank parchment and draw out a map of Ellova and Adreania for her to follow. "I know you have your own way of getting into Adreania but you could take my family's secret entrance." I circle the two trees on the map that hide the passageway.

She nods. "That will be faster."

"The orphanage marks the beginning of Beggars' Row when you get past the wall. The transition from Beggars' Row to the next district is marked by fine brick homes, and you'll want to start there, then make your way back towards the orphanage. They won't be expecting me, but they will recognize the leather bags. Written instructions for the elixir will be placed into each one."

She studies the map.

"I'll be right back." I disappear into my room. My work desk is still a mess of jewelry materials, scrolls, ink pots, and books.

From the bottom drawer I pull out the ornate silver jewelry box my father made for my mother.

My heart strangles at the sight of my parents' handwriting on faded letters. I bring them up to my nose. They have long since stopped smelling like her perfume, but I inhale anyway, the memory of lilac and lemongrass enough to imagine it lingers.

If I could speak to her now, would she understand my feelings towards Leon or mourn for me for making the same mistakes that ended her life?

After my father was no longer allowed to stay with us, she read them to me. I was too little to truly understand, but even as a dewling, I felt the love in her voice at every word.

After the enervation of her heart, when death hovered nearby, I read them to her by candlelight as silent tears streamed down her face.

I haven't opened them since.

A large key sits at the bottom, rusted on the edges. I take it and replace the letters. When I return to Viella, I hand her the key to the orphanage's stables. "Normally Cyanna opens the door for me, but my mother held on to one key in case we needed to get to my father in the mortal realm. Keep it safe."

She holds the key close to her chest. "I will."

"I have a favor to ask."

She mirrors my words back at me. "Of course. Anything for you."

I smile at that. "When you are on your way back, and only if everything goes smoothly, could you check on Farren?" Guilt eats at me that I have been gone so long.

"Oh, Izzy, of course I will."

"Try to get him to follow you home. I know he hates it here but maybe he will be curious enough to know where I went to follow you."

"I'll pack extra treats for our little friend."

Relief floods my chest. "Thank you."

He is fine; that I know. Besides sleeping with me at night, he spends sunup 'til sundown exploring the forest. Chasing butterflies and playing with the wild foxes near the cottage. Just as happy to hunt for his meals as he is to eat off my plate, but still, I miss my furry companion.

My sweet fox, how I miss you.

Before she leaves, I ask, "Is Lillian all right?"

Viella looks down at her shoes. "Well, she's certainly not pleased with the situation, but she knows how important this is." When she finally looks up at me, she says, "I do not have a reassuring history of leaving and coming back."

No, she does not, but that was a long time ago. "But this is nothing like that. I'm sure she is just scared. She thought she lost you once. Watching you rush into potential danger must be hard on her."

She nods, her eyes glassy. "I asked if she wished to speak to the temple guardians about the possibility of her and me..." Her voice fades.

Oh. They have gone through a dark time in their relationship, but they are so much stronger now.

Lillian loves her so fiercely, but I understand her reluctance. "She said no?"

"She said she knows without a doubt we are Zemras, but she's not ready. I fear she may not ever be, after the last time." Viella sighs, leaving without the beautiful smile that usually graces her face.

My already sorrowful soul twists for her.

I cannot have my happy ending, but I wish so deeply for my friends to find theirs.

~

I find Nueena in her greenhouse, tending to some flowers and humming to herself.

Time for all the confessions I have been holding close to my heart.

"Leon and I kissed," I blurt out, taking a seat on the ledge of a planter.

"*What?*" She lets out a quiet squeal of delight and rushing to come to sit beside me, eager for the tale.

"A few times actually. Back in the Gem Court, right after my magic attacked him, *more* than kissed."

"The Gem Court? That was a week ago! Why didn't you say anything?"

Guilt that I didn't tell her tightens my chest even though I know she will understand. As vivid as the day it happened, the memory forms of his warm body in the cool waters as we sink to the bottom of the spring. The taste of lochkiss on his tongue, rough hands all over me, soft sand beneath us.

"I didn't tell you because I know you worry about me. I wanted to keep what happened close to my heart in case he leaves so I could pretend it never happened, for my own sanity. At the spring, the crown almost killed him, and then the next moment I couldn't resist him any longer, couldn't shove down all that I've felt for him all these years. I showed him the cave where I went to hide as a dewling and told him about my mother. I truly thought the crown was going to kill him and I would lose him forever. It sounded silly but I just needed to be with him, more than I needed air. I lost all rational thought. I knew, deep within me, I needed to give in."

Her eyes are soft, filled with compassion. "So how was the kiss?"

How can I put into words the sensations I felt when his lips finally touched mine? Two years of dreaming about him was nothing compared to that moment.

I'm embarrassed at the giggle that escapes me. "It was everything I've been dreaming about. Beautiful. He kissed me as if madness had already taken him, but not the kind that destroys. I could feel the love and longing poured back into me, but instead of suffocating on it like I had been, it was like I could finally breathe. 'Til our fight about being Zemras."

"Oh, Del. Mortals cannot be Zemras." She says it with such gentle calmness, only seeking to protect me from my own feelings.

The ache in my head is getting worse. "I *know* that, but he will not listen to reason. Leon is..." I struggle to find the word that encapsulates how wonderful he is, what a caring and gracious man I have found. "...perfect, but he refuses to let go of a future we can never have. Even if we could be Zemras, he cannot tie his life to mine. The crown's magic would destroy his mortal body if we were to try now."

She nods. "That's completely understandable."

"Last night we went even further. In fact, if the attackers had arrived a few minutes earlier, they would have seen *much* more of me than I wished to share. I wanted to tell you, but Leon had almost died, again. The attempt to take me seemed like the important event to fret about. Plus, a gathering to discuss the threats to our lives is a strange place to announce that." I laugh. "Sorry, everyone, I know we have to prepare for a possible war, find out who sent those attackers and probably killed them so they cannot share what they know, plan a secret mission to Adreania to heal the mortals, somehow remove the crown, throw a coronation ball, and have a crowning day, but I kissed Leon and he gave me a toe-curling orgasm before saving me from being stolen away! Carry on. How many ships do we need?"

Nueena chuckles. "Does this mean you two are finally together?"

When I do not answer, she gives me time to think for a moment. She runs her jeweled fingers in the soil, and yellow blossoms follow her touch, rising into the air. With a wave of her hand, the flowers weave together to form a crown. Little purple buds follow, swirling around before placing themselves within the crafted bloom.

Nueena gently places the flora circlet on my head and patiently waits for me.

I reach up and touch the soft petals, such a sweet gift. "I'm not sure."

Nueena sees through me and takes a moment to collect her own thoughts before speaking. "Do you *want* to be Zemras with Leon?"

I do not know what the Zemra temple looks like, but I imagine a golden structure, surrounded by sparkling gems. Leon and I holding yellow crystals together, magic flowing around us. Beautifully bonded and utterly devoted to each other.

It's a nice daydream.

"Yes. No. I don't know." My heart twists but I try to keep the grief off my face. "I've never felt this way about anyone before, but it's dangerous enough for him to exist around magic, let alone for it to be *part* of him. I could not bear it. Mortals and magic are incompatible."

Nueena nods and looks up at the stained-glass ceiling as if it holds the answers we seek. "So few mortals have been allowed in Ellova, and we really don't know much about them. I suppose that just because a mortal has never been accepted into the temple doesn't mean it's impossible. Fae are able to have dewlings with them. That might mean something." Her expression is contemplative as she swirls a long braid around a finger, lost in thought. "You are right, though. You still have the madness to think about. I can feel Tavien right now; if his mind were in agony, I would experience his madness too. To tie yourself to someone whose sanity is bound to be lost might be too cruel to even dream about."

I nod, closing my eyes for a moment to give me the courage to say, "It's just that...no matter how much I want him, it's excruciating to love him knowing I will have to live the rest of my life without him. It leaves me aching to think that my only options are that he will die while I keep living for centuries alone or that I will die of a broken heart after losing him."

She lets out a low laugh but there's no humor in it. "Yes, I've felt this way about *you* for decades, Della. That doesn't mean we stop being friends. We treasure the time we have together; we always have."

I give her a small, sad smile and lay my head on her shoulder. We have talked about my early death before, but she has so many people to support her after losing me: Tavien and Vi, Lillian and Hiliyah, her parents and sisters. They will all have to mourn me too, but they will have each other.

I know I will have them too after Leon is gone but it does not bring me the comfort I need.

Nueena continues, "Magic is unpredictable and there are so few half-fae in history. We have no idea how long you will live. You have already far surpassed a mortal lifespan, but it doesn't mean that you cannot savor your time together. Maybe it's worth a few decades of happiness."

Fear grips my chest with my uncertain future bare before me. My mother wasn't strong enough to survive after losing my father. I can't know if I would be strong enough either. What if I never get this crown off and it kills me long before a broken heart does?

"I'm so scared, Nu."

She wraps her arm around my shoulders. "I asked my mother. She thinks that if you live outside Ellova, you might age with him. She said an Ellovian was shipwrecked on one of the dark islands once, and when he was able to sail back home decades later, he had aged, not completely like a mortal, but enough that it was noticeable. You, being only half-fae? Well, it might mean growing old together." She doesn't turn to look at my expression, but if she did, she would only see agony there. "It would mean the loss of your powers, but your mortal side might take over and learn to live without your magic. You are half-mortal. Dying from a broken heart might not happen. Not everything that affects the fae affects you the same."

I jerk back and balk at her. Dread fills me at the idea of abandoning my home and everyone I love here. "I know what I want: a lifetime with *both* of you. But I would not leave Ellova."

"You have the crown made specifically for a fae to be able to live in the mortal realm. It was just something Mother was going to suggest to you, since her *'mortals are forbidden'* speech went mostly ignored and now he is an Ellovian citizen."

We both giggle at that.

"I do not think I could have ever stopped my feelings for him, not with him here with me in this realm. My only path was to fall hopelessly in love with him, and now that I have, I feel trapped by time."

"He loves you too. That much is abundantly clear. Love is always worth the risk," Nueena says, "even if it is not forever. Be brave, Della."

 ueena, Tavien, Leon, and I spent the last few hours in the temporary apothecary. Dinner is spread out before us: vibrant red peppers stuffed with minced meat alongside flaky brown bread with fig jam, various savory pastries, and a delectable white bean soup with thyme and carrots.

Tavien uses his magic to hover a large feather quill and write the instructions for taking the elixir over and over again on one hundred narrow slips of paper. Most of the citizens of Beggars' Row are literate—thanks to Cyanna's lessons for any who wanted to learn—and those who are not can speak to their neighbors. It's too great of a risk to have Viella stay to administer it.

The anticipation of the evening leaves my stomach in knots. If this does not work, we will have no hope to save anyone outside Ellova.

We work in comfortable silence. Tavien and Leon, side by side, pour the vibrant blue liquid into crystal vials, handing them off to Nueena and me when they are sealed.

Once the quill has finished, the paper rolls itself and floats to me. I slip it into a small pouch, adding in a few pieces of jewelry. A dwindling pile of rings, earrings, and bracelets lies between Nueena and me. Since I no longer have coins, jewelry will have to be traded to purchase food for the Adreanians. I pass the small leather bag to Nueena, who tucks in one vial along with the instructions and ties it shut.

I can only hope it will be enough for now.

Although I try to remind myself that we have done all we can, that I've spent ten years trying to save those Jedrick forgot, but with this crown that decrees me queen, I'm left with the crushing sensation I have failed.

Viella will be the one to bring new hope now.

With thoughts of Viella comes a memory. "We need to remind Vi to walk across with Onyx instead of ride." I turn to Leon. "We learned the first time I snuck into Adreania that it can result in passing out and falling off my horse, and she won't have Nueena to panic like the world is ending."

"Oh, apologies for my alarm." Nueena places her hand over her heart in mock offense. "But if *you* watched *me* fall headfirst off my horse while in an enemy kingdom, you could not possibly possess the ability to stay calm either."

"Yes, but there did not need to be *quite* so much crying," I tease her.

Nueena flings a warm roll at me from her dinner plate, her fae agility ensuring the flying fare hits its target on my shoulder.

A rough knock cuts through our laughter and Tavien lowers the wards, expecting the mates, but Lillian stands alone in the doorframe.

"Have you seen Viella?" she asks, her voice slightly strained.

Nueena and I glance at each other, Nueena answering her. "No, not since the infirmary this morning."

"Actually," I add, "I spoke with her after that to go over her journey for tonight."

Lillian starts to pace away from the door. "I haven't seen her in hours, and I can't find her anywhere. I—"

Another knock and Lillian crosses the room in three large steps to swing the door open.

"Hello, my loves," Viella greets us. She wears all black with boots laced up in the front to mid-thigh, a dark hood over her head. Her short blonde hair is gone, and her dark wig is in a braid thrown over her shoulder under a thick hood. She carries a bundle of blankets tightly to her chest and kicks the door shut behind her.

"Where have you been?" Lillian moves towards her but stops abruptly when a muffled cough echoes around us.

My heart stops.

Leon clears the table we have been working on, shoving everything roughly to one end.

We both know that heartbreaking sound.

"Did you kidnap a mortal?" Nueena gasps. She brushes past a stunned Lillian and flips a corner of the fabric, revealing a small child, round ears peeking out in front of light brown curls. Sweat has her hair sticking to her pale face.

"Of course not. It's called *borrowing*. I plan on bringing her back," Viella retorts in a tone that implies she is quite pleased with herself.

Budding joy blooms in my chest. We will be able to test the elixir. The four of us have spent so much time creating the hope the mortals need, but I never could have dreamed I'd witness its life-saving magic myself.

That little trickster.

Viella plotted this. She wasn't nervous about sneaking into Adreania when I gave her the key to Cyanna's door. I don't know if I should be impressed or angry that she didn't tell anyone she was going to the mortal realm early.

Lillian certainly appears annoyed.

Before she can argue over her mate's actions, Leon walks over, taking the small child from Viella. "Where did you find her?" he asks, laying the little girl down on one end of the table and brushing his thumb over her bright red cheek. She stirs for a moment, her breath labored and rattling, but her eyes stay closed.

He tenderly presses two fingers to her neck. "Her heartbeat is weak." With the gentleness of a healer, he presses the back of his hand to her forehead. "High fever."

"I found her near the orphanage, heard crying through a broken window a few houses away. Her whole family is sick, all of them bedridden. The mother looked worse." Viella turns to me with a sad smile. "I told her I knew you. Did you know those you gave the gold coins call you the Midnight Altruist?"

The Midnight Altruist.

My heart leaps with amusement. I never had the opportunity to meet those I slipped coins to each full moon. Recognition was never something I sought; I only wished to help those forgotten by their ruler and keep all the mistreated citizens alive the only way I could. "I did not."

"Her mother said they owe you their lives and let me take her daughter to you. I explained about the elixir, how we had a cure but needed to ensure it worked before we could distribute it. I gave her my word that I would return her, hopefully healed."

"It was a dangerous risk," Leon says. He pulls down the little one's worn collar and I shudder at the violent purple rash around her tiny neck. Leon lowers the blankets, and we can see the angry rash descending down her emaciated arms. "She doesn't have much time left. If the elixir doesn't work, she will be gone by sunrise. Tavien, can you bring me a vial?"

Tavien quickly returns to Leon's side, uncorking one of the small elixirs and handing it to him. Leon cradles her head with one hand, tipping it back, her cracked lips opening just enough for him to administer ten drops of vibrant blue mixture.

We all take a collective intake of breath, Nueena and I reaching for each other's hand at the same time.

At first nothing happens, hopelessness ready to take root. The small child continues to take strained breaths, coughing through fitful dreams, but then her breathing becomes easier, each inhale deeper and deeper. The purple skin fades, retreating up her arms and disappearing along with the redness on her feverish face.

Overwhelming gratitude that it worked, truly worked, has me choking on a sob. Once the rash has faded, leaving behind unblemished skin, she slowly blinks awake, staring up at us, confused but not alarmed.

Nueena lets go of me and bends down. "Hello, my name is Nueena." She looks at Leon. "Can we give her some food?"

The little girl nods rapidly.

"Not too much," Leon warns. "She's extremely malnourished and will need to ease into a proper meal. Since the food here is incredibly rich, we will need to add some water to soup to make a broth."

The elixir worked and we're actually going to be able to save those dying in Beggars' Row. All that effort Tavien and Leon did was worth it. Tears stream down my cheeks. Leon accomplished what he set out to do. I could kiss him right now.

"How are you feeling, Mimi?" Leon asks softly.

My heart misses a beat. He knows her. What had Leon told me back in my cottage that first night?

"You are not the only one who spends time trying to help those who call Beggars' Row home. A few nights a week I provide medical attention there, including those at the orphanage."

This man, this selfless healer.

I almost blurt out how much I love him here and now.

Mimi looks up at him, eyes full of trust, and whispers, "Better, but Mama is still sick."

He gives her a bright smile, filled with reassurance. "She is going to be well again, just like you. Does anything else hurt like it did before?"

She sits up on her own and shakes her head.

Lillian brings over a small bowl for her. It's mostly broth but a few pieces of roasted chicken and vegetables float on the top. Mimi spoons it happily and is delighted when Tavien offers her a small piece of sweet roll that she eagerly dips into the soup.

"How old are you?" Tavien asks.

"I'm five. Where am I?"

"Somewhere safe, but we're going to take you home soon. We just wanted to make sure you feel better," Tavien assures her.

She nods and returns to her dinner.

Unable to keep myself away from Leon any longer, I wrap my arms around him. "Thank you," I whisper into his chest, his arms closing around me.

"Beggars' Row will be healed by dawn tomorrow. You saved their lives once again." He wipes another tear from my cheek.

"Me?" I ask. "You and Tavien did all the work! Nueena grew the ingredients."

"Yes, but you brought me here, trusted me when you had no reason to. You could have abandoned me in the forest the night we spent in your cottage, slipped out in the middle of the night," he says into my hair. "But you kept me close, and I was able to bring back Inara's diary."

"Why do they have pointed ears?" Mimi asks Leon, getting our attention, Leon and I breaking apart.

"This is a dream. Try to go back to sleep," he says kindly. Mimi nods, passing her empty bowl to him and lying back down with a yawn. Leon pulls the blanket over her. "She has older siblings. They were all newly ill last time I saw them. Hopefully they survived."

What we have done in this room, weeks of effort, hours of preparations, feels more important than ever before. I desperately need that little girl to wake up tomorrow and find her family free of the misery that the crown and Grayden have caused.

To live a long, happy life.

Lillian sits down and pulls Viella into her lap. "Why wouldn't you tell me you were going into the mortal realm early? Something could have happened to you, and I never would have known."

"I agree with Lillian," Nueena says. Her disapproving face could rival her mother's. "Did you tell *anyone* you were leaving?"

"Nu, I have endless respect for you, but as Spy Guardian, I do not need to let anyone outside of your mother know my whereabouts."

"I'm not asking as future Realm Keeper," she says, her hands going to her hips. "You have my complete trust that you can accomplish whatever dangerous task you stubbornly undertake. I'm asking as your *friend*. That was reckless."

Tavien sits on the couch, his pale blue eyes watching Nueena pace around the room.

"Oh." An embarrassed blush spreads up Viella's neck. "I appreciate the concern. I knew if I asked to bring a child here, I would be told it was too risky, so I didn't let anyone know of my plan. We needed to test the elixir or there was no point in me taking it all that way only to crush the hopes of the mortals we'd hoped to help." Her fingers gently move up and down Lillian's arms, Lillian's head leaning against her shoulder.

"How did the orphanage look?" I ask. "And Beggars' Row? Any sign of Grayden or his men?"

Viella shakes her head. "The orphanage has been abandoned, and the street was quiet. I saw a few guards on patrol, but they were at the far end, and I avoided them."

Lillian tightens her arms around her mate's waist at the reminder of the potential danger of the journey. "If I could just accompany you to the Divide, Vi—"

Viella shifts to the side and gazes down at Lillian, whose open expression is pleading. "My love, I will be back before dawn breaks tomorrow."

Lillian whispers, "I will have been driven mad by then."

Viella leans down and kisses the tip of her downcast lover's nose. "You need to trust me to return to you. Always."

Lillian's eyes harden but she does not ask again.

CHAPTER 10

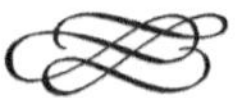

Leon, Nueena, Mimi, and I head down a narrow spiral stairwell, my anticipation for the evening growing with every step.

A floating crystal light guides us through the dark passageways 'til we reach an entrance, secret to most, at the base of the palace. There sits an unused kitchen Nueena and I have used for years to prepare the provisions for the mortals each month.

Leon sits Mimi on the counter as she eats the last bite of a soft cheese and spinach pastry, dressed in a warm gown borrowed from Nueena's youngest sister, Kaylena. She watches the little crystal light float around the ceiling, the flaky crust falling into her lap.

Nueena opens the back door to the kitchen, letting in wisps of cool early-evening air from the Merawood Forest, where Tavien waits with my horse, Onyx.

We all set to work.

I pour some dried goods into jars: purple rice, large beans, and finely ground brown flour. A task that is familiar and comforting. For the past ten years Nueena, Tavien, and I have prepared the provisions for my travels to the mortal realm, but tonight everything is different.

The elixirs' creation was triumphant, but this could end in joyful tears or tragedy.

Of course, I worried for myself when I slipped into Adreania on each full moon, but I knew no one was searching for me and my true identity was unknown. Tonight, though, Viella carries precious cargo with her, and I fear more for her than I ever did myself.

Tavien finishes wrapping up chocolate rolls in small blue handkerchiefs as Leon moves on to packing potatoes and I pour oils and spices into traveling containers.

Nueena hums to herself while she wraps the last of the crusty rosemary bread loaves in soft white fabric, tying the tops with strips of silk. I've seen plenty of the mortals making use of the fabric we wrap the food in to make new garments, or for ribbons in their hair. She smiles nervously at me; white flour streaked across her cheek.

Once we have enough wrapped, we bring it all outside, where Onyx is hitched to the small wooden cart that will make the journey to Adreania.

I hold out an apple to my sweet boy, and he happily devours it. I worry about his safety, too. Pressing my forehead into his cheek, I whisper, "One last quest. Bring her home safely." His soft snort is probably a request for more fruit, but I'll pretend he understands.

Once everything is packed up, all of us step into the forest to load the waiting cart Viella will be taking with her.

After a soft knock at the small kitchen door, Lillian and Viella join us under budding stars. Lillian with bags under her eyes, Viella's hand tucked into hers.

Poor Lillian.

"It's quite heavy, Vi. We can take out some of the bigger jars," Nueena says as she inspects the cart, prodding the bags of apples, potatoes, and leafy greens. "You have much to do. I do not wish for you to be slowed down."

Viella shook her head. "Absolutely not. If I'm going there, we must bring everything we can. What good would it do to heal them and give them nothing to begin recovering from their malnu-trition?"

Leon pulls out a letter and hands it to Viella. "You will find a mail bin right outside the orphanage. I understand if it's not possible, but if you could place this there, I would be most appreciative."

She nods, sliding it into her cloak's pocket.

I look at him curiously, but he only offers me a half smile instead of answering my unspoken question about the letter. Not that he has to tell me of his correspondence, but I find it impossible to be indifferent. Maybe he is missing a friend in Adreania? One of the princesses?

Everything we're sending will be left at Cyanna's orphanage for the citizens of Beggars' Row since going up and down the streets with food would draw too much attention. I secure the cart, placing a dark cloth over it to hide it from view.

Lillian and Viella stand close together, foreheads pressed together. "My mate." Viella says it so low I barely hear it.

"Yes, *mate*," Lillian replies, not quite with the adoring tone of her lover but with a hint of bitterness that surprises me.

Whatever Lillian is feeling fades quickly and an unexpected softness returns to her.

We give them a moment to linger in their love before Lillian helps Viella mount the horse with a reverent look in her eyes. Lillian gives her calf a squeeze before coming to stand next to me.

I wrap my arm around her waist, and she slumps against me.

She is taking this much harder than I would expect. Viella is capable and bright, trained in slipping in and out, unnoticed. Something much deeper is happening before them.

Viella gently places a satchel over her shoulder. The vials of the elixir have been wrapped up with care; Nueena enchanted the glass to never break.

"Ellova's grave, Vi. Please, be safe." Lillan's voice vibrates with distress, earning her an enthusiastic nod from Viella. "I know Izadella has safely brought provisions to the mortals every full moon for years, but I cannot calm my worries. Grayden is looking for her, for the crown, demanding a war, and there is a traitor from

Ellova still free. It was hardly safe before, and now it is even more dangerous." Lillian does not need to warn her of that, but I know by the desperation in her eyes she needs to speak of it anyway.

"As soon as I can see the palace again, I'll light up a fire sphere, so you know I have returned, safe and sound," Viella says gently to Lillian.

Leon passes Mimi up to Viella, who nestles the little girl in front of her, ensuring she is comfortable.

"Remember, you must listen to Viella," Leon tells her. "Whatever she says, you must do. She is going to make your whole family feel better. She's here to help."

Mimi nods, her little hands playing with Onyx's mane. "I will." She bounces slightly with a wild grin, delighted to be riding.

Nueena mirrors Lillian's worried expression but makes an attempts to send Viella off with a wobbly, encouraging smile. "If you run into Grayden's men, get Mimi home, but then you come right back. No matter what. Leave the cart. Leave the elixir. Nothing is more important than your return."

Tavien wraps his arms around Nueena's shoulders before whispering, "Ellova will protect her." We all bow our heads, sending out a silent prayer.

"I'll return swiftly." Viella softly snaps Onyx's reins, my beloved horse propelling the cart forward into the forest.

Lillian watches 'til they have completely disappeared. A lantern of crystal lights hangs near the door for Viella to find her way back. The moon's brightness fills the night sky with a soft glow that will make her journey easier.

"I'm going to wait here, if that's all right," Lillian says, staring into the forest. "I will secure the door after her return."

Nueena nods and we make our way out of the kitchen and back to our rooms.

CHAPTER 11

My nerves keep me quiet while Leon, Nueena, and I walk through the palace from our rooms. I carry a bundle of blankets, wearing my dark green hooded cloak. Leon is beside me with a large pillow, a bottle of wine, and a wooden plate of sliced fruit, soft cheeses, toasted bread, and cured meats balancing on top of it all. We follow Nueena and Tavien, who carry wine, glasses, and more blankets, 'til we pass the still waters of the royal natatorium and disappear into the hidden tunnel Leon and I arrived in. Illuminating crystals light our way through the tunnel that leads to the ledge overlooking the Merawood Forest.

It has been weeks since I brought him to Ellova, but it seems so much longer than that. Like he has always been here, was meant to be here, in my bed and at my side. Since his arrival, it has felt more like home than it ever has.

He must leave. The madness will descend. But at the sickening thought of him walking out that door, never to return, ripples panic through me.

The pounding in my head from the crown bothered me all throughout the day, and now it intensifies. I am grateful when Leon lays out our blankets, arranging the brightly colored pillows. Nueena snaps her fingers, and flame appears on her fingertips—a bit of Tavien's magic—to light the ceramic fire pit between us. She raises her hand and the space around us shimmers for a moment as a ward goes up, hiding us from any view below.

With the bright moon rising, the trees are clearly outlined below every star radiant in the cloudless night.

The perfect evening to share with friends. To relax before the extravagant events and my fear of an unknown future. At least for a night we can rest together and leave tomorrow's troubles at our feet.

I fill elaborate golden glasses with blackberry wine for us, handing Leon ours. Tavien tugs Nueena down to him and she accepts both of their drinks from me.

Not bold enough to slide into Leon's lap even though I want to, I attempt to sit next to him, but he sets the wine glasses on the ground and in one swift motion he pulls me down, nestling me against him. He slips his arm around my waist, securing me tightly to him, and the declaration of his desire sends an eruption of butterflies in my stomach. He drapes a blanket over us, his other hand passing me my wine.

Pressed against him feels so right.

A blush blooms on my face, the heat of it kissed by the cool night air, just like he does on my cheek.

Nueena and Tavien send us both sly smiles. When I look back at Leon, he stares down at me as he sips his drink with a satisfied grin. A sweet warmth caressing my chest at that look, before something swoops down, startling me.

Expecting an owl or perhaps a bat, I'm surprised to find a wild azure hawk has joined us.

Eyeing the food we have brought, its beautiful dark blue wings shine with the firelight. Leon tears a few pieces of meat and tosses them at the creature, who shifts towards him, devouring the tiny morsels. When all is eaten, the hawk comes closer, eagerly awaiting more, hopping onto his leg next to me.

I've never seen a hawk act like this, so unafraid of us.

They are rare but whenever I see them in the forest they are quick to fly away. This one seems incredibly docile.

"Hello there," Leon says, stroking its soft wings.

It closes its eyes at his touch, and I gingerly run one finger down its tailfeathers. "What a sweet bird."

"We should give it a name," Nueena suggests. "It doesn't seem wild. Maybe it belongs to someone and got lost."

Tavien is thoughtful for a moment. "Talon?"

"Lula." Leon smiles down as the hawk nuzzles his palm.

That is a pretty name, though it's hard to tell if the bird is even female. Once Lula finishes eating, she takes off into the air, circling once before flying away.

Leon watches her disappear into the dark sky. "Such an interesting bird."

We all nod. How odd.

"Hopefully it comes back." It seemed to have taken a liking to Leon. Maybe he needs an animal companion like I have Farren.

We spend the brisk night drinking and telling Leon our favorite stories from years ago, of our lives in Lavencia while we keep our eyes on the forest below. We will be waiting for a long while and so we drink the sweet liquid, letting the wine, Tavien's flames, and our laughter keep us warm.

The coronation ball is tomorrow. We have a week of festivities leading up to crowning day that will keep us all bustling, so it's lovely to rest before it all, even if the crown's unending pressure does leave my head aching.

Leon inspects his drink and turns to Tavien. "I believe your face is on my glass." He holds it up to the firelight, an impression of Tavien's profile shining in the flames.

Tavien snorts. "A Zemra ceremony gift from Del, a very long time ago." Their expressions of love and devotion now are the same as the ones they wore the morning they returned with their Zemra stones after their soulbonding ritual in the temple.

The fabric draped around Nueena's shoulders for warmth has fallen down to expose her skin, allowing Tavien an expanse to kiss when she leans back into him. Their purple Zemra stones glow like the glinting stars above us. "My Zemra."

He's called her that sweet title for decades and I've always found it incredibly endearing, but tonight it causes my chest to tighten painfully. Leon will never whisper that sacred word on my skin under moonlight.

Nueena must see something in my face and hastily changes the subject. "If all goes well, Viella will return soon. Mimi's mother will be so relieved when her daughter is healed." Nueena looks between Tavien and Leon. "It's the first step in saving the Adreanian people."

"One of many," Tavien agrees.

"Why are Viella and Lillian not Zemras?" Leon asks, sipping his wine, and my heart drops. He asks it so casually I could almost believe it's an innocent question, but I know what he's doing.

He wants to know everything about Zemras, and his words come back to me.

"What if that is something I want to share with you? Being Zemras? What if that is why we have been drawn to each other from the start?"

Tavien is the first to explain slowly. "They almost were, years ago."

Leon glances down at me but I avoid his eyes. His interest in Zemras, this insistence that is what we might be, will only hurt us.

"They hated each other at first," Nueena says with a short laugh, "but eventually fell in love. They were together for decades and went through all the steps to receive the blessings of the temple guides and my mother." She stops, letting me tell the rest.

They wouldn't mind us sharing their story when it's all common knowledge in the palace. It was all anyone could talk about for months, but I fear filling Leon's head with more stories will only push the subject.

"The night of their Zemra voyage to the hidden temple, Viella disappeared. When Vi was late to meet with the temple guardian to start the journey, Lillian went in search of her. Viella left an apologetic note on their bed, and no one saw her for twenty-five years."

Leon's sharp intake of breath against my chest and stunned silence is the reaction we all had before the tears for Lillian came. She has always been on the sterner side, taking her job seriously with no time for anyone's nonsense, but after Viella left, she locked up her heart.

It took many years and reuniting with Vi to even see her smile again.

"How could she leave if they loved each other enough to believe they were Zemras?" he asks. The question is genuine with a slight plea to it. I know we are not speaking about him and me, but it's a punch in the gut anyway. It's almost as if he's asking me how we could part from each other if love holds us together too.

Sometimes love isn't enough, Leon.

As if he can sense I wish to stand up and be free from his embrace for the end of this story, he holds me tighter. I somehow both hate it and love him for it. We both know out of the two of us, I'm the Viella in our story. He will fight to the end for whatever we have created between us—this beautiful connection—while I try to protect his mind and my heart from madness between us.

An owl hoots nearby and the crackling fire fills the silence.

Nueena spares me a response like the good friend she is. "Becoming Zemras might not be for everyone. When you go through the temple, your souls are bonded in ways that are unexplainable. It's a connection unlike anything else, as magical as the fae themselves. You are no longer alone in your own body. You can sense their strong emotions, experience everything with them, anticipate needs like hunger and sleep, even share pain and magic. Zemras are wholly exposed to each other. There is no hiding in the bond, no separation. It's raw and intimate in ways not everyone wants to experience or share so much of themselves."

Not all wish to be so vulnerable.

"Viella was terrified and regretted that decision as soon as she left, but she thought Lillian hated her, so she stayed away," Tavien says. "One of the many reasons Zemras are rarer than mates."

"Do you think they will try again?" Leon asks carefully.

I stare at the moonlit treetops, but I can feel his eyes on me.

Nueena shrugs. "If they wish to attempt the Zemra voyage, they will be allowed to try again at any time. But it's a decision one cannot make lightly, and not a quest for wavering affections." She reaches up to stroke Tavien's face with her thumb. "My parents are quite happy just being mates. Lillian and Vi might be too."

With the way Lillian said "*mate*" earlier, it sounded as if there was another name she wished to be whispered.

Maybe they will try again someday.

"What would have happened if they guessed wrong? Got to the temple and discovered they were never Zemras after all?"

A very real possibility for any couple.

"If the temple rejects a couple, they can never return. The pain of knowing you chose wrong and will never find your true Zemra is its own kind of torment. It is why most fae do not try unless they believe they are certain."

Would the temple reject Leon and me? It's a foolish thought, one I will never have the answer to, but imagining the doors opening for us spreads a warmth in my chest.

Just a dream.

Leon and I both look up at the lone shooting star that flies across the dark blue sky.

His lips brush my ear when he leans close. "In the mortal realm we have a tradition to make a wish when you see a star dash like that."

Once the last dust of the glitter tail fades, I return my eyes to his.

What would I wish for? To keep him here, untouched by time and madness. To have a life with him, free of threats and trepidations; for the hourglass on his presence to shatter. Hoard all of these moments and not count down the stolen ones we have now. To wake in his arms under morning sunbeams that end in sapphire nights of slow touches and fast heartbeats, never again feeling the cold touch of loneliness. A life with him filled with warmth and happiness.

Maybe he couldn't be my Zemra, but perhaps he could be something between the lover and friend I need.

I do not speak, but I lay my head on his shoulder, and he slides his arm around me to pull me close, his head on top of mine. We stay like that for a long time. Eventually, he slides his fingers into mine. Greedy for his touch, I welcome his hand.

Leon speaks in a low voice just for me. "I can see why mates would seek the temple despite the risks." He lets out a long breath, pulling me closer.

"Me too," I whisper back.

There is more that a Zemra bond can offer, but I'm afraid to say the words out loud, not wishing for even a moment to give him hope for him and me. To live without the other nearly guarantees an enervation death.

That is why Zemra magic only extends fae lifespans, ties them together, so one never needs to live without the other.

A secret I must keep from him.

Leon chuckles. His lips return to my ear, voice so low I can barely make out his teasing words. "I may not be your Zemra, but I sense you enjoyed our delicious time under the stars."

Heat returns to my cheeks at his reminder that he worshiped me in that moon-soaked garden before the soil ran red.

Before I can respond, Nueena gasps as she jumps off Tavien. A flicker of blue flame dances between the trees, coming towards the mountain. We all stand and watch the glow brighten as Viella rides towards the kitchen's back door, her flaming sphere following close behind.

A dark, frantic figure runs towards her. When Lillian is close enough, Viella dismounts Onyx and jumps into Lillian's arms. It is dark and far below, but we can see them faintly, swirling with joy, sharing a passionate kiss. They entwine in each other's arms for a long moment before Lillian gently places Viella on the ground. Lillian pulls Onyx and the empty cart, and we clink our glasses in celebration, drinking the last of the wine before we gather all we brought.

"Let's go see how it went."

CHAPTER 12

By the time we make it back to our wing, I can barely stand, my head viciously pounding. The wine helped with the ache there but the pressure there is unending.

Nueena promised to come to my room if anything had gone wrong with Viella's mission. I will need to wait to find out all the details, but I can sleep tonight knowing she is safely back in Ellova.

I slip on a short sleep dress while Leon is in the bathing room. When he finds me again, he swiftly places me in bed, turning the crystal lights low. Relief cascades down me when my head descends onto the pillow, lessening the crown's pressure. Leon climbs in next to me a moment later.

"May I help with your head?"

"Hmm, please." Even with my eyes closed, I recognized the pop of the strawberry oil, that sweet smell whirling around me. He swirls it on each of my temples, the pain slowly dissolving 'til I can think clearly once more.

The scent is intoxicating, lightning going straight to my core. Our strawberry kiss in the garden burns in my memory after he made a mess between my thighs with his tongue.

Curiously I ask, "What does it taste like? The oil, I mean."

I open my eyes to find him staring at me. Without looking away, he presses his finger to the opening of the bottle once more and delicately traces my lips with his glistening finger. First the top, then slowly down to the bottom, 'til he reluctantly retreats, his gaze hooded.

My own lust and longing are reflected back at me in his eyes.

The fluttering in my chest turns ravenous. The first night we met, I felt a pulling sensation I had never experienced before, a calling to the mortal man who had no interest in gems or gold but returned each month to my table just for a few words with me.

He corks the bottle and the urge to kiss him overtakes me. I grab his collar, pulling him down to me. His smiling lips meet mine. Leon's tongue follows the same path his finger had moments before, sliding into my waiting mouth. The oil is silky, mild with a light sweetness to it. I'm greedy for the strawberry-tinted taste of him, our mouths moving together in dizzying devotion.

Leon slides down next to me without breaking our kiss. I cling to him, wrapping one leg around him to pull him closer, but it's not enough. It's never enough. His strong hands navigate my body with a familiar touch, determined to memorize every curve.

The lust building in me is luminous, blinding me to every reason we shouldn't do this.

I groan in protest when his lips leave mine, but it morphs into a moan as his rough attention seeks my neck, licks and sucks, his hand on my cheek. My eyes slowly shut, drowning in the sensation of him.

Smooth and velvety, he whispers into my ear, "You have a healer in your bed, Izadella. There are *other* ways I can make you feel better." He laughs quietly at the shiver that rolls through me. "May I take that as a yes?"

"Y-yes." I nod frantically, stammering.

Leon slides his leg over me 'til he sits on my thighs, knees on the bed so as to not put his full weight on me, and he pours more of the fragrant oil into his palm.

He rubs his hands together to heat it before he starts just above my chest. Slowly building pressure, he makes his way up to my shoulders and squeezes the knots of stress there. His hands are blissful torture as they move up to my neck and back down again, releasing my twisted tendons in gentle waves. He makes his way down my arms and back up, smoothing as he goes. The distress I have experienced the last few days dissolves at his determined caress.

Leon's hands are magical.

He knows just where to massage to elicit my moans of satisfaction, manipulating my body perfectly 'til I am boneless beneath him.

Hands softened by the velvety oil return to my shoulders, varying his compression of the tightness he finds there, sweeping back and forth.

The tension I've held at the top of my body has melted away, but a new type of it builds at my center, wet and aching.

I am a needy, whimpering mess when his soft lips return to my neck, but a healing hand slides down, lowering the fabric of my sleep dress. Slowly, he kisses and teases my shoulder and chest in a new way. I jolt, my eyes flashing open when my nipples gleam with a few drops of the strawberry oil, his tongue swirling around each one. He caresses my other breast, his grasp firm. He moans into the peaked bud, lavishing each one with peppered kisses and demanding sucks, his other hand gently pinching, rolling it between his fingers, sending pleasure rippling through me.

He moves to lie beside me once more. One hand seeks deeper down my body, running up and down my hips. I spread my legs open, begging for his touch to soothe the throbbing need within me. Pleasure builds and I draw the fabric up to my waist, out of his way.

I gasp, clinging to Leon's arm. He drizzles the oil, anointing my center, strong fingers chasing the dripping liquid as it joins my own wetness. He slowly slides his finger up and down my slit, the ache blooming into sweet bliss.

"Leon!" I beg. "Please."

He swallows the words, his lips finding mine again. His kiss is soft, gentle, while his fingers pick up speed. Exploring me, teasing me, driving me mad. His hard cock presses into the side of my thigh.

We moan into each other's mouths when he slips one finger into me, thrusting and pumping. I lift my hips, meeting his plunging movement, his thumb circling my clit. His lips become my anchor as feverish bliss drowns me.

Ecstasy rises in overpowering waves, dragging me under.

My breaths come quicker and quicker. His tantalizing touch is divine, our kiss something closer to worship as he delicately slides in a second finger. His thumb keeps swirling around my sensitive clit while his fingers continue to pump into my pulsating core, searing him into my soul.

Leon keeps his rhythm with his hand, his lips returning to my breast, sucking the tender skin until I am bursting with pleasure.

The grind of my hips is frantic, demanding more from him.

I fracture completely with a broken gasp that draws his praise. "That's it, my love. That's it." His fingers never stop their quest to claim every rivulet of my release. He keeps pumping in and out of me, that wicked thumb applying the perfect amount of pressure as it whorls around my clit.

We're drunk on the afterglow, our kiss leisurely and sweet. His fingers slow, lazy, not leaving any part of me unexplored.

When I have finally caught my breath, his hand slips out of me. He once again brings his glistening fingers up to my parted lips, tracing them twice. His eyes widen when I open my mouth in invitation, my tongue sliding out for him. Leon glides his two fingers in, and my lips circle around them, sucking the essence of my arousal.

He captures my lips with his for another demanding kiss, our ravenous mouths sliding together with the bright strawberry taste on my tongue.

We stay like that for a long time before he breaks our kiss, righting my nightwear and pulling the blankets over us.

I reach for his pants, but he brings my hand up to his lips, kissing my knuckles. "How is your head?"

Oh. The pain is gone, the lightness of my lingering orgasm replacing the pain.

"Much better. Thank you, Leon." I kiss him again, letting my hands wander his body, but he stops me, closing himself around us and pulling me close. "Sleep, Strawberries."

Safe in his arms, I do exactly as he says.

~

"*I*zzy, Izzy."

I'm pulled from sleep by a giggly whisper in my ear. When I finally open my eyes, I'm met with Viella's smiling face as my sweet friend kneels beside my bed, hand reaching for mine. A small crystal light floats above her shoulder. The window beyond her shows a dark sky with dimming yellow and purple stars. She is still dressed in a dark brown traveling cloak with the hood pulled over and a bag over her chest.

"We're going to the temple! Tonight!" she says gleefully, practically bouncing when she says it.

My heart leaps for Lillian; I know she's wanted this for so long. "Are you sure?" I hope she isn't offended by my words, but I need to ask them anyway.

"Oh yes, I've been asking for us to try again for decades. I need to fix my mistake. I will not be scared for a moment longer."

I have dozens of more questions on the tip of my tongue, but Leon sits up behind me.

"Sorry! I didn't mean to intrude! Hello, Leon!"

He gives her a sleepy smile. "Hello. How did tonight go?"

"Oh, fine. Not a single problem. Mimi's family is healthy once more and her mother was distributing all the provisions when I left. Your letter to Queen Erenia was placed in the mailbox."

Jealousy slowly slithers around my gut. He wrote a letter to Grayden's wife? Why? What does he need to say to her? What would be worth the risk?

"Thank you," is all Leon says, smiling at Viella.

"Did you tell Nueena?" I ask, returning my attention to my giddy friend before me.

Viella nods enthusiastically with a dreamy expression on her face. She stands up and takes a step back to let me rise from bed, but we meet in the middle in a crushing hug. She's shorter than I am, which is rare for a fae, and I squeeze her shoulders.

"Ellova open the gates to the temple." I whisper the prayer into her golden curls as she nods, bouncing again.

"The temple will grant us entrance just as dawn breaks and we will find our Zemra stones." When we break apart, she has tears in her eyes. "I can feel it! We've waited for a hundred years. I think that's long enough," she says, laughing.

"Yes, I think so too!"

"I saw Farren! He let out the cutest little annoyed chuff when he realized you weren't with me, but he warmed up enough for some pets. He followed me for a while, but I think he realized I was headed back to the palace and scampered off. He's such a sweet fox."

A little bit of peace returns to me, knowing he is all right. "Thank you, Vi, thank you so much!"

I may need to find a way to bring him here, whether he likes it or not.

She pulls me into another short hug before heading to the door. "Next time you see me, I'll be a bonded Zemra!" She giggles and blows me a kiss before closing the door with a soft click.

"I wrote a letter to Erenia, telling her the truth of the crown. Besides Lyrora, she is the only one I trust, and she needs to know where I am," he explains and I'm relieved that he offers the truth freely to me without my needing to ask. He knew I would wish to know but would feel I have no right to ask.

"What is she like?" I try to say it casually, as if I am speaking of the weather, but I only know two things about the downhearted princess: that she is as beautiful as she is cold.

"She is sharp, notices everything. Passionate and cunning, she is always a step ahead of you. Erenia and I spent countless hours in the library together, both looking for an escape from the Fasaile men for an hour or two. She has many wonderful ideas to change Adreania for the better, but Grayden ignores every one, the bastard." He says the last words with such malice, but I cannot tell if they are on behalf of her or the oppressed people they shared a kingdom with.

"And the two of you never…" I let the words trail off and I immediately feel foolish for asking, turning my head away from him.

It shouldn't matter. He never owed me loyalty, and still doesn't, I realize with a stab to my chest.

Grayden will be locked in a dungeon soon and Erenia will be free of her horrible husband. Leon will return to Adreania with no attachment to me. Perhaps this is a pathway for them to be together. If they wish.

My thoughts betray me, and I suddenly see a vision so clearly, I break my own heart. The two of them reading together in the Adreanian library; they're curled together on a velvet lover's couch, her head on his chest with a small smile I've never seen her wear, and his hand on her thigh. Lost in the words but love found between them.

His warm hand slides across my cheek, taking my jaw in a surprisingly strong grasp and giving me no choice but to look at him, the night's glow illuminating his eyes. He stares at me with such intensity, such longing.

"Never. There has only ever been you." He kisses me softly under the moonlight, but when I lean in for longer kisses, he pulls me against him. "Rest." He holds me 'til my thoughts dance somewhere between reality and sleep, dreamy visions of a soft life with Leon.

CHAPTER 13

$\mathcal{I}$ wake hours later, the sky still dark. A cool breeze shifts the curtains and sends them fluttering around the stone window frame.

Leon's even breaths let me know I do not disturb his slumber as I toss and turn in the silk sheets for some time after.

Did thoughts of me torment him when he was in Adreania like they did to me before I fell asleep for the past few years? Dreams filled with moments we thought we could never have, and yet he is here. With his body pressed to mine, the room feels like home in a way it has never felt in the lifetime I've lived here.

Dawn finally arrives and I surrender to my scarcity of sleep. I leave the warmth of my bed, wrap a pale-yellow robe around myself, and walk over the magically heated marble floor. If I rouse Leon with the movement, he doesn't give any indication. I soundlessly cross the library into the shared living area and press my ear to Nueena's door. When only silence greets me, I push open the door a few inches and peer through the crack for a moment into the quiet room. I walk through the space, past their private sitting room, and make my way to the low bed, pulling back a corner of the thick blanket and slipping under it.

The bed shifts and Nueena rolls, blinking sleep from her eyes to face me, her night dress the color of marigolds.

"Good morning, sleepy Keeper of the Realm," I whisper, a note of song in my voice. "I do believe you have a coronation ball to rise for, and a full day of festivities awaits to celebrate you!"

She laughs, stretching her long arms above her silk-wrapped head. "I thought I would be more nervous, with all the court guardians here for tonight's celebrations and vows, but no, nothing but peace. Maybe the nerves will come on the coronation day."

"Or maybe," Tavien adds from behind her in a voice still sheathed in sleep, "there are no nerves because there is nothing to be nervous about."

"You know, your Zemra may have a point there." I give her a knowing smile.

Nueena just rolls her eyes, but they sparkle with joy in the sunbeams that greet her on this beautiful day, bathing the room in pink and yellow light. "Trouble sleeping?" She finds my hand above the blanket, squeezing our fingers together.

I nod on the pillow we share. "Headache and I had a giddy visitor in the night."

"Ah, as did I."

We giggle quietly like we did when we were kids hiding in a library fort made of Nyvenah's finest silk sheets.

"After all they have gone through, I have no doubt the gates will open for them." I look up to a portrait Nueena and Tavien have hanging on one of their bedroom walls, arms around each other. Their Zemra stones glow even in the oil paint.

Nueena nods. "They are incredibly different yet work exceedingly well together. You can just tell it's meant to be."

When we see them tonight, they will have their stones glowing bright on the dance floor.

A knock on the door reveals the beauty attendants who will start the long process to prepare Nueena for tonight, and we all must rise. Tavien informs me he will keep Leon busy while I'm with Nueena. He claims they have to pick up something for tonight, giving me a sly smile as he kisses his Zemra goodbye.

Nueena and I spend the day in her quarters.

After her rosewater bath, she is anointed in oils, and royal braiders sit on large pillows around her, weaving together several strands of her tight curls with long delicate gold strands that glitter in the sunlight.

Her sisters and Nyvenah join us, their hair styled with elaborate braids and intricate twists for tonight. Our day is filled with laughter, stories and a few tears from her mother.

As evening approaches, I leave and slip into my own dress, eager for whatever the night brings.

~

I return to my room to start the last of tonight's final touches for myself. I stay in my robes as I pull locks of hair into a loose braid to hide the crown, securing it with emerald-tipped pins, the rest falling in soft ringlets.

Leon is in the bathing room, the water rushing behind the closed door.

The small, planted tree in the corner of my room hosts my jewelry and I stare at the necklaces I have to choose from. I crafted them all. Some are delicate with small diamonds or dazzling precious stones, and others are extravagant with woven gold and gems the size of acorns that wrap dramatically around my neck. None of them fit the way the one I intended to make for tonight would have, though.

My throat tightens with grief that I lost my jewelsmith magic before I had a chance to make my emerald necklace. It may be foolish to mourn the loss of jewelry, but I had selected the perfect gems, the exact shade of my gown. It had taken months at the Court of Gems' private markets to find the perfect ones. The sketch of the design now lies abandoned at my cottage. Useless without my powers.

The front door to the wing opens and Hiliyah calls out to me. "Della, I have something for you."

I meet her in the main living space. Her smile is bright, radiating her beauty, and she thrusts a small, flat silk case into my arms.

"What is it? I already have my dress," I ask, confused.

Hiliyah giggles, her dark curls dancing around her. "No, no. This is for Leon but only if you wish him to share shades with you."

Sharing shades.

A fae claiming.

I carefully open the silks and find a masculine shirt cut from the lustrous green material of my gown.

"Oh, Hiliyah." My fingers float over the fabric. I am truly touched she would do this for me.

"Back at the shop, I know you told me you did not want—"

Her words are cut short as I throw my arms around her and she returns the embrace.

"Thank you," I whisper into the curve of her neck.

"There's a plainer option in there as well in case you change your mind," she whispers back. "Leon is a lucky mortal, even if it's just for tonight."

I'm the lucky one.

Leon calls my name and Hiliyah winks at me before slipping back out the front door.

Leon makes his way over to me, freshly bathed, his gray strands a stark difference to the black of his damp hair. He is also shirtless and wearing shined black leather breeches with knee-high laced boots that have small green leaves embroidered on the top cuff.

My heart skips several beats at the sight of him.

His laced-up breeches hang low on his hips, revealing his lean waist that tapers down to the vee of skin above the fabric, his taut stomach muscles on display, inviting me to trace them with my tongue.

I'm staring too long at his tempting waistband, and when I snap my eyes up, he is giving me a devious half grin, as if knowing my lascivious thoughts. His green eyes flare with an equally hungry expression as I approach him. Leon's slow gaze descends my body, the long panels of the yellow robe exposing my bare thighs as I walk barefoot to him. The robe is loosely tied too, putting the curve of my breasts on display. His eyes go out of focus for a moment but quickly return to my face, a hint of pink to his cheeks.

I step into his arms and stand on my tiptoes to give him a quick kiss. "Good evening."

"Hello. How was your day with Nueena?"

"It was wonderful. We need to get ready for tonight. We will be leaving soon."

"Is Tavien coming back? He left some clothes out in the library for tonight, but I seem to be missing a shirt." Leon waves a hand over his bare chest.

I do try to not look at his body anymore, but my eyes keep drifting down, so I turn it into an unconvincing nod. "Um, yes, I have it. Come over to the couch." The silk case holding his shirts is tucked under my arm.

We sit down, side by side, my bare thigh gently brushing his leg as I nervously cross and uncross my legs, torn between the desire to touch him and the rising urge to flee the room.

It may just be fabric, but the intimacy of what it means, what it declares to the world, twists my heart. I never thought I would share shades with anyone, never could have dreamt it would be with the mortal who stole my heart in a crowded ballroom.

But I fear this is just another part of me he will hold forever.

No one else will ever stand in Leon's place. No one could make me feel the way he does.

I will never share shades again after this night.

CHAPTER 14

"I have two choices for you," I say slowly, opening the wrapping and showing him the plain white dress shirt. The accompanying black vest has shimmering gold embroidery along the sides and ties tightly in the back like a corset. With its matching boots, this will go with either choice. "So here is one option. It's a popular style so you'd fit right in." I pass him the vest to examine the intricate threadwork.

"The shirt is very plain," he says, eyebrows crooking upward.

"Um, yes, it is," I murmur softly, suddenly feeling warm. The temperature hasn't changed so it must be me heating up with nerves as we stare at each other.

"Izadella…" He leans forward, just a few inches between our lips. It would be so effortless to brush mine against his. "What color is *your* gown?" he asks softly, looking at the light shirt, feeling the fine material between his fingers.

"Um…mine is dark green."

Leon's shoulders sink a little. "That's my favorite on you."

He looks up and smiles, but it doesn't reach his eyes. Too much longing there, a feeling I know too well. Oh, that green, the very shade of my dress, the color I selected months ago.

Because I wanted to match his eyes even if he wasn't ever going to be here, my own way of sharing shades with him.

He continues, "You said there were other choices?" A hint of hope colors his words.

Love requires bravery, to trust a part of yourself only the other soul can break.

"Yes, yes, I did." He refuses to break eye contact with me, and I take a deep breath, reminding myself not to be such a coward. "At Hiliyah's shop, when we were shop—"

He interrupts me, breaking out in a smug smile. "I remember. I told that ass Kole you'll be wearing green with me."

I cannot help but laugh. "In Ellova there is a tradition with colors at formal gatherings to show off their partnerships. It applies to any color, not just court colors—"

"Yes…shades," he teases. "I asked Tavien about it." He reaches up and pushes a loose strand of hair behind my ear. My cheeks must be pink with the heat of his sweet touch.

His fingers linger for a moment before he cups one side of my face, and I lean into his warm palm. "But I want to hear what it means to you." He whispers the last bit, eyes soft.

My heart races, the crown responding to the devotion in the caress. The magic flows faster inside me, and the potted flowers on either side of the couch erupt with plants hanging over ceramic edges, plump red strawberries dangling off bright green leaves and twining tiny white buds.

We both stare at the uninvited fruit that hangs merrily above the scattered dirt and, when we turn to face each other, burst out laughing, leaning on each other for support.

Maybe I should be embarrassed that this keeps happening, but his smile when it does is addicting. He knows what it means but thankfully hasn't mentioned it.

I'm the first to speak when our laughter finally subsides. "Well, there is a tradition with colors at celebrations. If you have someone that you are with, romantically, you wear clothing cut from the same cloth." I shrug, trying to downplay its significance in Ellova. "It's a way for everyone to know you are spoken for. Could be early courting or hopes of one day wearing the twin Zemra stones. The more events you wear color sets together, the further you are in the relationship. It also means more of my dances would be with you than with anyone else."

He smiles at me, earnest and open. "I like the sound of that."

"And you can decline on my behalf if anyone else wishes to dance with me."

"Oh, I *really* like the sound of that." He laces our fingers together and brings my knuckles to his lips.

My stomach drops. It is an electrifying touch, bringing an ache deep within me. I want his mouth on the curves that my robe barely covers. "It works both ways, you know. I can decline offers you get, too."

"Is that so? Hmm, I would dearly love to see that." He moves closer to me. "Izadella, what are you saying?"

My robe falls open over one shoulder as I turn to face him fully. I think he's going to kiss my face, but he leans to the left and places small, leisurely kisses on the newly exposed skin before moving upward 'til his lips are on my neck.

His warm breath on my skin sends a shiver down my body, and I moan as he speaks again. "Are you asking me? I want to hear you say it." And with that, he sucks the skin of my neck, teasing only to release it, swirling his tongue over the sweet sting.

"Yes." My reply is more of a whimper than a word.

"Yes, what?" he says into my skin, and I can feel his smile against the curve of my neck, his hand tangled in my hair.

I know words will surely fail me when I try to speak. "I—that is…if you…would like to match…with me tonight. I had a shirt made…for you. Leon, I—"

At the utterance of his name, we come together, and my body ignites.

Kissing him is sipping on blackberry wine under starlight.

I swing my leg over his, straddling him, and his hands go under my robe as our lips are crushed together, shirts forgotten. Greedy fingers roam down my body, grabbing for my backside, kneading at the plush flesh he seeks. His black breeches and my robe are the only fabric between us, and I grind my body against his hardness. He moans into my mouth at the scorching contact, deepening the kiss. His lips opens as I slip my tongue in and he meets mine eagerly, claiming.

I rub my fingers over his chest and shoulders, wanting no part of him untouched. He must feel the same as he can't seem to be still, roaming over my thighs, hips and backside.

I am bare under the robe, but he does not move to touch my throbbing center, instead going to my breasts, cupping them under the fabric firmly and using both thumbs to rub over my nipples.

His lips break from mine as he gazes up at me. He moans, "Izadella."

Leon grasps both sides of the robe's opening and yanks them apart, revealing all of me. I push my shoulders back to give him the full view of my breasts.

"Delicious." He takes me into his mouth, sucking, twirling his tongue over the light brown tip. I moan as my fingers glide through his hair, my hips grinding down hard against him.

I reach down for him, but before I can undo the laces to the formal breeches keeping us apart, the main door opens, and suddenly we are no longer alone.

Even though my back faces the entrance and exposes nothing, Leon draws the two sides of the robe closed, tying the sash together in a hasty knot. I chuckle at the alarm in his eyes and kiss his cheek before I peek over my shoulder.

Tavien lets out a boisterous laugh and immediately heads towards their room, giving us privacy, but not before he winks at me and slides the door shut. I sit back on Leon's thighs and turn to Nueena, who is grinning at the scene before her.

"Oh, I am telling Giles about this. He's going to love it," she says, laughing and leaning against the doorframe.

"You will not!"

Leon narrows his eyes in confusion, looking between the two of us and our identical smirks. "Who exactly is Giles and why precisely does he need to know about this?" he asks in a slightly possessive tone.

I run a hand over his worried brows, smoothing out the jealous expression, a thrill going through me. "He is a painter. Nueena's saying she's going to describe what she interrupted and have an oil painting commissioned of the moment she caught us."

Leon lets out a loud laugh and pulls me close, pressing his lips to my forehead. "Please do, Nu. I would like a copy, too."

As I cling to him, Leon stands up, taking me with him, and slowly lowers me to the stone floor. He turns me around with my body in front of him, and I'm about to step away, but when he holds me in place, I realize he's using my body to shield his hardness.

I stifle my laughter.

"While I truly hate to disrupt *whatever* is happening here, I do trust you both would like to attend this ball?" Nueena asks.

Nodding, I glance over my shoulder and Leon raises one eyebrow while he gives me a mischievous smirk that tells me he wouldn't mind missing the ball.

But Nueena adds, "Oh, that wasn't a question. Del is needed tonight." She feigns a stern look and follows Tavien into their rooms.

"We do need to get ready." I step away from Leon to hold up both shirts and he grabs for the white one. My heart sinks before he throws it over the small footstool near the table.

"I cannot believe you even brought a white shirt." He smirks down at me. "I am truly offended."

My eyes fall to the clear bulge at his waist, the evidence of just how very unoffended he is.

"Yes." I draw out the word. "It would appear so."

His lips are curved into a smile as he leans down, pressing them to mine before he whispers, "We are continuing this later, Izadella of the forest." He gives me a wicked smile and a last chaste kiss before we turn back to our rooms, one of his hands in mine, the other clutching the green shirt.

CHAPTER 15

*L*eon watches me with dark eyes as he dresses. I drop the robe before him and slowly slide the gown up my thighs and ample hips, turning my back towards him so he can lace it up for me, his greedy fingers running down my spine. Once I am secure, he leans down, kissing both shoulders.

Without ever saying the words, every one of his kisses and touches makes me feel loved and treasured. I'm greedy for the sensation. Unsure how I will go without it when he leaves.

Hiliyah's dress is spectacular. The fabric is the same rich emerald as Leon's eyes. Its plunging neckline reaches halfway down my stomach and leaves my full breasts open. The top and hemline are covered in delicate silk leaves embellished with small green gems that sparkle when I move, and the long, tight, sheer sleeves end in emerald-encrusted cuffs. The rest of the gown flows freely below my waist and has deep slits that show each side of my legs, reaching up to my hips.

I step away from Leon and twirl, the dress flowing around me, the decorative gems glittering with the movement.

The shirt Hiliyah made for him is perfectly cut to his body, and with an even darker corset vest over it, I have never seen anyone look so handsome. It takes my breath away. Joy spreads in my chest as I envision tonight: celebrating Nueena, representing my court, and dancing in his arms 'til dawn. Besides his rounded ears he appears like an Ellovian ready to attend the festivities. I do not miss the two daggers at his side, the sheaths matching his black attire, nearly hiding it from unsuspecting eyes.

He slips the pointed gold ear cuffs over his rounded tips before closing the distance between us, graceful and determined, as if he cannot bear to be more than a touch away from me.

"You look radiant, Izadella." We share a wide smile as he takes all of me in. "You are truly beautiful. I look forward to denying all other potential dance partners who think they have a chance with you. Tavien even said I could borrow a sword to ensure everyone knows you're mine." He places a hand over his heart. "And in my colors tonight, too."

"Your colors?" I raise one eyebrow at him.

"Oh, did you think I didn't notice that the fabric was the *exact* color of my eyes? No point in lying to me, my dear," he teases me.

I wish to deny it if only to wipe the smug smirk off his face, but my heated cheeks and shy smile betray me. "Well, you do have lovely eyes," I say, rolling mine.

He steps even closer, leaving no space between us. "Thank you for this honor."

"I'm warning you now, healer, I am a poor dancer."

He nods, understanding. "My only wish for tonight is to hold you close. Currently dancing is only the way I'm accomplishing it, as we are cursed to be interrupted." He winks at me.

A truly embarrassing giggle falls from my lips. "You say that now, but you may need to use those healing skills on yourself before the night is over." I look down at his shoes. "Those poor things."

He laughs but it fades quickly when he asks, "You're not wearing any jewelry tonight?" His eyes follow my hand as I rub over my collarbone, hating how bare it is.

"I do not think so. I had my heart set on a very special necklace I designed but—" My throat tightens, soul still raw from the loss of my jewelsmith magic. It is too painful to speak of.

Much to my confusion, Leon picks up a square, yellow velvet box that I hadn't noticed, off my bed. He carefully opens it.

Tears blur my vision at the sight of my emerald necklace before me.

A large teardrop-cut emerald sits nestled on a cushion, surrounded by small diamonds. Small leaf-shaped emeralds on each side of the diamonds go down slowly, getting bigger 'til they meet in the middle, with the largest of them hanging between the rows of the leaf emeralds.

I gape at him. How could he possibly have known about this necklace?

"Tavien wished for some history of the other kingdoms and offered to trade me for the scrolls, and I saw your original sketch back at your cottage and the loose jewels on your desk. I sketched out a drawing of it from memory. Hiliyah and Tavien helped bring it to life. I wanted to give you something to remember me by, and I hope in a few hundred years you can look back on it with happy memories and know how much you meant to me." He whispers the last part as he removes the necklace. "May I?"

I nod and run my fingers over the gems, speechless at the gift he delicately places around my neck. He clasps the chain and moves both of us in front of the bedroom mirror.

The sight of us takes my breath away, and I watch my reflection as tears roll down my flushed cheeks. Leon moves behind me and wraps his arms around my waist, pulling me close. "Beautiful. You look positively regal, my little gem. Like a queen. *My* queen."

We do look like royalty, like rulers of a far-off realm where mortals and fae can be as one, free of madness and untouched by time.

"Leon?"

"Yes, Strawberries."

"Just for tonight, can we forget about the future? Can we pretend everything will be all right?"

"Of course. Tonight, we are nothing but two dancers on the floor."

My voice breaks. "Thank you."

His lips press into my cheek, pulling me even closer, just two star-crossed lovers on the sparkling ballroom floor, unburdened all night with whatever tomorrow brings. I close my eyes for a moment, absorbing his endless devotion.

Someone clears their throat, and my eyes fly open again.

Nueena appears behind him in our reflection, smiling softly at our intimate embrace. "Apologies for interrupting yet again, but the court guardians are here for the procession, so we must leave."

Nueena is breathtaking.

Dressed in the gown Hiliyah designed, she shines as bright as the sun.

Her luxurious lilac gown is made of iridescent fabric and drops off the shoulders. Diamonds descend from her waist like falling stars amid silk flowers, gold adornments, and sheer drapery that gracefully descends down before flowing back up into panels that hang behind her.

Haloing her head are more of the silk flowers with the crown I made her—twenty-three points of various sizes coming out like the sun, crystals dangling from each tip.

I step away from Leon and take Nueena's hands in mine.

When we were dewlings, we hid in Nyvenah's extensive closet and wore her gowns that were far too large for us, and pretended we were at Nueena's coronation ball. We'd spin in circles and envision dancing to music in the arms of imaginary dance partners, parading around her parents' chambers, tripping over fabric. I would pick my favorite of Nyvenah's vast crown collection, dramatically bowing, and presenting it to Nueena before placing it on her head.

Nyvenah came back to her closet and found us fast asleep after hours of dancing, half of the contents of her wardrobe on the floor, one of her treasured crowns falling haphazardly over Nueena's curls.

Nueena has been dreaming of this night for so long.

We both lean forward, our foreheads pressed together, her hand tightly held in mine. No words are expressed. We do not need them as the excitement radiates off us.

Together we walk to the door, where Tavien stands. He pulls me into a tight hug, lifting me off the ground as I laugh. "Del, you look gorgeous!" He puts me down and turns to Leon. "You really will be needing that sword."

I playfully nudge my shoulder into his arm, thankful for my friends.

"Thank you for the necklace," I say to him, rubbing the stones that decorate my neck.

He points to Leon. "That was all him. He gave me the stones and provided the sketch."

"Who made it?" I ask.

"Lazalai."

Lazalai, Keeper of the Gem Court and my dear friend. Guilt churns low in my belly that I've kept such a secret from her. "I will need to thank her."

Tavien addresses all of us. "We have twice the guard count on duty tonight. They have been made aware of an elevated threat against the royal family, Della included. Tonight is a celebration but, Del, please be on guard. We still have a traitor in our midst."

I nod. "I will."

We all leave together. Outside the main doors to our wing is Nueena's family and their guard. Nyvenah has chosen the dress she can dance in and is now arm in arm with Alachite, who wears a formal jacket of the same color.

Nueena's little sisters, Vaylin and Kaylena, are dressed in different shades of purple to represent the Ellovian High Court. Both help their sister by carrying the train of her long dress.

Six guards stand with a flag of each court in golden armor, their faces hidden. Lillian stands in front of all of them and, for the first time in the many years I've known her, she is wearing a gown. The purple silk is so dark it appears almost black, with tight sleeves like mine; the rest is flowing. Her dress also has high slits, revealing three golden daggers strapped to her thigh. A long matching hair pin holds back the tight bun resting on the top of her head and is no doubt a weapon of its own.

A glowing yellow Zemra stone hangs around her neck.

They did it!

Soulbonded!

My chest swells with unending pride and elation for her. We make eye contact, and she rolls her eyes at my obvious excitement, but there is a smile on her dark lips, too.

I want to hug them both and shout with joy, but that must wait.

Nyvenah and Alachite lead the way, their dewlings trailing behind. Tavien's hand is low on Nueena's back as they make their way down the hall to the celebration of Nueena's coronation. Leon and I wait for them to pass us to join the end, the clash of thunder in the distance.

"Ready? I ask him.

We stare at each other as he closes his hand around mine, brings my knuckles to his lips, and whispers against my skin, "For a night with you in my arms? I've been eternally ready."

I have no words to express the burst of hope and excitement that erupts in my soul, but it's on his face, too, and maybe we do not need them.

CHAPTER 16

The guards hold the flags high; the court emblems embroidered in the waving fabric as the coronation ball starts

Leon and I are last in the procession behind the royal family. We walk slowly, and my stomach releases a flurry of butterflies as we make our way down to the stained-glass doors leading to the ballroom. They open on their own, bringing forth the deafening noise of merriment.

The ballroom is a vision of Ellovian Court purple and glittering gold amid vines and plants of all shades of green. Above the crowds of dancing fae are glowing luna moths fluttering lazily beneath the crystal lights and flora chandeliers.

The center of the ballroom is crowded with couples, most in matching colors, swirling around across the golden dance floor. Around the perimeter are round tables with decorative chairs and impossibly tall glimmering vases, bundles of white and purple roses with sparkling strings of diamonds coming down. Behind those tables are rows and rows of every type of food Ellova has to offer.

"The chefs and bakers have outdone themselves," Leon whispers to me.

"I can't wait to try everything," I whisper back. "Magic keeps everything hot so none of the palace attendants have to work during tonight's celebration."

The melody everyone was dancing to slowly comes to a natural stopping point, the musicians noting Nueena's arrival when the trumpet announces her.

Giddy excitement swells within me at the burst of sound.

Those in attendance watch with cheerful expressions and genuine delight, some even adding a respectful bow as they watch Nueena go by. She does not walk with her nose up as Princess Erenia does, but smiles, making eye contact with everyone she can, waving at the dewlings who jump with excitement, throwing purple petals in the air when she passes.

Alachite and Nyvenah follow Nueena and Tavien up to the stage, but Vaylin and Kaylena stay behind with Leon and me. We move to the front to watch while Nueena and her parents take their place on the marble dais built around a massive tree coming out from the ground.

Nyvenah stands before the Throne of Ellova. Alachite and Nueena sit on each side of her. Tavien stands behind Nueena, sword in hand, as Nyvenah proudly addresses the cheering crowd.

"Welcome to all who have joined us to celebrate the coronation of my daughter."

The crowd applauds with shouts of joy.

"Tonight, the celebration starts with dancing, dining, and drinking. By this time in six days, we will have the crowning ceremony, and you will have a new Realm Keeper. I know she will lead with justice and kindness, grace and passion." She continues her speech of how well Nueena will lead Ellova, over the roar of the crowd.

The guardians ascend in a single line and come to the dais. All stand before Nueena as she bows to them and the crowd before kneeling on a fluffed pillow facing the ballroom.

"Why did she kneel?" Leon wonders quietly to me.

"It's symbolic. She will put the courts and her throne over herself. Once she becomes ruler, she will lay the first stone in the foundation of a selfless rule. Since she has a Zemra, Tavien will be the one to assist her. It's symbolic that he will always be there to lift her up."

The room erupts and the entire crowd bows deeply back to her. Leon bows at the waist when I do. Once the crowd has risen, Tavien is at Nueena's side, raising her up, and gently setting her back on her feet, the music playing.

Alachite offers Nyvenah his hand. She takes it and they make their way to the dance floor.

Leon nods with understanding, but his expression turns dark. "It seems to be difficult to lead and to be selfless. The idea of a selfless royal is at odds with every ruler I have seen."

"You doubt her?" I ask, taking a step back.

His eyes widen with alarm. "No, no. Never. She is the first leader I've encountered who I believe will live by the vows she will make. It's just that the kings outside this realm are unfamiliar with the concept that their needs should come last."

"Is that not what will bring Grayden's downfall? Through war or at the hands of his own people? He would starve them and burn his land before he would have turned over the crown to Kalvorn, even if that was all they asked for. He would rather have the illusion of power at the expense of those who reside in his cursed kingdom."

"I doubt the king of Kalvorn will find Adreania worth fighting with now that the crown has left its grasp."

One can only hope. "If Kalvorn still seeks it, they will be searching for a long time," I add.

I wish to speak more of Kalvorn but Lazalai appears, pulling me into a tight hug. Her floor-length black hair is in one thick braid, adorned with jewels that swing.

"Della!" The gold pigments spread over her lips and pale cheeks glint under the crystal lights when she pulls back, smiling. She wears a yellow silk band that wraps around her neck and hangs down, hiding her full breasts, but leaves her thick legs and hips on full display. Yellow crystals in long strings drape over her arms and down her skirts, wrapping around her waist.

Joy at seeing her, gratefulness for my necklace, and guilt I've kept such an important secret from her bring forth a swirl of sentiments in my gut, but it settles on gratitude. For the necklace and for her unwavering love for me.

I caress the stunning gemstone adorning my neck. "Thank you, thank you so much!"

"Anything for you, my dear. Your friend is quite the gentleman." She winks at Leon. "A beautiful gift for you."

"She deserves a king's trove of presents," he says.

I laugh at Leon's prideful smile.

"Are you ready to celebrate all night?" Lazalai shakes her hips for emphasis.

I nod excitedly. "I've been ready for years."

"Delightful! I will see you out there."

She blows me a kiss and joins her multiple lovers on the dance floor, and I watch her leave with a smile. I know Nueena has glamoured the crown and it is unwise for me to remain near any of the Guardians for too long to ensure they do not sense it, but it is good to see her.

I gather my skirt and exit the throne area with Leon, ready to start the celebration. I haven't taken more than ten steps before Kole is suddenly in front of me, dressed in the blue-and-white colors of his court.

"You are finally here," he says with a sly smile, wine on his breath, holding out his hand.

He is bold to ask when Leon and I are so obviously a matching set. Kole's blatant disregard for our own traditions grates on my nerves, no matter our long history of familiarity. When I do not take it, he attempts to grab my arm with a laugh. "Let's dance."

Kole is an idiot.

Leon's hand strikes out to seize Kole's arm, forcing him to stop.

"Has the wine blurred your vision so early in the night? Or are you just ignoring the fact we are sharing shades?" Leon's biting words thrill me. His knuckles are white with the merciless grip he has on Kole.

Kole's eyes narrow on Leon and he yanks his arm away. "Oh, you are still here. I'm not asking you, whoever the fuck you are."

Leon wraps his arm around my waist, pulling me to him and out of Kole's reach. "No, you were demanding her, and I'm telling your pathetic ass, that's not happening. Not tonight. *Not ever.* Don't bother her *again.*"

Kole's drunken face twists in indignation at the slight. He steps up to Leon, anger radiating off him. "I don't take orders from a *nobody* like you."

"You do now, fishboy," Leon snaps.

Kole pulls his fist back, sending my heart into my gut, but Leon forces me away. The crown's protective magic emerges within me, but Leon strikes before it can release. He knocks Kole down with alarming swiftness, Kole's broken nose leaking blood.

Gods, this is beyond embarrassing.

Kole pathetically attempts to get up but stumbles.

Thankfully, Everett rushes over and grabs Kole by the arm, yanking him up. "Why can't you leave her alone, you idiot? You'd better pray Koray or Lillian didn't see you make a fool of yourself," he hisses.

"Oh, it's too late for that." Lillian steps out from the dispersing crowd who has mostly lost interest now the fight has ended. "Kole, let's have a chat with your Guardian about your behavior. Both past and present offenses."

I let out a relieved breath as a disoriented Kole is hauled away by Lillian, his eyes glazed with confusion.

I doubt she will seek a healer for him before speaking to the Court of Shells Guardian, Koray, about him.

Everett looks at me with apologetic eyes. "I'm so sorry, Della. I told him to leave you alone. He got what was coming to him. I'll stay close for the rest of the evening to make sure you are not bothered by anyone else tonight."

"That will not be necessary," Leon says in a possessive tone. "She will be fine, plenty of honeyguards and added protection nearby. Any other fools trying to steal her away will be dealt with."

Everett lets out a little laugh and shrugs. "Very well, I will assist the commander. Enjoy your evening." He turns to follow Lillian.

I may not need his protection tonight, but I do require something from his mother.

"Wait! Everett?" I step away from Leon. "When you see Camarra, can you ask if she can do anything about the weather?" I ask hopefully. I do not want anything to ruin tonight's festivities. "A storm seems to be rolling in."

Everett glances behind us at the dreary sky just beyond the large windows. "Of course." He gives a playful bow and leaves.

Once we are finally alone, an annoyed Leon steps closer to me. "What is Kole's problem?"

"He should have known better, but he was drunk." A lightness in my chest soothes me at Leon's unending protection and care.

I refuse to let an intoxicated fool tarnish our evening.

Leon opens his mouth to say something else, but I stand on my toes to kiss his cheek. His words die on those lips I love so much.

The tension releases from him. "Can we take this to the dance floor? I cannot resist more time holding you close." Leon asks with a greedy grin.

I hold out my hand with a laugh, and he pulls it to his lips, kissing the top of it, before steering me to the golden ballroom.

Our chests press together and we melt into each other. Other couples swirl around us, but I cannot tear my eyes away from the light in his, a joy I haven't yet seen in the short time we have known each other. He guides and I follow his lead, our bodies united and moving as one to the symphony of music that engulfs the room. All others fade away, only the two of us in this world.

"I'm sorry you had to experience that. Tell me what's on your mind?" he asks softly.

"That's all right. No one can ruin tonight. You simply won't allow it."

"That is exceedingly true, *my queen.*"

My heart skips a beat at the way he says it, with such devotion and warmth, like it was always on the tip of his tongue, waiting just for me.

The musicians lead into a new song meant only for lovers, slow and rhythmic. Leon's large hand presses low on my back, ensuring no space is left between us as we leisurely sway.

I want this. Forever.

Just him and me, on gilded palace dance floors or a simple one-room cottage.

My head is on his chest. His heartbeats are slow, unlike that of my fae heart, the heartbeat of a man with a mortal timeline.

I close my eyes. That is not what I wish to think of now. Not tonight, wrapped in his arms, a celebration surrounding us in its merriment. That is a thought for tomorrow's sunrise.

Tonight is to make a memory that will last for a lifetime without him.

Tonight is a beautiful lie that I will cherish, with no place for heartbreaking reminders of a future out of my grasp.

Tonight is a reminder that love exists and for a brief moment it graced me with its touch. I dig my nails deeper into the fabric of his evergreen shirt as if I could squeeze the thoughts of the future away.

CHAPTER 17

*L*eon and I dance all night.

The celebration of Nueena's upcoming coronation has no end in sight. Music and revelry fill the rooms of the Ellovian palace. We renew our energy periodically, stopping by the many tables displaying gilded trays of roasted meat and sugared fruit on each side of the marble ballroom. Fountains of deliciously sweet blackberry wine are ever flowing.

Eventually Nueena, Hiliyah, and Tavien join us on the floor and together we dance for hours. Nueena and I spin each other around to the rapid melodies, weaving between the other dancers. When the music switches to a slow rhythm, giving everyone a chance to catch their breath, Leon tugs me near, his arms tight around me.

Viella pulls Lillian into the ballroom. Lillian is not nearly as threatening in a dress and a soft smile only for her love. We all watch the two Zemras dance for a moment. Vi's dancing is graceful and fluid, a gift that has always come naturally to her. She spins and sways, her passion for the art of motion is beautiful to watch. Lillian's less so, but she looks happier than I have ever seen her.

Their eyes sparkle with joy as they dance with their Zemra. Soulbonded. Forever.

Nueena and I share a giddy look. I'm sure she wishes to rush over and congratulate them, as I do, but we give them their time together. They will find us later.

After all the wine, my face is heated and I seek out the crisp night breeze, the scent of rain in the air. I grab Leon's hand, and he follows me to a blissfully empty balcony that wraps around the ballroom. One side overlooks the city center and further down, the Merawood Forest on the other. Leaning into the railing and twisting my hair up in a bun to try and cool myself, I relax against the carved stone.

"Hello, Della, dear. I heard Kole was quite the prick this evening." Camarra's musical voice stands out among the revelry, growing louder at her approach.

Word spreads fast. "That he was, but thankfully your son handled him." She may be Everett's mother, who has always been kind to me, but I am still weary of her for withholding information about the harvest from Nyvenah. Along with the potential of her sensing the crown, I will only stay and speak with her for a few minutes. Any more than that, I will need to politely excuse us.

She joins Leon and me on the balcony, staring up, and we follow her gaze. No stars shine down on this joyous night. The sky is filled with storm clouds threatening our evening. "What horrid weather this is, and with fireworks ready to entertain," she muses.

We both turn to smile at each other, her yellow canary on her shoulder. "We are quite fortunate to have a cloudkeeper as a Guardian," I say.

"How right you are!" Camarra walks to the edge with a laugh, her hands rising with each step.

Lightning flashes above us.

I take Leon's hand and tug him back, giving her all the room she needs. He opens his mouth but closes it again when a brilliant wind swirls around her. She flings her hands forward, bracelets jingling, and the twisting wind flies upward into the dark sky. Her bird flaps its wings, holding on to her for dear life. Clouds shift as she sends more and more gusts, her hair whipping around. Her cloudkeeper's magic pushes back the storm. Massive gray clouds roll away, stars blinking back at us.

She lowers her hands and smooths out her hair with a bit of magic. "There. All is well."

"Thank you!" I add. "I will tell Nueena how helpful you have been tonight."

The Court of Green's Guardian just waves her hand. "It was nothing, enjoy the celebration." She gives us a polite nod as she leaves.

"That was quite impressive," Leon says.

"It's a rare gift."

The view is spectacular now and we can see smaller celebrations happening all over, fireworks exploding off in the distance.

He whispers in my ear, "Do you remember the day we met?"

"Of course I do. Two years ago, this month. How could I forget?"

I had thought it was going to be a night just as boring as every other bazaar. Rude courtiers, a crowded ballroom, greed fully on display. And then he was before me with wide eyes and a stunned smile.

"You looked beautiful. You wore a blue dress." He pushes a loose piece of hair behind my ear. "And you had on little diamond earrings. I'd never seen anyone so beautiful. I still think that. I was devastated when one of the other vendors told me you were married. Taken by another who wasn't me. The cruelty of it all."

"And yet, here we are, together."

He nuzzles my cheek with his. "Together."

The spires of Adreania's castle and the mountain range leading to Kalvorn catch my attention.

"Do you think Kalvorn is still looking for the crown?" I whisper.

"You wear a very powerful object on your head, and many will want it if it is discovered, but you do not need to fear Kalvorn or its king."

I wrap my hands around his neck, and he holds me tight. "How do you know?" I ask. The desperate hope in my voice is as clear as the night sky.

He stares at me with the softest smile. "The rulers of Kalvorn are kind and just. It's part of why Grayden hates them so much:

they are beloved by their people. King Zilas won't risk any of his citizens' lives to get the crown back the way Grayden would. Even if the traitor knows you have the crown here, Kalvorn does not."

"What do you think their queen is like?" I ask, picturing someone like Queen Erenia.

"I hear she is a lovely woman and beloved by her husband. They have one child, a prince. Married two years ago, around the time we met."

"I just want this damn crown off, so I don't need to worry about kings and their quest for power. To return to my cottage and the peace it holds, never to think of the crown again."

"We will find a way to remove it. There must be a key to unlocking it." He sounds determined and I almost believe him.

That is a worry for tomorrow.

I stand on the tips of my toes and kiss him, slipping my fingers through his hair. He kisses me slow and lazy, like we have all the time in the world, his lips soft and patient, tinted with longing. Our tongues meet and he tastes like blackberries and hope. One hand roams slowly over my back but the other one has firmly planted itself on my hip, his grip uncompromising. The jubilation is all around us. Cheers and toasts to Nueena's future reign.

More vibrant purple fireworks go off closer to us, and we break apart to look at the sparkle-filled sky.

Leon's hands slip around my waist, and he pulls me to his front so we're both facing the celebrations.

From our spot we can see so much of Lavencia below. The dancers moving to the music of the street musicians, children running around the city center. Most of the shops and homes have removed their own courts' flags to fly Ellova's crest, a sea of purple blowing in the wind.

As I lean back into Leon, he turns his head, and his soft lips meet my temple. We stay like that for a long time, gently swaying to the music that has followed us out. I reach up with one arm and hold his face, and he presses more kisses into my hair.

Shattering noises on either side of me draws a deep sigh from me. I know exactly what I will see. Enormous strawberry bushes reaching towards the sky have grown out of the flower planters on either side of the balcony. The purple roses that had been there before are now smashed at odd angles under the newly grown shrub demanding the space. A few more juicy strawberries have broken off, meeting the flowers already on the stone floor.

I should probably be embarrassed by now but I'm not. Smiling, I lean back again against his chest.

"Time to calm down, Strawberries," he says into my hair with a laugh. "Nueena is here."

Nueena steps out onto the balcony to join us. They each carry elegant crystal goblets filled with sparkling violet wine. The light from the ballroom behind her gives her an ethereal glow.

"Not a single planter is safe from you, Del." Tavien teases me.

I lightly slap his massive forearm.

"Truly," Leon's grin is mischievous, "I take full responsibility."

"A toast," Nueena declares as we each take our glasses, "to new friends and new beginnings."

We all agree in unison.

At the bottom of our glasses are frozen pearls to keep the liquid chilled, and they chime as we bring the crystal together. The wine is crisp and tart and I feel lighter after every sip.

"I'm going to get some food. Would anyone like something?" Leon asks.

"Yes!" Nueena and I say together. "Everything!"

"I will accompany you, then," Tavien says to Leon with a laugh. They walk off together back into the merriment of the ballroom.

I watch Leon leave before turning to my oldest friend. "The ceremony was beautiful. Did you see how Lillian was smiling?"

Nueena laughs at that. "I did. We will have to bring it up as much as possible, preferably in front of her sentries." We giggle at the thought. "Tonight was perfect."

"Feels like we were just dewlings running around the throne room, wishing it was the real event, and here it is."

She leans on the balcony, looking down at her vast realm. "Seems strange they're all celebrating *me*. I haven't done anything yet."

"They are all excited for a bright future with you at the helm! They love you." I lightly knock my shoulder into her, and she returns the tap.

"To Ellova's future." She holds up her glass, and the echoing *clink* joins the joyous chorus just below us.

Leon and Tavien return, each with a bottle of wine tucked under their arm. In each hand they have a plate covered in sliced meat, fruit, mini lamb pies, and fried potatoes. We all eat and drink straight from the bottles.

There is a rush of footsteps followed by shouts of joy as Viella collides with Nueena and me, turning us into a mess of tangled limbs and tearful cheers.

"We're Zemras! We're Zemras!" Viella steps back grinning from ear to ear. "The gates opened and we are soulbonded!"

"How was it, Vi?" I hold my breath, desperately hoping she tells us every detail. I must not be the only one; Leon's back stiffens besides me, and he leans slightly closer.

"It was like a dream. The temple is magical in a way I've never felt before. Crystals everywhere! It's a different type of magic. We found our stones! They glowed and the soulbonding ritual's magic took over. Just like that! We were one!" Viella's eyes shine with adoration as she gazes at Lillian, whose expression mirrors her own.

Lillian wraps her arm around Viella's shoulder. Their Zemra stones flare in affection with a bright yellow light.

"Sounds wonderful," I say, my heart full of love for my friends. "Why last night, though?" I think I know but I wish to hear it from them.

Traditionally, Zemra journeys are planned in advance. A group of close friends and family wait for the couple to return. To celebrate a bond with joyous revelry or grief, weather the weeping together.

Lillian is the first to speak, staring down at Viella with such devotion. "I've known she was my Zemra for many years. Even when she disappeared the night we intended to journey to the temple, I still knew. When we found our way back to each other, years later, I told her I may never be ready to try again, but seeing her ride away into Adreania, I just couldn't bear another night not being connected with her in every way possible, to not know if she was all right. It suddenly seemed so damn foolish to deny us the bond any longer because of past hurts. I had forgiven her a long time ago so what was I waiting for? I understand why she was so scared the first time. We could keep healing from the past while ensuring a future together."

We are all stunned into silence at Lillian's vulnerable words declared so openly. Becoming Zemras truly does change a heart.

"I couldn't change the past, but I can prove now, in every way, that we are meant for each other," Viella says in a dreamy voice.

They were always destined for each other.

Seemed so foolish to deny us the bond any longer.

My stomach clenches in distress.

Isn't that what I am doing? Denying what Leon and I have?

"Besides, I have this now." Lillian snaps her finger and a flame appears, dancing around her palm. It is not the blue light of Viella's fire, but mixed with Lillian's magic, it is a deep purple. "Just what I needed to motivate new recruits."

Nueena, Tavien, and I laugh, knowing she is merely joking, but one of Leon's eyebrows rises in concern.

Viella adds, "Sharing magic is incredible, sharing minds! It is the most beautiful connection, to know her so deeply. And the sex is astonishing. Best we ever had!" She laughs.

A flustered Lillian blushes. "All right, that's enough of that, my love."

Viella giggles, pulling on her arm. "Let's go back to the dance floor." As they leave, Vi animatedly tells her new Zemra about the sugar-covered lime pie she enjoyed earlier. Lillan is led away with a smile, her almost black-purple dress that matches Viella's, trailing behind her.

The Zemra stones around Nueena and Tavien glow too as he leans down to his love. They must be thinking of their own time in the temple.

When I glance over at Leon, the open longing on his face nearly takes me to my knees. Afraid of what is etched on my own face, I force myself to look away. In the distance, a large stone wall holds back a reservoir, moonlight reflecting off the dark water.

Leon follows my stare. "What is that?"

Nueena frowns. "The Airvell River that once flowed through the Merawood Forest into the mortal realm is blocked here. Realm Keeper Zarella let the waters free to bring peace and prosperity to Adreania but had the stone dam built when Drystan murdered her best friend. From what Del has told me, it was a great loss to the mortals. If I had enough magic to release it, I would. The enchantment ensures its healing waters are never returned to the mortals."

"Loyalty runs deep in Ellova," Leon says, glancing between Nueena and me.

"The mortals are right to fear the fae. Drystan started a war by taking Inara's life the way he did, and he was lucky to survive it. Zarella did everything she could for revenge."

"Remind me never to be on the receiving end of your wrath, Nueena, if that is the bloodline you descend from," Leon says with a short laugh.

"As long as you do not hurt Della, you never will be." She says it with a smile, a simple jest, but it holds so much truth.

Before Leon can respond, Alachite comes out to steal his daughter away for a toast with the Guardians, and Tavien follows, leaving Leon and me alone once more.

He holds me in his arms, and we dance on the balcony.

Why can't this night last forever?

The music is slow, leaving only lovers on the gilded tiles just inside. I relax in his arms, safe and content, only stumbling over the skirts of my gown a few times, laying my head on his chest, soaking up everything that he is to me.

Friend. Lover. Protector.

I stumble at a commotion on the dance floor. The dancers all stopped at once, all eyes on the dawn breaking behind us, before rushing past us.

"Fire!" One of them shouts.

Terror strikes my chest.

Lillian runs to me, Viella at her heels. "Della, your cottage!"

In the distance, part of the Merawood Forest is on fire. The tallest tree, the one planted in my backyard, burns brightest of them all, and I watch in utter horror as it goes down.

Farren!

CHAPTER 18

"FARREN!" I scream.

Farren might be inside my burning cottage. Trapped by the flames.

Bile rises in my throat, my body shaking, the magic feeling like it's going to boil out of me and burn me from the inside. Rip me apart. My skin can't hold it.

Farren was everything to me, the precious life that was mine to protect and care for.

I failed him.

I can't breathe.

"Della, Farren would have run away." Lillian gets to me before Leon does, but I step out of her reach.

"The wards lock from the inside at any danger. If he was inside when it start—" I'm unable to finish the thought. "It has to be Grayden," I whisper, tears streaming down my face.

"He can't possibly know that's your cottage, right?" Anger fills Viella's eyes at the sight of my home burning, her fists shaking.

Lillian's intake of breath is the only sound before I start screaming again.

The blinding pain of being split in half and molded back together rages in me. For the first time, I can feel my own magic swirling with the crown's, propelled by my emotions, both powers melding inside me. The agony and outrage of watching my home burn has my magic fusing with the crown's, bursting to the surface inside me.

Everything that is gold around us begins to melt, gilded rivers pooling at my feet.

Tall rose bushes turn black before the pots shatter, water rising in droplets from the blackened plants. The water from the pitcher on the drink cart rises with it.

Nueena and Tavien are at my side.

My eyes focus straight ahead but I can feel all my friends looking at me.

The magic's power feels like it's going to break my skull apart. My precious little fox might be dead, his home on fire, and the blazing anger that fills me is unending.

"Leon, stop! Come back!" Tavien yells.

Grayden thinks he can just burn down my forest? The flames, bright and hot, destroying the home my family built, the ancient place my ancestors used to forge the greatest magical creation ever made. Where the forger made a crown that would control such powerful magic that I now have.

I'm still screaming when I raise my arms up and focus on the small body of water that sits next to my beloved cottage, demanding the magic bend to my will. Calling to the natural metals in the lake. Commanding the iron and copper of the soil beneath it to rise. When I yank my arms back, the water rushes up into the air, rising above the flames. It moves like a wave spilling onto the fire, snuffing it all out with one motion, leaving behind only large tendrils of smoke rising into the starry night.

Nueena asks with awe in her voice, "Oh, Del, how did you do that?"

"Farren, my love," I whisper as my legs give out, and Tavien catches me before everything goes black.

~

a single fairy light floating above me casts everything in golden light and shadows. I wince as ice wrapped in cloth is pressed to my head where it's cradled in Nueena's lap in my bed. She takes the cloth away and puts it in the ceramic bowl next to her.

"You were burning up," she says.

I sit up as best I can. Everything hurts, like the first time I put the crown on. My head feels cloudy, with sharp, shooting pain behind my eyes. She brings a cup to my lips and pours sweet water into my mouth. When I'm done drinking, I lie back down on my side. All I want is answers. "What happened?"

Nueena rubs my cheek. "You put out the fire and collapsed. Tavien carried you to bed and you've been asleep for a few hours. Although sleep is the wrong word. You've been tossing and turning and mumbling. None of it made any sense."

"I'm sorry."

She shakes her head; face contoured in concern. "You were incredible! I don't understand what happened, though. I've never seen anyone outside of the Court of Shells control water in such a way." She brings the cold cloth back to my forehead and pats gently.

"I was just so angry. I could feel my magic again, just for a few moments while it fused with the crown's magic. I wasn't controlling the water. I was controlling the metals that exist within it." I pull up my legs to my chest and bury my head in my knees. "Farren..." His name is a broken whisper I barely recognize on my lips.

"He probably ran away. He is smart and fast and—"

"And territorial and curious. He probably tried to defend that stupid cottage. Remember when Kole tried to bring me flowers seventy years ago? Farren hid in a bush and bit his ankle when he knocked on the door." Tears slide down my face, and she leans down, wrapping her arms around me.

"Oh, Del." She moves her hand to my hair, pushing it back in a calming petting motion as tears run down her face too.

She loved him too, just like I did, and he loved her.

"Farren got away; I am sure of it. He was probably up in a tree, glaring down at Grayden's men. They probably ran screaming the other way, thinking him a dark spirit."

I laugh despite myself, despite the tears. He *would* do that, the little scamp. Nueena and I break apart, and I know the one other person I need right now.

"Where's Leon?" Another wave of dread hits me.

I frantically look around the room as if he is hiding to give us space in our grief. More tears come at the absence of him by my side. Where could he have gone? I need him here, now, at my side.

"Del…he…he left. Tavien tried to stop him. I'm sorry."

I sit up so fast I feel faint again, fear digging into my gut. "What? He shouldn't have gone! What if Grayden's men are still out there? He could be taken back to Adreania or killed." I attempt to get out of bed, but the world sways and Nueena rests her hands on my shoulders, gently pulling me back.

"Please try to sleep. My mother has sent guards from the Court of Swords to investigate what happened. Tavien is waiting at the back kitchen door for Leon's return. You need to rest. Whatever happened tonight took so much out of you." She moves to stand but I grab her hand and bring her back to kneel next to me.

"I never told him I loved him. What if something happens to him and he doesn't know?"

"He knows," she says softly. "You both look at each other as if you are raising the sun just for them. Whatever the morning brings, trust that you told him, just not with words." She squeezes my hand. "I'll leave my door open if you need me. Sleep."

"Thank you, Nu."

The crystal light reduces to a dull glow as she steps out of my room. The ache in my head is splitting me open, and I sob 'til sleep offers a merciful moment of peace from agonizing emptiness.

CHAPTER 19

The early-morning sky peeks through the sheer curtains fluttering in the cool breeze. Faint voices of tired guests linger in the palace.

It takes me a moment to realize I'm not alone. Soft dark fur lies across my chest. A wet nose tucks against my ear, with two black paws on my shoulders, and a tail wraps around my arm. Little puffs of breath tickle my neck as Farren sleeps serenely. A sob breaks out of me as I pull his body tighter to mine. Contented vibrations reverberate through my chest and into my bones as he begins to make a purr-like noise of contentment.

"My love!" I whisper, scratching his ears.

His eyes blink open and he licks the tip of my nose.

"Oh, Farren."

He purrs louder, but if he is here, that means...frantically, I look over at Leon sleeping next to me. He is shirtless in only a pair of low sleeping pants revealing a dark trail leading down, but my eyes go to the dried blood and angry scratches all over his arms.

"Did you do that?" I hiss at Farren, the sweetness of our reunion somewhat tainted at the red marks on Leon's skin. "Did Leon save you?"

Farren continues to lick my nose before he's had enough of my questions. He stretches and hops off me to find a new place to sleep at my feet.

"Good morning." Leon smiles up at me, his hair tousled. His hands find their way to the tops of my bare thighs, rubbing gently up and down them. "Are you all right?"

"Leon. What? Me? *Are you?* Farren! The fire! *You just left!*"

Leon wraps his arms around my waist and pulls me onto his lap, straddling him. I launch myself down onto him, our chests pressing together as our lips reunite. My hands are on his jaw, his beard shadow rough on my palms. I pour out my utter appreciation that he would run out of the safety of the palace for my beloved fox. Overwhelmed at his bravery, my tears falling on his cheek, and he pulls back.

"Hey, shh. It will be all right." He strokes my hair and presses his lips to the top of my head with sweet kisses.

"Is it all gone?" I whisper, desperate for the answer but dreading his response as I look down at him.

Sympathy fills his eyes, and I know his next words will hurt. "I am so very sorry, Strawberries. It is."

I nod silently before a new sob takes hold of me and I crumple on his chest. His arms are tight around me, rubbing my back over the soft fabric of my sleep dress.

"The forge still stands, though. Most of the building was made from stone, fire burning as bright as ever. Whatever magic kindles the flame has not gone out." He kisses my head again. I don't move, so he lifts my head in his strong hands and looks me in the eye when he says again in a low voice, "Grayden will get what's coming to him. I promise you that. You can hold me to it."

I nod and we stare at each other. Farren has come back to join us, lying on the warm side I've left behind.

"Your fox is a bit of an asshole," he says into my hair.

As I sit up to straddle him, laughter pours out of me with the tears still streaming down my face. "Oh, he is."

Farren glances up at us.

"Well, you are!" I tease my sweet pet.

With a huff he closes his eyes, unbothered by our insults.

"Where was he?" I reach out and pet the little terror, and he lifts his head to accept my attention.

Leon is quiet for a moment before answering. "Two of Grayden's men had him."

I jolt. "WHAT?"

"They were soaked, had two washed-out torches, so they must have started the fire. Grayden wasn't there, unfortunately. I would have loved for him to meet the end of my sword. I think Farren attacked the guards. One was holding a very bloody wrist, cursing at him, as they were leaving the cottage."

"They were taking him back? But why?"

Leon can only shrug. "I'm not sure but I can guess. Grayden is a hunter. His chambers are filled with his trophies spiked to the wall. He had them shipped from Versairen for sport. I imagine they were bringing Farren back as a gift for Grayden, maybe trying to get a little favor from their new king. They had him tied up with rope. Foxes have never been seen in Adreania, he would have been quite the novelty."

I reach over and pick up Farren, holding him in my arms, cradling him against me like I did when he was just a kit. He lays his head down on my arm and purrs again.

"What happened to Grayden's guards?"

Leon is quiet, not making eye contact with me, nervously twisting the ring around his finger. After a long moment, he sighs and looks up at me. "I killed them."

I stop petting Farren and stare at him. "You what?"

"I know how you feel about me murdering Grayden's men, but I couldn't leave them in a comatose state like the last ones. They set your home on fire and were bringing your pet to be killed for sport. They deserved it. It brought me immense pleasure to take them from this world. All I could think about was what would have happened if you were there. They would have dragged you back by your hair to Grayden. Even without the crown, he gave you an order to come to him when he became king, and you fled. We don't know how he knew it was your cottage. Don't think for a moment they would have shown you the mercy they begged me for. Death was the price they had to pay."

I do not know what to say to any of that. "But we can't be sure it was me they were after…"

His fingers tighten on my thigh. "They burned down your home. Even if you weren't the target, they were willing to kill whoever lived there. One man's death was fast. The other was… slower and he was persuaded to speak freely about his intent. They had orders to kidnap you. Apparently, when you didn't show up, he sent soldiers to…bring you to him, and someone revealed you do not live in Adreania. They found your empty store, nothing there to make any jewelry. No record of Arra existed. Or her husband and children. We both are missing and have apparently been seen flirting at every bazaar for two years. Grayden was told you actually live in the forest."

"Who told him?"

"That he didn't know. He was just given orders to find you and bring you back with whatever force was necessary." That last part he speaks slowly, anger simmering in his words.

"I don't know what to say. Thank you doesn't seem like enough, not nearly enough." I look on the floor next to the bed and see his green dress shirt from last night covered in blood.

The perfect night ended in bloodshed.

"Well, it wasn't *all* for you," he teases. "I do like the little guy. I think he might just like me, too." His hand lifts from my thigh, reaching out to pet Farren, who snaps at his fingers. "Maybe the feeling isn't mutual yet. Perhaps a few more slices of bacon are needed."

We both laugh together, and it is as sweet as honey.

He turns his head and meets my lips. I kiss him like I've never kissed him before. I want to consume him, for us to be welded together forever.

For one agonizing moment I thought I lost both him and

Farren. That Leon was about to leave my life as quickly as he entered it. I love him and the feeling is overwhelming.

I need to tell him how I feel.

To show him with my words and my body and I will not hold anything back from him.

CHAPTER 20

I kiss his cheeks, his jaw, his neck.

"You *saved* him." Pressing my lips to his skin where his neck and chin meet, I lick up his neck, earning a moan from him. "You *killed* for him."

As I kiss him just below his ear, I can feel the ragged breath he takes at my touch. He nods and is about to smile when I sit up on his lap, lifting the short sleep dress over my head.

Bare skin fully on display, my honeyed center opened wide just for him.

The only thing I wear now is the emerald necklace he had created.

His smile falters as his insatiable eyes move rapidly all over me like he can't decide where to look first.

I toss the fabric to the side, where it lands near Farren. He lets out a small growl and hops off the bed, heading into the library.

Leon's hands go to my breasts when I lean down. He teases the nipples between his fingers and rubs his thumbs over them reverently.

"Come here and let me taste them." He ever so slightly pulls at them for me to follow his request, but this is not about my pleasure;

it is about his. I laugh and I slide myself back, sitting just above his knees, out of reach of his eager hands.

He rises on his elbows, watching me with lust-filled emerald eyes.

"Where are you go—" Desperately he watches my hands as I unlace the binding tying up his pants. I take my time with it, rubbing the front of his pants in between pulls.

He lifts his hips, seeking my touch, before he tries to sit up and bring me closer. I stay out of his reach when the fabric has been undone, needing only for me to open the front to reveal what I want to taste. Leaning down, I kiss the small trail of dark hair leading me to my carnal raving. My kisses are light at first but slowly I press harder, my tongue swirling on his skin as I go lower at my leisurely pace, tracing down his glorious body. His head dips back and a low moan leaves him, his breath fast and jagged.

"Izadella, I—"

Whatever he is about to say is cut short as I open his pants and his hard cock springs upward. My mouth waters at the sight.

I smile down at him. "Oh, yes, this will do nicely."

I reach for the strawberry oil he left on my nightstand and pour a small amount into my hand. He watches me, breaths uneven, eyes wide with longing. After rubbing the oil on my hands, I slowly lick up one finger. He groans at the sight of what's to come for him.

Taking his cock in my hand, I slowly pump up and down. His hips lift off the bed at the teasing strokes, urging me to go faster.

"Strawberries, you don't have to." It comes out quickly, like he feels the need to say it but no desire for me to pause.

"I know." While one hand rises and falls, my other holds the base as I lean down. His eyes are unblinking as I bring my lips down over the head of him, lapping at his hardness. My palm presses down on his hips gently to try to prevent him from raising as I take him inside my mouth. His thickness is impressive, and I move up and down, occasionally pausing to suck the top or lick from base to tip, voracious for his pleasure.

The sensation of him in my mouth, his enjoyment rolling

through him, the power I hold over him in this moment—it all has me aching between my thighs.

Anytime he tries to speak, it comes out incoherent, a series of moans and curses. His rough hands tangle in my hair. He wraps my copper locks around his hand, guiding me up and down his dripping cock.

I love every sound he makes.

We make eye contact; his mouth opens slightly with his lips turned up in an expression of delightful awe. With a pop, I take my mouth off him and smile up through my lashes as I drag my tongue up to trace his veins. Keeping my eyes on him, I press my lips over his head and take him into my throat, deeper and deeper each time.

I squeeze and pump with my hand where it meets my lips.

His thigh muscles are straining under me as his hips try to increase the speed, desperate for more, and I give it to him.

Anything for him.

"Izadella, I'm so close. Please." He begs over and over again. *"Please."*

Who am I to deny this selfless man the completion he seeks? Pumping and sucking over his tender skin, I offer him up what he desires. His hands tighten around my hair, pulling it. The tension shoots a bolt of lust straight to my dripping center.

I moan at the touch, dragging one hand down his chest, my nails trailing pink marks of desire.

The vibrations send him over the edge, proof of his pleasure hot in my mouth, and I drink it greedily, sucking and savoring the salty taste of him mixed with the sweetness of the strawberry oil that still coats my hands. All the while, I gently pump to ensure I've taken every drop.

I pepper soft kisses to his sensitive tip, sucking the head in one last time as he jerks his hips. An expression of ecstasy is etched on his features.

His breath is ragged, chest rising and falling rapidly. His eyes darken as I sit up higher on his thighs, his cock resting on my curls, sliding my own wetness over him. I take my hands and rub the oil over my breast, teasing them for his visual gratification.

Leon's eyes darken and it sends a thrill up my spine. His devouring stare tells me he is ravenous for me.

He quickly sits up so he can lick each nipple clean, moaning into my skin, and his hands squeeze my backside as he does 'til I break us apart.

I slide off a panting Leon, his eyes on me as he watches with a half-smile.

"You need a bath. You have blood on your arms." I gather some soft robes for us. "Let's go, healer."

"I did try to rinse it off before I got in bed with you."

"Oh, how romantic." I bat my lashes at him.

"Anything for you, Strawberries."

CHAPTER 21

*L*eon stands, stretches, and tugs me in for a long, slow kiss before we make our way into the bathing room with its heated pool. He steps in, dunking himself, and drains away the blood-tinted water before refilling it.

With hungry eyes he stares at me as I stand bare at the top of the bathing pool stairs. Some of my hair has fallen in front of my breast and rounded hips.

He rises and holds out his hand. "Come here, Izadella." He guides me as I slowly enter the water with him.

The pool isn't very deep, going up to my waist. Leon pulls me to him, and the hardness between his thighs pushes up against me.

Leon relaxes in one of the built-in seats, watching me. I brush his dripping hair out of his face and pour in floral-scented cleansing foaming oils. The hot water bubbles, hiding most of the tiles at the bottom of the pool and Leon's stiffening cock.

This feels so right, him and me, our bodies pressed together. Whatever ties us together, that pull towards him practically glows in my chest, its warmth burning away all of my fears.

He takes my face in his hands and kisses me, adding more and more passion to it. I wrap my arms around him, clinging to him. I need him closer.

Our time together may be cut bitterly short but at least I will have known true love.

We will have truly known each other's souls.

I will make enough memories with him to sustain me for the years I will spend missing him, craving him, mourning him.

To soothe the ache of a forever without him.

I chose him.

'Til my mortal side takes me from Ellova and we will be together again in death.

We can get married, in a mortal ceremony.

Be husband and wife.

I can see it so clearly. A small ceremony in one of the Gem Court gardens. Walking down the aisle in lace like the mortals wear. No crown atop my head, just a sheer veil. Leon standing there, waiting for me with glassy eyes that match my own. Golden rings I made just for us. Tear-filled vows that surpass death. Sweet cakes and sparkling wine, dancing under the stars with our friends.

It's not a Zemra soulbond, but it will be enough.

He is enough.

"Leon, I need us to be together. Whatever time we have left, it's yours. Let me be your *wife*. I don't know what we are going to do about the mad—"

"Izadella, you are worth any madness."

My lips collide with his; it is not a gentle kiss as he did before. This time it is wild and raw. One of his hands spans my waist, and the other plunges under the water, trailing down my body 'til he reaches my throbbing core. Two fingers pump inside me as I moan into his mouth. His tongue slips in on my cries, and his thumb goes to my clit, pressing in slow circles sending me bucking against him. He takes advantage of my arching back and sucks desperately on my breast as his thumb goes faster and faster.

His touch builds fire within me, the pleasure rising, my hips bouncing at his attention.

My orgasm snaps like a bowstring. "I love you." It slips out of me as I gasp but I've never spoken truer words.

I *love* him.

He cups my face, something like awe on his. "I love you endlessly, Izadella. I have since the moment we met."

Our hands are frantic over each other's bodies, lips parting, tongues tasting. I reach between us and wrap my hand around his hard cock, slowly moving up and down. He lets out a small gasp at the contact.

Leon looks delicious like this, his broad chest glittering from the water, eyes blown wide with obsession.

My lips trace his jaw. "Let's get married."

"Izadella," he whispers, "marriage would never be enough for me. I need to have you anchored to me, body and soul, our magic and minds intertwined, interwoven 'til death."

Drunk on such sweet words, I shift to kiss him, but he pulls back.

"My queen, I need to tell you something."

"Later. I need you inside me." I am hollow and aching between my thighs as I pump him under the water.

He breaks us apart and takes a step back from me, his face turning from pleasure to pain. "I haven't been honest with you, in the way you have with me, and I'm so sorry for that but I need you to trust me."

Dread starts low in my gut, twisting the lust out of me. "What are you talking about?"

Our magic?

"You love me, but do you trust me?"

Something is wrong. I can see it in that pleading expression he wears but I answer honestly, "Yes. I trust you."

He holds up his right hand, the gold band glinting. "You were in Adreania, using a fake identity to help its citizens, and so was I."

My stomach drops.

Leon pulls the ring off his finger. There is a popping noise, and he shifts in front of me, his once-mortal form growing taller, bigger, his chest expanding. Soft rounded ears lengthen, coming to points at the end.

Fae ears.

Our magic and minds intertwined.

His hair has the same silver streaks, but it is longer now. I've taken so many steps away from him in the water I hit the edge of the pool. He doesn't reach for me or make any movements, just watches me with sorrow.

"When Alvina made the crown for Inara, she also made her a ring. The glamour ring. I know this is a lot to process but I love you. This changes nothing about us. I just need to be honest now. I was in Adreania attempting to steal the crown back from Jedrick. It's rightfully mine, but I don't care about it anymore. You don't need to worry about any madness or a mortal lifespan. We can be together for centuries. We can go to the Zemra temple and be soul-bonded. Maybe we can get the crown off with our magic combined." He gives me a smile that holds both guilt and hope. Pleading eyes beg me.

He's fae.

He let me believe he was mortal.

I broke a law to bring him here, showed him Ellova's existence. Risked the safety of all who live here.

Told him my secrets, Ellova's secrets.

Let him sleep in the royal wing, so close to its heir.

He let me *agonize* about loving him and I have no idea who he even is.

Convinced me he was mortal.

All to take the crown?

Liar.

Liar.

I scream and I do not stop.

When we were children, Nueena and I would play a game where we would see how fast we could get the honeyguards to come running. We would hide under tables or behind thick curtains and let out a bloodcurdling scream. Well, Nueena would; I would be hiding with her, giggling.

Nyvenah thought it was good practice for them and allowed our reign of terror to torment the poor honeyguards for years. Lillian wasn't commander then, just a honeyguard at that point.

Now my door is broken open with a brutal kick from Lillian's heel. The jeweled lock rolls away on the floor.

Just like when we were little, honeyguards storm in, swords drawn and ready to defend.

It is Lillian's arms I feel around my waist, lifting me out of the shallow pool and away from the stranger who stands before me, my screams echoing around us. She drapes her shoulder cape around my naked, shaking body and pushes me behind her.

Leon's devastated eyes bore into me, or at least some twisted version of him. His pointed ears mock me. How could I not have known? This fae male in the pool looks like Leon, same black hair with streaks of gray. The same face, but like all fae features they are more sharp, more beautiful. He has grown almost a foot, shoulders wider, muscles that weren't there before, a bigger frame, a dominating force. He doesn't look like a lean healer anymore; he looks like a warrior. His expression is one of distress and shock.

We must wear the same pain.

My chest aches from all the hope I had in him being ripped out of me at his deception, his lies. Whoever he is, he is not Leon. His face crumples when my tears mark my face with my own misery.

"Strawberries, please…please let me explain."

Cavernous agony splits open my chest, so raw and real I claw at skin. Pink slashes rake under my nails.

Leon takes a few steps forward.

Lillian's weapon points at his tortured expression. "Don't. Move." Her low voice was menacing.

"I can explain." He holds his hands up, trying to portray he is not going to attack.

"I never want to see you again." I rip off my necklace, slamming it to the floor.

His eyes go wide, and he stumbles in the water, anguish blooms on his face. "No, you need to let me explain! IZADELLA!" he shouts after me, his voice cracking, but I've already started to run, the broken sound of my name chasing me out of the room.

Tormented agony emanates from deep within me, fracturing, breaking.

I sprint out of my room, grabbing a dress I'd left draped over a chair on my way, past the living space and into the hall, where I collide with Viella. Kaylena is close behind her.

"Oh, Della!" Viella takes in my tear-streaked appearance, naked except for Lillian's wet cape.

"I didn't know!" It's the only thing I can think to say, the only thing screaming in my head. Viella puts her hands on my shoulders to steady me as I shake.

"It's okay. Come on." Viella turns to demand, "Kaylena, head back to your guards right now. Do you understand me?"

Kaylena looks between us. "But I want to stay with Delly." She gazes up at me with bright eyes. "Why are you crying?"

"You need to go right now. Go back to your rooms!" Viella's tone is not to be argued with, and Kaylena runs back down the hall.

I clutch at my chest, swaying at the pain.

After Kaylena turns down to where her rooms are, Viella pulls me along, holding my hand down a few gilded halls over to the wing she shares with Lillian. I plant myself and pull back on her arm. "I need to speak with Nueena. Immediately! This can't wait. Where is she?"

Viella has an iron grip on my hand and continues to drag me with her, my chest burning. "You are as naked as a newborn dewling. Hold on a moment." She hurries us into her chambers and holds the dress I was carrying so I can slide my arms into it.

"Put this on." She shoves my dress over my head, but she freezes when I let the cape fall away, pulling my dress down over my hips.

"Oh, *Ellova's grave*, Della, your chest." Her eyes are wide with horror and filled with tears.

Dread pools like lava in my gut, a torment under my skin; my own magic has ruptured in my chest. I know what I will see, and I can't bear it. I shake my head uncontrollably.

Leon didn't just break my heart.

He killed me.

An enervation death.

CHAPTER 22

LEON

"IZADELLA!"

More honeyguards pour into the room, circling around the pool, swords at the ready and bows raised. Lillian has her sword drawn and pointed at me.

"Who the fuck are you?" she demands.

I ignore her questions and continue screaming Izadella's name over and over again, a burning ache in my chest at hurting the love of my long life like this. Being honest with her was not supposed to end like this. Bitter regret and anger brew inside me into a lethal rage.

I finally turn to face Lillian, her indignation mirroring my own.

"I need to speak to Nueena," I say in a low voice.

Her laugh is humorless. "You think you can make demands? Do you know what we do to spies here? I warned you what would become of you."

Narrowing my eyes, I respond, "Yes, yes, wilting minds, dungeons and such. I remember what you said to me on my first day here. There's been a misunderstanding, one I will be happy to explain to Izadella or Nueena—"

"Get dressed, traitor," Lillian says through clenched teeth. She walks over and kicks my crumpled, bloody clothing from the floor into the pool.

Gods, why didn't Izadella listen to what I had to say? She said she loved me, said she *trusted* me. My chest twists with the guilt I've been carrying since the day I met her in that damn forest.

I want to argue with Lillian, but clothing is better than standing in this pool, naked, surrounded by swords at my throat. I would hate to be killed naked.

A male needs a little dignity in death.

I dress as quickly as possible, sitting on the chair to put on my socks and boots. The shirt is ripping apart in the sleeves. Everything is too tight now. The pants, the shirt, the damn boots. Before any guards could stop me, I grab her necklace off the floor and pocket it.

A honeyguard waves his hand in front of me and my wrists are bound with a dark blue light. It's pointless to fight them; it would only make it worse. I go to repeat myself, demand to see Izadella, but unending alarm bells sound around us. The palace shakes. The crystal lights above flash red.

Lillian's face changes from angry to murderous. "WHO DID YOU BRING!"

"I DIDN'T BRING ANYONE! NO ONE KNOWS I'M—"

Fuck.

Erenia does, but we had a plan a year in the making. She wouldn't risk it.

Lillian shoves me into the main living space.

Tavien walks in without his signature smile, and shame builds a fire in my gut. I loathed lying to him, to all of them.

He stays a safe distance away and some of the guards come to make a half circle around him. Anger floods me, causing my fist to clench, as if I would attempt to harm him. He is one of the few friends I've made in over a hundred years.

My rib cage feels too large for my body, painfully so, like my soul is trying to escape to chase after her.

"So, it's true, then? Who are you? And let's try the truth this time, all right?" He says this so casually, as if he's mentioning something insignificant.

"My real name is Zilas."

Tavien's eyes narrow at me. "There's an army outside, one that Nyvenah is about to eviscerate after declaring them enemies of the realm. She has a duty to protect Ellova against any and all threats. If you do not start talking, that forest will be painted red and you'll have so much blood on your hands your soul will never know a moment of peace again. I highly doubt an army shows up for one without much importance, so I'm going to ask one last time. Who. The. Fuck. Are. You?"

We stare at each other but finally I say, "I'm the rightful King of Kalvorn. It's just taking me longer than I hoped to return."

He lets out a bitter laugh. "A king, huh?"

Before I can explain, Lillian speaks first, glaring daggers at me, her hand tight on the hilt of her blade.

"Well, the only thing we actually know about him is that he's a fucking liar, so let's not bet on that one." She gives a mocking bow and waves her hand in the direction of the front door. "After you, Your Majesty."

Honeyguards shove me into the hall, and we make our way out of the royal west wing. The red lights continue to flash.

I wish I could ask how the alarm system works, but in my current position they don't seem in the mood to share any more of Ellova's intricacies. A shame, really. Kalvorn still uses bells as alarms. At least they did when I left a hundred twenty years ago.

Lillian stops. Her face pales and one hand flies up to cover her chest. "Something has devastated Viella. Tavien, take him to the command room." She sprints away towards her Zemra, abandoning my arrest.

It spreads new panic within me.

If Lillian can feel in their bond that Viella needs her, does that mean Izadella needs me, too? Are they together? Before I can ask to follow, honeyguards push me down the hallway.

We arrive in a flurry of movement. Guards and attendants rush out. Camarra and a few other guardians rush in. Their eyes focus on the bonds of light securing my hands. Lazalai gasps and starts rapidly signing to Reyna, both guardians shooting daggers at me with their eyes.

Nyvenah moves to stand in front of me, wearing an expression only mothers wear when they are truly disappointed.

I'm taller than her now but I still shrink under her gaze.

"And here I thought we would be welcoming you into our family. I see I was mistaken."

"No, that is still going to happen. One day we will be able to laugh about this." It's a poor jest as all eyes in the room continue to stare at me, disgusted looks on the faces of those who love Izadella the most. Anguish rolls through me as I think of her beautiful face frozen in ecstasy in the pool and the screams of fear moments after.

I will never be free from the sound of her terror at seeing me.

"Oh, I very much doubt that, as Izadella said she never wants to see you again," Lillian says in a sardonic tone.

"She's in shock and I wish she would have waited for me to explain myself before jumping to conclusions about my intent here. Nothing was done to her with premeditated falsehood. Everything got out of hand and some things were more important than the truth at the time. She is owed that now, I know, but there are forces at play much bigger than my feelings for her."

It pains me to say it, and I don't even believe it myself.

Nothing is more important to me now.

"Is it your intent to get a great many mortals killed today?" Nyvenah motions to the balcony and I walk with her. Below is the forest and indeed a small army, most in filthy clothing, that waits at the base of the mountain. Many of the women are from Beggars' Row, strong and healthy, their children clinging to their legs or tied to their backs. Unlike when I cared for them as they lay dying in bed.

Mimi stands with her two siblings and their mother. This isn't an army; these are asylum seekers trying to get to Kalvorn.

The elixir truly worked. I never expected so many of them to live. It's the only bright spot to all of this.

They all stare up the mountain, but I know they can't see us. The glamour makes it so they only see a false cliffside.

"They have been yelling for King Zilas. Can I assume they mean you?" Nyvenah drawls.

Alachite puts himself between his mate and me, arms crossed protectively.

I nod, looking down.

Queen Erenia, Grayden's wife, is gazing up. Our eyes meet for a moment, but she stares right through me. My loyal hawk, Lula, sits on her shoulder, its blue wings flapping in distress.

Fast-approaching heels echo in the hallway as Nueena makes her way in the crowded room at a full speed. "Ellova's fucking grave. Where is Della? What's happening?"

She charges right at me but stops when she gets a full view of my true fae self in chains. Shock and rage battle on her face at the sight of me, rage winning. "You fucking liar! We *trusted* you!"

With every word she says, she steps closer to the guards, moving in 'til she is right in front of me.

"She loves you." She says this without venom. It's almost a whisper. The heartbreak I feel is suddenly reflected in her eyes. "She *loved* you."

The sensation of my ribs breaking open one by one tears into me. "Please let me explain. I—"

Her fist connects with my gut in a blast of pain, the force so unexpected it brings me to my knees. "Damn it, Nueena," is all I get out before her knee connects with my nose, breaking it. Throbbing pain and the tang of blood meets my lips. She makes a fist again, pulling her arm back like a bowstring.

I brace for the pain I deserve but Tavien moves between us, his hand covering her fist.

"My love, as much as I would love to see you annihilate him for his utter betrayal, he claims to be the king of Kalvorn."

"Thank you, Tavien." My words are mumbled as blood runs down my face into my mouth. Spitting it on the golden floor at Nueena's feet would be disrespectful.

"Do not thank me. I do not wish for my Zemra to hurt her hand,

and I want you *gone*. Before we decide what to do with you, you need to start talking."

I stand up and spit the blood into a black plant—my love's doing, no doubt. The reminder I've caused Izadella pain is a gut punch greater than any Nueena could harm me with.

No longer needing to hide what I am, I call to my magic. The shattered bones in my nose slowly slide into place. As the pain fades, I know the bruising has, too, but something is wrong in my chest.

That is when I feel it.

The fracture where the ache from hearing Izadella say she wishes to never see me again. Not just heartbreak, no, so much more than that. Icy fear spreads at the realization.

My healing power is leaking out of me.

Enervation.

I frantically send my healing powers to my chest, trying to undo the consequences of my own broken heart, but my magic simply passes though, fading out of me instead of repairing.

Every night I slept with her in my arms, pulling the crown's magic out of her, healing her as it ravaged her mortal side. It has taken so much of my power and what is left is slowly fading, unable to save myself.

My face remains neutral, hiding my dread. My healing magic is buried so deep under the crown's, it takes longer to obey me. For now, the crown's magic flows out of me first.

Nyvenah and Nueena watch my nose slide back into place. I can explain my powers later. For now, I must go back to the beginning of all this, the beginning of Kalvorn, and I tell them everything in hopes that they will allow me to see Izadella one last time.

CHAPTER 23

IZADELLA

An enervation death.

Lines of golden cracks, the width of my finger, run up between my breasts. It glows faintly, and my metal magic slowly seeps out of me. The fracture on my skin will soon take over my body, like gilded lightning strikes across my skin, 'til I'm gone.

I'm going to die just like my mother did, crying out in pain while my magic abandons me.

I will be nothing but a corpse for Nueena to mourn.

"Leon, he—" I wrap my arms around my chest, holding tight, as if I could keep my gilded magic, my life force, inside me.

"Nyvenah will know what to do. We can fix this." Viella's red-rimmed eyes meet mine with such compassionate concern.

I choke down a sob. "He isn't who he said he was, or *what* he was. He's not mortal. Leon is fae!"

Her mouth is a perfect *O,* frozen in shock before she says, "How?"

"He took off what he claims is Inara's glamour ring that Alvina made. One moment he was mortal and the next he was...not." Nausea rises within me, the pain in my chest growing white hot. I rub my hand over the spot.

"Lillian feared he wasn't who he said he was. But where is he from?"

"I'm unforgivably foolish! I BROUGHT HIM RIGHT HERE." My legs give out, and I fall gracelessly to the floor, sobbing, my breaths becoming jagged gasps.

The floor rumbles.

"Oh, oh, the vines! Della, you need to calm down." I look up and the vines are growing and crawling into the room.

The palace shakes again.

Viella gets to the floor and holds me. I cling to her as she rubs my back in a soft soothing motion. "Della, honey, *please* calm down. We can handle anything, but you need to relax. Where is he now?"

"Lillian has him," I gasp out.

"She will know what to do. She will find out who he is and why he's here. Nyvenah can decide what to do with him."

"Isn't it obvious? He never loved me. He just wants this horrible crown." I grab it and pull. The pain is immediate and searingly hot. I only cry harder, a miserable mess on the floor.

"Well, he can't have it, whoever he is. He can bring a whole army if he wants. He—" Piercing bells ring frantically all around us.

Viella freezes. "Ellova's grave," she whispers and fear bleeds into her eyes.

Panic eclipses my own grief. "What is that? What does that mean?"

I've never heard this sound before. Three booming bells in a row followed by three seconds of silence. The pattern repeats itself over and over again.

"Get up!" She yanks me up and races to one end of the room, lurching open an armoire, revealing nothing but weapons. "We're under attack!"

Viella throws on a set of golden armor with a terrifying amount of weaponry. I take a step back at the sight of her.

She looks just as fierce as Lillian.

"I need to find my Zemra and you need to get to the command room. If it's Grayden, we can't let him get to you."

I gape at her, and she shoves me through the door into the hallway.

"We need to leave, NOW!"

Someone screams my name down the hall. Everett races towards us.

"Izadella, I am to bring you straight to Nyvenah in the command room. They're waiting for you. Vi, Lillian is in the west wing and there's an army outside."

I nod numbly and turn to Vi.

"I'm going to find Lillian. Stay with Nyvenah," she says.

"Okay," I mutter, and she gives me a long look before giving me a hug.

"It's going to be all right. I just know it," she whispers in my ear. I don't respond but wrap my arms around her roughly before she pulls us apart and dashes away.

"Come on." Everett takes my hand into his and guides me as we run, the echoing warning bells causing my head to throb. He wears leather gloves that grate on my skin as he tugs me to safety.

How could Leon do this to me? He lied this whole time about who he was and why he was here. Let me believe he would be dead in a few decades, that he would have allowed the madness to over-take him just to be with me. Letting me believe that loving him could break my heart, that I could *die* from it. How did he think I would react? That I would blindly trust the stranger in front of me?

Leon was never a helpless mortal I needed to protect from Grayden.

He was the one I needed to be protected *from*.

I brought him to Ellova and had him recognized as a member of this court. The ways that he's broken me can never be fixed. He held my whole heart in his healer's hands only to break it so easily. The pain from his betrayal slices every part of me.

I choke on another sob.

"We have a full army ready to defend us. We can crush whoever is at our steps," Everett says confidently as we arrive at one of the small stairwells only used by honeyguards.

"It's not that. I'm aware of the power of the Ellovian armies," I say through trembling lips.

It takes me a moment to realize he is taking me down into the depths of the palace and not up towards the command room that overlooks the forest with its clear view of whoever is attacking us.

"What, did the mortal break your heart already?" His tone turns mocking.

I nod my head, but violent dread makes me pause. How did Everett know that Leon was mortal? Or at least pretending to be.

Nyvenah wouldn't have told the court Guardians about Leon, would she? I know he was forbidden from being here, but still. Did Camarra tell Everett? Why would she tell her son? He's too far down the chain of command to have been given that information.

I swallow slowly, focusing all my energy on acting as if I'm not terrified. An icy feeling is crawling down my back. The instinct to run away from him takes over.

It was Everett.

"Something like that." I force my voice to sound casual, but it wobbles.

The stairwell is narrow and dark with no place to escape. When light appears below us, I prepare myself to break away when we reach the next opening and escape.

Is he the one who took the sacred navlue fruit? Or maybe worked with the person who did? Is he working with Grayden?

The tree only grows in the throne room in Ellova.

Someone told Grayden's guards the exact location of my cottage to burn it to the ground.

The bastard, the fucking bastard.

"Oh." He makes a small *tsking* noise. "Did I let it slip?" His smile is unbelievably cruel when he turns. His gloved hand almost crushes mine when I try to bolt, but he's faster and stronger, shoving me roughly against the wall.

The crown's magic rises within me, but the stone stairwell we are in has nothing to help me.

An ice-cold collar is clamped onto my neck.

Iron.

The flow of the crown's magic slows but never fully leaves. The vibrant magic has been a consistent presence since I put it on my head and now feels muddy and distant in my veins.

"Someone is waiting for you across the Divide," he whispers in my ear before his hand is around my throat. I claw at him, kicking where I can. When I open my mouth to scream, he shoves a small bundle of red and black leaves past my lips.

The numbing in my mouth starts immediately and he presses his rough hand over my mouth, keeping my head jammed up against the stone wall.

Vedesdron.

The poison growing in the balcony garden in the Adreania castle.

Footsteps grow louder, someone is racing up the stone stairs towards us. Hope surges into my soul.

Please be Nueena. Please, please be Tavien.

Kole arrives with pink cheeks, out of breath from running up the stairs.

That spark of hope vanishes.

"Everett! We are needed—" He stops, taking in the sight of me pinned against the wall, slowly losing consciousness, Everett's hand over my mouth.

Kole glances down at the iron collar. He narrows his eyes at us, demanding, "What the hell is going on?"

My captor is swift with this deceit. "Izadella is a traitor to the realm. She brought an enemy army to Ellova's gates, ready to attack. I'm taking her to Nyvenah immediately!"

The numbing sensation spreads over my face to the top of my head, but I use all the energy I have left so slowly shake my head, which rolls to the side, hanging limply.

"I find that hard to believe, Ev," Kole says slowly, his hand going to the hilt of his sword. "What's around her—"

Everett releases me, unsheathing his sword. Kole doesn't have time to block the weapon as it plunges into his gut.

I collapse and Kole's body slams to the ground next to me, blood gushing from him. We stare at each other, horror frozen on his face as he gapes at me, tears forming in his eyes.

"I'm—sorry," Kole whispers.

Everett brings his sword down again, piercing right through Kole's side. He rips the blade out again and sprays the wall behind him with blood.

Kole's last words hang in the air.

My terrified mind struggles to process the gore and loss in front of me. Everett just slaughtered his best friend of a hundred years as if he were no more than a pig for dinner.

Kole's blood seeps down the stairs, pooling onto the next step.

If he would do that to his friend, what would he do to me?

Everett kneels down to yank me off the floor, tossing me over his shoulders like I'm a bag of flour, knocking the breath from me.

He walks through the blood, leaving a trail of crimson footprints behind us, leading me to my own devastation.

I try to struggle against him, but my eyes feel like stones as I fight to stay awake, the poison pulsing through my veins. The blackness comes in waves.

Leon's name echoes around me over and over again and it takes me a minute to untangle the fog in my mind to realize it's me, calling for him. What is left of my heart shatters completely.

CHAPTER 24

LEON

Zilas, Fae King of Kalvorn
Firstborn royal heir of Kalvorn Throne
Descendant of the fae-born
Queen Inara and Prince Kalden Fasaile

I have one chance to try to earn their trust back.

One chance for them to believe I was never in their midst with malicious intentions.

"I left my kingdom long ago to steal back the crown, but it is not what I want anymore. I only wish to be with Izadella. To explain to her that I am Inara's descendant. Grayden's bloodline is a false one. Queen Inara fell in love and had an affair with King Drystan's brother, Kalden. They had a half-fae child together, Princess Arelia, the missing princess, but she was never lost. When Drystan killed his wife, Kalden took their daughter and ran to what is now Kalvorn. Princess Arelia is who should have inherited the crown, but Drystan had it and passed it to the son he had with his wife after he murdered Inara. Grayden's line never should have had the crown. They stole it from *my* line."

"Do you have proof of this?" Alachite says. "Your words mean little to us now."

I turn to Nueena. "Did you or Nyvenah give me access to the garden? Before it burned, when we were growing what we needed for the elixir? The first time Izadella grew strawberries, you found us in each other's arms."

Nueena and Tavien glance at each other but do not speak their confirmation, so I continue, "That garden once belonged to Alvina, Zarella, and Inara, a place where their descendants would always be welcome. You never granted me access because I never needed it, much like I suspect Izadella never needed it either. It is our birthright."

"Who sits on your throne now if you are here?" Tavien asks.

"My younger brother."

Nueena says, "I wish you had trusted us with this information earlier. We could have been allies from the start. With your lies, you risk two wars. Honesty now will not help you."

Guilt has been a constant companion this entire time, and now it sinks its claws deeper into me. "I know, but everything got carried away in the forest the night she was forced to wear the crown. One moment I had the crown within my grasp but—" I swallow hard. There is too much to tell. "She showed up and she somehow managed to get the crown before me. I couldn't leave her after that moment. I had hoped she would trust me enough that I could reveal everything to her in time. It devastated me but I was prepared to never be with Izadella after Jedrick and I snuck out of Adreania. I thought she was happy with her fictional husband and children and that would've been enough. I knew she was meant to be mine even when I thought she was mortal, but I had a duty to my kingdom to return what was taken from us. Yes, I wanted the crown, of course. I tried for a hundred years to get it, but I do not want it now. It can only be removed in—" I can't finish the sentence.

"Why didn't you tell her who you were?" Nueena demands.

"I was going to. I wanted to every day I've been here. I longed to be honest, but you have to understand that at the beginning, everything I knew about Izadella was a lie. While I was—and continue to be—enamored with Izadella, the feelings I had for her didn't erase wisdom. I didn't know if she was loyal to Adreania when I found her, and I'm not in the business of sharing my deepest secrets with a stranger, no matter how beautiful. I spent two years pining after someone I thought, for multiple reasons, I could never be with. So, I just treasured our few hours together in the same room for the past two years. I constantly had jewelry commissioned I neither wanted nor needed just for a reason to talk to her." I sigh deeply.

I've only slept for a few hours in the past two days, and bone-deep weariness is settling in.

The crack in my chest spreads under my shirt.

I take a seat, everyone staring down at me. "I wasn't the only one who saw all her beauty and talent. She didn't go unnoticed by Grayden. He was quite open about all the things he planned on doing. Invading Kalvorn, instituting mandatory service in his armies. He always wanted Izadella. It didn't matter if she was married. He doesn't like not getting what he wants, and if her imaginary family had been real, they'd already be dead. I would have killed him myself, but he is never without his guards.

"I thought maybe once I was king again and we were both safely in Kalvorn, we could start a true friendship. She and her family would be safe, and I would have the crown. Honestly, I hoped her husband was old or sick, and maybe *something* could happen in the future. Selfish of me, I know. Then Izadella got the crown, and I didn't know if she would go running back to Adreania, but it turns out, nothing was real. She was a descendant of the Forger, who made the ring I used to deceive everyone."

"Where did you get the glamour ring?" Nueena asks.

Her face is unreadable, but I hope she can hear the sincerity with which I share my story.

"From my mother. It's been passed down through my family. Fae and mortals live side by side in Kalvorn, so it never needed to be used."

"What was your plan after that?"

"I had hoped Izadella felt the same way about me, even though I was lying, as she was. That one day I would reveal myself to her and she would wish to be my queen. I had the royal birthright, and she had the crown. It felt like destiny."

Nueena lets out a little laugh. "Ruling is not something Della desires."

I nod. "Yes, so I have learned. She has the crown three kingdoms seek and she doesn't even want it. Della refused to come back to Kalvorn with me, and short of kidnapping, I couldn't—wouldn't—do anything but make sure she was safe, so I convinced her to let me stay with her. I had no idea where she was going but wherever she went, so would I. Ellova is more myth than fact, and with the crown out of Adreania, I could've gone home empty-handed, but it wasn't all in vain. Grayden didn't have the crown; it was in the hands of Alvina's bloodline. For a moment I considered heading back to take my place as king, but I would be an awful protector of my kingdom if I didn't at least see what Ellova was. My kingdom is only a mountain range away from you and I needed to know if you were a threat, if I needed to prepare for war from both sides or inquire about possible alliances."

"That I can understand," Nyvenah says slowly.

I smile gratefully at her. "I know I've hurt Izadella and probably all of you, but the people at the gate are not your enemies. Grayden's wife has led a rebellion, and she knows who I am. I got out a letter letting her know where I was and why I didn't meet with her like we planned. I told her not to come here, though. Her instructions were to take everyone loyal to her—or at least hostile to Grayden—and head to Kalvorn."

"So, you need to go back?" Alachite asks skeptically.

"I do. I have a lot waiting for me, but I was hoping…"

Nueena crooks an eyebrow. "Hoping for what?"

"That Izadella would want to return with me."

She laughs at me. "And what? Be your queen? You get the crown no matter what?"

"I don't want her because she has the crown, Nueena. I care about her. I'm in love with her. I know she is my soulbonded mate. When she thought I was human, she still chose to be with me. Now we can share a fae lifetime together. Kalvorn does not have a Zemra temple, but I know the legends we were told, what Izadella has explained. I know the Zemra magic extends fae lifespans so they are tied together with their mates. She is my Zemra; I know it. I can feel it every breath she takes near me. Nueena, neither of us will have to bury her. We will never have to grieve a half-human life. We would *both* get her for centuries longer."

Nueena's eyes are glossy. "That's for *her* to decide, not you. You aren't soulbonded yet, and you will be fortunate if she even speaks to you after your deception."

Her words widen the ache of agony within me. "*Please* let me see her. I need her to understand." Even if there is no physical wound, the pain of all this feels like I am bleeding out before them like the night I was attacked.

Nueena shakes her head. "She said she never wants to see you again, and I'm going to honor that choice 'til she tells me otherwise. As of right now, I can only take your word that you mean no harm to my realm. Either I can throw you into the dungeon for your clandestine infiltration, or you can leave Ellova and *never* return here."

Could Izadella truly live without me in ways I can never live without her?

"Don't make me leave her. I will return to Kalvorn. They are about to go to war, but she has to know I never meant for it to turn out like this." It's a broken plea. The doors open and hope rises that Izadella has returned, ready to trust me, but I'm a fool for even thinking it.

Viella runs in, tears streaming down her cheeks as she nearly trips over herself, Lillian at her heels.

"What's wrong?" Nueena reaches for Viella.

"Della," Viella chokes out, pressing her hand to her chest. She opens her mouth to speak but sees me and snaps it shut.

"What's wrong?" Panic roars in my chest. "Is Izadella hurt? Does she need me?"

Viella sneers at me. "You don't get to know anything else about her."

Her words cut deep. I know she is only being a good friend, but desperation to know what is wrong, feels like an execution.

I should tell them all what I am experiencing, that causing Izadella such pain has broken me irrecoverably. That I need to see her one last time before my enervation death. But I cannot be sure how they will use such vulnerable information.

"You deserve the dungeon, but I think it's time you leave," Nueena says, taking Viella's hand, and heading towards the doors but turns to me. "If you believe you have found an ally here, you are sorely mistaken. Whatever war Kalvorn finds itself in has nothing to do with us. New wards and glamour will be added to ensure you *stay out*. If you attempt to return, it will have deadly consequences, and your kingdom will be an *enemy* of Ellova."

CHAPTER 25

IZADELLA

When I open my eyes again, my chest burns, like liquid fire was poured into me.

Everything is blurry but I know where I am. The secret kitchen at the base of the palace, with the door leading into the Merawood Forest. The lingering scent of cakes and baked bread from Viella's trip to Adreania mixes with the sweetness of the open forest door.

Everett dumps me on a flatbed cart. Pain explodes when my head slams into the wood with a crack.

"Kole stumbled upon us, nearly ruining everything," he seethes.

A woman is speaking, a low voice I recognize but cannot place. "You are fortunate I discovered that on my way down here. His body is disposed of, but you were a fool to leave such a bloody mess. The army outside is from Adreania, rebels of some kind, and they're demanding King Zilas."

"Why the fuck would the king of Kalvorn be in Ellova?" Everett's annoyance is clear.

"That man with Della was no mortal. He is the fae King of Kalvorn. He swore to leave and not come back if Nyvenah didn't attack them. He has been in disguise. They're leaving now. Go, go! Do not get caught!"

Quick heels hit the ground, a door slamming behind her.

Leon has been King Zilas the entire time.

A king who disguises himself as a healer.

Only in Adreania to get the crown.

King of the kingdom about to go to war for it.

He has a queen.

He never wanted me at all; he just wanted what I had.

Never loved me.

Everything was a lie.

Everett yells at someone and I can barely make out a head of soft reddish-golden hair almost identical to mine.

He roughly pulls my head back, fist in my hair. "Put them on her, now!" Everett hisses and another woman sobs softly. She comes into view, and I know that tear-streaked face. She is the servant I collided with in the castle as I ran away from Grayden the last night I was there, just before Leon found me in the garden. We share the same devastation and fear in our eyes.

"I'm so s-sorry," I mumble, barely able to speak.

She nods and drags over a set of chains, puts them around my wrists, and connects them to a metal loop on the iron collar around my neck.

"Get this on." Everett throws a bundle of fabric at the poor woman.

Blackness rolls in and out.

The woman tries to speak but it comes out as a whimper.

"Shut up!" Everett all but growls, "You will get on this horse with your hood up and hair down. Follow that group swiftly once they leave. If you say or do anything, King Grayden will deal with you. Ride straight into the forest. I will be waiting. We are heading back to Adreania. If you do exactly as I say, I might tell His Majesty to let your family live."

A black Ellovian battle horse is tied to the front of a cart and I almost weep with relief that it is not Onyx.

He's trying to make it seem like I left with Leon?

My words are slurred from the Vedesdron. "Y-you will die for this treachery. Nueena *will* f-find me. I promise you that. She will never let you get away with this-s."

"Oh," he says, his voice full of malice, "I already have."

My world goes dark again.

~

I wake with a pounding headache that has me wishing I were still asleep. The sound of the ocean beating against the rocks is close by, and a gray, cloudy sky hangs above me.

My thoughts are muddled. Flashes of Leon in the pool, shifting to fae, and Everett's betrayal. My mouth tastes like ash from the Vedesdron. Panic shoots through me. I struggle against the chains wrapped around me, still tied to the cart.

"Fuck," I whisper.

A soft laugh I've heard many times since I was a dewling echoes behind me. I turn my head as much as I can to face Everett. He has a knife and is slowly cutting pieces of the navlue fruit while making eye contact with me. "You should still be sleeping."

"Not with my luck today."

He doesn't respond.

I take a giant gulp of air and let out a bloodcurdling scream that sends an ache into my lungs. Everett's arm comes down with the knife. I turn my head, terrified, squeezing my eyes shut. The knife is embedded in the wood an inch from my ear. The impact vibrates the whole cart.

"Scream all you like. We're very far from anyone who will care."

"That might be true, but those who do care will be on their way."

Everett leans down over me with a sinister smile that chills me to my very bones. I never thought I would see a look like that on his face.

"You will be surprised at how little they could do even if they knew you were here. Which they, in fact, do not. Do you really think I would leave a little trail for them to follow?"

Anger seizes me and I try in vain to break free of my chains again. "You are such an asshole, Everett. I thought we were *friends.* I can't believe you would do this. Your mother will die of shame."

"Die of shame? Della, Camarra is helping me." He holds up the navlue fruit. "Where do you think I got this from?"

I open my mouth to speak, to demand the truth, but it all makes sense, and my stomach drops at the realization. The salt-tinged air coats my tongue.

"That man with Della was no mortal. He is the fae King of Kalvorn. He swore to leave and not come back if Nyvenah didn't attack them. He has been in disguise. They're leaving now. Go, go! Do not get caught!"

Camarra was the woman's voice I heard in the kitchens.

She is Ellova's true traitor.

My heads spin that a court Guardian would do this, help her awful son work with such a horrible king for a grasp at power.

The servant woman who placed the chains on me hides behind the cart, sobbing.

I wish I could comfort her.

A horrible creaking noise of rusting metal is an assault on my ears before a door is slammed open.

Everett's smile widens.

The vile king of Adreania moves into my view, with a few of his guards around him. His approach is slow. He's clearly in no rush, and the clothing he wears is much finer now, with golden embell-ishments and silk. An iron circlet sits atop his thinning blond hair, a poor attempt to recreate the crown he lost to me.

Grayden leans down and asks, "Comfortable?" His putrid breath on my cheek.

"Extremely," I remark dryly.

His answering smirk is cruel, and he straightens. "Were you followed?"

Everett shakes his head. "Not that I could tell. It was chaos when I left. No one noticed me."

"Good. How did you get her out?"

"A little army from Adreania showed up. Would you like to know who was leading it?"

Grayden looks bored but waits for his response.

"Your wife!" Everett says this in a delighted tone, clearly meant to annoy Grayden.

"That's impossible," Grayden says, his eyes narrowing.

"Oh no, Erenia was there with many of your traitorous citizens behind her, her own little rebellion. They made quite an entrance. Demanding King Zilas of Kalvorn. They seemed to think he was there being held prisoner instead of just following this one around like a pathetic dog to get the crown." Everett inclines his head at me. "Your queen seems to have been working against you with him. Probably fucking him, too."

His words are a knife in my chest, a bitter reminder that I truly do not know Leon. He said he never had feelings for Erenia but I can't believe any of his lies.

"So, Zilas was after the crown as well. I was right to ready my army against him."

"You do know him as another." Everett revels in his reveal. "Zilas has been in your employment for years; he was your father's healer, Leon. I'm not sure how he was mortal here and fae there, but I recognized him the second I saw him in Ellova from my time at the bazaar."

Grayden balls up his fists. "We need to prepare for him to come after the crown again."

Everett and Grayden keep discussing Zilas and Kalvorn and war, but the rushing in my ears fades their hateful voices away in a small gift of mercy.

The hollowness that was inside me is replaced with a pain that tears apart my heart so viciously I can no longer breathe, my face burning with some jumble of anger and embarrassment.

I was so foolish to think love had finally found me, that Leon had actually wanted me for who I was and not the power I possessed. Of course he demanded to follow me to Ellova. He only sought the crown and said anything he could to stay near it. He'd made me feel treasured and adored, beautiful and loved.

Lies.

Lies.

Lies.

I squeeze my eyes shut. These monsters do not get to see me cry over Leon or Zilas or whoever he claims to be.

"Who the fuck is Izadella?" Grayden asks, annoyed.

"Your royal jewelry maker." Everrett kicks the cart I'm on, jostling me. Asshole.

Grayden looks down. "So, Arra was a fake name." He glares at me but then his eyes trail up to the crown. "Why is it gold?"

Everett seems irritated at Grayden's ignorance over an item that has been in his family for thousands of years. "Because she has magic. The crown is alive again. I told you if the one who wears it holds magic, the crown will react differently. She's been growing shit all over Ellova. It's tied to her emotions. Unfortunately, you're going to have to keep her happy if you want anything to grow here."

"I have no intention of her experiencing any happiness again after what she stole from me." Hatred burns in Grayden's eyes.

Everett rolls his. "If you want it to seem like you're in control of the magic and providing for anyone in Adreania, you have to at least not torture her. You'll have thorns growing everywhere. Hardly the bounty you promised your starving citizens. Emaciated soldiers make for a poor army."

"Get her in the flood dungeon," Grayden demands and turns to the woman. "Get back to your station. Dinner is starting soon."

She chokes on her sob and bolts from us, her reddish-gold hair flying behind her.

One of the guards pulls the cart following in her direction, wooden splinters pricking me as it wobbles over the hard-packed sand.

The dark castle towers over me, a reminder it will be my tomb.

Built into its rocky base is a small prison cell that faces the Elbasan Sea.

The cart is dragged inside with a final bounce and rolls over the smooth ground.

The cell door that faces the rising tide is slammed shut. The wall is made of iron bars close together that offer no sanctuary from the bitter chill that rushes in from the dark sea and gray skies.

Everett picks me up and drops me on the floor behind the cart, muttering under his breath, "Have a good night."

"I've tried so many times to kill my father but never attempted this way. I'll be eager to see the results. We have some time before high tide. Let's celebrate the crown's return," Grayden says to Everett as they leave. "We will send her body back to Kalvorn, as a gift for Zilas." The rest of his men follow, walking up a steep staircase that leads up to the castle.

I lie down among the tangles of seaweed littered on the moss-covered stone floor and cry myself to sleep.

CHAPTER 26

IZADELLA

Freezing water touches my feet and I curl in on myself. The ground is covered in a light dusting of sand that grates on my exposed skin. The tide laps at my legs and I frantically sit up. It reeks of mold, rotting seaweed, and salty air. Ocean water has slowly filled the dungeon. I look up and see seaweed hanging at the tops of each of the doors and some on the stairwell.

They're going to drown me.

Raw rage fills me, and I scream and scream and scream. Not to be rescued but to release some of the pain slashing me from the inside.

Rage at what Leon has done.

The lies he whispered on moonlit skin.

That he made me believe he actually *loved* me.

Agony that I will never see Nueena and Tavien again.

Tortured that Farren will think I abandoned him in Ellova after what he survived last night.

"Ellova's grave, shut the fuck up," Everett says, annoyed, outside my briny cell.

I snap my head in his direction. "How could you?"

He drinks from a golden chalice. "Do not take it so personally."

Asshole. "Seems impossible not to."

He only shrugs. "Think whatever you need to, Della." He takes another sip of his drink.

I have one question for him. "You told Grayden you recognized Leon? How?"

Everett rolls his eyes. "I've been meeting with the king for months in secret. Zilas never saw me, but I saw him. If I had known he was the king of Kalvorn, he would have been dead on sight. It would have solved so many problems. Just like I saw you at the bazaar. So many dark corners to hide in and watch."

My stomach twists at his dark smile.

"It was funny to listen to Grayden complain about you. This mortal jewelry maker with a family who wanted nothing to do with him. What I can't figure out is why you were there. It could not be for the coin. You have *everything* in Ellova. I wouldn't be surprised if you had access to the royal family's treasuries."

At that, it's my turn to grace him with a smug smile. "We all have our reasons for the choices we make. You just happen to choose terrible ones. And yes, I do have access to them."

"Try to remember you are the one in the jail cell here." He has the gall to be reading the novel I lent him.

"Are you seriously enjoying my book right now?"

He shrugs, turning a page. "I want to know how it ends."

Delighted to spoil the ending for him, I bellow, "The hero solves the riddle, saves his brother who slew the serpent, and earns the maiden's love, and together they win the war."

The book snaps shut, and Everett throws it at me. I duck even though I'm still bound, and it slaps against the slick wall, falling into the water. My book is ruined, but it was worth it, and I snicker at the utter ridiculousness of it all. The bottled-up stress of the past few weeks pours out of me, turning into cackling laughter.

"You won't be laughing soon." He seethes.

"Everett! What are you even doing here? What can you possibly gain? You want the crown? I can promise you; it's been a *miserable* experience."

"I want the power the crown has," he says in a haughty tone.

"You think Grayden is going to share power he doesn't have? With you?" My laughter continues.

"You don't need magic to have power."

"Yeah, but it sure fucking helps, Everett. It really fucking helps."

His smile is an evil, twisted thing. "Guess it's pretty lucky we have you, then, isn't it?"

I stop laughing at that.

He tsks. "Oh, not so fucking funny anymore, is it?"

"What is funny, what will give me endless joy, will be seeing Nueena rip you to shreds."

It's a glorious mental image. Her magic tearing him apart, Tavien's flames incinerating what is left.

Revenge for taking me, revenge for his treachery.

"Nueena isn't coming. When we left, she was a little preoccupied with the army at her doorstep demanding a king she didn't know was right under her nose. Zilas promised to leave and not come back if Nyvenah didn't attack them. He rode away with them. You know who else rode out just after the army left? That servant girl with red hair on a Ellovian war horse. A horse that looks suspiciously like yours. Everyone in the command room saw *you* leave, chasing after your beloved healer, fleeing your home forever to be with him."

Panic rises faster than the icy waters. A broken "No" slips out of me.

Nueena thinks I've abandoned her? Abandoned Ellova? All to chase after a mortal man who has done nothing but lie to me?

No. No, she knows me better than that.

Everett murdered his closest friend. He cannot fathom a friendship like what Nueena and I have shared for over a century. He has lied to everyone. How could he possibly understand what it is like for someone to understand you as much as you understand yourself?

Nueena would never believe I'd run off to Kalvorn without telling her or without begging her forgiveness on my knees for risking the security of Ellova.

She would know how devastated I am, having unknowingly brought a possible enemy to our realm.

But what if she thinks I've fled in shame?

"And Zilas never loved you anyway. He was after the crown, so don't hold your breath for him to care that you're here either."

Even if Leon did have real feelings for me, he thinks I'm safe with Nueena in Ellova.

The water is up to my waist, filling the dungeon.

The numbness spreading within me is not from the frigid waves but from one realization: no one is coming.

CHAPTER 27

LEON

Guards escort me down the staircase into the unused kitchen where we prepared Viella for her journey into the mortal realm. Nyvenah follows as we make our descent deep below the palace to the base of the mountain, and she unlocks the door with a wave of her hand. "You've done enough damage. See that you do not attempt any more."

I can only nod. The wide door opens, sunlight pouring in, and I step into an unknown future. The door slams behind me.

Erenia jumps at my sudden appearance. I turn around just in time to see the entrance has disappeared into the mountainside, glamoured completely.

Dread devours me.

I run my hands over the rocky mountainside, the sharp rocks scratching my palms. I slam my fist into the rocks on the mountain side and rest my head against it. There must be a way to convince Izadella of my true intentions before it's too late.

I need her to let me back in, but for now, Adreania's more vulnerable citizens stare back at me. I must help them. Return to my home, my people.

I've been gone far too long.

Lula's long, dark blue wings flare out, catching the breeze, and she lands on my shoulder. My azure hawk lightly pecks my ear in greeting, allowing me to pet her gently.

One of the Adreanian rebels brings me a horse but I choose to find my way back to Kalvorn on foot, passing off the animal to someone else who needs it more as we walk in the direction of my kingdom, eager to meet with my brother. Callen must be briefed on everything that has happened.

What will he say when I tell him I've met my soulbonded mate and that she has the crown I once sought? That the throne he's kept for me will be his forever now?

"Let's head out!" I yell at all those around me. "There is food and shelter in Kalvorn. We will find you new housing, and you can start over."

A shout rings out from the back of the gathered group. "Are you really the king?"

"Yes, my brother is on the throne in my place 'til I return."

The weary faces that stare back relax. Reluctant hope appears. The Merawood Forest's thick canopy of the trees shades us from the beating sun. These people followed me, trusted me when they were ill as they do now with their lives outside Adreania. I've let too many people down today and I will honor whatever promises Erenia has made to them. They deserve a place to be safe and happy, not used as a villainous king's personal shield.

But every step away from Izadella is agony.

Breaking my heart a little more, ushering in my death that much sooner.

I know she is my Zemra.

From the moment I saw her across that dreary ballroom, I knew. Her essence called to me, screamed at me to keep her near, protect her, love her, worship her.

Her brown eyes seared into my soul, forever changing me the moment they met mine at her booth. My body demanded I claim her, my heart yearned to truly know her, and while every part of me ached with an unwavering awareness that her soul and mine belonged to each other, my head still screamed for me to run from her. She threatened everything I had been working towards, a distraction I couldn't have but desperately desired.

It was endless elation and torture all at once.

When I found out she was fae. That we felt the same about each other, that she was drawn to me in the same unexplainable ways I was to her. I knew then what we were to each other, why I couldn't let her out of my sight.

To never see her again because of my own mistakes is anguish I've never known. I won't entertain the idea that such a thing could ever come to pass.

No matter how much time I have left.

She *is* my Zemra; she needs to know that. Even if we could never be truly soulbonded.

I just need to give her time—space to remember what I mean to her and who we could be together. No matter what happens, she will always have a place at my side and in my heart.

I will crawl on my knees and beg if need be.

The forest is peaceful. The trees stay still, apparently seeing no issue with my departure and keeping their branches to themselves.

Erenia catches up to me. "What the fuck is going on?" she demands.

My anger at everything rises in me, but this is my friend who has suffered greatly. "We had a plan," I say roughly. "You needed to wait 'til I became king again or head straight to Kalvorn if you must."

"Yeah, well, what was I supposed to do? I waited as long as I could. We all did." She motions to the small army of people behind her watching us carefully.

"I told you to just go straight to Kalvorn, *alone*. My brother would have believed you if you had shown him the letter."

"You did say that, and we *tried*, but you actually haven't spoken to Callen in a hundred years, so *you* have no real way of telling how he would react. I, however, do. We were attacked on sight. No matter how many white flags we raised, no one from Kalvorn would let me get near enough to let me explain that you were *planning* on returning. Even if they had, I would have had to explain that I had no idea where you were and why you never returned to Kalvorn with the crown but *please let us all stay*. For all he knew, we were a trap sent by Grayden. A large group of citizens from the kingdom he's about to go to war with just shows up with a promise that we know you, my only proof a letter."

"Erenia, that letter had our invisible family seal on it. He would have trusted what was said."

She rolls her eyes. "I would have loved to show him if your army did not attack. Everyone in Beggars' Row was healed and Grayden demanded they go to the front lines. He was going to force them to be the first to attack Kalvorn, the first to die."

Fuck. "Of course, Grayden would take any hope these people had and destroy it."

"We were all just planning on staying in the forest, but your letter arrived, explaining where you were. I had to track you down. It's time you return to your throne and become king again. Kill my husband to stop the war, Leon. Pursuing your little jewelry maker will have to wait."

I purse my lips.

Erenia's voice cracks when she speaks again. "Zilas, I just want to go back *home*. He's waiting for me."

The lover she left behind when she agreed to marry Grayden. We've spent so much time in the castle, miserable, longing for the ones we couldn't have. That pain bonded us in many ways.

That and our shared hatred of her husband.

Her tough exterior breaks for a moment. I pull my dear friend to me and squeeze her shoulders tightly. "I know. I'm going to get you back to him. You will be free of all of this soon, I promise."

Our embrace is brief, and she wipes away a single tear before she straightens her back. Her cold, calculating face returns. "Where is it?"

I know she means the crown but with so many listening ears it's not safe to tell her the details—how I've long since attempted to get it back, how Izadella got wrapped up in my quest, how she is far more precious to me now—so I simply say, "I'm working on it."

"I'm sorry," she mutters. "We really did wait as long as we could.

We just need to take everyone somewhere safe. If you can provide ships, I'm happy to take anyone who wishes to join me. They can build new lives for themselves across the sea, but I need to leave as soon as I can. I need to speak to my father and break the alliance between Adreania and Versairen. Versairen will only have one ally now and it will be Kalvorn."

"No, you're right. Everything went to shit once Jedrick died. I should've returned sooner. I have nothing to show for my efforts for the past month. You can take my fastest ship."

"Thank you. It didn't work out with her?"

"Arra is not speaking to me at the moment. I think I may have spectacularly ruined everything I've built here." My voice breaks. "She hates me."

Izadella trusted me. Trusted me with her body and her heart. Trusted I was who I said I was. I waited too long to tell her the truth, and it has cost me everything.

Erenia's face softens. "Let's just get you back on your throne. You can make things better from there. I'm sure she will understand one day. We have a war to stop."

I do not bother to tell her that a dying king has no place on Kalvorn's throne.

The journey into the forest is slow with so many families. I shove down the desire to go back to Izadella's cottage and sit in the ashes just to feel like she is near again.

We reached the wide tree Izadella and I used to travel here, the magic thrumming through the roots beneath my feet.

"What is this?" Erenia asks.

"A tree portal. We need to get to Kalvorn fast. Stay here with them. I'm going to ensure a new one can be opened into my castle."

I push the ivy that hangs over the hidden doorframe into the dark hollow, finding the hand-shaped carving. I slip my fingers into the wood connecting to it. Whatever enchantments this tree is made of takes hold of all the magic within me. The sensation tugs at me and I am thankful for the sweet release of power.

The ground rumbles and I stretch my magic to the northwest, picturing the royal gardens of my childhood so clearly, spiral

cypress trees that surround the blooming flora, the marble fountains and greenhouses. The branches of the portal magic shoot like
an arrow ahead, forging its path. The shaking gets more violent,
more of my magic being siphoned to create a new portal tree. I can
sense the roots deepening and growing.

Finally, it stops, and I am overwhelmed at the fragrance that
drifts in from my mother's lavender garden.

Home.

I step out onto the ruined grass. A huge tree has burst out of the
center of the perfectly kept lawn. Kalvornian castle guards arrive
with swords raised and bows drawn surrounding the new portal.

One guard lets his arrow fly, opting to shoot first and ask questions later.

I make no attempt to dodge the golden arrow; the skilled archer
hits his mark, piercing my chest. The arrowhead tears through my
heart muscles, rupturing the organ, blood vessels bursting. Blood
seeps down my chest as I wrap my hand around the arrow, ripping
it out of my flesh, ignoring the pain. My healing magic rises to the
wound, slower than it ever has before, but it stitches every part that
was damaged, renewing and restoring inside me 'til it is whole
again.

I throw the bloody weapon at my feet.

"Go find your king. Tell him his brother has returned."

CHAPTER 28

IZADELLA

The icy water rushing into my jail cell bites at my skin. Tiny needles pierce every inch of my flesh. Every second is a reminder this freezing prison will be my grave by high tide.

All so Everett can have this miserable crown.

A memory pops up, and I turn my frozen body towards him.

The water laps at the steps where he still sits above the water, watching me. He moves each time the water nears his feet 'til he sits on the top of the dry steps, clear of the moss and seaweed that litters the bottom.

The perfect view for my last few minutes of breath.

My teeth chatter together when I talk. "So, this-s is the p-plan? Watch me die and grab the crown off my c-corpse?"

"Well, if you could remove it yourself and hand it over to me, I'm sure Grayden could find other uses for you."

Bastard.

"You-u fell off your ship during that winter storm-m and were reported lost at sea for days. Did you wash up-p on Adreania's shore? Is that how you and Grayden met? Did you convince him you could control the crown and form an alliance to take over Ellova-a?"

His jaw tightens and I know I'm right. "Something like that."

"Everett, I *mourned* for you-u, cried over you. Nueena and I both did. I would expect this type of betrayal from Kole, but *you*? We've been friends for a century. P-please, just tell me why. I'll be dead in the next few minutes anyway. Give me that closure."

Everett watches me struggle in the water, and for a brief moment, regret peeks through before it is washed away. "I'm made for greater things than just being an ocean guard. I *demand* greater things than being the son of a guardian whose own title isn't even passed down. Here, if you have power, you hold on to it."

"You think you can have Ellova?"

He rolls his eyes. "Even I'm not foolish enough to try and take Ellova by force. Six courts against one malnourished kingdom of useless mortals would be a waste of future soldiers. No, once I have the crown in a few minutes, I can use the magic to restore Adreania."

I still laugh through my rattling teeth. "So, becoming king of the mortals is this master plan of yours? King Everett, ruler of nothing."

"You forget what it was like in the years Adreania had a fae on the throne. It was once a prosperous kingdom thanks to the crown. Once it is restored, it will have been worth the effort. Adreania is allied with the biggest kingdom across the sea. Versairen has fleets of ships ready to set sail towards Kalvorn. After all, they kidnapped and killed King Jedrick, beloved ruler and father. They are well within their right to declare war on that lying king to protect Erenia's interests in Adreania. Grayden has discovered something I want about Kalvorn. They have magic. He could never be ruler of a fae kingdom. But with the crown, I could. Your precious king will be joining you soon in the afterlife, if that brings you any comfort." He smirks at me.

The water splashes around my chest and the chains have me nearly submerged, trapped to the wall. It's the light greenish hue of the sea surrounding me. The tide drags and pulls at my body, fear consuming me.

Anytime I ever thought about my death, I assumed I would die in Ellova, after centuries with Nueena and Tavien.

Nyvenah told me once that a spot had already been designated for me in the royal family's mausoleum next to where Nueena and Tavien would eventually join me in an eternal resting place among past Realm Keepers.

It was an honor I didn't believe I deserved, but Nyvenah had decided that all of her children would be buried with her and that was that.

Something slimy slithers past my leg.

Fucking eels.

Water rises and rises. I try to stay afloat but my chained leg is weighted down. I'm going to die in the fucking cursed castle with its prick of a king.

The coldness of the water makes my body ache, my dress heavy as I kick my feet to stay above the tide, desperate for my last moments of precious air.

I should have told my family how much I love them. How I knew I would never be alone, with Nueena there after the night my mother died and Nyvenah held me as I cried for hours. How my friends feel like home now.

Leon.

Even if he was a liar.

I love him.

I lied too. I should have listened to what he had to say. I should have trusted him as he trusted me.

It felt real. Every caress, every kiss, every word.

The truth in his touch.

I thought I would never find love, and I was going to die after only experiencing it for a moment. Maybe this was the cruelest part.

The water is up to my nose, and I can go no further. Once the next wave rolls in, I'll be pulled under. I close my eyes and take one last gasp of air to buy me a few more seconds of borrowed time.

Ellova, please save me.

Agony rips into me as death prepares to greet me. I kick and kick but it's no use.

It can't end like this.

Why wasn't I given more time?

My lungs burn and burn from holding in my final breath. My last terrified thought is of Leon as my body finally forces me to inhale. I gasp with a sob no one can hear, not ready for death. My chest expands and precious air rushes in. I expect biting water to fill my lungs, to die choking, but nothing happens. I take an experimental breath and then another.

I can still breathe.

The lochkiss.

That blessed bubble Leon and I used to swim in the spring.

Where we had our first kiss.

I start laughing and cannot stop. Maybe fate has yet to forget me. The joy of being alive fills me with a warmth no one in the castle can take away.

The look on his face will be priceless.

I pretend to drown, dramatically thrashing around, grabbing at my throat. Truly, it's a performance worthy of the Royal Ellovian Theater.

Finally, after a few full body twitches, I let my body relax, floating listlessly, pretending to truly have drowned but keeping my eyes open just a sliver to see him.

After a few minutes, the bars open and Everett dives into the green water illuminated by the torches lining the stairwell above.

If we were in Ellova, he could part the waters with his magic, the waves his to command, but here in this dreadful place he is as powerless as a dewling.

He barrels towards me, ready to take the crown for himself.

Just before he reaches me, I snap my eyes open, startling him, much to my delight.

I blow Everett a kiss, little bubbles floating up to the surface, and give him a playful wave of my fingers.

He bares his teeth and his fist flies towards me. I brace for impact, but he grabs the crown and pulls. Pain rips through me, but a strange electric shock of the crown's magic pulses out, and Everett jerks before going limp and floating towards the surface.

Unfortunately, the fucker can breathe underwater.

I may not be able to protect myself, but the crown will. Even with the iron collar, some magic cannot be stopped.

My head aches but I start laughing again. This time it's hysterical, the combination of relief and horror.

A small school of silver fish swim in and out, exploring the new places the tide has brought. Tethered to the wall by the chains, my body bobs leisurely, rocking with the freezing undercurrent.

I doubt Everett is dead. He will try again and again 'til he gets what he wants, but for now I'm alive and will survive the night.

For now, that is enough.

CHAPTER 29

IZADELLA

J'm awakened by crashing waves and the thump of footsteps. My watery prison has lazily retreated into the sea, and I am alone in the damp cell. Everett is nowhere to be seen. The door rattles as guards rip it open and swarm me. They undo my bindings, put fresh chains on my wrists, and drag me up the stairs deep into the castle. Grayden sits on the extravagant throne I saw his father on so many times before. The guards around him have their arrows drawn at me.

To his side stands Everett, alive and well. His lip is pulled up in anger. Behind them is a large tapestry with the Adreanian crown. *Loyal to who wears the crown* is sewn in bright gold lettering.

Leon said I am the ruler of Adreania, that the throne is my right as I hold the crown, but dripping water onto the polished floor, half-drowned, I've never felt less like a queen.

Everett follows my gaze, his expression shifting as he starts laughing so hard at me, he nearly falls over, clutching his side.

Grayden's expression matches someone who discovered they stepped in horseshit. "Oh, what is it now? You are testing my patience, faerie."

"Della, do you seriously think having the crown makes you queen?" Everett faces Grayden. *"Loyal to who wears the crown.* Isn't that your law? You have it everywhere in this damn castle." Everett snickers, turning back to me. "The captive queen."

The guards glance at one another, and given the tight line of Grayden's lips, it does not go unnoticed. "Take the collar off her."

Someone's hands are on me, removing the iron weight. The crown's magic rushes back inside me and I stumble for a moment. It's a light weight on my head, a comfort now, filling that empty ache only magic can fill, even if it's not my own. Power rolls through me, but before I can make any attempt to use it, the side doors open and a disheveled Cyanna walks in with more guards. The gut punch of seeing her in chains nearly knocks me over.

No.

No.

What is she doing here?

My mortal cousin's red, tear-filled eyes match her splotchy cheeks, but she otherwise appears to be unharmed. "I'm sorry."

"It's okay! I understand!" I lie, trying not to let my devastating anger show. No matter her intentions, no matter her heart for those in need, Grayden will kill her, and her blood will be on my hands.

Magic surges inside me, reacting to my rage, as if it is begging to be set free.

It was so fucking foolish of her to come back here. Any chance I may have found to escape will now be useless. I could never leave her behind, will do anything to keep her safe. Grayden will deliver the final blow, but she has built our coffin.

My nails dig so deep into my palm I have to force my fist to flex so I don't break through skin.

She knows her ruinous return will harm me. The guilt is obvious on her face. "I came back for more children, but they were all gone."

Gone? What does she mean by that? Did the elixir not work? Are they all dead?

"The place where you sent me," Cyanna begins slowly, "they are like you."

Of course they are, if Leon is fae and she was sent to his childhood home. "I know."

Grayden speaks in a low voice. "Any sudden movements or attacks will result in a very nasty punishment for you both."

I nod, not breaking eye contact with Cyanna. No matter how angry I am at her, I mouth, *I'm so sorry,* and she gives me a small, wobbly "Me, too."

We will both die here.

Ignoring Everett, I take a deep calming breath and walk up to the throne. "I'll do whatever you wish. If I can. This isn't my magic. It's not under my control."

"I want to win a war." Grayden sounds like a petulant child demanding everything that isn't his. "I want Kalvorn."

What does this horrible man want me to do about that? "War is not something I am familiar with."

"Everett says his sword was made by you. Is this true?"

My eyes flick to Everett and I pour all my hatred in his direction. "Yes, it's beautifully crafted, encrusted in sapphires, sand from his favorite beach mixed with the gold on the handle so his grip would never slip, even in water. All the other water guards were *so* jealous of him. I refused many valuable trades when they begged for a similar one. It was a beautiful gift for a dear friend."

Everett looks away like the coward he is.

Grayden rolls his eyes. "I do not care. I want more of them, thousands of them." He hurls a long wooden branch at my feet. "Turn it into a sword."

I smother my urge to laugh at the ridiculous request, and it soothes my ire at Cyanna. "Everett, is that something you said I could do? Are we adding lying to your new king to the list of your many transgressions?"

His eyes narrow at *your king.* "The crown has limitless power. I have no idea what it can do, but I intend to find out."

The wooden stick is rough, the ends of the bark rotting, but I close my eyes. I imagine the parts of the sword in my head, clear as day. The hilt and the blade, pommel and cross guard. The weight and sharpness of it. I cannot have Cyanna harmed because of me.

If that means arming soldiers for a war against Leon's kingdom, so be it.

He made his choice, and I shall make mine.

Magic flows through me and into the wood; it vibrates in my hand. It grows heavy, but not with the weight of a weapon. The branch is alive again. Bright green leaves grow from it with clusters of small pink buds blooming, their fragrant aroma only lasting a moment before the petals fall to the floor. What's left collapses in on itself, becoming bulbs, growing to plump green apples.

My heart sinks.

"I can't control the magic. Wood cannot turn to metal." I walk up to the dais stairs, bringing the bounty up to Grayden, who takes it. The apples are perfect and the guards stare at it with their mouths open. I wonder if it is the magic that surprises them or the food they have never seen. "I did try. If I had access to my own magic without the crown stifling it, I could make what you requested."

"Very well, bring the orphan keeper to me," Grayden drawls, snapping his fingers in the direction of a weeping Cyanna.

"NO!" I scream as guards grab my arms and force me to kneel. "Don't touch her!"

Grayden ignores me, ripping off an apple and handing it to Cyanna. "Eat."

She glances at me with wide, fearful eyes and I rush to reassure her. "It's okay. It's safe. I was growing strawberries, and they made these delicious little tarts." When she doesn't move, I whisper, "I promise."

Her hand trembles as she brings it to her lips. I hold my breath as she chews.

"It's delicious and crisp," she says before taking another large bite. The guards watch Cyanna chew with hungry eyes.

Grayden stands, walking slowly down the stairs away from his throne, each step a threat towards me. He taps the branch on his palm. "I did not ask for fruit, did I?"

Guards grab my arms, holding me in place as he closes in. He brings the heavy branch back, ready to swing, but my magic rises up to protect me, the castle rumbling beneath our feet.

Heavy doors slam open, grabbing our attention. Princess Lyrora bursts in so quickly, she must have been eavesdropping on the other side.

"Stop it!" Lyrora pleads with her brother, her guard behind her.

Grayden lowers the branch and swings it in the direction of the door. "Get out of here, Lyrora!"

"No! Every tree outside has turned to ash, Grayden! Whatever you're doing to her needs to stop! You promised Adreania prosperity and all you have brought it is despair. Everyone outside is panicking!"

Shouts and wails are coming from outside.

"Get her the fuck out of here!" he screams at her personal guard.

"NO!" she says defiantly as she is pushed away. "You're going to destroy everything!" Her voice slowly fades, still trying to convince her brother to stop.

Grayden's back is curved, and he's breathing heavily. He throws the branch at my feet. "You'd better learn to control that crown quickly or the orphan keeper is *dead*. I do not want apples. I want weapons." He turns to return to his throne. "Return her to her cell."

As I am dragged away, I realize my neck is bare.

CHAPTER 30

IZADELLA

I'm dumped on a thick pile of seaweed the tide left behind in my ocean dungeon.

My pain comes out of me in a bloodcurdling scream. I scream and scream 'til I choke on the guilt and grief, rage and terror.

The thick, light green seaweed beneath my fingertips withers at my touch, which only makes me feel worse.

Whatever fight I had in me flees and the tears return once more. I do not try to stop them, letting heartbreak tear me apart from the inside for hours.

My sobs steal my breath. The agony claws at my chest as I lie listlessly on the brutally cold floor, unrecognizable lamentations sputtering over my lips. My magic twists out painfully.

Everett's words about my emotions controlling the crown come back to me.

The seaweed has shrunk, brown with decay in my hands.

I did this.

What else has the magic done while I've been here?

If my grief and despair is causing this, I need to shift my emotions, or at least try to.

Princess Lyrora said the trees had turned to ash, the crown's magic reflecting my inner turmoil.

I *need* to learn to control it.

Grayden will kill Cyanna if I don't.

I take deep breaths in and out.

he first people to be hurt by the crown's continuous quest to destroy will be those on Beggars' Row. I cannot let that happen. I did not spend decades caring for a forgotten community just to deliver the final strike.

I focus on my happiest memories, those in my life that I love.

Nueena. Her kindness, her grace. How proud her family and I are of her finally stepping onto that dais to sit on the Ellovian throne, claiming her rightful place as ruler of Ellova, like she was born to do. Her strength is remarkable, her loyalty to Ellova unwavering. We are all lucky to have her and I will never get to see that.

My soul cracks again, the wound opening wider and wider.

Leon.

I shove the thought away and try to think of all my favorite moments with Nueena over the years.

The tea parties we had as dewlings.

When I gifted her a sphere of solid gold for her birthday, which I used to make her a new necklace every morning I was at the palace, to match whatever gown she was wearing.

The shining in her eyes of pure joy when she told me about her first kiss with Tavien.

The year after we finished our schooling and traveled around Ellova, exploring the courts, just the two of us. We ended up at the seaside palace and convinced a group of water guards that we wanted to join the Shell Court. Had them take us out on their ship and instead of learning how to sail, we laid out blankets, soaking up the sun in little more than strips of fabric.

Leon.

Nights spent reading with Tavien by the fire or listening to him teach history to dewlings. Exploring the many libraries of Ellova together while Nueena went off to meet court Guardians.

Long summer days swimming with Viella in the royal natatorium.

Dancing all night under the stars in the Gem Court parties with Hiliyah, our goblets full of sparkling wine.

Lillian's insistence I be knowledgeable on swords so I could always protect myself. Training sessions at dawn. Finally besting her just once before she had my ass on the floor.

Leon.

The night of my mother's burial, Nyvenah took me back to the Ellovian palace, insisting I had a place with her family. I thought it meant I would just be given a small room in the palace, but instead she walked Nueena and me into our newly furnished royal west wing.

I was never alone after that.

Leon.

No, I won't think of him or his betrayal. How could he have made me think he loved me? I was nothing but a stepping stone to get what he wanted the whole time. It's almost too painful to think about, but he had to have cared about me, even a little. When we were both pretending—Leon, the mortal healer, and Lady Arra, the married mortal jeweler—he liked me.

Before I had this wretched crown on me, when it was just him and me under the full moon, tortured, yearning for a stolen moment and secret touches we were never allowed.

He had taken vows to care for the king, forbidden from anything outside of his service to the crown. Came to my booth every month, commissioned jewelry he barely glanced at, time and time again, just to talk to me.

Years before this awful crown, I had nothing to offer him as a king, yet he was there at every bazaar with heated eyes and kind words, watching as I sold jewelry to the spoiled and heartless court of Adreania. The weight of his wanting had been expressed at every opportunity. The pull of us towards each other, like planets rotating around the same sun of burning desire. When his stupid vow to Jedrick was in his way and a false mortal family in mine, he never looked away.

I wanted him when I knew I couldn't have him.

I want him even now.

For two years I yearned for his touch, and when we finally collided that night in the forest, something changed. Every day we were together in Ellova, it felt like home with him.

My eyes burn from tears that won't stop flowing.

I cannot concentrate on his betrayal. That will only lead to pain, so instead I choose to believe what he felt for me was genuine. That the love I felt in his kiss, the truth of it in his touch, was honest and real. That I will not die here but I will see him again, an explanation on his lips just before mine are.

I loved him. I still love him.

He must have had a reason not to tell me 'til I told him I loved him. I didn't trust him then but maybe I can trust him now.

Magic spills from my heart at my love for Leon.

Movement in my hand startles me as the withered seaweed plumps up, color returning.

"Impressive," Grayden drawls behind me. I roll over and scramble to sit up. He forcefully slides a plate of food, some of it falling off the plate, and tosses a bottle of some kind underneath the metal bars towards me. "Eat. I need you to have some strength."

The meaty aroma sends a stab of pain into the aching emptiness of my stomach, but I make no move to take it.

"It's not poisoned." Annoyance drips from every word, as if I am being unreasonable.

"Well, considering you attempted to drown me last night, I don't think I will take your word on that."

"That was before. I see your true purpose now."

My skin crawls.

"What do you want?" I lean against the wall, ignoring the food in front of me and appear as if his presence doesn't terrify me. I fold my shaking hands together on my lap, trying to hide that fear.

"I wanted to see what you would do without the collar. You should see the trees outside. Adreania has never seen such green-ery. Well, not since the last time it had a fae queen on its throne."

His smile is oily as he throws something into my cell. "What does it say?"

The iron rolls over the stone floor, and I slam my fist over it, not bothering to read it. "I know what it says."

Loyal to whoever wears the crown.

"Here I thought the real value was the crown, but I see now that you hold what I actually need. Everett was intended to wear it, claiming he could handle it, but you will be far more fun to control."

Fuck, whatever he wants will be awful and I shove down the hopelessness hammering into me.

"I've already told you; the crown does not obey my command. It's not my magic to possess. The crown was only ever intended for Inara. The Forger keyed it to only her, and after her death, the crown, like all fae-keyed items, will choose who can control it." I hope he can see the hatred in my eyes. "Believe me, if it had chosen me, you would have taken your last breath days ago."

My throat burns from my words, the reminder that I have not had anything to drink in nearly two days. I pick up the bottle and sniff it. The mild scent of honey entices me to take a small sip. The drink is some sort of watered-down ale, but it has an aftertaste of medicinal bitterness.

When nothing happens, I take another long swig of the warming drink, letting it heat me, a new strength returning.

"Adreania was once a great kingdom. It can be that again with the right queen."

His predatory eyes rake over my body, the crown on matted hair, my filthy dress, and the scratches and bruises peppering my arms and legs. My stomach turns at the implication.

I'm tired of this conversation. Tired of this man.

"You already have a queen. Her name is Erenia Caslow of Versairen. You know, daughter of the king whose armies you plan on using to take Kalvorn. I highly doubt her father will look favorably on you remarrying."

He scoffs. "Erenia is no queen of mine. She is a traitor and will be dealt with accordingly. She spent an extraordinary amount of time with the healer the past few years, but now I know he was actually a king. She perhaps sought to aim even higher than just my princess." Cruelty covers his face. "Everett said you and the healer were inseparable. Did you think he was only fucking you?"

A seed of jealousy takes root even after everything Leon has done. Grayden has to be lying, though.

He's trying to bait me. I can see it in the gleam of his eye, his hideous need to drag me lower in whatever way he can. He knows his wife would never risk her life like that, nor would Leon.

I will not give him the satisfaction. "What Leon did while he was here is none of my concern, nor do I care what he does now." It hurts to say it.

I hope it's convincing.

Grayden stretches out his legs on the stairs, getting comfortable. "The orphan keeper told us everything, you know. We found her trying to find children to sneak out of Adreania. One threat and she sang like a canary. She told us you came once a month to bring food and medicine, how you refused to let those children starve. How very *noble* of you. I'm going to guess you wish to continue ensuring the safety of those children? What of the orphan keeper's life?"

Dread fills every space inside me. My voice breaks. "I—I will do whatever you want, if it's within my power. P-Please, just don't hurt them."

"Eat," he says again.

His threat forces me to crawl towards the food. I expect the worst but it's a hearty meat pie with a thick crust.

I know his next words before he speaks them, but they still stab me in the gut with panic. "We will marry. You will become queen and will grow whatever I want, bring prosperity and health back to Adreania. If you obey, I will not murder your new people and loved ones in front of you. Do we have a deal?"

Of course he does, as if I would refuse him. Cyanna was a fool to return but I need to ensure her safety anyway.

His grotesque grin taunts me.

All those dreams of a short lifetime with Leon fade away as I am faced with the reality that I'll be forced to wed a monster.

"We have a deal."

CHAPTER 31

LEON

It's been over a hundred years, but I am *finally* home.

Yet again, I am surrounded by guards, and I am escorted inside my castle. The anticipation of once again rejoining my brother has my heart beating rapidly, nerves twisting in my gut.

Kalvorn's throne room is still as magnificent as I remember from childhood, and it stops my heart for a moment. While Ellova's palace is bright with rich colors and vibrant flora, Kalvorn's castle is filled with sun-soaked greens, gilded touches, and cream walls. The golden throne gleams under lavish chandeliers where it sits empty under a marble archway, emerald fabric draped over sandstone pillars above lush greenery that lines the walls.

The Elbasan Sea glitters below the castle, the soft calls of gulls filtering through the circular windows. The air is tinged with salt and the sweet citrus of the nearby orange grove, which thrives in Kalvorn's temperate climate thanks to irrigation from the Airvell River.

Those doors swing open and my brother, Callen, appears, commanding his guards to leave us.

I've pictured this moment countless times since we parted, when I was sent away at seventeen to retrieve the crown.

Callen, only fourteen, stands on the rain-soaked dock, eyes cast downward. I hold one ticket to board a ship to Versairen in my hand. I've clung to it with so much fear it's crumpled in my fist.

My mother's last words to me echo in my memory. "Do not come back without that crown, Zilas."

My younger brother embraces me one last time, his small frame shaking. The movement against my chest clogs my throat. "Come back, no matter what. With or without the crown, just come back." His words are hidden under rolling thunder.

Now, he breaks out into a run at the same moment I do, racing over the shining malachite floor. We collide roughly and hold each other tight. A missing piece of me slides back into place at our reunion. Tears spring to my eyes. The crashing wave of love and familiarity, no matter how much time has passed, could ascend me into the clouds.

A weight is lifted off my shoulders at the sensation that I've made it back, that if I must die, it will not be in the rotten kingdom of Adreania but with my brother.

To be born and to greet death here.

He slaps me on the back. "*Zilas!* You've returned! We will plan your coronation at once," he shouts joyfully and we pull apart. It echoes around the elegant throne room that as a young prince I dreamed would be mine.

I need to be honest with him, but his joy at my arrival is such a gift after all that has happened.

We look so similar; it's part of the reason we were able to fool everyone when I left. How he could easily pretend to be me after I disappeared. He has no gray in his hair, though. I may be slightly taller, my hair longer, but our features are nearly identical, the same bright green eyes.

Those eyes stay locked on mine, never glancing up at my head, devoid of the crown I was meant to return with.

"Are you well? We got word that Jedrick had died and we feared the worst." His smile is stretched wide, his hands on my shoulders as if to remind himself I am truly here.

"Callen...I—" Words suddenly fail me. I despise ruining the joy between us at this treasured reunion. To tell him he will lose me just as quickly as I've returned. I slowly undo the first few buttons of my shirt, revealing the proof of my enervation death's swift arrival. Bright white scars crawl up my chest. "My coronation will be unnecessary. I thought I would return with the crown and a queen for Kalvorn, but I have failed on both counts."

His face falls in devastation with a broken whisper. "No!" He knows, as I do, a cure does not exist but hope still returns to his words. "But your magic? Can you not heal yourself?"

"I'm afraid not." I close my eyes and try once more to save my own life. My healing magic gathers within me, but when it reaches my chest, the magic slips out of me like sand through an hourglass. I shake my head. "Any magic I use attempting to heal it just fades out of me."

"How did this happen? Where is the crown now? If we can get it back, surely it has enough magic. We will take it by force this time, send out the entire Kalvorn army." His resolve to save me is commendable.

With a deep sigh I say, "I have much to tell you."

"And I you," he says with an ache in his voice. "You are an uncle now."

Callen has lived a full life here, and I want to know everything. "Yes, I heard through whispers at the castle you are a husband and a father to a little prince now." No matter the heaviness between us, we have much to celebrate. "I wish to meet them!" I glance around to see if anyone has joined us, but we are still alone.

Callen wrings his hands for a moment. A guilty expression crosses his face before he straightens with determination. "Before you meet them, I have a confession. I know she was betrothed to you when you left Kalvorn, but Estelle is my *wife*. I married her two years ago, but I loved her long before that. I did try to delay the marriage, for you to return, but we—no." He takes a deep breath. "*I couldn't hold back from her. I swear, I kept our true identities a secret for as long as I could. She arrived to be your queen, but she was meant for me. I could sense it in my bones, my being. I had no way of contacting you in Adreania. She may have been the fiancée

Mother chose for you, but she was always meant to be mine." His throat bobs. "I understand if you hate me. It is a betrayal I do not expect forgiveness for."

I am stunned by his words. *I understand if you hate me.*

I'm more wounded that he thinks I possess the ability to hate him, than I am at anything to do with Estelle, a woman I hardly knew.

I take in all of his words, his desperate need for me to comprehend how much has changed since I left. Perhaps if I had never met Izadella, I would feel differently. If I returned with the crown, ready to marry, only to discover they had fallen in love. That loss of loyalty might eat at me, but I now know the crushing weight of loving someone you think is another's.

When I thought Izadella was married to a mortal man, I was convinced he was unworthy of her. She'd been so close to me in those midnight hours but eternally out of reach. I'd cared so little of her husband when I knew she was fated to me.

I imagine Callen must have felt the same relief and joy when I freed Estelle from our engagement, as I did, learning Izadella was never truly married.

Callen's apprehension keeps his face guarded and transforms into surprise when I yank him into another bone-crushing hug. "I understand, truly."

He quickly pulls back, shocked at my response. "What?"

"The news of your marriage did seem rather soon after I broke off our arranged engagement, but how could I harbor ill will towards either of you? If you found love in my absence, I am exceedingly glad for it, and having a child? What a blessing! You've had much placed upon you, and my quest for the crown took decades longer than I had hoped. You are my brother, and you deserve every bit of happiness. You stood in my place for a century. For that I am grateful. How could I harbor anything other than gratitude for your sacrifice and joy for your marriage?"

He deserves all the happiness one can find in this long lifetime.

Callen's eyes shine with relief and it is his turn to draw me in. "Thank you." It is a broken sound dipped in bliss. "I've missed you,

Brother. You should have come back sooner. We don't need the crown; we need you. Mother was wrong to demand so much."

My heart swells with gratefulness.

When we finally break apart, I ask, "I have missed and thought of you daily. Have the two of you been happy?"

He sags in relief, and his answering smile is that of a man desperately in love. "Immensely so. I never knew true happiness until her. Estelle is everything to me. It would have broken me completely if you returned and demanded your union proceed." He pauses for a moment before asking, "Why did you end it, though? Did something happen?"

I nod, grateful to talk about Izadella with someone who cares for me as only family can, someone who may take a moment to hear my side and understand I never meant to hurt her.

We may have been separated by mountains and irreplaceable time, but I know my brother will not judge me for the mistakes I have made this month, or how the weight of my withholding the truth from my soulbonded mate might have cost me everything.

"At one of Jedrick's midnight bazaars, I met a mortal woman named Arra. I knew I could never wed anyone who was not her. I sent you that letter the moment I returned to my rooms that evening. I've been with her for the past month. She is my soul-bonded mate; of that, I am sure. She is meant for me as I am meant for her."

His words are ripe with pity, "A mortal? Zi, that will not end well."

Delight flares deep in my chest at the childhood nickname. "Well, I suppose it worked out rather well in the beginning. She is fae like us, only pretending to be mortal, as I was. She was just quicker with her honesty. Her name is Izadella. It is a long story best shared over strong ale, but she has the crown."

Sadness softens his face. "Is she who you thought would become queen?"

"Yes." I tell him most of everything that has happened in the past month. I leave out the existence of Ellova. One secret I will keep for now.

By the end it is a knife to my chest at the reminder that Izadella and I will never sit side by side on that dais, a crown of Kalvornian emeralds upon her sunset strands. I take a deep breath, pushing down the heartache of hurting Izadella so badly it will kill me.

"My heart breaks with yours, Brother. We *will* try and find a way to save you."

"Nothing can be done but there is much to discuss. Grayden plans on marching troops here soon."

Callen rolls his eyes. "Yes, he made that very clear when the two of us met in neutral territory on the Elbasan Sea. He raged and raged at us. I told him I could lift all of Adreania's sorrows in exchange for the crown. His refusal was swift. Our spies tell us that kingdom is even worse than we knew. I do wonder what army he plans on using, since food is about to run out and riots are starting every day."

"I know Grayden all too well. Please take his threats seriously. He will burn Adreania to the ground if he thinks it will get him what he wants. He does not understand that the root of all of Adreania's problems *is* the crown. He truly believes Kalvorn holds the magical key to a thriving kingdom."

Callen laughs humorlessly. "The crown will soon be the root of our problems, too. It has been siphoning our magic for years, just far more slowly than it has in Adreania. It has only been within the past few years we have truly felt it. Now that you have returned and the crown is no longer there, Kalvorn will have a brighter future. If it comes to all-out war, we shall navigate it together."

"That we will, Cal." I have no doubt my brother can handle whatever is coming.

He appears to search for the right words to say and settles on, "We have no idea how long the enervation will take. As the rightful king of Kalvorn by birth and by blood, you should rule for whatever time you have left."

I cannot read his expression. Does he wish for me to rule?

The need to prove to Izadella that she is most important to me clashes with my desire to be a good brother and a great king to Kalvorn. He has spent a century waiting for me to return, and before I met Izadella, being king was all I wanted but everything has changed.

I am loath to speak my next words, but I have made up my mind.

"I must rescind the throne and any claim to the kingdom of Kalvorn. I will not give Izadella a single reason to think I desire the crown more than her. She is the last descendant of the Forger, and what she chooses to do with the crown is up to her. Our family has no claim over it anymore."

His expression hardens but he finally says, "I can understand that. There is nothing I would not sacrifice for Estelle."

"I know you have been a beloved king to a thriving kingdom. I am truly sorry I cannot take this burden from you. Everything has gone so wrong."

The space between us is thick; much has been left unsaid. I wish to know how his life has been without me. Ruling Kalvorn and pretending to be me must have been difficult.

He looks me up and down. "You need rest."

My answering laugh is dry; I'm sure I do. "Yes, I have not slept much the past two days. It has been…" I search for the right word. "…rough."

Callen takes a deep breath. "Your room has been kept ready for you. I ensured it was tended to weekly. I figured even when you returned, you would wish for the room closest to the library. I will have food and drink sent to you. We can discuss Grayden and his senseless war later."

"Thank you. That is very kind."

"You did not arrive alone. Who are those with you?"

"A group of travelers from Adreania, fleeing Grayden. Please see they are all treated well. I would do it, but I'm not sure who would listen to me. Grayden's wife, Queen Erenia, is leading them. Please let her know where I am if she needs me."

He nods, lost in thought. "I will."

"Thank you. And for what it is worth, I am truly sorry." I leave him on the dais, standing next to the throne that is truly his now.

My bedroom is warm and inviting. I was terrified the last night

I slept here, over a hundred years ago, when I was being sent off to learn medicine far too young to somehow, against all odds, find a way to get close enough to a king to steal the crown upon his death.

I climb into the silken sheets, terrified once more, but this time for fear that I've lost Izadella forever.

CHAPTER 32

LEON

All day and night I dream of Izadella. Her tears of betrayal haunt me, the agony I've caused stark on her beautiful features. I run after her endlessly through the haze of my guilt, hallway after hallway, but she is never within reach. Her sobs echo inside my head as the dream fades and reality returns. I wake with the grip of contempt for myself, my magic slowly leaving me.

How long will it take 'til I am empty of everything that makes me fae, freeing me of my own torment?

I must find her. I have not begged at her feet for forgiveness yet. I have too much left to redeem myself for before I leave the land of the living so quickly.

When I rise, I tie my black-and-silver strands back and find new clothing waiting. Boots of fine leather shine, dark breeches stitched with impeccable quality. A green high-collared shirt with a long row of emerald buttons and golden embroidery that swirls down my arms.

This clothing is fit for royalty, but I miss what I wore in Ellova. Who I was there.

Not a king, not a healer.

Just hers.

This was not how I thought my triumphant return would be.

Instead of joyous cheers of arriving with a dying Jedrick freely ready to give me his crown, I find myself drowning in guilt and anger, shame and longing for Izadella. I go in search of my brother. When I knock on the door of his private study, the guards that flank its entrance let me pass.

Callen is writing a long letter, his desk neatly organized with official papers and scrolls, his royal seal on them all. His hair stands at odd angles from his hands running through it. He keeps this place immaculate, so unlike the chaos of our father before him. A grin tugs at me at the reminder he is a far better leader than our apathetic father ever was.

He greets me with kind curiosity. "How are you feeling?" He glances down at my chest, frowning at the hidden scars he knows are there.

"Better. Please know I have no intention to abandon this family. Izadella needs time away from me, and until she seeks me out again, I wish to assist you in any way you need." It is possible she will never attempt to find me, but I refuse to give up hope. "I am sorry yesterday was not the reunion you may have hoped for."

My brother nods. "You must do whatever it takes to get your mate back in the time you have left." His eyes soften. "You will always be a prince here. In the meantime, I would like to make you my advisor. You have valuable insight on Adreania we can use against them. Once this war and Grayden have been dealt with, Kalvorn can enter a new era. I delayed a great many things in your absence. Decisions for this kingdom I felt were your place to make, since I was not its true king, but now..." His words fade and he does not need to speak of the grief we both share.

"There is no time for me. Make this kingdom your own. I hope I live to see it continue to flourish."

"You would have made a great king. Once Kalvorn knew of your sacrifice, your bravery to try and retrieve our ancestor's crown, they would have loved you. Please know even if you never sit on the throne, you will always be its true ruler."

I am touched by his words. "Thank you. You have stewarded

this kingdom with honor. Tales of your kindness and prosperity are known in every corner of Adreania."

"I have many grand ideas for the future of Kalvorn and will want your thoughts on all of them."

Pride shines within me. "I look forward to hearing your plans."

"I think it is best that we reveal our deception to the kingdom. They will understand and you will be seen as the hero prince you deserve to be. Prince Zilas—"

"Just Leon. I would like to go by Leon."

His answering grin makes me chuckle. "Prince Leon then."

"Where is the current prince?" I've missed my younger brother, but I have another reunion I am eager to have with my cousin, Sailon, who has been masquerading as the youngest prince.

Callen sighs. "About a month ago, a ship arrived from Adreania, one specifically meant for you. Imagine my disappointment when it did not hold my brother as intended but a myriad of malnourished orphans. A mortal named Cyanna was escorted to the family estate per your request. Estelle has been ensuring they are all treated well and received everything they need. Sailon has been accompanying her. They returned this morning."

The Tullewood Estate, the place our mother hid Callen, Sailon, and me for enough years that she was easily able to switch us before sending me away, the rest rejoining the court.

The estate where I intended to send Izadella and her false family. My stomach tightens with the reminder of nights I spent twisted in guilt over my feelings for a married woman.

How greedy I was to have my future Zemra all to myself.

I cared little for her husband. If she wanted me in the ways I needed her, nothing was going to stop me. I imagined sending her to Kalvorn, finally revealing myself as king, hoping she would agree to be my personal jewelry maker. I would continue to commission countless pieces I had no need for, just to spend time with her. Hours for us to be alone, to get closer, dishonorable as it might have been.

A thundering boom from inside the throne room put us both on alert. Callen and I both take off running. Some of his guards try to protect him, standing in his way, but no one makes any attempt to deny me entrance. A large crack runs down the center in front of the dais. Roots rush upward through the malachite tile, branches swirling around themselves to form a tree in the center of the throne room, small purple buds blooming.

Only one person has the exuberance of power and enough confidence to arrive in a potentially hostile kingdom in the middle of their damn throne room.

Nueena.

She steps out from the beautifully twisted tree, Tavien standing protectively behind her.

Guards surround my brother, swords drawn. Archers hold their bows high.

My heart lurches in my chest. "Don't attack her!" I yell, but it is too late. Panic shoots through me as fast as the arrows flying towards her. If we have killed the heir to the Ellovian throne and Izadella's best friend, Kalvorn will be nothing but ash by the time Nyvenah is done with us.

Tavien waves his hand effortlessly, a shield of sapphire flames swirling around her like shadows and smoke. The arrows hit his protective magic with powerful precision, but they collapse into dust at his Zemra's boots.

"Thank you, my love," she says, not looking back.

I turn to my brother. "If you do not wish to start a war, tell your men to lower their weapons."

He nods in confusion. "Stand down!"

The guards obey their king and step back.

Nueena does not even glance in his direction. She only stares with an annoyed glare, approaching me.

My heart beats rapidly. Whatever reason she is here must have to do with Izadella.

Rage and power come off her in waves. Following Nueena is an amused Tavien, who looks around the room, soaking up the details, and speaks before Nueena does. "Beautiful castle. Can't believe you roughed it in Adreania for so long."

I give him a small smile. I didn't think I would ever see him again, so I choose to be thankful for whatever has brought them here.

"Where is she?" Nueena asks me, her tone sharp.

My stomach twists into painful knots. Dread spreads down my body. Did Izadella try to find me and Nueena managed to arrive before her? I don't dare hope Izadella came after me, but why else would Nueena be here? My love's heartbreaking last words make her chasing after me seem like exceptionally foolish wishful thinking.

"Nueena…I haven't seen or spoken to Izadella since I left Ellova. She told me she never wanted to speak to me again. I left with the Adreanian rebels and—" This is clearly the wrong answer to give her.

She shakes her head. "Don't play dumb with me, *Your Majesty*. I know Della is here. Now go get her and tell her she belongs with us in Ellova. She can come willingly, or I can sling her over my shoulder, but either way I'm not leaving without her."

"I swear, if she is here, she has not revealed herself to me. Believe me, right now I'd want nothing more than to see her, speak to her, explain everything."

"You think I believe that for one moment?" She laughs but it has no humor in it. "She has not been seen since *you* left. She was spotted on *her* horse, leaving with *your* little army, following you! Save whatever bullshit lies you have. Tell Della that I already forgive her for bringing a lying spy into my realm. We have fought before and we will fight again, but I'll be damned if she does not stand in that room with me when I'm crowned Realm Keeper."

"Nueena, I—"

"We have been talking about that day for a hundred and twenty fucking years, and I might be livid at her for running away but she will return with me. If you have taken her against her will, do not be surprised when I march every soldier under my command back here to retrieve her the very second I'm in full control of the Ellovian army!"

The knots at the bottom of my stomach tighten. How can Nueena not know where she is?

Lost for words, I stare at her. It has always been obvious that their friendship ran deep, but starting a war is loyalty beyond words. She takes after Zarella in that way. It is a comfort to know Izadella will be so loved by those in her life after I fade from it.

I wanted to be one of those people to love her like that. "I promise you I haven't seen her."

She narrows her eyes. "Della loves Ellova. So, I understand how distraught she would be, knowing she led an enemy into our home and shared far too much information with someone who could turn around and use it against us. First, she says she never wishes to see you again and the next moment she's riding off with your army. Something I would never have believed if I did not see it with my own eyes! I cannot fathom why she would have changed her mind so easily after what you had done."

How can no one know where she is? What if she's not safe? What if she's alone in the forest?

"I am not your enemy, Nueena. No one here is, but we need to find her, immediately." Panic bleeds into my being. Air is harder to take in. Something is wrong; I know it.

"He hasn't shared anything with us, if that's what you are implying."

Nueena glances at Callen in obvious irritation at our conversation being interrupted, a bold move to stare like that at a king in his own castle.

I didn't want to bring him into this conversation yet, but introductions are inevitable. "This is Nueena and her Zemra, Tavien." I turn to face my brother, dreading this interaction. "And my brother, King—"

"Still pretending to be Leon?" Nueena laughs dryly. "Little late for that now, isn't it?"

I take a deep breath. "No, he *is* the king of Kalvorn. I abdicated the throne shortly after I arrived home yesterday, so any war you wish to start will be with him, not me."

CHAPTER 33

IZADELLA

I'm tossed into a carriage shortly after being forced to agree to a marriage to Grayden. He faces me while two guards sit on either side of me. I suspect it's only to make me uncomfortable, or perhaps he's so afraid of my power he won't ride alone with me. It's not long before the carriage is hot with the press of bodies. The guards are both massive in size, forcing me to hunch my shoulders to squeeze between them, a dull ache already spreading up from my back to my neck.

The pressing wound in my soul opens a little wider as I remember how Leon's hands felt rubbing my back during my bleeding. How warm and strong they were as they traced the outline of my spine and down my hips. Hands of a healer, reverent and confident. I can almost feel the phantom touch of his rough palms caressing me.

The touch of a lover, not a liar.

I refuse to cry in the carriage, but the weight of Leon's betrayal slices deep into my soul.

My eyes water, and Grayden's cruel gaze watches me, smiling but saying nothing. He's simply basking in my sorrow. I expect nothing less from him and I find I can't possibly hate him more than I already do.

I stare back at my future husband. If he's waiting for me to cry or beg or even ask where we are going, he will be waiting a very long time.

I imagine taking down the giant gold-framed royal portraits in the throne room, taking a hot poker from the fireplace and slicing the canvas, carving black streaks down his blank expression. After I destroyed the painting, I would break down the frame. Solid gold would be too heavy to hang so I would guess it's a wood frame behind it. Perfect firewood for the forge. I would watch the wood burn and then take all the metal left behind and melt it down in the forge. I see myself with my powers again, taking the gold, molding it into a sword. I would take that sword and run Grayden through with it.

The rubies I'd put on the hilt would be just as red as his blood.

It's a nice daydream.

Grayden leans forward in his seat, plenty of room on his side, not breaking eye contact. My face must give away my thoughts, the desire for vengeance seeping out of every pore.

"Oh, I will enjoy wiping that look off your face." The smile he wears is cruel, and I return the look.

"And I will enjoy watching life leave your eyes when this is over, Your Majesty." I spit the last words out, but it only widens his smile. Whatever he is about to say dies as the carriage comes to a halt. One of the riders next to us dismounts and opens the door. Grayden steps out first, barely stepping on the ground before a guard shoves me out the door.

I miss the steps, tumble down, and collapse into the dirt. As I try to collect myself, a rough hand grabs me by my wrist, the bones grinding in his grip as Grayden launches me up and pushes me to walk. The dungeon and carriage had both been dark, so it takes me a moment to adjust to the sun. The little gasp that escapes my lips does not do justice to the feeling of dread at the sight before me.

Dirt covers my feet as I stand in an empty field filled with hundreds of long dirt rows.

As far as I can see, it's desolate earth. The wind picks up, swirling the dirt in the air for a moment, making me cough. A few trees are scattered around but they are dead, too, their tips blackened with decay.

"This is the fae's fault," Grayden chides. "This was once a fruitful valley, but your wicked magic has stolen what was mine." He glares at me.

I don't bother to correct him that so many are dying because his ancestor killed the fae queen. That it was his own family's fault that the crown demands magic and when it can no longer have it, it will take life in its place. First from the soil, then the animals, and finally the life force of mortals.

"You are going to grow me something." It is not a question. Maybe some part of him does care that his people are starving.

"Once again, I can only say I will try to give you what you desire." I'm desperate for the crown to care about anyone else's safety beyond my own, to know the horrifying consequences of my failure and do *something* to prevent it.

"I would desire nothing more than to take a sword to your neck, but I will not make my ancestors' mistakes. It's useless on my head. I do not possess the magic it needs, so that means you will do as I say." He waits expectantly.

I can only nod at him.

"This field is empty. Let's change that, shall we?" he drawls.

The people of Adreania deserve to eat. This barren field has so much potential. It could grow potatoes nicely, although with my thoughts constantly returning to Leon, I will probably only be able to grow an endless sea of strawberries. I can try to do potatoes in one field and different greens in the others, but my powers will probably give out. It's unpredictable, and if I pass out, Grayden will probably just leave me here. I should focus on smaller things, maybe those petite red potatoes Tavien likes roasted with rosemary and butter.

"You have to understand; I do not have control over the magic. I swear. I will try. I would give anything for the crown to obey, but that's not how its magic works. Everett must have told you that. He was lying to you if he said the crown is something to command. It does not grant wishes."

"Try or the orphan keeper dies."

I fall to my knees in the soil. My fists are clenched at my side, focusing myself to stay rooted in the dirt and not launch myself at him. Through gritted teeth I ask, "What vegetable would you like me to grow first? Potatoes are the most filling, but perhaps I can—"

He cuts me off.

"You will not be growing food. You will be growing Vedesdron."

Dust fills my mouth as I balk at him.

Insidious bastard.

"Your people are starving! Sick and dying, and your first act with magic is to grow poison over food?" Staring at him, my fist start to shake, fingernails sinking into my palms.

He arches an eyebrow at me. "You refuse me?"

I lower my head. "My apologies, I did not mean to question you. I'm just doubtful I can grow that."

"Try."

I close my eyes. I try to think of the poison. I imagine the balcony garden where I stood with Leon the night all of this started. Vibrant pink flowers next to a small patch of red buds with dark leaves. Vedesdron. Planted next to geranium Leon grew. What had he said about it?

I planted them almost two years ago. Geranium. It reminded me of you. One night a month never seemed like enough.

I shove thoughts of Leon away; it will only bring those fucking strawberries.

Vedesdron, Vedesdron, Vedesdron.

The red veins that snake through the pitch-black leaves. The horrid taste of it as Everett shoves it down my throat before the numbness takes hold and blackness follows.

Will Leon know I grew it when it's used against his Kalvorn soldiers? Will he hate me for helping Grayden murder them?

Not nearly as much as I hate myself right now.

I dig my fingers into the ground, dirt clumping under my nails.

The crown's magic rolls through me, pouring out into the soil. Not the angry, protective power like when it thought Leon was attacking me at the spring. Not the sensation of love and devotion that blooms the strawberry plants with thoughts of him.

This is something new, something extraordinary.

Guards gasps all around me, followed by soft, excited murmurs.

Life blossoms beneath me. More and more magic leaves me and I sway, trying not to fall face-first into the ground, my body overwhelmed by the sudden loss of it. Never has so much power been drained from me at once. I try so hard to focus on the poison, but even before I open my eyes again, I know I have not grown it. Tears pour out with it, my heart sinking.

Ellova's grave, Cyanna, I'm so sorry.

Every row for miles is filled with ruby reds, rich purples, and vibrant greens.

Through the black spots in my vision, I can make out the thick asparagus sticking up, ready for harvest, next to overgrown ferns with bright red berries. Wide flat leaves with deep red stalks of rhubarb. Potato leaves with rows of purple flowers turning into green potato berries near it. Peppers and fat purple eggplants. Leafy tops of tomato plants blow gently in the wind. Hanging pods of wild butterbeans. Rows of white, brown, and cream-colored mushrooms. Further down are vast lemon, pomegranate, and apple orchards and, of course, rows and rows of strawberries.

It's beautiful. But not what he wanted. He snaps his fingers at someone, and one of his men, with eyes just as cruel as his rulers', slams the iron collar back around my neck.

"Pity." Grayden stands over me, blocking the sun as he slaps me across the face. I collapse; the blow slams my face into the dirt. I cough, spitting up blood.

From this angle, I can see what grows close to the soil. The magic did listen to me for once.

I could laugh. "I did what you asked. All of these plants have at least some part that is poisonous. Look at all these nightshades! The tomato leaves, roots and stems; rhubarb leaves; those red and green berries. Don't be fooled. Some of those mushrooms are safe, but that row right there—" I point behind him. "—is death cap mushrooms."

He narrows his eyes at me. "You are a liar."

"Summon your farmers and alchemists. They will tell you. You think your soldiers will go to war for you while they starve, while their children starve? Feed your people while you have the chance, *husband.*"

He slides his tongue over his teeth in an irritated motion before turning to the guards on horseback. "Well, don't just stand here. Fetch some fucking farmers."

The riders nod and take off in the directions of the small farms in the surrounding areas.

Grayden inspects one of the plants. "Put her in the carriage while we wait."

Drained from the day, I don't struggle when the two guards who rode next to me drag me back and put me inside. I lie back, trying to find a comfortable position.

One of the guards pauses before closing the door. "Thank you," he whispers. "My daughters have never had fruit before."

I nod once. "Where is Cyanna?"

He shakes his head, shrugging, and closes the door behind him.

I curl up on the cushioned bench inside the carriage and nearly cry with how nice it feels after two nights on a stone floor. All I can hope for now is that the farmers will confirm what I told Grayden and that it will be enough to appease him. Enough to keep Cyanna safe.

For now.

CHAPTER 34

LEON

*Q*ueena is stunned into silence, something I doubt happens very often, but she soon finds her words. "Why did you abdicate?"

Her suspicious look brings a bitter taste to my mouth. She's right not to trust me. I would feel the same in her position, but I'm at a loss as to how to help her understand.

I don't want to have this conversation with anyone but Izadella. This conversation should be private. It should have happened in the bathing pool, just Izadella and me. She deserves to be the first to know how I feel about her, what I'm willing to give up, what I *have* given up.

The seeping pain in my chest returns. She should have given me a moment to explain. I thought I'd earned that.

I'd assumed that she felt what I felt; that she knew I would never hurt her.

I sigh deeply. "Because I doubt Izadella will accept my feelings for her if she believes I only want to be with her because of the crown. I will be honest with her that I was trying to get the crown in Adreania, that it was my birthright, but I do not want it anymore. I'm in love with Izadella and want to be with her, wherever she is, *whoever* she is. She's made it clear she wants nothing to do with ruling and that's fine. She doesn't need to rule to change the landscape of the kingdoms."

Nueena eyes me suspiciously. "You really gave up your throne just for her?"

"She is my soulbonded, my future Zemra. I can feel it. There is nothing I wouldn't give up for Izadella. No title or kingdom is worth losing her. In my absence, my brother has been a kind king. He will continue to be a just and honorable—"

"Well, I certainly wouldn't call him *that,* with the whole marrying-your-betrothed bit."

All eyes turn to my cousin Sailon as he enters the room. He is shorter than I, but we have the same build. His green eyes are lit with mischief. Any excitement I had for reuniting with him dies. That was not something Nueena needed to know at this moment.

"Shut your mouth!" Callen hisses at our cousin.

"*Betrothed!*" Nueena says, her fist balling. "You disgraceful brute."

Fucking Sailon. I take a deep breath before turning to face my brother.

Guilt slowly bleeds into Callen's features.

"Sailon, I am aware of that." Speaking to Nueena, I add, "Yes, before I met Izadella, I was part of an arranged marriage. Callen and Estelle married after I sent a letter home breaking off our engagement the *very night* I met Izadella." I hope Nueena can hear the sincerity in my voice. "I risked being discovered by Grayden to send a message breaking off my marriage agreement two years ago. I knew Izadella was my future Zemra the moment I met her. I could neither explain it nor deny it. I would marry her or no one at all."

Callen looks pale but straightens his shoulders. "That was admirable of you but," He clears his throat. "—I believe this conversation would be best had in private." He glances wearily at Nueena. The last thing I need is to have Nueena running to Izadella and telling her that I was engaged to a woman I hadn't seen in over a hundred years on the night she and I met, but I will not hold any truth back from her.

"No, Nueena can hear all of this," I say flatly. She is still glaring at me when I turn to explain, "Estelle and I only met once when we were dewlings. She was the daughter of my father's war advisor."

Nueena looks unimpressed with this new information.

I continue, "A few years later, I received a letter from my mother on our arranged marriage while studying medicine in Versairen. Like everything when it came to my mother, it was short and to the point, only stating that once I returned to Kalvorn with the crown, I would be wed to a suitable noble she had selected to be my future queen. Since we didn't know how long I would be gone, a royal wedding would eventually be planned if I returned with the crown."

An arranged marriage was not a surprise. My parents did not marry for love, and I did not expect anything more. When I was young, the idea of a queen when I returned was alluring, but as the decades passed, it was just another burden placed on me like all the rest.

Earn a place of esteem within medicine to be sought after by royals, become Jedrick's personal healer in Adreania, retrieve my ancestor's crown, return to Kalvorn, take my place as king, enter into a loveless marriage to someone of noble birth, and rule a kingdom I haven't been in for over a century. Give every part of me to my kingdom.

Give. Give. Give.

"Leon did not do anything wrong," Callen says in my defense.

I send him a small smile of gratitude.

"How can I believe anything you say?" she asks, hands on her hips.

"The night I met Izadella, she told me she was married with children, and I knew she and I didn't have a future, but it still felt… wrong for me to be pining after someone with Estelle at home waiting for me. Estelle deserved to find someone who could love her, and apparently, she did. I had been gone much longer than I planned, since I missed my opportunity with Jedrick's father."

Callen moves closer to me. "Leon…maybe this isn't…"

I turn to Nueena. "That's why I was in Adreania, to try and take back my birthright as the descendant of Queen Inara and Prince Kalden. The crown should have been mine. I wanted it back. Jedrick was letting his people die and Grayden would be far worse. The crown protected him, though." I turn to my brother. "What is Sailon referring to? What else happened while I was gone?"

Callen gulps. "Yes, well. You were gone for a long time. After so many years of waiting before she even arrived, she was devastated that I kept pushing the wedding date without any way to explain beyond exposing our ruse. She wrote countless letters, asking to come to the castle and go through a proper courtship, to plan the wedding. Eventually her horrible father got tired of waiting and left her on the castle steps in the middle of the night ten years ago, demanding she be made queen or she would be disowned, the alliances between our families broken. We couldn't delay forever when everyone thought I was you. There was no reason to continue extending the timeline, so we moved her into the castle. I...we...got close."

"Close?" I raise one eyebrow at his tone. My only thoughts of Estelle over the years were how difficult it must be to wait for endless decades for a royal marriage she was promised so long ago, a union that kept being nudged further into the future with each year I was gone. I certainly didn't expect love, but I had hoped to make it up to her by being an attentive and respectful husband, someone she might wish to build a friendship with.

"Hello, Zilas," says a small voice behind me.

I turn to face our newest guest, who I can only assume is my new sister-in-law. "Hello, Estelle. You look well."

Dark brown ringlets hang down her back. Her wide blue eyes shine above a sprinkling of freckles, her sharply pointed ears sticking out between her curls. My eyes immediately go down to her rounded belly and the two children she is with. Her young son gleefully tries to escape the tight hold Estelle has on his hand.

A son who appears to be older than their marriage.

On her other side is a girl with messy curls who must be at least nine. While the prince looks like Callen and me at that age, she is a perfect copy of Estelle.

She notices her mother's apprehension and leans into her side.

So, Callen's and Estelle's feelings went well beyond the two years of marriage they shared, years before I had broken off our arrangement.

Maybe I should feel betrayed that my brother fathered multiple children with my fiancée while I was away risking my life, but the anger never comes. Callen said Estelle arrived ten years ago; she must have conceived the first year she was here. If I had returned a decade ago, I would have had to marry her and never met Izadella, would have robbed my beloved brother of his own happy ending.

Nausea rises at the thought.

Estelle looks guilt-ridden and tense, barely able to walk so late in her pregnancy but clearly ready to grab the little ones and leave at the slightest sign of conflict between my brother and me.

When I glance back at my brother, he is staring at his wife, devotion and love radiating off him. I have a niece and nephew.

The realization warms me.

Two young royals of Kalvorn, just like Callen and I were. A princess who will one day rule Kalvorn.

"This is Elona, our daughter," Estelle says softly.

The young princess politely curtsies before looking around me and waving at Nueena and Tavien. He seems amused by all of this. Nueena gives Elona a kind nod of acknowledgment but returns to glaring at me.

"Baba!" the young prince happily yells at my brother, continuing to reach out for him.

I follow as Callen walks towards Estelle and both children smile up at him with adoration. He picks up the youngest with the softest expression.

"Atlas, this is my brother, Leon, your uncle," Callen says to his son.

The boy grins wildly at me. He reaches out with his tiny hands, and I gently take him from my brother.

I find myself in awe that these dewlings are of my blood, and I wish yet again that Izadella were here to meet my family. That she would want to be part of this, if she ever forgives me. I never saw myself as a father, but did she want children?

Whenever I thought about our uncertain future, it was just the two of us and that's all I desired.

"We have much to discuss," Callen says quietly.

How the hell did he think he could hide this when I returned if I never ended the engagement? Sleeping with the king's promised bride wasn't treason, but infidelity was the highest form of disloyalty even if it all worked out for the best.

I hand him back his son. "And another time we shall."

Nueena and Tavien take in all of this, letting us have our complicated family moment, and I am grateful for it, but Callen has his family with his mate and I'm desperate to find mine.

I return to Nueena. "I may not know where Izadella is, but now that you've told me she is missing, you can't possibly expect me to let you leave without me. If you do, I will follow. She can reject me all over again, she can hate me for it, but until I know she is safe, I will not stop searching for her."

Nueena shakes her head. "When I find her, I will let her know all of this. She can decide if and when she seeks you out again. I will personally bring her to you if—"

"No, I am leaving with you." My words are final. Nueena will not leave without me. She opens her mouth to argue but I angrily rip open the top of my shirt. The emerald buttons scatter, echoing around the throne room floor. My white enervation scars crawl up my chest. "Now do you believe how much I love her? Breaking her heart broke mine and I need to see her. One. Last. Time."

Nueena and Tavien wear mirrored expressions of horror, glancing at each other. Something like mourning reflects back but I do not feel it is for me.

Her eyes are glossy when she finally nods. "You are neither forgiven nor trusted, healer. We can go to the cottage. If she's still in the forest, she's probably there."

I turn to my brother, about to apologize for my abrupt departure, but he is already behind me with a dark green traveling cloak and our father's sword.

"I would like to meet this Izadella. Bring her home." Callen embraces me and emotion clogs my throat. He slips me some kind of rock.

When I pull back, two moonstones gleam in my palm.

"These are traveling crystals; they use the same magic as portal trees. Crush it and it will immediately bring you here. I do not want you ever to be far from home without a way to return quickly again."

Overwhelmed by my brother's care and everything that has happened in the past day, I push down the desperate gratitude and despair, not letting it overtake me here. "I will see you soon. All of you. We will have a proper reunion when that time comes." No matter how much I loath to leave my family, I have to find Izadella. She must know the truth about who I am and how much I love her before my time runs out, but dread consumes me.

Something is wrong; I can feel it. We must find her before it's too late.

Izadella, my love, I'm coming for you. Hold on.

CHAPTER 35

IZADELLA

*O*nce we return to that dreary castle, I am escorted up a steep flight of stairs, past open, beautifully carved, black marble doors—one of the few things not made of iron—and shoved through them.

The bedroom furniture is all a deep crimson that would fit more in the Court of Swords than this awful place. The curtains are well made and hang beside large windows on the far end of the bedroom, overlooking the midnight blue sea. Overgrown plants take up each corner, and the iron walls have been covered with tapestries depicting faraway places. Pillows of all shapes and colors cover a high bed.

A cheery fire brings a wave of warmth that caresses my frozen skin. Relieved tears spring to my eyes.

Gowns worthy of a princess hang in an open armoire. A few handmaidens come out of the bathing chamber; fragrant oils added to the bath drifting out. Three walk beside each other, leaving empty buckets still steaming.

An older woman with short gray hair, pale skin, and a kind smile steps before me in dark clothing. "My lady, my name is Vera. King Grayden has instructed us to prepare you for dinner."

Two lady's maids behind her hold gilded hairbrushes and the small pots of pigment meant to enhance beauty.

I roll my eyes. "May I guess? He will have me painted like a doll for dinner so I can hear what an absolute honor it is to be his bride, or he will kill everyone I care for in the fucking kingdom. Am I missing anything?"

She looks alarmed and shakes her head. "I was just instructed to prepare you for dinner."

"What's his least favorite color?"

"My—my lady, that I don't know."

"Fine, find me the ugliest gown in this damn castle."

She shrinks into herself. "He has already selected the gown."

Bastard.

"Well, I'm so very glad he could carve out some time in his busy schedule of terrorizing his kingdom to have an opinion of the dress I wear. Let me speculate: it's very revealing, isn't it?"

She purses her lips together apologetically.

I take a deep breath and head to the bathroom door. None of this is their fault, they are just trying to survive here, as I am.

After stripping off torn clothing, I dunk myself under the blissfully warm water. If they wonder about the streaks of gold tainting my skin and indicating my imminent death, they hold their tongue. They rub me down with oils and someone brushes my hair. The women all stare at the crown.

"You can touch it if you like," I say.

They all lower their heads at the same time.

"This isn't a trick. It only reacts to someone with magic or if someone is trying to hurt me."

The youngest one, who looks to be around seventeen, slowly reaches out and touches it with a single finger. "How can you wear it if you are a woman?"

Vera hisses at her, "Hazel, do not ask such questions!"

Hazel lowers her eyes again, but I am quick to pat Hazel's hand. "Cause the Fasaile line is full of *liars*. Remember, the first wearer was a queen. It was made for a fae woman, by a fae woman. Male heirs to a false line hold no power with this crown. Anyone can wear it, but only the fae can access its magic."

"And you have some?" another woman asks carefully, eyeing my ears.

"Well, not with this on." I motion to the collar. "But yes. I'm part fae. Magic is real."

"So, you are queen now? You wear the crown?" Hazel asks with so much hope it tears at me.

"It seems so but there is not much I can do to help anyone." These women here must have been Erenia's lady's maids. "Where is Queen Erenia? Are these her chambers?"

"Yes, it is, but she disappeared. Many people did." Vera offers no further explanation.

Did Grayden have them all killed? My stomach plummets at the thought. Where could they have gone?

Where is Cyanna? What if she is hurt?

My dark thoughts haunt me while they dress me in a tight red gown that flares out at the bottom.

It's sleeveless and low-cut. My breasts are pushed up with a bone-crushing corset. The golden cracks are spreading, crawling up my chest to my neck. Everett will immediately know what is happening to me.

He will be in quite the celebratory mood when he tells Grayden the gold on my skin means my ending is truly inevitable.

The crown is all but Everett's.

My death will be a kindness. Maybe I ought to thank Leon. He may have broken my heart, but in the end, it will spare me the horrors of being Grayden's plaything. His captive. A wife in name only.

Not Leon's wife. Grayden's.

I need to stay strong, so I push back against the suffocating misery that threatens to drown me. Weeping will not help me, so I allow numbness to spread like wine spilling from a goblet, swallowing me whole.

Vera mournfully places silver cuffs on my wrists with a strong chain attached to the collar. Too glamorous to be for prisoners, it must have been made for me, as the tops even have some diamonds placed on them.

Chains meant for an obstinate queen.

My hair hangs loosely down my back under the crown that is on full display for the first time since I've been forced to wear it. They paint my lips red just before I'm escorted downstairs into the depths of the chilling castle.

All servants here have my despair and pity, but the royal artists deserve my condolences as well. The walls are lined with paintings of Grayden. Vain and vile man. Each painting is slightly different but with the same smug look on them. On some, he's riding a horse into an imaginary battle. On others, he is standing in a golden room covered in fur and jewels. He must have been commissioning these for years.

One of them shows him with Erenia at their wedding. Her melancholy is captured on canvas even on that day.

I am ushered into a long dining room decorated by even more paintings of Grayden. They hang on the walls alongside wide flags with the crest of Adreania on them. Thousands of candles light the room. The large windows show a dark sky, rain clouds hiding any stars.

At the end of the dining table, places are set for four. Grayden sits holding a full glass of wine. "You look ravishing. Shame we have to keep that collar on, but you can't be trusted."

Everett is on his left, dressed in the finest clothing I have ever seen him in. His fork clatters to the table. His face shifts from shock to malice, eyes on my glinting chest. "Enervation scars? He really did break your heart, didn't he?" His laugh echoes around me as he sets down his golden chalice. "Oh, Della, he couldn't have possibly been worth it." He makes a tsking noise. "Didn't you learn from your mother's mistakes? You should have let Kole have you. At least he actually liked you." Everett smirks and no matter how much I've seen it since being captured, it brings fresh horror that I once called him my friend.

That he would speak of the friend he murdered so casually.

Refusing to acknowledge Everett's or Grayden's comments, I start piling food on my plate. "I would like some wine."

"Well, of course." Grayden snaps for a servant, who pours the ruby-red liquid into my glass, but I grab his instead and start to drink it. At least I know it's not poisoned. He smiles at me cruelly while drinking the new glass. "You are going to make such a beautiful bride."

"And you will make a dishonorable husband."

He slams his knife down, causing me to jump in my seat. He has embedded the blade in the table, half an inch from my hand. "You will show me respect. Everett's little experiment with the drowning showed that the crown has some protections for you, so as much fun as we could have…" He reaches over and rubs up my thigh.

I force myself not to move. It is no doubt not the reaction he desires, so I don't give it to him.

"…I won't take my chances."

Through gritted teeth, I calmly say, "You will remove your hand from me, and you will not touch me again."

He digs his fingernails into my skin, marking it. "You and I are going to be married very soon. Once we are, you will be locked in your chambers and you will grow crops and poison as often as I say."

"I'm not a summer market."

"Oh, but you grew these?" He points to the glass bowl in front of him and leans in close. "What are these?"

The fruit gleams, dark and juicy, like the ones growing in Nueena's garden.

"They are blackberries," I say flatly.

He stands next to me, moving the hair off my shoulder and I force myself not to recoil at the touch. "Are they edible?"

I debate for a moment if it's worth lying about. "Yes."

"Eat one. How do I know it's not poisonous?"

"It is not, and I do not want one."

He grabs a handful of the fruit. Before I can move, his other hand takes hold of my hair. Everett's eyes go wide as Grayden pulls my head back with a violent jerk and he tries to shove the fruit down my throat as he did at the last bazaar with the navlue fruit. This time, though, the crown's magic roars at the offense. With the collar, all it can do is send a sharp jolt of electricity through his hand, but it is enough for him to release me. Fuck him.

He cradles his hand to his chest. "You bitch!"

Everett chastises him like he would a dewling. "I've already told you the crown responds to her emotions and will not allow anyone else to touch her."

I pop another berry so he will not attempt to harm me again, a headache starting. The berries are sweet and harmless. When I do not descend face-first into my soup, he eats a handful, chewing slowly.

"Interesting," he says, flexing his wounded hand.

I gulp down more wine, not wishing to be sober for this meal. I must find a way to escape this nightmare. I need to get back to Ellova, to Nueena, and maybe find Leon and let him explain.

"What do you think is the greatest risk to the lives of the people of Adreania?" I ask, bringing a spoonful of soup to my mouth. It's bland, so bland. I miss the rich food of Ellova. I even miss the sweetness of its cuisine.

He has the audacity to look bored with the question, as if the well-being of his entire kingdom is as trivial as the weather. "The sickness. Its effects on the reproductive health of the Adreanian women." For a moment I am surprised by his answer, but he follows with "Sickly women cannot birth me soldiers."

Pain bites into my hand. My grip on my spoon is so tense, my hand throbs. Of course that's all he cares about. The power an army brings, not the lives of the women the illness has devastated, the mourning of sick children and empty wombs, bitter tears from the loss of motherhood.

Tavien will make more elixir and Viella can deliver it. As long as no one in Beggars' Row says how we got in, it could be delivered. They have to bring it here anyway; maybe I can trade it for my release. "What if I told you I have the antidote?"

He sits up in his chair, putting down the goblet of wine he was lazily drinking moments ago. "Do it. Grow it!" he demands.

"I've already grown it, and if you release me, I will give you more, boxes and boxes of it in just a few short weeks. A few drops to each woman and child who suffers from it, and you will have happy and healthy citizens again. You will have no need to go to war with Kalvorn over it. They don't have anything that will help you. You would fight a meaningless war over something I would hand over to you. What do you say? My release for it?"

He sneers at me. "I don't believe you, nor do I trust you."

"You do not have to trust me. I can prove it."

The doors open, and Lyrora arrives in a cobalt-blue gown and the delicate sapphire tiara I made her the last time I was here willingly. It looks as lovely on her as I imagined it would. Grief knocks on the door to my soul with the realization that her tiara was one of the last times I was able to use my magic.

Her guard slides her next to me and bows before stepping away.

"Hello." Lyrora gives me a half smile.

"Hello, Your Highness."

Grayden laughs. "No need for such formalities." He faces Lyrora. "Izadella here will be your new sister shortly."

The color drains from her face. "But what of Erenia? Our alliances with her kingdom, her father?"

"Erenia is a traitor and not fit to be queen." Grayden stabs his steak. "She has been replaced. I will announce it to the court tomorrow."

"She ran off with your father's healer to be together," Everett announces gleefully.

She laughs at him, the delighted noise echoing around us. "I can assure you, they did *not*. What a lie to tell, Prince Everett, what a lie."

I nearly choke on my wine as I cackle. "Did he tell you he was a prince?"

Everett's cheeks have a tinge of pink to them as his eyes shoot daggers at me.

Lyrora glances between us, confused. "He said he was prince of the faeries."

I laugh even harder. "There is no such thing. He has no ties to royalty. His mother is an *elected* Guardian of her court, but that gives him no title or birthright. He is what you would call a common sailor."

Lyrora lets out a small giggle with me. "That is interesting."

"When he helps me take Kalvorn, he can have whatever title he wants. He can be king of the fucking faeries for all I care," Grayden says.

I lean toward Everett. "I cannot wait to tell Nueena and Tavien this."

He leans forward, too. "You will be dead before you can utter a single word."

It wipes the smile off my face and widens his.

"Who are they?" Lyrora asks.

"*Actual* fae royalty," I say proudly. "My family."

Everett snorts. "They aren't her family. She was their little orphan pet. Her family was exiled for creating the very crown she wears now. It brought destruction to the fae realm, and the Forger was banished for it. Her family line is a shameful one."

Everything he says is meant to hurt me, but I will not give him the satisfaction. "Yes, it is. Just like your family line will be shamed for your treachery."

I could strangle Everett. I focus all my energy, calling to the crown to attack him, but nothing happens. He sits there alive and well.

Useless. Fucking. Crown.

I thank a servant who has come to refill my water, watching her add more to everyone else's but Everett's. She leaves only to return with a different pitcher to fill his chalice.

"Are you drinking water from home?" I ask suspiciously. Does he know of the healing effects of the Airvell River? Is that how he has been able to stay here unaffected by the loss of magic?

His sly grin before he takes a long drink is answer enough, and I hate him a little more.

Dinner is mind-numbingly dull. Grayden and Everett spend it discussing grand war plans that they have no means to achieve, like two dewlings with delusions of grandeur. Hours later, I am finally allowed to return to Erenia's rooms.

Guards are stationed outside the doors, and the room is up on a high tower. With no faith in my ability to climb down, I accept this is my new prison.

At least it is warm.

CHAPTER 36

*I*t's well after midnight when a soft tapping noise comes from behind one of the large paintings. My heart beats wildly, hoping it is Cyanna somehow. I take one of the lone candles with me as I head to the source of the sound.

"Izadella?" the soft voice of Princess Lyrora drifts in. "There's a latch under the painting."

I trace along the underside of the frame, searching for the lock, and the painting swings open when I hit it. Lyrora is dressed in a thick nightgown, her guard carrying her through a narrow pathway carved into the stone, illuminated by a single oil lamp on the wall. He steps in, gently sets her down in one of the plush red chairs.

"Thank you, Henrik."

He smiles at his princess and leaves again.

Sitting beside her, I can't stop myself from asking, "Have you spoken to Leon?"

Her face falls. "No, I'm so sorry. We don't know where he is. I haven't seen him since the night my father went missing." She looks at the crown. "Well, died, I suppose."

Guilt I have no reason to carry leads me to explain, "He died naturally. No harm came to him. I'm sorry for your loss."

Lyrora only shrugs. "I care more about Erenia and Leon now. They have been more family to me than anyone I share blood with. Hopefully, she made it back to Versairen and Leon back to Kalvorn." She reaches out for my hand. "He liked you so much. He was practically giddy on bazaar nights. I have a jewelry box full of your pieces simply because he wanted a reason to talk to you. Even when he thought you were married and knew nothing could ever come of it, he still cherished every moment in your presence. Whatever happens, please know that. You meant *everything* to him."

Her words send a flurry of grief and longing inside me. "How do you know I'm not married?"

"Your shop was raided, and not a soul ever saw you with a family. Plus, no records of you exist. I checked. Be thankful you have no family or husband. Grayden wouldn't have let any of them live if they had been real."

I shudder at that. "Your sibling is…evil."

"I learned that many years ago when he killed all our other brothers to ensure he was the only one in line for the throne. He is evil in ways I can't possibly understand. I'm so sorry for what he is about to force you to do."

"Me too," I whisper.

Henrik returns, holding an ancient book. We're silent again before she takes a balled-up napkin from her gown's pocket. It's a white satin square with red splotches on it. Slowly she unwraps it and three strawberries lie in the middle, one slightly smashed, its bright juices staining the fabric.

"It smells like Leon," she says. "They have popped up everywhere. Is it safe to eat?"

"Yes," I whisper, tears forming.

She opens her mouth and bites down, eyes closing as she chews slowly. "I've never tasted anything so sweet."

Henrik bends at the waist, watching as her tongue darts out over her lips. She feeds him the next bite lovingly, and he, too, lets out a noise of happiness at the taste.

So young and in love. I hope someday they can truly be together.

He holds the book out to his lover. She flips towards the middle and turns the book to me.

Inara in her glamoured human form is there on the page. Even though the painting is old, the golden ring she was wearing, the one Leon wore, is still visible.

A small passage about the crown near the bottom.

The fae crown was made for Queen Inara by Alvina Vanabalt, known as the Forger. Her Majesty is quoted speaking of Vanabalt as the greatest goldsmith and craftswoman throughout all kingdoms and a close friend to Queen Inara.

"What do you know about Inara?" I ask, tracing my ancestor's name with my finger, bitterness growing with every letter. Alvina was the greatest goldsmith. Inara never should have asked her to create the crown in the first place.

"The family lore says that after she married King Drystan for his kingdom, she became a cunning adulterer who quickly fell into bed with Prince Kalden and conceived a child with him. They plotted to kill her husband, but Drystan got the crown he felt he deserved after he killed her. Both Kalden and the child were never seen again."

"She never wanted his kingdom!" I'm not sure why I'm bothering to defend my ancestor's closest friend after the pain she has caused my family.

Lyrora shakes her head. "Yes, I know. My family's history is filled with lies. Drystan was just as evil as all the men who came after him. He was a terrible and cruel husband, and his brother actually loved Inara."

I wonder how Leon got her ring. "Thank you for showing me this."

"I have to go, but I wanted to be sure you know that they've announced Erenia's death and his marriage to you in front of all the courtiers. The kingdom is being unruly, people rioting and deserting their posts, protesting the war. You have brought new crops, new bounty, and he thinks it will bring back a little peace before he can go to war with Leon for Kalvorn."

"Wait, you knew about Leon too?"

She seems surprised. "That he is the King of Kalvorn? Yes, he told Erenia and me. It seems everything has gone wrong, but I'm very glad he was able to trust you with his true identity."

Her words sting like a slap in the face. "I've been with Leon in the fae realm for the last month—"

Delight shines on her face and she interrupts, "Oh, he must have loved that!"

"—but he didn't trust me, at least not when it mattered. I was the last to know. He only graced me with the knowledge he was not who he said he was minutes before I was taken."

The pain in my chest is a reminder of that moment.

"Oh." Her eyes are so genuine. "I'm sorry to hear that, but I'm sure he had his reasons. Time with you was all he wanted."

"Yeah," I say flatly. "That and the crown."

"Izadella, does he know you have it?" Conflicting emotions dance over her beautiful face.

"He does. He was there the night I was forced to put it on. I thought he loved me, but it seems he wanted the crown more." It's bitter even to my own ears.

She purses her lips. "It sounds like the two of you have much to discuss when you're reunited."

I know of only one solution to every problem: ending the war, ensuring Grayden does not harm Cyanna or the children in her care, stopping my forced marriage, and ensuring the reign of terror on the Adreanian people ends.

Grayden cannot live.

The guard moves towards his princess to return her to her rooms, but I grab her arm. "I desperately need your help. Tomorrow, ask Grayden why I can't simply make him a new crown, a magic one. My ancestor created this one. I need to get to my forge. It will look suspicious if I offer it."

Lyrora and her guard look at each other, unsure.

"Please. Grayden can't be ruler anymore or he's going to get everyone killed. I'll grow every food imaginable for you, and this kingdom will overflow with prosperity, but I need to get out of here. If I am back in the Merawood Forest, I'll have access to magic again and he will have to take off my collar if I am to make him anything. Then I can strike."

"Can you make a new one?" Apprehension coats her words. "One seems to have caused more than enough trouble."

I laugh without humor. "I can't make anything right now, but I have ideas."

Pour melted gold over his head, use a sword I have on my desk, strangle him with vines. Countless ways I can make him pay, but I need magic. I need him to believe me and take me home.

She bites her lip but nods. "All right, if you are sure, but please be careful. He will know if it's a trap."

"Then we need to be very convincing that it's not. If I can end your brother's life, are you prepared to rule?"

Lyrora gapes at me. "Women cannot be rulers here. I would need to marry."

Her guard stiffens beside her, a flash of agony distorting his handsome face, but he is quick to hide it. When she looks up at him with wide blue eyes, her own longing is mirrored back.

She needs to see herself as the ruler she was born to be. "Do not let men tell you that you cannot have what is freely given to them."

"But—"

"You could be the new queen of Adreania. Lead it with compassion and kindness. Be everything your brother never was and so much more. You actually care about your people in a way he could never fathom. I'm sure you'll have an ally with Kalvorn when Leon returns."

"You have the crown. *You* are our ruler; it's our law. Loyal to whoever—"

"Yes, yes, *I know*, but I don't *want* to be a ruler. I want to go back to being a jewelry maker." My voice cracks a bit. "I want to go home. If I could take the crown off and give it to you, I would, believe me. If I knew how to remove it, I'm sure *Zilas* would have stolen it by now."

"No, no, Leon isn't like that!" She opens her mouth to argue again with me, but I wave my hand.

"It's not important. The only thing that matters is that you are prepared for whatever tomorrow brings."

Lyrora nods slowly. "Well, I suppose I'm the only heir left. I cannot say my father prepared me for anything other than to be a bride for some foreign noble, but yes." She straightens her back. "If you manage to kill my brother, I will take over the throne."

Her guard's chest puffs up with pride.

"Where I'm from, the fae realm, we've only ever had women rulers. My closest friend, Nueena, is about to take her mother's place as Realm Keeper. If I survive this, I will introduce you to her. She has been preparing her whole life, so she will have plenty of advice."

"I would like that." Lyrora's hopeful smile fades. "Just be prepared for what will come should you fail."

It's a punch to the gut. There are countless ways this could all go wrong.

She and her guard depart, leaving me alone again. Once the painting is locked behind them, I lie in Grayden's wife's bed and think of all the ways I can kill him. My violent imagination grows more and more unrealistic with every idea, but the rage within me sings at each thought.

I just need my forge.

~

The planning of the extravagant event that is to be my wedding falls on me, so I spend the morning trying to be as uncooperative as possible. When asked for colors I would like, I choose a horrible green shade, a dull yellow, and brown. Only the greedy nobles are allowed to attend the wedding feast, so I demand boiled frog legs, jellied eels, and onion pies with extra pig liver, much to the dismay of the pompous courtiers attempting to assist me, trying to earn my favor.

By midday I am escorted back to my pretty prison. The lady's maids once again paint my lips and eyes. Tonight's gown has a neckline so high it covers the gold on my chest and reaches my neck. It's a pale gown the color of snow with silver embroidery on the corset and hem and down the long sleeves. They adorn me with rings and bracelets, all silver. They leave the collar, but all other chains are removed.

Everett knocks but does not wait for a response, entering with a wicked smile. "What a beautiful day it is."

"Fuck off." My glare only amuses him more.

He holds the door open, holding out his arm, motioning me to leave. I roll my eyes and brush past him, hoping to walk alone to dinner, but he easily catches up.

"Oh, but you look so lovely. I don't think I have ever seen you in that color. So much yellow for you Gems." He pretends to look thoughtful. "Though I do suppose the only time you would wear white is in a Zemra ceremonial dress, but that will never happen."

His words hurt exactly how much he wanted them to. I do not hide the devastation on my face. Too hopeless for anger.

I stop in front of the throne room doors. "I would love nothing more than to remove the crown and slam it on your head. I've never wanted it. I will be dead soon. Why must you add cruelty?" I stare at him demanding an answer. "Were we ever friends?"

Everett's face hardens. "I do not need friends. Having them has gotten me nowhere. You ruined everything! Grayden and I had a plan. I was there the night his father died. I was meant to have the crown! Now let's go. Your future husband awaits."

I scoff at him. "With any luck I'll be dead before that ever happens."

His smile grows cruel again, sending ice down my spine, but he looks past me. "Looks like your luck has run out again."

Slowly I turn. Vera holds a long white veil slightly faded with time, tears in her eyes.

A wedding veil.

No.

I gasp out, "I do not need that. The wedding isn't—"

Vera walks towards me with glossy eyes. "I'm so sorry, Highness. They forbade me from telling you."

No, I will not marry that cruel man. I try to flee but Everett expects that; his arms lock around mine. I kick and thrash just like the last time he dragged me away from Leon in the garden, but now Tavien is not here to protect me.

The wide doors open and Grayden walks in.

The throne room is filled with courtiers dressed in their finest clothing. My blood boils in my veins at the sight of them happily eating the food I grew yesterday. Bastards. They are drinking wine and finding seats in the rows and rows of chairs, a long empty aisle down the middle. On the dais, in front of the throne, is a wedding arch.

No flowers, no decorations, just my future tied to a horrible man.

Horror spreads like fire throughout me and I snarl at him, the sound full of rage. How dare he force me to marry him. How dare he try and turn me into his little pawn.

"What the fuck is going on?" Grayden angrily demands. He wears all black with a white sash, the same silver embroidery across his chest.

A matching set.

Seeing Grayden in his wedding attire sparks new fury within me. I choke on an angry sob. Leon is the only one I ever wanted to tie myself to. He is who I wanted to spend my life with.

The only one worthy of being called my husband.

Gods, where is Lyrora? We had a plan. I'm desperate to get to the Merawood Forest.

Two guards escort a miserable Cyanna to the large hallway we are standing in. Whatever fight I had in me drains out of me and I go limp in Everett's arms.

"That's better," Everett says in my ear, his tone mocking.

More wedding guests arrive at the end of the hall. "Get her out of their sight 'til the wedding," Grayden demands.

Vera opens a door. "She is not ready yet, Your Majesty. I need more time." Her words are strong but her hand shakes on the handle.

He rolls his eyes. "You have three minutes. I want this wedding done and over with." He storms back into the throne room. Everett finally lets me go and I follow Vera into the small sitting room. In one corner a round table sits near large windows, a fine porcelain tea set for three, and couches on either side.

The deep crimson tablecloths and small hanging pots with tendrils of soft green leaves reminds me of Erenia's rooms.

Leon's words come back to me, the ones from the gardens just before the strawberry plants swirled around him with my affection. *"The days leading up to the bazaar were agony for me, waiting to see you again. Erenia once tried to suffocate me with a pillow in the middle of tea when I spent an entire afternoon talking about you."*

"Is this Erenia's tea room?" I whisper.

Vera nods, surprised. "Yes, she took tea here every morning, and in the afternoons, Princess Lyrora would accompany her."

And because I need to know, I ask, "Did anyone else join them?"

She is thoughtful for a moment. "Yes, that missing healer, if the king was sleeping. I heard a rumor among the servants that she ran away to be with him, but they only ever seemed to be friends to me."

I sit in one of the plush chairs, overwhelmed that Leon once sat in this room, thinking of me. Separated by realms, we both sat with our friends, who listened about our constant feelings for each other for years.

Both of us longing and lying to each other. Something deep within us recognizing fae souls meant to be together.

A fae king pretending to be a mortal healer.

A jewelsmith pretending to be a mortal woman.

If we had just been honest together from the start, would any of this have happened? We could have started over as ourselves. No lurking madness, no hourglass of slipping time stealing our future. Were we destined to enjoy spending decades together, becoming mates? We were fated and it all fell apart. Is he my soulbonded?

My Zemra.

Vera pins the veil to my hair, our reflections in the brass mirror. A veil is such a mortal tradition. I refuse to be tied to anyone but Leon, but everything feels hopeless in new, horrible ways.

Grayden's wife. What a wretched dishonor.

Someone knocks on the door and to my endless displeasure it is Everett, Cyanna at his side to ensure my continued obedience.

"Come now, bride. It's time for your little wedding." He laughs while I stand and walk past him without a glance, making my way out the door.

Cyanna has a new gown, dressed like a courtier, her hair clean and lips painted.

I hold out my hand, and hers slips in. Words fail me, no reason to ask each other if we are all right. How could we be? But we squeeze our hands, forgetting words that could never soothe our broken souls. I try to pour out my love and regret into that touch, feeling it returned to me. I will do anything to keep her safe, even marry this monster, and whatever else he asks of me.

Our moment is tainted too soon, as Everett grips under her arm and yanks her away from me. "We will be sitting in the front row, a reminder of what will happen if you choose to ruin this."

Her lip wobbles but I shake my head while she is dragged away. Her eyes stay on me during the long walk to the front. The pain of her misery is yet another knife in my chest.

Lyrora is nowhere to be seen, and any hope we could convince Grayden to take me away is lost now. The ballroom where I had spent so many nights stealing moments with Leon is filled with courtiers. When they see me standing at the doors, they all rise from their seats.

Vera whispers, "It's time." She holds out a bouquet of flowers for me and my heart stops. It is entirely made up of fragrant roses and vibrant geraniums. The petals are full and bright, and I cannot breathe.

No.

"Where did these flowers come from?" My voice is hollow, like my heart.

"Not many flowers bloom here but I found a small balcony garden which thankfully grew some. Aren't they lovely? Whoever grew them took great care in their growth."

The ballroom fades away, and I am transported back to my bedroom, the first time Leon stood there so many weeks ago.

He picks up the bottle of perfume I wear every day and brings it to his nose. "Floral, with something citrus underneath. Roses and geraniums? With a hint of what I would guess is lemons." He breathes it in again. "Definitely a summer lemon."

"Impressive. A man who knows his scents."

He places the bottle back on the desk with care. "Jedrick was a late sleeper, and I enjoyed tending to my medical garden in the misty mornings, the one we met in. I have roses and geraniums planted there, too."

My heart skips a beat. When I was in that garden in the Iron Castle, I saw those flowers. "Is that right?"

"Oh, yes, I planted them almost two years ago. Geranium leaves can be used as a pain reliever when placed in teas, and rose oil is good for the skin." He turns and walks over with soft eyes to where I lean against one of the bed trees.

"The scent also reminded me of you. One night a month never seemed like enough."

I bring the flowers to my nose and inhale deeply. My tears fall onto its delicate petals and disappear.

He grew this for me; he loved me even then. Long before the crown, long before he knew I was fae, he loved me.

Now he will never know how much I love him in return.

Music swells, a mortal tune I only vaguely know. "Your Highness," Vera pleads, "you must walk now."

The memory of Leon and me fades away and my horrible reality returns.

Grayden waits under the arch, impatiently tapping his foot.

My tears do not stop. Footsteps grow heavier with each step. Grief guides me down that aisle.

Every stride is a reminder that any future with Leon is over now, the loss of our future laid out before me as I am forced to marry another man.

I finally reach the dais, every part of me wishing I could turn and run, but that would cost Cyanna her life. Trumpets play, my ears ringing from the blast as I stand next to Grayden, the crowd cheering.

He spins lies of Princess Erenia's betrayal and abandonment

that led to her death. His voice booms around the room. "Fae Queen Izadella is my new bride. You eat the fruits of her magic tonight. She will bring back prosperity and wealth to Adreania. The crown will be our greatest asset in the war with Kalvorn."

More cheers follow.

"The crown has chosen her to be our queen. Tonight, we celebrate our union with a wedding like no other."

An old man in plush robes joins us, I can only assume to wed us. I've never attended a mortal wedding. In Ellova we have mated unions and Zemra ceremonies, a celebration with loved ones and a chance for the couple to show off their stones.

My mind must want me to suffer more: a vision of Leon and me is crystal clear. He waits at the end of the aisle, our friends with us; bright stones decorate our neck. The thought is painful, and I shove it away.

There is only Grayden now.

We face each other. He holds out his clammy hand, and through gritted teeth he spits out, "Make this quick."

The man nods quickly. "Do you, King Grayden Fasaile, son of Jedrick Fasaile, take Izadella of the fae to be your queen?"

"I do." He says the words so flatly, as if his wedding is a trivial event.

The elderly officiant turns to me and recoils a bit when he meets my glare. I understand it's not his fault I stand before a monster to wed but he strikes the last nail in my coffin with his final words.

"Do you, Izadella of the fae, take King Grayden Fasaile to be your husband and obey him in all ways?"

No, I fucking don't

Grayden's hand tightens in mine, motivation to speak.

"I—" I cannot bring myself to say the word. "I—"

An explosion behind us has courtiers screaming, glass breaking, and the throne room descends into chaos. Hope surges so quickly my head spins that it's Leon coming to save me but pouring into the crowded room are men with makeshift weapons. Theodore and Clive are at the front. The royal armor they wore to escort me to each bazaar is gone; they fight alongside the healed men of Beggars' Row.

Adreanian rebels clash with Grayden's men.

My heart soars and for the first time since I've arrived in this shit kingdom, happy tears fall on my cheeks as more and more rebels arrive, ready to take back their kingdom. The castle guards may have superior weapons, but they are outnumbered.

The elixir worked and they now have a fighting chance to rise up against their tyrant king.

I'm desperate to escape, not wasting this distraction, but Grayden anticipates my movement, snatching me before I can run. Guards surround us. "I want every traitor alive, and in the dungeons," he yells at them, dragging me through a hidden door to some sort of small armory and finally lets me go. Lyrora and her guard are close behind us.

Everett shoves Cyanna into the secret room with us and she reaches for me. I pull her close while Everett and Grayden argue. She trembles in my arms. I wish I could get her out of here. All she has ever done is help those in need. "I'm so sorry," I whisper into her hair. "I'm going to find a way to get you out of here."

She nods but does not speak. Every moment here is wretched. I can feel her sorrow.

A pounding on the door makes me jump. "GIVE US LADY ARRA!" Theodore shouts, his fist banging again.

I need to live long enough to thank him for halting the wedding, for trying to save me now.

"They want the crown!" Grayden seethes.

I glare at him over Cyanna's head, desperately wanting to scream that they do not seek the crown. They could no more control it than he can. They want him *dead*. Those of Beggars' Row can now stand up instead of being used to fight a war they could never win, all because of the healer king that sat under his nose for years, my friends, and me. Oh, to see the look on his ugly face.

Lyrora makes a frustrated noise, gaining the attention of the whole crammed room. "Damn it! Why not have her make you a new crown?" she angrily points at me. "She is a fae jewelry maker and her ancestor made the one she wears, did she not? Why can't she make you one so you would have magic of your own to command?"

Grayden whirls on me with hungry eyes. "Can you do that?"

Letting go of my cousin and backing up a step, I stammer, "Y-you are mortal. The magic would not work. Surely you know this by now…"

"What about Everett?" he demands, inches from my face, pointing at my once friend. "He has magic! Can you make him one? If he has the crown's magic, we will destroy Kalvorn in a day."

Trying to appear frantic, I look between the two men. "No, no. I have nothing I could create with. Adreania has no magic here!"

Everett's face is feral with delight. "But your mother's forge does. You have made many, many magical items! You can recreate the crown!" He turns to Grayden. "She is half mortal. That might be why she cannot control the magic. I am full fae. It would obey me! We need to go to her forge! I know where it is. We can have it by tonight." They both turn to me with the same terrible expression. Greed and dishonor, cruelty and wicked delight.

"Please, Everett." I picture never returning to Ellova and my tears come easily. "Don't do this. You would not be able to control it!" I almost smile, nearly give myself away at the look of unearned confidence he now wears.

"Watch me, Della. Watch me."

CHAPTER 37

IZADELLA

Dark gray clouds threaten to drench us as we race away from the chaos that consumes the castle. Guards ushered us through a secret stairwell built for a rebellion, taking us to a stable to secure horses for our journey to my forge.

I glance over at Cyanna, who is tied up, as I am, riding with Everett to ensure my cooperation. At least Everett is more respectful of Cyanna's personal space than Grayden is of mine.

Grayden is pressed to my back as we ride together through the dead forests of Adreania. Thick woven rope cuts into my wrist, reddening my skin. One of his hands holds the reins while resting on my thigh as if this is a casual garden ride among lovers. They take the long way and I'm grateful that they don't know the quickest route even if it means more time with Grayden so close.

He wraps around my waist tightly, his arm far too high up my stomach with his thumb occasionally swiping on the underside of my breast.

"I'm so looking forward to finishing our little wedding." His lips curve into a smile on my ear and my stomach plummets with nausea at the thought.

Anytime I try to lean forward, I'm roughly pulled back to him. I would jump off but one of my ankles has been tied to the saddle, ensuring any attempt to escape will have me dragged by the horse for the remaining journey.

It's tempting, just to get his hands off me, but I'm unwilling to risk Cyanna's safety or my plans to escape. I try to relax. If the crown perceives I'm in danger, I risk getting us hurt. His hot breath is on my neck, and I spend most of the ride imagining breaking every bone in his hand.

One of Grayden's guards calls out from the back of our caravan. "Your Majesty! The castle!"

He whips our horse around so quickly I nearly lose my balance.

Grayden screams in rage, but delight fills me. Through the rain, the Adreanian flags are ripped away and replaced by white ones that look much like bedsheets. The rebels have taken the castle and surrendered to Kalvorn before the war even started.

They did it!

"We need to go back!" Grayden demands.

Cyanna and I share a secret smile while Everett yells, "No! Once I have the new crown, we will destroy them all! Those traitors will pay in ways they cannot fathom. We need to hurry."

Grayden snaps the reins, and our group picks up speed through the harsh terrain.

The moment we cross the divide into the Merawood Forest, Everett and I release the same sigh of relief as magic returns to our veins.

With the iron collar on, the crown's magic is weak but flows freely again in my blood, bringing with it warmth. I can even feel my own magic again, unreachable and under all the other magic trapped within me but there, like a caress against my very soul, waiting for the day it can be released.

Ready to command gold and silver again.

With the magic returning, new pain races across my shoulders, up my neck, up to my jaw. The golden cracks deepen, spreading. Glittering reminders of my enervation death as the magic leaks out of me again. Unseen, but a gut-wrenching reminder.

The forest is quiet, *too* quiet.

Finally, we arrive back at the forge. The trees surrounding it are blackened stumps on the forest floor next to my burnt and crumbling cottage.

I want to curl in a ball and mourn, sob 'til I have nothing left but the magic seeping out of me.

The place I shared with my mother, the beautiful home generations of women survived exile in. Where my father made me my first wooden sword to practice with. Where Nueena and I met. The first night Leon truly met me.

Decades of memories. Lost.

It is too much, losing everything.

Seeing the remnants of my life shatters what's left of my heart, but something else starts within me. Those shattered pieces burn with white-hot anger. This is all Grayden's fault. He sent his guards to destroy my home.

The idea of watching him die in the ashes he created satiates me enough to focus on what I must do.

When the guards unbind my ankle and help me down, Grayden removes the icy collar. I nearly crumple at the rush of endless power returning to envelop me, but he grabs my arm, holding me up. Everett stands near the doorway with a stoic Cyanna in front of him, a dagger at her throat. Her beautiful face is expressionless but the tear streaks on her cheeks betray her fear.

The agony here leaves me breathless.

The small army Grayden brought surrounds us, some near the ruins of my cottage but most stand on guard around the perimeter.

My head throbs.

"Get to work!" Grayden shoves me towards the forge with eyes full of hate. I fantasize about throwing boiling gold in his face.

A backup plan.

Unlike my destroyed cottage, the forge was made to be fireproof. I open the door and all the windows so as not to suffocate Cyanna with the heat. The workshop is just as I left it. Without my jewelsmith powers, I find one of the dusty circlet molds and ready it on my desk. I pour nuggets of gold in the crucible and place metal containers directly into the magical fire. It burns brighter; the blue flames are more vibrant now that it has work to do.

The stone hearth is large. I could easily fit inside. No one could hurt me there, I used to play in it as a dewling, but that would leave Cyanna alone.

I turn my back to Grayden, and I let my fingertips dance in flames for just a moment.

Grayden tries to come over to see me work but steps away from the blistering heat. "Hurry up!"

"I cannot lower the melting point of gold. Let the fire do its work," I snap.

Grayden must have thought this wouldn't be a time-consuming creation. While the gold starts to melt, I pray to Ellova that no one in the palace sees the smoke and tries to investigate.

I cannot have anyone risking their lives to retrieve me, no matter my fate in the mortal realm.

Cyanna screams, trying to drop to the floor with her arm over her head when I spin around. Everett reaches for her, but a flaming arrow shoots through his palm. He yells in anguish, cradling his hand to his chest.

Grayden grabs me, slamming the iron collar around my throat, screaming for his guards.

Panic pulses in me as the magic is cut off.

What is happening?

Cyanna runs towards me. Another guard grabs her, but she elbows him in the nose, scrambling away just before an arrow goes right through his eye. Pride and hope she can escape replaces some of my panic. Chaos erupts around us, more burning arrows meeting their marks and taking out the few of Grayden's guards that followed us into the workshop. I yank Cyanna behind me as I try to shield her from the fighting. Everett rips the arrow out of his melting skin and lunges for me, but my fist connects with his nose, breaking it, sending him stumbling back.

Hope shatters my horror.

Outside, Viella and Tavien are fighting with sapphire flames in their hands. Lillian's gold swords, lit with her purple flames, clash with the iron ones of her enemies.

My sobs echo off the stone walls.

The joy of seeing them is short-lived. If they are here—that means…

My heart plummets in fear as Nueena and Leon burst through the forest with identical expressions of furious vengeance, running straight into danger. Leon is fae again, his ears poking out from his gray-and-black streaks. They both make a run for me.

Air is impossible to get into my lungs, horror and elation shredding me apart.

Leon is here. He came for me! Even when I said I never wanted to see him again, he races towards me, crushing anyone in his path.

Nueena shouldn't be here! Ellova needs her. Gods, if something were to happen to her, her family would never recover!

Adreanian iron soldiers clash with Ellovian honeyguards, their purple capes blowing behind them.

Tears sting in my eyes at the sight of that beautiful color.

Grayden's guards outside try to intercept them, but Nueena strikes them down with a blow of magic. Leon moves alongside her, meticulously slicing and stabbing with graceful merciless retribution, the two of them an unstoppable force making their way through the trees to get to me.

They leave rivers of blood in their wake on the forest floor.

My heart stops beating as two more guards descend on Nueena, but with a flare of magic taking them out at the knees, both men collapse, howling in pain as they fall, legs at awkward angles.

Purple thorny vines shoot up from the ground, wrapping around their arms and legs. The building shakes from her power.

Everett runs out of the forge, sword in hand, and lunges at Nueena, who is just outside. I scream her name; she turns just in time. Her blade slides into Everett's side, blood gushing out of him.

More of Grayden's guards try to form a circle around the forge to keep anyone from getting inside.

I rush towards the door, holding the doorframe, about to warn her about more guards coming while she's occupied with Everett, but I only make it a few steps when pain explodes in my stomach, stealing my breath. My knees make a sickening crack as I hit the stone floor. I reach for the source, finding metal tearing through me.

An iron sword protrudes out of my stomach. My blood runs off the sharpened edge, splashing on the forge's floor. Everett staggers away before he falls to the ground in front of me, holding his side, and I think for a moment he was the one who stabbed me, but it wasn't him.

It was Grayden.

Nueena races into the forge, screaming, finally reaching me, "No, no, no!" Tears stream down her face as she gently takes my cheeks in her hand, kneeling in front of me.

More guards race to attack Leon, who breaks through their numbers, screaming my name, the sound echoing around the forest.

Everett raises his sword behind Nueena's back.

NO!

He slams the sword down and I use my last remaining bit of strength to push her out of the way, knocking her to the ground, his sword driving through my chest. Blood flows down me in rivulets on my already stained white dress.

Was everyone in my family cursed to die in this fucking cottage?

Nueena scrambles to get to me. "You're going to be okay! You have to be! Della!"

A scream of rage rings out.

It sounds exactly how I feel, but it's not coming from me.

Leon finally reaches the workshop and charges at Grayden, who is trying to escape. The cowardly king lunges to avoid Leon's blade and raises his own to block the attack. Grayden is only mortal and so much slower than Leon. His emerald-and-opal sword finds Grayden's chest, sinking the silver blade straight through him until the king slams into the wall behind him.

A small painting of Nueena and me as dewlings falls off at the force.

"You are a vile abomination, and you will *never* get near her again!" Leon wraps his hand around Grayden's throat, blood pouring to the ground from his chest.

"Fuck you, healer."

"It's *King Zilas,* you pitiful fuck!" Leon squeezes. Black veins spread under his hand, and Grayden's eyes redden, blood running out of them. Something snaps in Grayden's neck, his head rolling to the side. Dead.

Good.

"Della, *please, no, no, no, no!*" Nueena pleads, sobbing. "Leon, fucking save her! LEON!" She and I stare at each other. This was not how it was to end, but I am already halfway in the grave. She needs to live. For her family, for Ellova. She opens her mouth to speak again but her face freezes in shock.

Blackness slides across my vision but I force myself to stay present for a few more moments with my closest friend.

To say goodbye.

I'm desperate to say that I'm sorry, that I love her and everyone else I call family who risked their lives to save me, but when I open my mouth, the words never come, only blood.

Everything is fading away. The pain, everyone in this room, Leon, but I hope he knows. Even after all that has happened, I love him. My magic snaps away from me on the inside, floating away.

Leon races towards me, anguish distorting his perfect face. He slides on his knees to get to me, the ashes of the forge scattering around us. Leon's roar of rage is the last thing I hear as I take my last shuddering breath.

The scent of strawberries and blood reaches me, but Leon never does.

CHAPTER 38

LEON

I race towards Izadella, screaming her name despite knowing I will not reach her in time. The light in her eyes, so full of pain and regret, fades. Anguish shreds my soul; grief drowns me as I slam into the ground, sliding over the stone floor, and finally pulling her to me.

Tavien is on my heels, dropping to his knees next to us to pull a weeping Nueena into his arms.

I'm too late.

Izadella's body, pierced by two iron swords, slumps in my arms. Dead.

Blinding agony, the likes of which I have never known before, burns me alive.

No, no, no.

How does my heart still beat? How has my body not collapsed from the knowledge that she's gone?

The crown falls off her head, gliding down her curls and I grab for it midair, the metal scorching to the touch.

It's finally in my hand. This crown, the very object I've spent a century attempting to get. Limitless magic radiates off it and up my arm, the ground shaking beneath me at the loss of its wearer.

My birthright.

Everything I sought before I knew her.

Before I knew what she was to me.

My Zemra.

It means nothing to me now. Claiming the crown would mean I risk losing my own magic, and with it, any chance of bringing her back to me.

I will not allow death to take her from me, *never.*

I shove the crown at Nueena, needing both of my hands for what I am about to do. She gasps but takes it from me.

If anyone can handle the uncontrollable magic it holds, she can.

Tears stream down my face. "Izadella, my love, it's going to be okay. I love you, Strawberries. I love you. *I love you.*" I wrap one arm around her, her blood soaking me.

I rip the swords out of Izadella's lifeless body, and my stomach rolls with nausea. The sight and sound of metal sliding out of her will haunt me 'til the day I die. This is a living nightmare. It slices into my soul even though I know she's dead and can't feel it.

I tear open her destroyed gown, and a new torment burns through me, severing my soul in half.

Her chest is ruined like mine, golden enervation scars revealing just how horrendously I've broken her heart. Those marks on her flawless skin are proof that my lies would have taken her life.

The suffering I have caused.

I will *never* forgive myself.

My deceit almost took her from me forever. I should have done more to earn her trust, and we would have both lived.

Her blood coats my hands and I press my shaking palms to the exposed, bloody skin of my Zemra's chest, shoving my healing magic into her, *demanding* it save her, to heal what I have so wholly broken.

She *must* live.

My hands glow with an ethereal radiance, and her body jerks as my magic tries to force her body to knit back together. My vision blurs. Every bit of magic I flow to her is agony inside me, like my body is being ripped apart with the sudden loss of so much of myself, but I will give it all to bring her back, no matter what it takes. If I have to pass from this world to give her life again, then so be it.

My body sways as my healing power strikes her chest like lightning, flooding her body with its restorative light over and over again. Her stomach and chest gleam bright out of the places where the swords tore through her.

Every second she doesn't breathe is torturous.

I choke on my suffocating sorrow. The thunder in my head leaves me unable to think properly, my own magic leaking out of my enervation scars. Tears pour down my face, falling onto her bloody body.

This heartache is an execution.

I scream in rage. No matter how much of my own magic is poured into her, nothing happens.

My panic overpowers every thought in my head. My magic is sluggish, running out, but I shove it into her heart, striking it again and again with bolts until my healing magic is nearly gone. Her heart must be restarted before the magic can heal any other injuries.

Holding her lifeless body is agony. If Izadella truly dies, I will have nothing to live for.

I will follow her to the soil if I cannot save her.

My head spins, relief nearly knocks me over when her precious heartbeat returns, weak, but proof that she lives. I wipe away the blood on her stomach in time to see the light fade and her skin fuse back together, not even daring to leave a scar on her perfect chest.

Those horrid golden streaks across her body retreat back into her chest as if they were never there.

She's alive.

Not even the grave's merciless grip could stop me from being with her.

I pull her to my chest, burying my face in her neck. Gratitude overwhelms me with her soft breath on my skin.

I didn't lose her.

I will *never* lose her again.

It will take hours for her to be fully healed, but we can take her back to the Ellovian palace. She can rest in her bed with Farren while I beg for forgiveness. I close the torn fabric of her dress as much as I can.

My last drop of healing magic swirls in my finger as I run it over her dry, peeling lips. Softness follows my touch until the skin is plump and kissable once more.

I would give anything to know my lips would be welcomed as they once were.

Tavien yells as Everett appears from outside the forge. He propels a distracted Nueena out of his way, grabbing the crown from her.

"It's mine now!" Everett cries in delirious laughter, slamming the crown on his head.

Tavien positions Nueena behind him, his fist erupting in protective blue fire and shadows around them.

For a moment nothing happens.

Everett is out of breath; his good hand pressed to his wounds gushing at his side. The crown shifts from gold to a violent crimson, glowing angrily as if it were freshly removed from the flames of the forge behind him.

His victorious smile slips away, his face twisting in pain, and his bloody hands claw at the burning crown he should never have put on.

Blood comes out of his nose and ears; crimson tears leak from his eyes. He frantically tries to remove the crown, but it's too late. He was a fool to think he could control the magic inside, to think such a powerful keyed item would accept him.

An unworthy, evil man who had brought harm to the crown maker's last descendant.

He screams. His pale skin turns a sickly green, the crown shining brighter as Everett is torn apart by the crown's magic, and I am filled with pure delight at his death. The shredded pieces of him shift into brown leaves that flutter to the floor in a pile. The crown sits on top.

His death was not painful enough, not nearly what he deserved, but at least he is dead.

Nueena moves towards it, but Tavien tries to stand in her way. "*Please*, don't touch it."

Transfixed, she whispers, "It calls to me." The ground shakes as she steps closer to it.

Tavien wraps his arms around her, dragging her back. She pulls his hands off her body, slipping out of his desperate grasp as he pleads, still attempting to pull her away from it. "We don't know what it will do to you!"

"I do," she says in a quiet voice, looking back at him. "It will be keyed to me. It has chosen me. Trust, my love."

He sighs, no longer trying to get in her way. "I will always trust you."

She kneels where Everett just stood, reaching out for the crown. I rock Izadella in my arms and watch in awe as Nueena's touch returns it to a glistening gold.

More of Grayden's guards surround the workshop as Nueena gently places the crown atop her braids. Her eyes glow an iridescent purple, and a blast of power shatters all the glass in the room as it fits perfectly on her head.

The fire in the forge winks out.

Her voice booms, echoing into my bones, power rippling through her. "Get her out of here."

Every part of me aches but I do not hesitate, picking up Izadella, who stirs in my arms. She opens her eyes slowly at Nueena's voice, staring between her and me in confusion. I run towards the door, and we exit the forge, rain pouring.

Lightning flashes above us as Izadella blinks up at me, confused.

"Leon," she whispers, affection in her eyes. She reaches up to cup my cheek. "You came for me."

No matter the agony inside my body, my heart might burst in my chest with hope for us. "Always, my love."

She doesn't despise me. The relief nearly sends me to my knees.

Her gentle hand moves upward towards my hair, her fingers touching the pointed tips of my ears. Those beautiful brown eyes of hers widen and a kaleidoscope of emotions pass over her face.

She settles on anger.

"You lying, deceitful asshole!" Her voice is rough. I need to get her some water. "Go back! Take me back to Nueena."

Guilt guts me.

The only part of me she can reach is my ear and she yanks.

Hard.

"Fae! This whole time!" She fumes.

My joy at holding her, alive and angry in my arms, causes me to laugh. I hold her tighter against my body, the rain running down, down my smiling face.

"Do *not* smile at me, you lying piece of—"

"*You're alive!*" I shout to her over the rolling thunder and rain. "Punish me for eternity if you wish, but you live. I thought I would never see you again, Izadella. I have so much to tell you but not now." I tuck her even tighter against me while she thrashes, and I run over downed tree branches and through muddy puddles.

"Put me down! Nueena! NUEENA!" she yells, but she immediately coughs and tucks her arm protectively around her stomach, sending my heart plummeting.

"Stop moving, my love! You are healing. Please rest and let my magic restore you. I can't explain everything, but I need to get you somewhere safe."

She groans, rubbing her hand over the spot where she was stabbed, probably noticing my healing magic is still working inside her. "Leon, it hurts."

I can sense my healing swirling inside her.

"I know. I know. I'm so sorry, Strawberries. I'm so very sorry. The damage done to your internal organs was devastating. Your body will need time to recover. It will only be painful for a little while longer."

"How?" is the only thing she manages to get out. Her eyes flutter closed, and her body goes limp again.

"I promise I'll explain everything."

The forest shakes with an explosion behind us and I whip us around.

Nueena is unimaginably high in the sky, shimmering purple light pouring out of her. Lightning flashes across the sky, followed immediately by the crash of thunder.

One of Grayden's men jumps in front of me, his sword ready to strike. I am about to twist my back and accept his attack, but he is suddenly struck by violet lightning. There one moment, vanished the next.

Nueena is high above us, one hand pointing to where the guard had been completely obliterated.

"Thank you, Nu," I yell.

More of Grayden's guards enter the forest, ready to fight, unaware that their leader is dead.

Another explosion of magic rolls off her and the ground rumbles again. Some kind of shield stretches for miles at the Verge, soaring upward. Lightning flashes again, followed by screams of men who have done wicked things for their king. They swore to die for him and now they shall.

Nueena has sealed off Ellova from the rest of the world, sealing us out.

"That's Tavien's to deal with," I mumble aloud, "You can hate me later if you wish, but I need you alive so I can spend a lifetime earning your trust back."

The rain drenches us, washing the gore from her in bloody rivers. Lightning flashes and illuminates Izadella. Her long hair is tangled, and her lips are in a frown with her brows furrowed, angry with me even after she has fainted.

She has every right to be.

My stomach twists at the sight of the blasted collar still on her. I lay Izadella gently on the moss-covered forest floor. I take a deep breath and run my fingers over it to find some sort of lock. I do not have my glamour ring so I cannot return to my mortal form to do this. My fingertips blister instantly against the iron. I grab each side, hissing at the searing pain, and pull with all my strength. My blood slicks the metal, but I rip the collar in two. The pieces fall to the ground, and I toss them away from her. My hands are a burning, bloody mess. Painful, but nothing compared to the pain of tonight.

Guards shout in the distance.

Scooping her up again, I pull her tighter to my chest, offering the warmth of my body. The forest is nearly black with the storm. Every direction looks the same. Rain pours down, and Izadella's soft breath on my neck and the movement of her chest are my only peace.

I need to get her somewhere safe.

Ellova is now protected by a glowing shield, so that direction isn't an option. Too many guards are still in the forest. It's tempting to bring her to Kalvorn, but she will awaken just as angry as before. I will not take her against her will like Everett did.

I fear I have already done too much. The damage I've caused is too permanent to risk taking her away from her home once more and adding to my list of offenses.

Best to keep her close to Nueena, even if she's a deity in the sky now.

I close my eyes and take a deep breath to block out the rain, the thunder, the faint heartbeat of the woman I love in my arms.

I feel a sudden pull in my center and I focus on it. I've never felt this before but it's there, a beacon drawing me northeast towards the mountains between Ellova and Kalvorn, past the forest. Letting that tugging feeling guide me, I push myself to follow it.

"Izadella?" As I walk, I give her a small shake, but her head just limply rolls to the side. Sighing, I adjust her to face me. She smells like herself, a light, lovely scent even the rain can't wash away.

"I'm sorry," I doubt she can even hear me over the rain bombarding us. The occasional roll of thunder is my only company as I trudge through the muddy forest.

With every stride, I feel that pulling in my gut growing stronger, like a moth to a flame, until the sensation that tugs at me is all-consuming. Calling me to move faster.

Dark clouds roll past to reveal patches of bright stars, but we are both soaked to the bone, and she shakes from the chill.

Trees space farther and farther apart until we reach the base of a mountain as the sun's first rays of light arrive.

That tugging sensation has led me to the base of a mountain where a wide cave is carved into the stone.

It's hidden and away from any danger, so I carry her over the threshold.

CHAPTER 39

LEON

I am overwhelmed by the ancient magic that swirls around us in this cave.

The large door opens on its own and crystal lights slowly glow to life, illuminating a long hallway.

Rose quartz stairs lead to a large circular door of carved emerald surrounded by diamonds and it's twice as tall as me. The short hallway is dark but the carvings on the wall are distinctly fae.

The walls are covered with delicate carvings of fae embracing, of animals in pairs running and jumping, of stars and moons, of births and deaths. The end of the hallway leads to another circular door similar to the one outside. The floor of the cave is covered in small, shining river rocks.

Izadella has stopped shaking, curling herself into me and occasionally releasing a soft moan of relief.

I step into the hall.

The walls of the massive cave are made of sharp, pointed crystals that glitter and glow from within.

In the center of the room on a large dais is a sanctuary of some kind with stairs leading up to it from all sides. Four onyx pillars hold up the roof where gossamer white curtains flow down. A bed sits at the center.

The warmth of a bubbling hot spring off to the side catches my attention. As tempting as it is to take Izadella straight to the bed, where she can rest, the dried blood that mars her skin is a gut-wrenching reminder I nearly lost her forever. The spring lures me to wash these memories away.

I carry Izadella into warm waters, gently laying her on its edge.

Relieved at this opportunity, I dunk myself, running my fingers through my hair, and stay under for a moment, letting the magic cleanse me, as if it could erase all the ways I failed Izadella as easily as it washes the grime on my skin. When I break the surface, my once-filthy clothing is pristine.

My hands no longer hurt, and when I hold them up, the blisters from the iron collar are healing. Interesting.

I pull down my collar, and my scars still gleam on my chest. I did not expect a small pool of water with some healing properties to cure me, but I am disappointed just the same.

If I had been honest from the start, she would have never fled, never given Everett a chance to take her from me. That is guilt that will never leave me.

I reach for Izadella, holding her to my chest. I carefully dip her in, swirling us in the center, erasing the evidence of her capture and brief departure from this world.

Her dress is no longer a rust color, stiff with her blood and dried mud. The fabric flows gently in the water, returning to white but still torn apart.

The crystal-clear water pools in my hand and I pour it over her forehead, the rivulets washing away the blood there, too.

I had hoped the water would wake her, but I know healing magic takes time, and sleep is best, but I'm desperate for the sound of her voice. Even if she is angry with me, even if she repeats the words she spoke to me in her bathing room, I just need to hear her.

I never want to see you again.

What if she wakes and her wishes haven't changed? My stomach twists at the wretched thought. I will respect that choice, but it might break my heart in the way I broke hers. I would deserve it.

No man, mortal or otherwise, deserves it more.

Oils and soaps line the edge, and I am thankful for whoever supplied them.

With one hand, I pour some into her hair, using my fingers like a comb to brush through her tangled locks, tilting her head back into the water to rinse the lather away.

Finally, she is outwardly cleansed of tonight.

I settle on the built-in seating around the hot spring and prop Izadella up, letting her lean forward, her cheek pressed against my chest while I wring out her hair 'til it is damp. I twist it into a bun on the top of her head before I pick her up, carrying her like I would a sleeping dewling, her head resting in the crook of my neck. I treasure every breath that flutters against my skin.

I walk her up the stairs and through the curtains, guided by the glowing lights in each corner illuminating the space. The floor glitters with polished crushed crystal and in the center is a hollowed-out square filled with pillows and blankets. Surely someone is caring for the temple; the pillows are free of dust and the air smells sweet and clean.

It's probably sacred to the Ellovian fae, but it's warm and dry and soft for her to sleep on, so I can hardly bring myself to care.

I would be lost without her. I never wish to leave her side again. If she chooses to live in Ellova without me, I'll sit waiting at the forest gates forever.

I lie down next to her but give her enough space that if she wakes and still hates me, she won't find me crowding her.

I desperately want to pull her into me and hold her, feel her breath on my cheeks as she sleeps. I resist though, pulling back my hand each time I reach for her, fighting the urge to curl up next to her and beg for forgiveness.

CHAPTER 40

LEON

The pillows move next to me, and I open my eyes to meet Izadella's teary, warm brown ones staring back at me. The temple is dark around us but enough light from the dull light crystals allows me to see her.

"Leon?" Her confused voice is so soft.

"I'm right here. You're safe." My throat tightens at the last word. The staggering guilt I feel weighs heavy on me.

Izadella nods slowly, closing her eyes again. "Safe. With you." She wiggles her body closer to me, sinking deeper into the bed. "Home."

"How do you feel?" When she doesn't respond, I hope she hasn't gone back to sleep, but moments later her eyes flare open with panic.

"I died!" Izadella swiftly gets up on her knees, pawing at her shredded dress, rubbing both hands over smooth skin. "I was *dead*, I died and then magic I've never felt before. Oh, Ellova's grave. The crown is gone!" She clutches her bare head, running her fingers through her hair, her shoulders curling in with relief.

"It is," I say calmly, sitting up and letting her process all of this.

"Where is the crown now?"

"It chose Nueena and is keyed to her now."

"That doesn't surprise me at all." She smiles softly but it fades just as fast. "And she's okay?"

"Yes, she was able to control the magic. Quite the sight. A little terrifying, actually."

She gapes at me, rubbing her temple. "You healed me?" Her fingers graze her chest, finding no scars. "You brought me back, didn't you? I felt your hands on me."

My responding smile wobbles a bit. "Of course I did. You do not get to leave this life without me, and we have much to live for. Tavien was right when he said I wouldn't let something as trivial as death separate me from you."

"Oh, Leon," she whispers, her voice cracking slightly. My chest tightens at the sound, which for the moment is devoid of the rage I felt from her last night.

"Please, lie back." I take her hand and guide her down into the bed.

"Where is Cyanna?"

"I'm sure she is safe. Lillian and Viella were there, too. They will probably take her back to Ellova 'til you return."

She nods at that. Worry still shines in her eyes when she asks, "Are you all right?"

"More than all right now that I have you back. Are you in pain?"

She shakes her head, leaning forward and touching our foreheads together. "No, just a little sore."

Tension floods out of me and I crumple with relief that maybe not everything is lost between us.

"Are they dead, too?" she asks, not needing to say the bastards' names.

"Yes, painfully so. Grayden with a sword and Everett by the crown. He put it on, and it killed him, turning him into a pile of dried leaves. I would have been impressed if I weren't so terrified I had lost you."

She is quiet while she stares at my head but finally asks in a small voice, "You are not wearing the crown. You could have taken it for yourself, for Kalvorn. Why didn't you?"

"Because I could have lost my healing magic the moment I

needed it most. The crown overshadowed your jewelsmith powers. There was no way for me to know if it would do the same to me. I couldn't risk it. The crown would have meant *nothing* if you had died in my arms." I lightly run my fingers over her cheek, and she closes her eyes at the touch, leaning into my palm. I expected her to move away, but she doesn't. A seed of hope rises in my chest.

"Thank you. Are you going to tell me who you really are now?"

I laugh at her light tone, relieved to find no anger or betrayal in her voice, just a soft, patient question. "Well, I was King Zilas of Kalvorn, but now I'm just Leon. Well, Prince Leon."

She opens her eyes; brows pinched in confusion. "And you are no longer king because…?"

My honesty is all I wish to give her now. Maybe if I lay everything down and beg at her feet, she can forgive me, understand what I did, why it was so important.

I focus on the only thing I care about right now: her.

"Izadella, I'm in love with you, and I have been for a long time, since the moment I met you." She looks like she is about to say something, but I cut her off. "I wanted to tell you earlier, but I didn't want you to ever doubt that my feelings were genuine and had nothing to do with the crown. I am the descendant of Queen Inara and Prince Kalden Fasaile."

"Well, that explains the ring, but what about the crown?"

"Since it was Inara's crown, my family tried to get it back many times with assassins and armies. My great-great-uncle got close but ultimately died trying."

She moves to lay half of herself on my chest and gazes down at me. I take her other hand in mine, gently rubbing my thumb on her arm. Just this touch is healing the agony that dragged me down like an anchor these past few days.

I love her so fucking much.

"Such effort for an uncontrollable item."

"We knew the power it had. My parents are both fae and they longed for the crown to be restored to us. Like in Adreania, the crown was slowly siphoning Kalvorn's magic. The main difference was that we had the Airvell River to replenish it, unlike Adreania. The only thing we knew about the crown was that it was removable at the point of death for mortal kings. So much of Adreania is laden with iron since Drystan grew paranoid over attacks from the fae to retrieve the crown, and iron is deadly to us. I was chosen for the task because I was born with a rare gift. The last fae to have healing magic as strong as I have, was Queen Arelia, Inara's missing daughter. I could heal and that could be its own weapon."

Her face softens. "What happened next?"

I press a kiss to her palm. "I was sent across the Elbasan Sea to Versairen and attended the best medical academies. When finished, I created an identity and built up an excellent reputation that got me recruited to the Iron Castle to serve Jedrick's father."

Her eyes widened. "So long ago."

I chuckle. "Yes, but when I failed to get the crown from him, I left for long enough that no one would recognize me, and I went through the academy training once more before returning to Adreania, posing as the son of myself. I developed a reputation for my skill, combining real medicine with my magic to boost my successful treatments, and soon enough Jedrick summoned me to serve him as his healer. I feared Grayden did something to the previous healer, but I had no proof. I just wanted the crown so I could go home, and once Jedrick trusted me, I started poisoning him with everything I could think of."

Izadella jerks her head back, but she doesn't reprimand or judge. "You were?"

"Yes, and I never felt bad about it either."

"Thank you for killing Grayden," she says in a tiny voice.

"I wish he weren't dead so I could make his death so much more painful. I could've made it last for days with every conceivable horror. He deserves nothing less," I growl, bitter remorse is a reminder that I wasn't there to protect her. "I'm sorry—"

Her soft hands reach my face. She leans down, her lips finally back on mine. I close my eyes and give in to her. The anger bleeds out of me.

We stay like that for a while, passionate kisses turning into lazy, slow ones. My arms wrap around her waist, clinging to her, until she pulls away to let us breathe.

"What really happened the night I got the crown?" She gently slaps my bicep. "The truth this time."

CHAPTER 41

LEON

"Only the truth from now on," I vow to her, and I mean it, bringing her hand up to my lips to kiss her knuckles. "A few months ago, Jedrick told me he had to live as long as he could to keep Grayden out of power since he didn't have it in him to kill his only living son. He was weak and I offered him a way to help Adreania after he died. He quickly agreed and I revealed myself to him. He was never kidnapped. When Jedrick was close to death, he arranged for two of his guards to get him out of Adreania and meet up with one of my soldiers in Kalvorn. I followed in case we were caught by Grayden. The plan was that when Jedrick died, I would take the crown and return to my place as Kalvorn's king. I told him Kalvorn and Adreania would merge into one kingdom and flourish once more, but it was always my intention to place Lyrora on the throne."

"Why wouldn't he have let Lyrora inherit if he didn't want Grayden to rule?" Izadella asks, annoyed.

"Jedrick would never let a woman have power. But before any of that happened, I needed you safe. I wanted you to escape before all the chaos and potential carnage. You would have gone to Kalvorn, and even though you were married, or so I thought, you would be near me. That was enough. To have you happy and safe in Kalvorn even if I couldn't have you. To know the family you loved was safe, that your children would never again know empty bellies and cruel kings. Even if you being so close would drive me mad with desire, I would take whatever crumbs of your attention I could get. I'm ashamed to say I was already plotting ways to get you alone again as often as I could. I knew what you were to me, even though I had no idea how it was possible for a human to be my mate. Your soul called to me from that very first night."

Her eyes glimmer with tears. "I felt it, too."

I wipe away one that escapes. "I was going to commission royal jewelry, repairs of old family heirlooms, anything for a moment of your time, your talent. I was greedy for every second with you. All of my dreams came to an abrupt halt when I found you on that forest floor with the ground burnt black around you and the crown on your head. At first, I was just terrified for you, that it had hurt you in some way."

Guilt pulls at her beautiful face. "You must have been angry with me."

I laugh. "I waited for the blinding outrage to come, for the overwhelming grief that I had wasted a century of my life just for the crown to slip from my fingers like it had done for generations before me, but it never came. The crown was out of Adreania, I was a king, and you had the crown. I knew it meant something, validation we were destined to be together. I wanted to toss you over my shoulders and take you straight to Kalvorn, to crown you queen and tell you everything."

She laughs and it is a glorious sound. "That would *not* have ended well for you."

I join in her humor before taking a long breath. "I was so close to revealing myself, but then you said you were going to Ellova, the birthplace of Inara, a place I didn't think existed anymore. I followed you because I loved you, but I also had a responsibility to my kingdom to find out if Ellova would be friend or foe to us in the upcoming war with Adreania. I had to put my people first at that moment. They are all descendants of Ellova, too. Maybe they could return, to know the true heart of magic again. I'm so sorry I hid who I really was from you. It was never to truly deceive you."

She stares up at the dark ceiling, appearing to collect her thoughts. "I wondered why you took to learning my identity so well. The fact I wasn't a human named Arra didn't seem to faze you. In fact, you seemed oddly delighted that I was fae," she teases with a small smile.

My chest feels lighter with every word I speak, the truth flowing out, and I'm desperate to tell her everything, to have no secrets or lies between us ever again. "Oh, I had never been so happy when you told me you were fae, too. It was further proof we were destined to be together."

"And the journal?"

"Lyrora found it hidden away in the Royal Library and shared it with me. She thought it may include something about the healing magic Inara brought with her when she became queen. I understood some of it, but Inara had written in ancient Ellovian and I wasn't a very good student when my tutors attempted to teach me the language as a child. It was actually Lyrora who sent a message to me through my hawk, Lula, that you had been taken. She let us know where you would be last night."

I squeeze her hand, drawing it to my mouth, and press my lips to the soft skin.

"Anything else I need to know?" Izadella sounds a little tired. Maybe we should sleep some more. I hate the dark crescents under her eyes, a reminder of her mistreatment at the hands of dead men.

"I renounced the throne of Kalvorn. Callen will remain king and retain the name of Zilas, ruling in my place. I'm just Leon now."

Her eyebrows draw together but I cannot tell what she is thinking. "Is your brother truly a good man? A kind and just ruler?"

"Yes. He is what Kalvorn needs and deserves. He's a family man, as well. Apparently, I became an uncle while I was away." She smiles at that, but it fades when I speak the next part. "My mother died when I was in Adreania, but she had many plans for me while I was away. One was that when I returned with the crown, I would immediately marry, so I left knowing I was betrothed."

Her eyes narrow.

I press on quickly to get past this part. "I sent a letter the night after I met you, cutting it off. Turns out my intended bride had fallen in love with my brother long before that and had already had two children with him by the time I sent the letter. My brother and I had a long chat about it when I returned home."

Izadella blows out a puff of air. "*Multiple* children? You are a kind brother to forgive that, but I suppose fate was playing a part in all of our lives." She pushes me onto my back and lies over me once more with her head resting between my head and shoulder.

I pull my arms around her and inhale deeply.

"I'm forever sorry, for every lie and half-truth," I whisper in her hair, kissing the rosy-golden strands. "I couldn't reveal anything to you until you chose me! Chose me over your fear, or anything else. Revealing myself meant revealing my kingdom, my family, my people. I needed to know you loved me the way I loved you. I thought that was the best way, but clearly, I was wrong."

"Trust goes both ways. I should have listened to you, allowed you to explain. I forgive you." Her words are soft.

"I have not even begun to earn your forgiveness. Izadella, I saw the golden marks on your skin before I brought you back." I choke on the words. "I cannot believe I hurt you so badly. I broke your heart so completely."

A tear slides down my face, but she is quick to brush it away with her thumb. "Everything went wrong so quickly but I know you never meant to hurt me. I forgive you." She must know I need to hear it again, not believing her because she whispers, "I forgive you. You came for me. You fought for me and brought me back to life."

"It's not enough, but I will try for as long as you let me make it up to you," I promise.

Her response comes in the form of a long kiss. Each press of her lips and swipe of her tongue brings me hope everything will be all right.

Finally, she rises off me, stretching her arms above her head. The low cut of her neckline draws me in, making my mouth water.

"I'm starving. Prisoners aren't exactly fed well. One of the many downfalls of imprisonment. Let's go find Nueena and see what the kitchen has for us." She smiles down at me, but it falls when I don't smile back at her. "Oh no, where is she? Nueena!" She stops yelling when I pull her down, holding her face in my hands.

"The last time we saw her, she was hovering in the sky and placing a wall of protective magic around Ellova. I don't know where she is now, but we can't get through it. I'm sorry; I tried. The forest is filled with iron guards looking for you, or her, or us. It's not safe out there. Do you remember?"

Recognition fills her face, and she yanks herself away from me. "We need to go find her. She came for me! I need to be with her! I need to know she's okay!" She rises quickly from the pillows before I can stop her.

"Izadella, we cannot reach her right now."

"Wait, where are we?" The moment she stands, the crystal lights illuminate the cave. Her flabbergasted expression freezes on her face as she looks around the crystal cave. "Oh, fuck."

I jump up, ready to grab my father's sword. "What's wrong?"

She's staring at me, lips in a perfect *O* and eyes blown wide.

"Leon, we're in the Zemra temple!"

CHAPTER 42

IZADELLA

Oh fuck, we're mates.

Soulbonded mates.

Leon and I stare at each other.

"We're Zemras?" he asks quietly.

I laugh in wonderment. Not just lovers, not just mates, but Zemras.

For the first time, I truly take in the beauty around me. The floor shines with smooth crystals and stone in all shapes and sizes, the reflections from the lights above decorate the crystal walls with rainbows.

The temple accepted us.

We will be connected in ways we cannot fathom. Our magic, our lives. We will never be alone in our minds again. We will share everything, know everything about each other.

It is both terrifying and enchantingly beautiful, lighting up every part of me with unbridled joy.

My breaths come out too fast.

Zemras.

Zemras.

I never could have imagined this moment truly happening, never dreamt of a soulbond. We were meant to be together. It was not infatuation or lust, but our lives and hearts woven together before we ever knew each other. We were bound in magic and would always experience that calling towards each other, that pressing need to never be parted.

He was meant to be mine. Forever.

We would share our magic, our *lifespans*, and I would have a full fae life. My family will not have to mourn me for hundreds of years. I get to spend that time with Leon, being loved by him. He brought me back to life and now I get to live, truly live with him at my side.

I'm dizzy with the joy of it all, my anger with him fading away.

Panic blooms in his expression as the blood drains from his face. "Izadella, I swear I didn't know what this was. It was warm and dry. I would have never gone in if I had known. I wouldn't have taken that choice away from you!" He grips my hand, anguish in his eyes. "We need to leave *immediately*."

My body is so filled with joy I can't comprehend his words. How have I not floated away with happiness? I beam at him, needing him to reflect my elation. "Leave? Leon. We need to complete the Zemra soulbonding ritual." I grab his face, desperate for one long kiss, but he steps out of my reach.

What is wrong with him?

"We can't." His words are strained, hopeless.

My stomach twists in fear at the pain on his features. "Ellova's grave! Leon, we are Zemras, we—the stones! We must find them. I don't know how we do that. Normally there's a temple guardian to guide us. It's like a marriage ceremony."

I don't know how to explain how important this is to someone who didn't grow up knowing the stories, wishing for their own journeys here.

Tears well up in my eyes, the eyes his own won't meet. Why isn't he happy? Why won't he share in this joy with me?

He just spoke of how much he loves me.

I tug on his arm again, trying to urge him away from the door, but he pulls me to him.

"Strawberries, I never needed a temple to tell me you were

meant for me, but we can never become bonded Zemras." He presses his lips to my forehead, standing as still as a statue.

Is this a nightmare? Am I still dead and this the bitter afterlife?

Anger bursts out of me and I shove at his chest. "After all that we have gone though, all your lies I endured, and all my heartache...it was supposed to have been worth it. Why even bother bringing me back if you intended to break my heart like this all over again? Now we stand in the Zemra temple, a place I never thought I would be, with proof that you and I are meant to be together forever, and you don't *want* me anymore?"

My words slice at me deeper than daggers, my head spinning, but they hurt Leon, too.

He tries to take me in his arms again, but I sidestep him, my fist balled at my side.

"No, no, never! Of course I want you, Izadella. You and I are meant to be together. We just can't soulbond," he pleads with me. "*I love you.*"

"No!" I shout, my resentment echoing off the crystal walls. "You do not get to tell me you love me and then deny me the one thing I didn't even dare to dream about wanting." Tears stream down my face.

"We can be together, *will* be together, but I can be your Zemra in title only. Why can that not be enough? To know what we are to each other?"

I glare at him, hoping he can sense all the pain he has brought me, the sorrow his words are causing. "Give me the reason or I walk out of this temple, and you will *never* see me again. Nueena will wage war on your kingdom if you ever try to find me."

"Izadella, please, I—"

Then it's over.

I found love for the briefest of moments and that is all I will ever know. "Let's go, then. I wish to find my family." My voice is hollow, shoving down the rising pain and regret threatening to swallow me whole. I turn to run, to leave a part of myself in this temple and never look back, but he grabs my arm.

"I'm dying."

The fight drains out of me leaving only shattering pain. "What?" I whisper. The ache in his voice tells me he speaks the truth.

He lets go of me and rips open the top of his shirt.

I gasp at the scars. They are the same ones I bore before he healed me, and I know exactly what fate awaits him to carry them on his own body. My heart can barely handle this devastation.

"It happened at the same time yours did, in the bathing pool. I couldn't handle the pain I caused you. We cannot be Zemras because it will only cause you more suffering. I will not do that to you. You and I *will* have a beautiful life together while we can. I want to spend every moment with you I have left. I will always love you, more than you will ever know, but I will not let you tie yourself to me just to be driven mad by my death through the bond. You have gone through so much already. Let me love you to the very end." His voice breaks at the end, sending ripples of torment within me.

I stare at him in horror.

Did I truly find my Zemra only for it to end like this? I refuse to be denied a life with him beside me. The very thought sends agony to every part of me.

"Your healing magic?" Surely, he can fix this.

He looks down and shakes his head, trying to hide his misery. "I did try. I promise I did, but nothing worked. It's nearly gone now, like whispers of smoke when I reach for it. My powers have been depleted and my fae life force is draining out of me."

Gone? How can it be gone?

I step close to him, forcing him to look up at me. "Did you use the last of it to save me?" I whisper. Now it's my turn for my voice to break.

One of his hands cups my face, his thumb running over my bottom lip. "It was worth it."

My soul aches to shatter, to fall to the floor and sob, but I am prepared to fight fate with claws and teeth.

Zemra magic is wholly different from other types. It is meant to preserve souls. That's why lifespans are tied together, so one never needs to live without the other.

That magic will save him.

Before he can stop me, I grab his hand and pull. Hard. He stumbles forward but stays upright as I yank him towards the other side of the cavernous space.

"We need to find our stones. They are incredibly important." We reach a small dais with marble stairs leading up to it. "Nueena said the stones choose us."

"Izadella, *please.* You would feel every moment of my fading from this world if we completed the bond. I would love *nothing* more than to truly be your Zemra. I just would never wish to bring you pain, especially the kind you will experience if we become Zemras."

I dig my fingers into him and take a deep breath, knowing he will argue with me at every point. "I'm fully aware of what an enervation death feels like, and I'm not choosing this lightly. Your death will break me whether or not we're soulbonded. Your healing magic brought me back from the dead. Zemras share magic. Let me try to save you, too. The crystals will amplify the magic you have left. It could be enough—"

"Izadella…"

"I understand you wish to save me from devastation, but, Leon, we have to *try.* I would rather be Zemras for a day, for an hour, than to only have you as a lover. If you are going to die, let me at least know what it is like to truly call you mine. Let our souls be as one for whatever time we have left."

Gods, it feels like begging, and I hate it, but I refuse to leave here unbonded because of his stubbornness.

He hesitates, but I can see him start to succumb to my wishes.

I squeeze his hand, gentler this time. "Please, stop being so noble. Back in the garden, when you first arrived, you asked me a question. If the roles were reversed, and I were the mortal and you were the one to live on without me, would you still tell me it's not worth it? Now I'm going to ask you the same thing. If I stood where you do, would you deny me a Zemra bond?"

Leon stares at me with so much longing it hurts me. "I would not."

"So why deny me now when we have a chance to save you? Please try. *Please* give us the opportunity of a life together. If we leave here unbonded, you die, but if there is a chance we can share magic and I can save you, just as you did me, we have a shot at a long and happy life together, as Zemras."

The cruelty of it all. To find my Zemra only to have him slip away from me.

He shakes his head "And what if it doesn't work? I will not break your heart again. I will not be here to heal it. You can survive my death if you do not experience it with me. You are strong! I know you can. You have so much to live for, so many here in Ellova who love you."

"Please, I cannot lose you after what I've gone through. Zemra magic is powerful and ancient. We have no idea what it can do for us."

"My love—"

"We deserve a future together. The stars aligned for us to find each other. Every tear and heartbreak brought us here and this cannot be the end. I need you!" My words fade until they are a wisp between us. "I don't want to be alone again."

I'm desperate to ease the devastation that flashes across his face. "What if it doesn't work? What if our magic together is not enough and you feel everything through the bond? My agony at abandoning you, my fear of harming you in ways I can never repair? The loss of time with my brother? The anger at never knowing my niece and nephew?"

"Why are you the only one who gets to sacrifice for love? A bit hypocritical wouldn't you say? You would gladly share my pain. Why stop me? You will feel all of that but let me share your burden. That's what love is; what a soulbond is. It's the sharing of pain and joy."

Leon will not hear my words, determined to die the hero, so I step up to him. His short beard is rough against my fingertips when I take his face in mine. My lips meet his and I let my longing linger there. Our kiss is slow, allowing us to taste each other's sorrow.

He holds me so tightly that his fingertips might leave a memory there forever. When we finally break apart, I expect him to keep fighting me, but instead he says, "Anything for you."

CHAPTER 43

IZADELLA

Leon presses our foreheads together. "We will try. If that is what you truly want, I will not deny you. I only seek to protect you, even if it's from myself, and I wish to spend every last moment proving my love to you."

Relief floods me. Even if this doesn't work, we have to try.

A soft grinding noise comes from one side of the cave. Anticipation has my stomach in knots when an ornamental basin held up by an onyx pillar rises up out of the crystal floor. Leon steps protectively in front of me.

I peer around him. "I think it wants us to go up there."

He nods, remaining between the basin and me.

"I can tell you wish you had a sword right now," I tease him, trying to release some of the tension between us. "Such petrifying bowls about."

"I *do* wish that," he retorts. "This might be a sacred place but it's unfamiliar and I'm feeling quite uneasy at the moment."

I squeeze his hand. "It may be cloaked in secrecy, but I think Nueena would have mentioned it if the temple was unsafe."

He nods, giving me a small smile. "Perhaps we must face a series of dreadful trials we must overcome to prove our devotion."

I snort. "Gods, I hope not. I think dying is all the excitement I can handle for the next century."

No, only hope and happiness ahead of us. I refuse to believe anything else.

The basin is filled with viridescent water. A flickering light starts to glow in the center. The liquid ripples and my hope rises just like the two shards of crystal do. They look exactly like Nueena and Tavien's but are a deep emerald, rather than their purple ones.

They're gorgeous and all ours, meant for *us*, if we choose to take them.

"Leon, once we pick up our crystals, the ritual will begin."

I've dreamt of this moment, but I suddenly feel small. He will be able to feel the depths of my desires, how deeply my heart feels things.

We turn towards each other, and he cups my face with both hands. "Izadella, there is no part of you I do not already love. You are the fire that burns within me. To forge our souls together would be the greatest honor of my life."

His lips touch mine in a kiss that is so incredibly sweet. Leon was always meant to be mine. I can feel it even now—the draw to him and now to the crystals that seem eager to be ours.

We break apart, both ready to take each other as Zemras, prepared for whatever might come.

I hold my breath as I pick one up, Leon following my lead.

Our Zemra stones glow in the palms of our hands.

"Oh." Unfamiliar magic swirls around us. The soulbinding magic tugs at my chest, settling into every part of me, flowing in my blood and sweetly sinking into my bones. It twists in my soul, my own magic shifting, changing. It's beautiful.

With the way Leon's chest rises, I know he feels it, too.

We lean towards each other at the same time. The moments our lips touch, an explosion of power within me nearly takes me to my knees. A swell of my magic collides with Leon's, dancing together between us in the blissful merging of our souls and fae abilities before slamming back into our chests. New emotions—*Leon's* emotions, how precious I am to him—rush into me.

My own adoration and respect for him races into his soul, how long I have loved him, how deeply.

His very soul sings to mine. Leon's endless devotion, over-whelming love and gratitude come in waves with an undercurrent of guilt over his deception. I know he can feel my own guilt that I wouldn't trust him.

I break our kiss. How can I relieve the crushing weight of his pain? "Oh, my love, it's all right. I understand and I forgive you. I do!"

He lets out a long breath, nodding at my words.

Every part of him—his essence and his fading life force—swirls within me. The hollowness is a sharp ache that shoots through the bond from both of us. Where once an internal palace held his healing magic, now lays a cavernous loss in his soul.

Beneath it all though, is the hovering shadow of death.

No, no, no. The Zemra magic was supposed to heal him.

I weep furious tears, slumping in his arms as torment erupts in me. Leon tries to flood the bond with love but my anger at the Zemra magic, that the bond will not save him, burns so much brighter. His guilt over allowing me to push for the soulbonding, while heavy, only feeds the flames of my misery.

"Shhhhh, my love." He holds my face with his strong hands. "We knew this was a possibility."

"No, *no.* The magic was supposed to heal you! Something is wrong!"

This is all my fault. If I had simply listened to what he had to say when he revealed himself, I wouldn't have broken both of our hearts. Everett never would have taken me. I wouldn't have been murdered.

He is going to die because I did not trust him.

My guilt and shame threaten to drown me.

I don't deserve a Zemra.

He shakes his head furiously, wiping the tears from my cheeks. "At the coronation ball, you asked me if we could forget about the future and pretend everything will be all right, just for one night. Do you remember?"

My anger has my teeth grinding together, but I nod. How could I forget?

He continues softly, "I will ask the same of you right now. We are going to forget the future. Tonight, only you and I exist. Our bond is a vow to each other. No matter what happens, let us have these moments. Let me give you one night where we are truly Zemras with no fear, no doubts. *Please.*"

Shoving down everything that hurts, I let his love fill me, calm me.

One night. The only thing we can promise each other now. "If this is all we have, I give every hour remaining to you."

I waste no moment, letting my greed for him and the sensation of safety in his protective arms flood me with delicious warmth. Our lips come together once more, slow and sweet, our emotions entwining. The love we share for each other shines within us— tender, obsessive, and fiercely protective—as a wave of passion sweeping me away.

I never wish to leave his embrace. Hunger for him takes over me, the likes I have never known.

"I love you, Leon." I tremble, overwhelmed with gratitude that he is my Zemra. If fate blessed us with each other but cursed us to have only a short life, we must make the most of every opportunity.

His hands move to my hips, gripping the torn fabric he finds. "I've always loved you."

He takes my face for another tender kiss as more tears stream down my face. I'm desperate for him, totally and completely, longing to be forged together with our bodies. My lips are on every part of his skin, his hands all over me. I want to crawl into the pillows with him and never leave.

Leon sheds his clothing. I trace the taunting enervation scars on his skin, a reminder my future is being ripped away from me, that I will be alone, as I've always been. He shakes his head, drawing my hands up and kisses my fingertips. His lips are a reminder of what we have now, and I hold on to that.

I pull off the remains of my wedding dress in a graceless motion, throwing it to the floor. Oh, how I will enjoy burning it.

Leon pulls me back to him and his lips brush mine, like he's never tasted anything so sweet. It feels like he imprints his very soul into mine. His hands are gentle and leisurely moving around, exploring and teasing. Lightning courses through my veins and an ache for him pulsates in my core. My body has longed for this moment before we ever met.

He is home, my universe shifting us to the center of it.

I need this moment with him, just him, to forget about everything that haunts us and to truly be together.

Leon's lips move to my jaw, and his hot mouth is all I can think about. I'm desperate for him to be inside me, nothing keeping us apart.

"I need you, right now. Please." With my stone in one hand, I push him back towards the bed. At the last moment he spins us, and I fall first into the bedding.

He moves down between my thighs, spreading me open, resting my legs on his massive shoulders.

"And I need *this*." His head swoops down into my cunt.

My breath hitches and I am lost in pleasure, the bond heightening this moment. My only thought is of his tongue and the many ways he could make me come with it.

His licks are frantic, shifting from long and slow to fast little circles around my clit. His fae hands are so much bigger now and he spreads my slit wide before him, teasing my entrance until I beg him to fill me. Leon thrusts two fingers into my blistering heat. Pleasure rises inside me. My panting, moaning, and screams echo around the cave. Damn it, his healer's hands know exactly what they're doing. As I'm splayed out before him, back arching, he uses his mouth, tongue, and pumping fingers to bring me over that edge.

Sucking on my swollen clit, he moans as he licks the proof of my arousal away.

My thighs shake next to his pointed ears, my breaths ragged, and yet he doesn't stop. He dips his fingers back in and hums his delight as his fingers slide in and out of my pooling essence while his thumb rocks over my sensitive bud. It's bliss. All I know is this unending pleasure. It's breathtakingly too much and not nearly enough.

"Leon, *please.*"

"Oh, Strawberries, your pleas are sweeter than honey." He kisses the inside of my thigh. "But I've waited years to fuck you, dreaming of it every night. I *will* be taking my time, so you'll need to beg harder than that."

He presses leisurely kisses and slow flicks of his tongue to my dripping cunt, adding a third finger, stretching me, priming my body for him. His touch is euphoric as his thumb moves faster. I cannot keep still, rocking my wide hips in time with his fingers and tongue. I cry out again, my second orgasm overwhelming me until I'm shoving his handsome face away, too sensitive for any more of his eager attentions.

His lips glisten with my release. "Beautiful, just beautiful, and all *mine.* What an honor." It's practically a growl. His voice is so rough I whimper with desire.

Leon crawls up towards me. His hands are all over my body in frantic, possessive motion, and his pupils are blown wide with lust. He leans forward, squeezing my breast, and playing with the tight tip before lavishing attention on the other with licks and kisses. While he teases my breast with his mouth, his hand slides between my legs, seeking my clit again, but it's my turn to torture him.

With my teasing touch, I grasp his cock, pumping the thick length of him, paying special attention to his tip. With his fae body, he is much bigger than the last time I held it. I see now why he spent so much time ensuring I was ready to accommodate his new width.

Leon pries my fingers off him. "Not 'til I'm inside you, my love. Then you can have all of me."

My legs are eagerly stretched out and ready for him.

He moves his cock to my entrance, but he pauses, eyes roaming my face. "Are you ready?"

I've lost the ability to speak, the lingering pleasure silencing my very thoughts. I can only nod enthusiastically at him. His lips curve into a feral smile when they meet mine. I kiss him back until I'm gasping and squirming under him. The stretch of him entering me is almost too much, even though he moves slowly. Our pleasure fuses together, amplifying it with every one of his shallow pumps filling me up and applying more pressure as he slides in and out with gentle hip thrusts.

"Please, tell me if I'm hurting you," he says with such care.

Tears of joy spring to my eyes and I shake my head as I cling to him.

I do not want him to be my sweet mortal healer at this moment. I demand my powerful fae Zemra to *ruin me*. To make up for all that lost time between us, for the time we will never have. To sweep away the feeling of frozen seawater prisons and fear-filled days apart from him.

To fuck away the feeling that I was lost, taken from him forever, trapped behind iron walls with men who only wished to harm me.

I need him to kiss away the dread of losing him.

Make me forget about the map of enervation scars on his chest pointing to my destruction.

When his striking length is finally all in, he gives me a moment to adjust to the pleasurable pressure between my thighs.

Our bond is glorious, alive with love, lust, and passion, an endless sea of pleasure and belonging.

Two bodies, one soul.

A strangled sob escapes me, my euphoria enveloping me, consuming me like a forge fire. His pumps slow, letting me catch my breath with his stiff cock still inside me. I press soft kisses to his cheeks and neck.

His strong hips continue their rocking, his speed increasing with every thrust. "I love you, Izadella. You, your body, us."

I chase the feeling of pleasure rapidly intensifying within me again, its throbbing need to tumble over the edge with him.

We need this forever, our hands and lips on each other.

Blinding devotion in every taste and touch.

He's *mine*. Never to be parted, never alone.

The thought makes me giddy. His love engulfs my soul as

another orgasm builds. His teeth graze the underside of my breast before his lips find my other nipple.

Tired of my breasts receiving all of his affections, I grab a fistful of his hair at the back of his scalp and tug his mouth free. He grunts in amusement, and his answering smile is near-feral, his lips finally returning to my mouth, our tongues reunited. He sears my lips with one last rough, demanding kiss, consuming my ragged breaths before looking down at me.

His arms shake, eyes unfocused, his control dangerously close to breaking.

Leon grasps the back of my neck to keep me in place as his hips snap against me, over and over again.

The gentle Leon I fell in love with has vanished, replaced by something deliciously brutish, determined to consume all of me. Uncompromising strength pounds into me, my breasts bouncing, and he watches the way my body ricochets with every thrust. Hungry adoration and greedy eyes. His cock grinding against my inner walls brings a new type of lust, different from his fingers and tongue. Leon pours all of his emotions over us.

Hips strike fast; he removes himself before slamming back, encouraged by my whines of pleasure.

His movement becomes erratic, but it hits everywhere I need it to.

The pressure of his cock deepens as his speed increases, over-powering my senses. His worship of my body and the desperate way he touches me are exquisite.

I grip the sheets, his hips thrusting me with such force, such determination, I scream his name.

"Am I hurting you?" he gasps out. His distress at the thought is a balm to my soul, but something flickers inside him. Just for a moment, a tiny flash of healing magic, so small it's almost not even there, as if the very idea he has hurt me was enough to bring it forth one last time.

I grab that spark, holding it so tightly, not letting it fade away. My own magic swirls around it. The fire within me that melts gold in my palms joins that small burst of him and the magic we share between us. Our Zemra stones flare, magic shifting inside of us.

That spark of his healing magic combines with mine, growing and growing.

Leon keeps moving, lost in our bond as it is flooded with longing and lust. So much pleasure swells between us that I'm overtaken with wonder as that healing magic bursts within me, rushing to my now-luminous hand.

Awestruck, I shove my palms against his chest, right over those horrible scars. They light up at my touch, as if liquid gold flows there, glowing. Another thundering orgasm takes over me, but this time Leon follows me over that edge, erupting inside me with heated force.

Leon gasps. The scars fade until his chest is perfect once more, a new strength returning to him. That hollow place inside him fills up and overflows with his own magic, but it holds something new there, too.

Our combined magic.

He's healed! Whole and stronger than ever.

We stare at each other in wonder until I begin to cry. Pure joy descends into our bond and Leon quickly turns over on his back, settling me over his hips.

"Izadella," he says, eyes blown wide, but we are both lost for words.

I lay my head on his chest, my tears hitting the place the scars used to be. His strong arms go around me, one hand circling my back, the other in my hair.

I'm not going to lose him.

He's going to live.

His gratitude overwhelms me, sending even more tears spilling out of me.

We have our future back and brighter than ever. My half-mortal lifespan is tied to his fae one. The hourglass that burdened us shatters, taking with it all that haunted us.

Everything we thought we had lost has been restored.

"You did it. You saved me." His words send ripples of elation through the bond. "Thank you."

We are Zemras, forever. Unburdened by mortality and a cruel fate.

I lift up my head and find him staring at me with so much love in his eyes it's nearly blinding.

"I told you it would work."

"Izadella, darling, I will never doubt you again."

I giggle at that.

We lie there for what feels like hours, no words needed, every feeling shared through the bond. Every sensation of love and precious devotion swirls between us. We both drift in and out of sleep, soothed by the satisfaction of our orgasms and lazy touches.

I trail my finger up and down his tipped ear, a smile on his lips.

"Viella was right about Zemra sex. How are you feeling?" he asks, still slightly out of breath.

"It was perfect." I kiss his cheek, softly murmuring, "Better than everything I've ever fantasized about."

Leon's lopsided grin turns wicked. "I wish to know more about these fantasies."

"Later. I want to return to the palace and tell everyone of our bond!" I slip out of his arms, and he groans with displeasure but follows me. Soft, golden robes of silk have appeared on the foot of the bed.

Once we are done dressing, we search for a door with a direct path back home, not wishing to leave the way we came. A portal tree, perhaps, or a long tunnel.

A throat clears behind us.

"Hello, my dewlings."

CHAPTER 44

IZADELLA

light flashes and Nyvenah stands at a back entrance that was not there before. Her glossy, joyous eyes stare at the two of us. Her smile, so full of pride that matches mine, fills my heart with elation that is overshadowed as fear spikes within me.

No, never in me. In Leon.

I turn to ask why, but he quickly moves me behind him, his body tense, and he shoves his Zemra stone into my hand.

"Nyvenah, I promise we did not seek out the temple. I stumbled upon it when we needed shelter and Izadella was unconscious. I did not know what this place was until she woke up and explained it." He walks backward, pushing me with him. "Any Zemra temple law we broke was unintentional. I will not be separated from her again. I am not Ellovian. Any attempt to separate us will result in war."

Leon waves his hand, and a small dark gem appears out of thin air. He slams it into the ground with a blast of magic.

No! I do not wish to leave! I reach one hand out for her.

Nyvenah's shouts to stop are drowned out by the swirling wind. Leon throws himself over me before the temple spins around us. "Hold on!"

His twisted terror at losing me once more blasts my soul, and the whirling wind makes it hard to breathe. We spin and spin, the sensation so much like that of a tree portal.

Endless waves of his emotions cloud my thoughts. Leon's hand secures my head to his chest, the spinning finally slowing down.

When we stop, he doesn't let me go. His panic continues to flood me, and I know he can feel my anger rising.

He's taking me from my home. Even if he would never take me somewhere unsafe, wherever we're going is not where I wish to be. I need to find Nueena. I long for my own bed and to be reunited with Farren.

I push against his chest, and he reluctantly releases me with heaving breaths.

I'm ready to release my anger at him but Leon's fear keeps rising uncontrollably. Shaking, he says, "She can't take you...Won't let her...Mine." His voice is sharp as daggers.

Is this how he felt the whole time I was away? I'm drowning in his fear and guilt. It's endless within him. My own anguish at the sight of him is not something I can keep from him, and it only adds to his guilt.

I need to convince him no one is coming to take me from him.

Nyvenah will not punish us for finding the temple in a moment of great need. Her smile when she found us told me that, but Leon clearly did not understand. We did not seek the temple like Nueena and Tavien did; we did not break its laws.

She did not gaze at us with disappointment or dread that she must dole out punishment like she once did with her own daughter.

Nyvenah knew what having a Zemra would mean to me.

"Oh, Leon, it's all right." I wrap my arms around him, attempting to settle his soul from his swell of sorrow.

"No, it's not," he rasps, pulling me tighter against him. "Hide... Never parting."

I don't know how to calm him, and he pulls back suddenly, grabbing my hand to leave.

We stand on a dais in an elaborate gold-and-emerald throne room.

For some odd reason a tree is bursting in the middle of the room.

Has Leon taken me to his home, to Kalvorn?

The main door opens, and six guards of some kind rush towards us but stop when they see him.

"Leave us! Now!" Leon bellows and they quickly follow his instructions.

Once we are alone, I shove him onto the throne. "We're not going anywhere, Leon."

"*Please*, we have to, I just got you back." He attempts to stand and I grasp his shoulders, pressing down as he stares up at me with helpless eyes of emerald, his panic still overwhelming, but at least he obeys.

Euphoria flares within me. The throne he sits on is gold!

My jewelsmith magic rushes to greet me in a blissful reunion. It shines within me, whirling, desperate to be released when I touch the curved armrest.

I nearly collapse with joy at its return.

With my magic back, I feel whole once again.

It burns with loving fire in my veins, an effervescent caress on my soul.

Happy tears spring to my eyes. I never thought I would have my magic back, the magic of my mother and the women before her.

The sensation of it is glorious in my veins.

Leon must feel it too, the elation that erupts when the gold beneath his arms swoops up like water, glinting as it moves. I command the metal to wrap around Leon's forearms, cuffing him to the chair. His eyes narrow at his newfound confinement, and when he tries to lunge forward, he cannot.

A new type of heartache flickers in him, in me. Does he think I'm going to leave him here and return to Ellova alone?

I slide one knee, then the other, on each side of his legs, settling over him. He continues to struggle against his bonds, so I take his face into my hands.

"Leon, my love, my Zemra." I place a soft kiss on his lips, a bulge quickly growing between us. "No one is going to keep us apart for entering the temple. You didn't know where you were. I was lost to the realm in a deep sleep, and you needed to keep me safe. We did not seek out the temple purposely, so we never knowingly tried to break the sacred temple laws."

I circle my finger around the headrest, stealing some of its gold.

No one will notice.

My magic sings to me. Following my command, the metal stretches out to a thin chain that swirls around my Zemra stone, leading up to a necklace. I fasten the sparkling emerald around my neck.

It glows when it touches my skin, and a tear slides down my face.

To be able to use my own magic to create my Zemra necklace is the greatest gift Leon has no idea he has given me.

He may have abdicated the throne for love, but he is Kalvorn's rightful king by blood and now a piece of his throne, his birthright, will always be with him.

Leon's shoulders slump when I place his Zemra stone around his neck.

The stones are what amplify our bond. If we are not holding or wearing them, our connection will be weaker, and the further away we are from each other without them, the harder it will be to sense each other.

Now that both stones rest against our flushed skin, our emotions vividly tangle together.

I try to reason with him. "Nyvenah was truly happy for us. Nueena and Tavien finding the temple was a carefully calculated act. They knew they were breaking the law. They spent months researching and innocently asking questions as if they were just curious. Tavien snuck into restricted libraries. Nueena lied when asked why she had such an interest in the temple. The law states that those who *seek* the temple are at the mercy of its punishments. Did you seek out the temple? Did you know what it held inside?"

He shakes his head violently, his long hair falling into his face. I push back the black-and-silver strands, my fingers tangling in them while I hold his head up to look at me.

"*No,*" he rasps. "I only sought to keep you warm and safe. That's why I went inside. We cannot be sure if we are immune to its punishments. I was not ignorant of its law." His breathing is wild and strained, his yearning for me burns in our chests.

Panic and pain still overshadow any other emotion I can sense from him, his eyes wide in distress, distrust etched in the lines of his face.

I wish to bring him peace in a way only Zemras can for their mates.

With trembling hands, I make my way down his chest, caressing the skin there. His cock and my core are only separated by the slip of fabric at his waist. He is so much broader in his fae form, thick with muscle, beautiful in that way only fae can be. Lower still I go until I reach the tie of his robe, unraveling the knot to free his length. Leon lets out a deep groan when I take it in my hand, his head rolling back against the throne as I slowly move, peacefully pumping it.

Need and gratitude overshine his fear, longing for me replacing his need to hide me away. Good. My own desire to soothe away his sorrow with my touch, my body, grows wild within me.

I center myself above him, slowly lowering onto his waiting cock. "Strawberries," is all he moans.

Raw lust fills us both, impossible to tell who felt it first. His pleasure dances with mine, and our magic swirls together.

My new bond is far more intense than I could have ever imagined. Desperate need for him floods me once more.

Measured movements quickly become frantic. Leon's fists are balled and white-knuckled with want at his inability to touch me now that the gold of the throne ties him down, but I know the tease is adding to the moment, anticipation joining the constellation of his emotions.

Each powerful thrust of his hips meets mine with a desperate motion, the movement of my breast has his tongue sliding over his lips with lust.

I laugh and sit up, leaning forward to grant this unvoiced desire.

He moans again as he takes my nipple into his warm, waiting mouth, teasing it.

I slow so he can take his time with each breast, hips shifting with delicious leisurely rocking, hitting the perfect place within me.

The building of pleasure fades, so I chase it again, gliding myself back down and rolling against him at the perfect angle. We moan together.

Him. Us. It's delicious.

My hips rise and fall, pumping over and over again.

I grip one of his shoulders for balance as I rock myself on his cock. His eyes track my other hand as it slides down my stomach to my clit, gliding over the wetness in a rhythmic motion 'til I'm shaking.

His love and desire pour onto me through the bond like a waterfall.

Our entwined desire and lust for each other are an experience like no other. I had always heard sex with your Zemra was different, but this borders on otherworldly, unending ecstasy.

The connection between us is an endless ocean of love and desire. I know his soul as deeply as I know mine. Every facet of him shines like a diamond within me. Our very being swirls together in a joyous meld.

Leon and I break apart, collapsing against each other through the waves of our overwhelming orgasm. His hips sweep upward to extend my pleasure and it has me moaning all over again, gasping and clinging to him.

While I try to catch my breath, he presses featherlight kisses to my shoulders, his satisfaction and gratitude gracing me.

His emotions are calmer now, his breaths labored in the aftermath of his release, and we stay close together on the throne. My arms are wrapped around his neck, and I kiss him softly on his lips and cheeks, neck and shoulders. I let my everlasting love for him flow. His eyes close and a tear slips out that I brush away. Each press of my lips erases a little of his shame and guilt, freeing us both of the torment of his soul.

"Do you trust me?" I whisper into his lips.

It takes him a moment to open his glassy eyes, and he slowly nods, expecting what I'm about to say.

"We must return to Ellova soon. I will not miss Nueena's coronation, and I need to see my family. No one will try to take me, I promise."

"We will find clothing here to change into and return."

Satisfied he will not attempt to take me anywhere else, I touch the golden throne. My magic swirls out of me and into the metal, releasing Leon's arms and returning the carved armrest as if it had never shifted its shape.

Being able to freely use my magic again has brought its own type of renewal to my soul.

His forearms are deep red from the friction, but before I can feel guilt over my magic, he rubs each arm once, his healing magic erasing it. I wish to kiss him but before I can rise on my toes, his lips are passionately on mine, sensing that desire within me. It is intimacy I could have never imagined.

When we finally break apart, he intertwines our hands, and we leave the throne room.

The windows we pass reveal glittering stars fading into dusk.

"The temple's doors only open at dawn. How can it be night again?" I ask him, guards in the hallways bowing to Leon.

"Best not to question the magical love temple." That earns him a giggle, and he adds, "The hours seemed endless when I thought you wouldn't awaken but you did sleep for most of the day."

Once we reach his room, I immediately explore, eager to know everything about his past. It is a beautiful space, yet an emptiness has a hold here. Plenty of books, maps on the walls, drawings of plants and animals, family portraits, and a few wooden toys, aged with time. Proof a young Leon lived here, but now it's more of a museum than a home.

My heart aches for his young self, thrust into a duty he couldn't escape. He senses my pain for him and attempts to soothe it through the bond.

Now that he is free, I wish for him to truly live for himself, free of the weight of expectations. What type of life does he want?

He quickly changes into clothing worthy of royalty. The dark green vest is delicately decorated with golden swirls over a fitted tunic. Emeralds dot the ends of his collar with a gold chain that hangs over his chest.

Handsome and all mine.

Lust builds in us, and I am about to pull him down to the bed, but we are interrupted by a strong knock at the door.

"Leon, are you there?"

A different type of excitement blooms in my chest as Leon's eyes light up.

"It's Callen, well, Zilas now, as he will remain as king," he says to me before calling to his brother, "One moment! Do you mind getting Estelle and we shall meet you at our library? Please have some attendants bring food as well, whatever is ready."

"Of course. We will see you in a few minutes." His brother's voice fades away.

Leon glances down at my silk Zemra robe. "We need to find you something else to wear." My torn wedding dress is forgotten on the floor of the temple, not that I wish to ever see it again.

He opens the wardrobe and pulls out a black tunic and a belt.

I roll up the sleeves and belt the shirt. With the top of the robe hidden, it appears that I am wearing a skirt of some kind. He pulls out a light traveling cloak towards the back and secures the brass clasps at my neck.

He leans down for a quick kiss, and I savor it.

"Ready to meet your new family?"

"Oh, yes!"

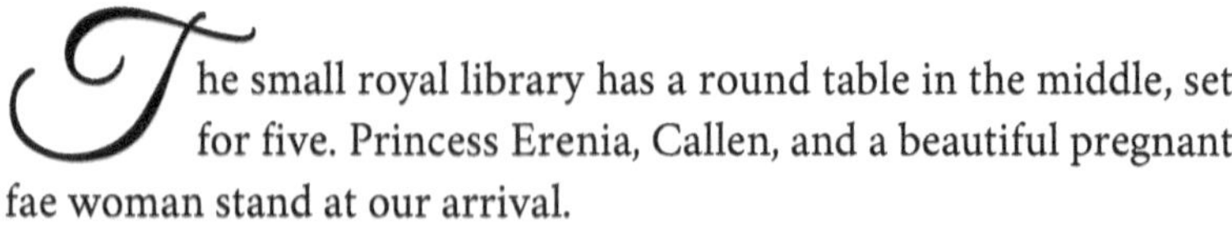

The small royal library has a round table in the middle, set for five. Princess Erenia, Callen, and a beautiful pregnant fae woman stand at our arrival.

I give them a polite curtsy, which only amuses them, Erenia stepping forward to hug me.

"I'm glad to see you are all right," she says.

Her icy blue eyes still hold deep sadness, but her smile is genuine. She steps back, allowing Leon to stand next to me, his arm draped around my waist.

His pride is luminous and overwhelming in our bond.

"This is Izadella, my Zemra. My love, this is my brother, Callen, and his mate, Estelle."

"Zemras?" Estelle whispers, her eyes wide on our glowing stones. "So, the myths are true? The Zemra temple still exists?" Her words are so full of longing.

I smile softly at my new sister, understanding that feeling. "Yes, it is hidden in Ellova. We have laws surrounding it, but when I return home, I will let the temple guides and Guardians know another fae kingdom deserves access to it, too."

Estelle and Callen exchange a look so full of love and hope my chest bursts with pride.

It's beautiful that Leon and his brother have found such transcendent love in the midst of uncertainty. Tyrant kings, impending wars, crowns set to destroy, and years apart, separated as children. Yet, they stand here, finally reunited with the loves of their lives by their sides in the castle they were born in.

How generous fate has been.

Leon guides me to the table, our hunger gnawing at us. "I need to ensure Izadella eats something. Please join us."

I give him a tired but grateful smile. The urge to feed me and pull me back into his bed tugs at him but he knows I must eat. He can sense that beneath my rising hunger is apprehension at being so far from home, missing my friends and family.

We must return soon if he is to truly soothe that ache for me.

His own concern at returning is there, too. He believes me when I say we will be spared any punishment for our unbidden journey to the Zemra temple, but he fears he may have made the situation worse by taking me. I know my family will understand.

"Erenia, when do you set sail?" Leon asks.

"Tomorrow, if the weather allows. Lyrora has sent a ship with all of my belongings. A few Adreanians who wish to start a new life in Versairen will be joining me. There is much my father is unaware of, but I will ensure a continued alliance with Lyrora and now Kalvorn."

Callen raises his glass in her direction.

"Thank you for the coin bag that last night I saw you. That was very generous." I say, when she thought I was just a mortal in need of funds to escape with my family at the last bazaar.

"It was entirely selfish." Erenia's smile is sly. "I hoped it was enough for you to get wherever Leon was going so he would have something else to patter on about besides his obsession with the pretty jewelry maker."

I giggle at that. It seems both of our friends are astoundingly good at embarrassing us.

"Well, it all worked out in the end. I hope your arrival home and reunion is everything you wish it to be."

Her shoulders relax and she nods, glancing down at her plate. Something unspoken passes between them, brotherly affection and hope for her. Whatever or whoever is waiting for her in Versairen, I hope it brings her peace.

"How did you know you had healing magic?" I ask Leon, sensing Erenia wishes to be alone in her thoughts. He is devouring roasted fish in a creamy sauce and seasoned vegetables, so Callen speaks first.

"I broke my arm when we were dewlings. Everyone was making such a fuss over me, and little Leon asked with all sorts of annoyance, why don't they just heal him? We all stared at him, so he threw down his toys, walked over, and healed my arm."

Leon smiles at the memory. "At first it was only small animals, and I never mentioned it to anyone because I thought we all possessed the same magic. My mother was delighted at my power, and when I decided at ten, I wanted to be a healer, it gave her an idea. My mother still had Inara's ring, passed down from generations. So, she snuck it out of the family trove one night to test it. Without the ring when she touched the iron wall, it burned, but with the ring turning her mortal she could touch the wall without pain. If it was the only way to be with the king at the moment of his death, someone needed to pose as a royal healer. So, she tested the ring on me, and it turned my body mortal with some kind of glamour, but my healing power remained. You know the rest."

"I'm sorry you have lost a family heirloom." It was probably the only thing they have of their ancestor.

Callen waves his hand. "I just wanted Leon back. That crown seems to have brought more pain than power."

Truly.

His family asks me plenty of questions between bites, and I share openly with them about myself but any answers about Ellova are vague. Only that it exists and the joys of living there.

Estelle and Callen tell us how they fell in love nearly a decade ago. How he knew she was meant to be his mate from the moment he saw her, but she was engaged to Zilas. He hid the fact he was pretending to be his brother for as long as he could but almost lost her in the lie and was finally honest with her. They had their first child soon after.

Towards the end of our short meal, I have one question left. "How did Kalvorn come to be?"

Callen kindly explains their history. "The day Inara died, Kalden wasn't there to protect her, and it devastated him. He couldn't allow his daughter to grow up in that court and was able to get her out. For a while, Drystan thought the princess had been kidnapped, but he would never have let her inherit the throne anyway, so he didn't search for her. Kalden kept Inara's glamour ring that the Forger had made for her. He gathered all his soldiers and told them that their king had murdered Inara, who had transformed the kingdom with bounty and goodness."

Leon continues the story for his brother. "Unwilling to stay in Adreania, he offered them a choice: stay and serve Drystan or leave with their families to form a new kingdom. Those loyal to him chose to leave, and in the dead of night they packed up everything they needed so they could start new somewhere else. Kalvorn. Prince Kalden of Adreania became King Kalden of Kalvorn, and he raised his daughter there. The young Princess Arelia eventually became queen and accepted many fae who had been locked out of Ellova when they left at the end of the war with the mortals, when the glamour and the Divide went up. They needed a magical sanctuary and Kalvorn was their haven."

"So, mortals and fae are able to live together here?" I ask hopefully, thinking of Cyanna. We could visit each other without fear.

Leon smiles at my hope. "Yes, the Airvell River runs through Kalvorn, too, and the mortals there found out that by drinking the water, they lived longer and were protected from the ill effects of magic. The waters also imbued the land with magic for the fae to be comfortable. We live in harmony."

Joy shoots through me. Cyanna will have a beautiful life here. "I can see why you were so desperate to bring me here when you thought I was mortal," I tease Leon.

"Mortal or fae, I just needed you near," he says softly.

We stare lovingly at each other 'til Callen coughs, reminding us we are not alone, and we laugh at that.

Once the meal is complete, we say our goodbyes with promises to return.

Leon and Erenia speak in hushed voices for a few minutes, and she tearfully hugs him goodbye.

"She has someone waiting for her at home," he explains as we walk down the hall alone. "Her time in Adreania was horrible, but I have a feeling a great life is ahead of her now."

Hope drifts in the bond. Goodness is ahead for all of us.

CHAPTER 45

IZADELLA

I'm eager to return home, so Leon finally leads me back to the Kalvorn throne room once more.

Confused, I ask, "Why is there a tree in the middle of the floor?" It couldn't have been there intentionally as the beautiful green flooring lies in shattered pieces scattered around the thick trunk. The delicate leaves are a soft lavender hue that reminds me of Nueena, and my heart twists with longing to be reunited.

Leon's amusement floods me. "That was Nueena's doing."

"What? Nueena was here?"

His laughter fades and a darkness replaces it. "When you were taken, she came looking for you here. She had seen you leave and thought you went after me."

I stop him in front of the mighty tree, a monument to Nueena's loyalty. "Everett had a servant girl from Adreania with hair like mine pretend to be me. He intentionally made it seem like I left with you so Nueena wouldn't try and find me."

Leon's answering smile is amused. "I guess he didn't understand Nueena very well after a century of knowing her." He stands very tall and attempts to sound like her. "Don't play dumb with me, *Your Majesty*. I know Della is here. Now go get her and tell her she belongs with us in Ellova. She can come willingly, or I can sling her over my shoulder, but either way I'm not leaving without her."

Tears well up in my eyes, and when one falls, Leon is quick to wipe it away. She came for me, after everything. Gratitude for her overwhelms me and he draws me into his arms. "I was so scared she was going to find out I was taken and try to retrieve me. I knew she would have. I know she is the most powerful fae in Ellova, but none of that matters in Adreania where we can't use our magic. I couldn't be responsible for her death."

Leon cups the back of my head. "I'll let her tell you the whole story, but I thought she was going to burn down Adreania when she found out you were taken. Let's return to Ellova. There are many who wish to see you whole and well before them."

I nod, pulling him into the thick, hollowed-out tree. One of his hands slips into mine, the other on the bark. His power connects with it and the traveling portal magic swirls around us. It only takes a few moments before bright light pours in.

Leon's hand tightens in mine, his apprehension rising. As eager as I am to run into the palace, I need him to be at peace. "You have every right to be in Ellova." I never told him about Nyvenah's gift.

"When Nueena came to Kalvorn looking for you, I returned with her. It was…" He searches for the word. "…tense."

I imagine it would have been. Loyalty runs through my friends like their own blood. "Leon, they saw me die, and you brought me back to life. They all would have lost me if it weren't for you. No matter their opinions of you before, you are my Zemra, and all will be forgiven."

"Even by Lillian?"

Laughter rolls out of me. "Well. *Almost* all of them will be forgiving." His answering smile warms my chest. "Actually, you do have every right to return to Ellova with me. Nyvenah had you recognized as a citizen of Ellova and an honored member of the Ellovian High Court. I have the scroll back in my rooms."

He is taken aback. "You didn't tell me?"

Hurt drips into the bond and I'm swift to answer, "I know. I am sorry. I was just trying to protect my heart, but we know how that turned out." I let out a little laugh.

He scowls at my jest but nods. "That I can understand. Becoming your Zemra and an Ellovian in one day. What a wonderful privilege." He leans down to kiss me quickly. Sensing my eagerness to see my friends, he takes my hand, and I follow him into the moonlight.

The expansive courtyard garden just outside the Ellovian throne room is hidden in the soft evening shadows, the blooms closed 'til dawn.

One honeyguard rushes inside as we approach. Her fellow guards greet us warmly, opening the large doors at my return. The long room is brightly lit with rows of encased crystals and columns wrapped in vines along the walls, fully decorated with banners and flower garlands for the coronation tomorrow.

Nyvenah sits at the driftwood table just before her throne. The navlue flowers are about to fully bloom, the plump fruit hanging low on its branches.

The woman who raised me gives us a kind smile as she stands. "Before you run off with my dewling again, Leon, since you did not knowingly break the Zemra law, I will not punish you for it."

I smirk at him as the trepidation lingering within him fades and he lets go of my hand.

"Nueena has filled me in on the events of the past few days." Nyvenah holds out her arms to me, eyes glossy. "Welcome home."

I rush into her embrace, clinging to her. "Is Nueena okay?" I am desperate to be reassured of my friends' well-being.

"More than okay. She has much to tell you." Nyvenah pulls back to search my face, hand on my cheek, and I find sorrow on hers. "Did they hurt you? I never thought Everett would betray us like that."

I lean into her touch. "I'm all right now. Grateful he is dead. Is she ready for tomorrow?"

"Yes. Waiting for you, of course, but everything will be perfect for the coronation," Nyvenah says, pride in her voice.

We exit the throne room and follow her down a long, well-lit hallway and up to the royal west wing. With every step closer, I grow more and more excited, running the last few steps to the doors that open at my arrival. In a rush of movement, Viella launches herself at me, crying. Leon is instantly at my back, so I don't get pushed over and take her down with me.

"Della! Ellova's grave! You had swords sticking out of you! It's going to haunt my dreams." Her face is tear-streaked when she pulls away to assure herself I'm uninjured.

Lillian comes up behind her. "We really need to work on your defense in combat. The swords are meant to stay *out* of our bodies."

I laugh, knowing that is her way of saying she was worried about me. "Thank you, both of you, for coming after me. I am forever indebted to you."

Viella waves her hand. "What are friends for if not to run into danger to save your ass?" she says with a sniffle.

A gasp cuts through the air.

Nueena is there in her doorway, a jarring guttural sob breaking from her. She holds Farren, who whines when he sees me. We bolt towards each other. My chest tightens painfully and I'm crying uncontrollably, too, as I reach for her and my precious fox. She hauls me to her, Farren snug between us, licking my face. She looks regal with the crown glittering on her head and a matching golden gown.

I kiss her cheeks as she laughs. "I thought you were dead!"

"Well, it wasn't a lack of effort on Grayden's part, but I'm here now." I pull them both tighter against me.

When we finally do pull apart, she turns her anguished expression towards Leon. She opens one arm, welcoming him to join our teary reunion. He leans into us, his lips brushing the top of my head in a gentle kiss.

I stand between them as they hold me, safe in Ellova, soothed by Farren's soft purrs, and the last week washes away in a cascade of emotions, the fear and anguish flushing out of my soul, Leon ever-present within me.

"That bastard stabbed you," Nueena whispers into my ear.

"Death will need to wait a little longer now. Fate has blessed me with a Zemra who possesses healing magic."

She rears back in delight. "Let me see your stone!"

We separate so I can reveal my exquisite glowing emerald.

Nueena turns hopeful eyes on Leon. "What of your enervation death?" she whispers to him.

His smile to her is as bright as morning sunshine. "She has both my magic and our shared powers, so she used it to heal me completely. Her lifetime is tied with mine now, so she will not part from you until I do."

Nueena makes a noise that's half laughter, half sob, a warm, broken sound, as she squeezes me against her.

I am no longer bound by a half-mortal life.

A fae lifespan with Leon at my side.

I have a lifetime ahead of me with my Zemra and the family I forged. To see Nueena rule Ellova for centuries.

My legs give out but they both catch me easily and we all sink to the floor as one. The warmth of pure happiness radiates within me, dancing with Leon's own happiness.

Thundering footsteps race down the hallway into the room.

Tavien slides on the floor to us, wrapping his arms around the three of us. "Excellent work not dying, Del!"

"We have Leon to thank for that," I say, smushed between them.

When we all finally stand up again, I present my emerald to him. Tavien shouts with joy, extracting me from our Zemra, my feet leaving the ground in a crushing hug.

"Welcome to the family," he exclaims to Leon. The two of them embrace like brothers with hardy pats on the backs.

Soft arms slide around my waist; a head pressed to my back. For a moment, I think it's Viella, but red hair is the first thing I see.

Cyanna.

She weeps while I hold her. My sweet, sweet cousin. "Della, I'm so sorry I went back. Kalvorn was just so wonderful. It just broke my heart knowing I could bring more children to Leon's estate. I had no idea about the elixir or that Princess Erenia would help those in Beggars' Row escape."

I would never expect anything less out of her heart. Of course she would go back, thinking death still had its clutches on the Row, leaving new orphans in its wake. How could she possibly know we were working to save them with the elixir?

The past few days have been horrible. I need her to know how terrible I feel, too. "I'm sorry you were so mistreated in Adreania and they used you against me."

We stay like that for a while, gently swaying. The memories of her trapped in the castle with me are a knife to my gut.

She finally pulls back, stepping away from me, wiping tears from her eyes. "Seeing Leon kill Grayden was worth it, though, and the crown choosing Nueena was spectacular."

I turn back to Nueena. "Are you okay?"

She takes the crown off and fear spikes in me, but nothing happens. "I'm completely fine. It's woven its magic with mine. I have complete control over it now." She places it back on her head and smiles at me, wiping at her eyes. "You were—" She stumbles over the word dead. "—gone. Leon grabbed the crown off you and gave it to me. Then Everett ripped it away and the stupid bastard put it on. Killed instantly. It was everything he deserved."

The reminder he is dead still feels like a cold drink on a scorching day. "What about his mother? She knew he took me. She revealed who Leon really was right before Everett snuck me out."

Cold rage paints Nueena's face. "She disappeared once we realized he was the one who took you, but we will find her. We know she was giving the navlue fruit to her son to give to Grayden. She will receive no mercy when she is found."

I take her hand and pull her down to the couch, Leon and Tavien on our sides. Cyanna and Viella take a seat on each armrest, Lillian behind her new Zemra.

"Tell me everything that happened after that. Leon said you were in the sky?" I ask, wishing for every detail.

She laughs. "Once Everett died, the pull towards the crown grew with each passing second. It's the greatest keyed item ever made, and keyed items will always choose who can control it. Once I put it on, it was like a piece of me I didn't know was missing slid into place. The magic was overwhelming, but Ellova's grave, it felt wonderful! Before I even knew it, I was floating in the air, striking down every one of Grayden's guards. The ones who surrendered were spared. The ones that kept attacking, well…The Merawood Forest has a few more bones of our enemies in its roots. I put a protective wall around Ellova to ensure that no one from Adreania would try to seek revenge for their king."

I add, "Lyrora is now ruler of Adreania and I promise she is as glad of his death as we are. She may even throw a parade in your honor."

She and I both giggle at that, but her smile fades. "When I finally came down to the ground, you were both gone. Lillian, Viella, and Tavien searched for you in the forest. I looked from above. We thought the worst, Del. There was so much blood."

I look towards Leon, who fills in the gaps in my own memory.

"I just ran, needing to get you somewhere safe, not knowing even which direction to go. I could still hear the Adreanian guards. I wasn't going to let them find you. The farther we walked, the more I felt this tug deep within me. I couldn't have gone anywhere else if I tried. I simply followed it all night, not knowing it was leading me to the Zemra temple. I walked right in with you."

"That is incredible!" Viella squeals. "All of us Zemras now, how marvelous!"

Lillian pierces Leon with a sharp look, one eyebrow in a perfect arch. "And you thought the best course of action after that was to kidnap her?"

Leon raises his hands up for his defense. "That is a fair question. Yes, Nyvenah appeared and I thought we would be punished. I knew what happened to Nueena and Tavien, locked away from each other. I had just lost Izadella. I would not be separated from her for any reason ever again, temple laws or not. I took her to Kalvorn, where she convinced me, we could return."

We share a look, and I know we are both thinking of the way I rode him on his throne.

I quickly change the subject before a blush can tint my cheeks. "With Grayden and Everett dead and the crown off my head, everything can return to as it always has been. You will be crowned Realm Keeper. All will be well once more and with the crown's magic within you, there is no limit to what you can do."

Finally, some peace.

Nueena's shoulders tug back with pride. "And my first act as Realm Keeper will be to restore all the damage the crown has done to Adreania. After the coronation, we will meet with Queen Lyrora. The crown stores enough magic to rebuild her kingdom, restore its fields, and finally get the harvests they desperately need. We will help in any way we can."

"I can talk to my brother," Leon adds. "Kalvorn can help Adreania rebuild as well. Izadella will need to speak to let those from Beggars' Row know it's safe to return now."

"I do have one question," Nueena says. "Del, how did you survive wearing the crown? The magic it held was too great, so much fae magic for your mortal body. I know I took some from you but…" Her voice cracks. "Ellova's grave, you shouldn't be alive."

Before I can shrug, just as confused as she was, Leon speaks up.

"Actually, I was siphoning off the magic so it wouldn't destroy her."

Nueena and I both stare at him.

He had been saving my life this whole time.

Every day he was here, he was healing me. His love and devotion caresses my soul. My wobbling smile meets his smitten grin.

"Oh, Leon."

"Every time I touched you, every night you slept in my arms, I took as much excess magic as I could. My healing magic works with touch, and being fully fae from a powerful bloodline meant I could withstand absorbing endless magic and healing all the damage the crown was inflicting without you even knowing it."

"That was why I felt so much better waking up with you and miserable when we were apart." My eyes water, overwhelmed with gratitude and love for him.

He leans down and places a kiss on the top of my head.

"It's late. Let's give the new Zemras time to themselves," Tavien suggests.

Nueena yawns, leaning against Tavien. "It is. We should all get some sleep."

We share one last hug before we part.

The balcony windows are open, letting in the cool night air of the Merawood Forest, a hint of flora from the wing's greenhouse. A reminder I am safe, surrounded by those who love me, the scent of saltwater dungeons and iron castles long gone.

CHAPTER 46

LEON

Izadella and I arrive back to her rooms, that soft yellow bed a welcome sight. Her rose and lemon scent is everywhere, and I breathe deeply. I truly thought I would never be back here, never again hold her in my arms, tangled in the sheets she laid alone in for years, dreaming of me the same way I dreamt about her.

She takes off the traveling cloak and shirt, reaching for the tie of the temple robe. I place my hand over hers and she allows me to undo the knot.

"Do we need to return this to the temple?" I ask, sliding the silk fabric off her rounded shoulders, bending down to kiss each one. She is bare before me, and I stare down at her exquisite body. Exhilaration rolls through me, and she laughs, wrapping her arms around me.

I find the spot on her neck I know she loves and take the skin there into my mouth, earning a breathy moan, the tantalizing sound shooting straight to my throbbing cock.

She whispers, "No, we will need them for our Zemra celebration."

Zemra celebration?

I pull back. "When is that?"

"Well, had our journey to the temple been planned, it would have been immediately after the temple visit." She gives me a playful slap on my chest. "Which would have been explained had you not whisked me away to your kingdom, Your Highness."

It's meant to be a tease, I know that, but it cuts deep, as it should. It seems I've taken yet another thing from her. When I try to step out of her embrace, guilt enveloping me, she only pulls me closer.

"Forgive me," I rasp.

She shakes her head, her copper curls swaying around her. "I may not like your choices, but I understand why you made them." Her smile is soft and comforting. Too gracious for the hurt I have caused.

"I would still like to celebrate, if you would." I try to keep the pleading from my voice.

"Of course. We will plan something together."

Her soft lips find mine, her love in the bond fighting against the remorse of my transgressions. She undoes each of my buttons as we kiss, breaking apart so I can toss my clothing to the floor.

We are tired from the long day, but our slow kisses and soft touches continue after we have pulled the sheets over ourselves. She spreads her legs wide in invitation. Her desire is a sweetness in the air and a longing in the heart she has given to me.

Tonight is not for the greedy grinding and frantic obsession of earlier, but tender and graceful.

I slowly slide into her, pouring devotion out of me. Her velvety whimpers with each long thrust are its own kind of magic. Her cry of pleasure brings my own. Sated and safe in my arms, my love and adoration drift out of me as she falls asleep. I need endless nights like this one.

* * *

Icy fear grips my chest, pain shooting through me. It's disorienting, and for a moment I grab for my sword before I realize the agony is coming from our bond, from Izadella.

She is asleep, tossing and turning, sweat glistening in the moonlight down her face, moaning in her sleep. Her beautiful face twisted in terror. "No…no…no."

Her fear is so palpable, nausea churns in me. I hold her face in my hand, slowly stroking her cheek. "Wake up, my love. Please wake up."

Glossy, terrified eyes jolt open, and she tries to quickly move away from me, her fear bursting open. I let her go even though it's the last thing I wish to do. She frantically looks around the room, taking in her surroundings, confusion gripping her, and it guts me.

"You're safe in your bedroom in the Ellovian palace," I reassure her in a gentle tone. "You are here with your Zemra. Everything is all right. Grayden and Everrett are dead."

My own panic and guilt that she is upset mix with her dread.

I fear that our pain coming together in the bond will make it all worse, but instead, it soothes us both. A reminder that she and I are one, our souls tied together.

She blinks at me, tears falling, but the pain within her fades when she recognizes she is truly safe. Peace spreads over us at whatever that damn nightmare had brought, calming us both. My Zemra nods, moving towards me, letting me wrap my arms around her and pull her close.

I give her space to process whatever was going on in her mind while she lies on my chest. I get impressions and feelings, but I will never know exactly what she went through. She does not want my guilt, but unfortunately, I do not believe it will ever truly leave me.

She had every right to run from me. I had chosen the worst moment to reveal myself to her. Yes, it was Everett who had taken her, but I opened the door for that bastard, and for that I will never forgive myself, even if she has.

"What were you dreaming of?" I ask. "If you'd like to speak of it, I would like to listen."

She is quiet for a moment but slowly she tilts her head up to me. "I was back in that horrible water dungeon. Everett was there, just waiting for me to drown. Cyanna was there in the water with me, but she didn't have the lochkiss and she fell below the waves. I didn't see her come up." She pulls me tighter to her. The memory is still so fresh.

I gently rub rhythmic circles on her back, my other hand in her hair. "I'm—"

"*Don't.* Don't say you're sorry," she grumbles into my chest.

I pause at her request, but it will not be the last she hears of it. Instead, I think of everything I love about her and let that flood our bond.

We lie there in the dark, the night breeze a caress over our skin. I want her to share her burdens with me, to let me carry her anguish in my own heart so it is lighter for her. I will not have her suffering in silence or let evil men steal her peace.

"I thought I was going to die there."

Her haunting words hang in the air.

"You were incredibly brave. You didn't deserve even a moment of your time there. You stayed strong. Lyrora sent a letter the morning of your wedding." I growl the final word. "It said you had a plan to kill Grayden and to meet you at the forge. That's how we found out where you were. Pride doesn't begin to express how I felt. You did what you needed to do so you could return to Ellova. You didn't let those bastards break you."

"I thought of you often. I thought everything about you was a lie, but I remembered those two years when we were both lying to each other every night at the bazaar. I had nothing and was no one there, but you saw me."

Seeing her was the only thing keeping me going towards the end. I despised every moment I was there, and she was not. The urge to return home in shame without the crown seemed easier than staying, but then she would return to sell jewels, and I could make it another month.

Even with the lies, even with the distance.

I swirl a piece of her hair around my finger. "Yes, our souls called to each other from that first greeting. The crown was only an object that brought us back together. It was never yours and never truly mine. But if you hadn't put it on, we would never have found each other again. I'm exceedingly sorry for what you endured, but I will be eternally grateful for another chance at a life with you. I only wish I could have been the one to kill Everett instead of his own foolishness."

Alarm fills me when her chest rises quickly, and for a moment, I think she might be crying but when she lifts her head again, her smile is bright.

"You should have seen the look on his face when I could breathe underwater. He was so certain he was about to get the crown, and there I was, very much alive. I even blew him a little kiss. It just enraged him."

The image she paints is a delight and I laugh with her under the moonlight, midnight tears forgotten.

CHAPTER 47

IZADELLA

The palace is alive with excitement at the upcoming coronation.

I hold the necklace Leon had made for me, calling to my metal magic. The part of me I have missed so much hums to life in my fingers. The gold at the bottom gem shifts at my touch and drips down, swirling around the edges of my Zemra stone, attaching it to the necklace so I can wear both.

Leon takes my hand as we enter the crowded throne room in our formal clothing, sharing shades of greens and golds to match our stones.

Wooden seating has been arranged in many rows. We move to the front for the best views, saved for the guests of honor. Each of the court Guardians sits with us, waiting for their time to walk on the dais to present their gifts to Nueena, but with one noticeable absence.

Camarra.

Seed Keeper, Guardian of the Court of Green, and Everett's mother is still missing. I hope they find her so she can stand trial, but I never wish to see her again. She has the same eyes as Everett, bright with a false warmth. They both hid their deceit deeply and had us all fooled.

Memories flood back of that seaside prison I'd expected to die in. Sadness claws at me, the reminder that death hovered so near for days on end at Everett's hand, that his mother had known of his plan. Encouraged his deranged ideas of power.

Leon feels my pain, his own joining it. The intimacy of the bond. No way to hide, but maybe we never needed to. His regrets slip around his soul as his arm does around my shoulders, his soft lips pressing into my temple. He is so warm, our love for each other pushing away the darkness like sunshine against storm clouds.

I lean against him, eyes closed, soaking in the beauty of this soulbond, the magic tying us together forever. How breathtaking it is to know without any doubt how much his devotion and reverence for me is sweetness in his soul.

He pulls me deeper into his arms, so grateful for my forgiveness, overwhelmed as I am at my love for him. I'm so lost in our connection I don't notice Kaylena approaching until she jumps straight into my lap.

"You're back! You're back!" she shrieks with joy and grabs both sides of my cheeks, squishing my face together. I stick my tongue out and look at my nose. She squeals in delight, her giggles echoing around us.

Viella sits next to me, Lillian following with Vaylin.

Music swells, and the room stands as one.

"Lili!" Kaylena reaches out for Lillian, who can hold her higher than I can. Lillian takes the youngest royal from me, twin smiles on their faces, and Kaylena waves at the crowd behind her.

I'm practically vibrating. My excitement makes me giddy.

Leon wraps his arms around me, swaying us from side to side to release some of my energy. I have waited so long to see Nueena ascend the throne.

The doors open with a blast of trumpets. Tavien and Nueena follow her parents down the rose-petal aisle, each row bowing silently as she passes by.

Her smile grows when she reaches our row and graces us with a small nod. Pride shines on all of our faces. Viella sniffles next to me. I link our fingers together and squeeze. She steps close, resting her head on my shoulder.

"It's finally her time." Viella's words wobble, filled with emotion.

I can only nod, lost for anything to say. This is finally happening.

Alachite follows Nyvenah, who gracefully walks up the steps of the dais, followed by Nueena. They turn to face the crowd under the sparkling lights surrounding the navlue tree while crystals on strings branch out in every direction, attaching to the smaller trees around the ballroom, making the whole ceiling glimmer.

Nueena stands before her realm with regal grace in the Court of Ellova purple. Around her neck is a band of flowers, with sheer panels crossing over her chest and over her bare arms that swoop low behind her. The sweetheart gown underneath is a darker shade with enchanted bright roses that get larger as they go down the sides of her hips, golden leaves under it all.

She kisses her parents on each cheek and stands in front of the twisted tree and entwined ivy of the Ellovian throne. Shimmering gemstones that represent each court are set in an arch just above the throne's high backrest. Behind them is the magnificent statue of the goddess Ellova, standing tall, spiral moss climbing up her stone body. Carved hair reaches her feet with an enchanted flower crown just above her beautiful frozen smile.

Five empty marble pedestals are on one side of Nueena.

Tavien stands just to the side of her. His eyes shine just for his Zemra, love and devotion chiseled in every bit of his handsome face.

Nyvenah speaks. "Welcome to a new era as my daughter takes my place as Realm Keeper. Each court may present their gift of loyalty. It is the greatest honor to pass stewardship of Ellova to my daughter. She will make us all proud as Realm Keeper." She takes a step back as we all sit down.

The last of the navlue blossoms bloom, signaling the start of the coronation.

The Guardians from each court stand, making their way to Nueena, who now stands next to the first pedestal.

The golden guard who carries the yellow flag of the Court of Gems follows Lazalai, who strides up the steps and bows dramatically, a yellow silk pillow in her palms, presenting the gift that shines under the crystal lights.

"From the court of artisans, your creators of art, your guardians of culture." She holds out the elegant necklace with its bright citrine stone the size of a walnut and offers it to Nueena, who laughs at the flourish with which the necklace is presented to her before joyfully accepting it.

It would show favoritism for her to wear the necklace tonight, so it is laid carefully down on the pedestal, but I do not miss how her eyes linger just a moment longer on my court's offering.

I helped design it with Lazalai months ago. Nueena glances at me and I give her a mischievous smile.

The Court of Shells ascends the dais next. Koray, the Wave Keeper and Guardian, holds a long fishing spear covered entirely with bright white pearls, delicate light green gems, and seaweed that artfully hangs over pale purple sea glass wrapped around a sharp coral tip. Their short blond hair falls in front of deep blue eyes as they bow before Nueena.

"From the court of the tide, your wishes in the waves, your hand in the current."

Nueena accepts the gift with graceful hands, bowing to Koray before turning to place the spear gently against the second pedestal. They reach out their hand to Nueena, who takes it, squeezing it affectionately. Koray leans in, whispering what must be kind words as Nueena's eyes turn glossy. She smiles gratefully, nodding before Koray exits the dais.

Following behind Koray is someone I have never seen before, her face downtrodden. She carries a golden cornucopia with shaking hands, filled with enchanted preserved fruit, grains, and vegetables that lie atop a base of golden wheat that falls loosely out of it, all of it wrapped in green ribbon. The bounty of Ellova sits on a satin pillow the color of moss and she offers it to Nueena.

"I am here on behalf of the Court of Green. You have all of our deepest apologies for our Guardian's absence. Please accept this gift from the court of provisions, your hand in the soil, your realm kept nourished." Bowing deeply, she passes her gift over.

Nueena accepts it with a kind smile, adding it to the third pedestal.

Bria, the Guardian for the Court of Swords, strides up to the throne, her crimson flag standing out among the pastel shades that paint the ballroom. On her deep red pillow, almost the same hue as her hair, she holds out a long obsidian dagger set in an intricate silver handle.

With her voice loud and clear, Bria declares, "From the court of defenders, your blade and your bow, shield and arrow."

Nueena takes the dagger and moves it in her hand to admire the way the light reflects off the jagged black stone before setting it down.

The last court to present their gifts is the Court of Ink. Reyna gracefully approaches, two small moon moths in her hair. Her gown, the same shade of pale green as their wings, drapes down low, revealing her copious tattoos. Nueena's smile at the librarian is wider than of all the court Guardians she has greeted tonight.

The guards stand, holding the black Ink Court's flag proudly. One holds a thick scroll wrapped around two golden spindles.

Reyna's hands are energetic in their motion, her expression one of pride for a dear friend as she makes vows for the Court of Ink.

I whisper to Leon, who moves low, so my lips graze his ear, "From the court of wisdom, your history preserved, your knowledge everlasting."

When Reyna has finished, Nueena's golden eyes are a bit glassy, and she takes the scroll Reyna presents to her. Nueena does not open it but holds it to her chest for a moment before adding it to the line of gifts.

The Guardians all stand before her as Nueena bows to them and everyone behind them. The entire crowd bows deeply back to her. Once the crowd has risen it erupts in cheers and the music plays.

Alachite stares at his daughter, pride shining in his eyes.

Nyvenah approaches the navlue tree next to the Ellovian throne. Its deep purple branches display its beautiful flowers, the fruit dangling from it, perfectly ripened. The rare and sacred fae food only grows when a new heir is to be crowned.

She takes the sacred fruit, places it on a silver platter, and holds it out to her daughter, who peels the bright green rind.

It's a deeper shade than the one Grayden forced me to eat. His cruelty and the phantom flavor of it sours my stomach but I shove the memory away. Leon's anger boils in the bond, so I stand on my toes to kiss his cheek.

Just a passing pain. I won't let dead men taint my closest friend's coronation. It is a blessed day.

Once the fruit is completely peeled, Nueena savors each piece. The rest of the hanging fruit will be pressed, and the juice will be served at dinner to the royal family and guests.

If Camarra were here, she would play a role in this part of the ceremony since she tended to the tree, but Nueena waves her hand, all of the flowers swirling towards her. Using her magic, she brings the flowers together in a long garland that floats behind her and hangs over the throne's headrest.

Now is the moment.

Queen Inara's circlet still glitters on Nueena's head, but her mother places the Realm Keeper's crown on her daughter. The golden swirls hold large diamonds and bright gemstones, with tall points that end in amethyst. It nestles perfectly inside the circlet, almost looking like one headpiece.

Nyvenah holds Nueena's hand up to the crowd. "I pass on this crown as a symbol of your royal leadership. You now take my place as Realm Keeper."

Tears well up in my eyes and the crowd cheers as Nueena sits on her new throne, Realm Keeper of the Fae.

As the throne acknowledges she is the rightful heir and accepts her new rule, it transfers to her the magic of Ellova. It swirls around her, rising up from the throne. The magic glitters and glows, rushing into her. She was powerful before, but now all of Ellova's magic is at her fingertips.

A rumbling starts low beneath the Ellovian throne, shaking the floor. Nueena's smile falters, quickly replaced by panic.

Someone behind me screams.

CHAPTER 48

IZADELLA

Dread pools within me when the shaking grows stronger. A blast of magic comes from Nueena that shatters the windows around us.

Viella and Lillian throw their bodies over Vaylin and a crying Kaylena, Viella using her magic to create a protective barrier around them.

Nueena jumps off the throne and rips Inara's crown off her head. The gold quivers before the gilded color drains from it, turning it pale as moonlight. It hovers above her hands before it breaks into four pieces, falling into her open palms.

Leon tries to stop me, but I run past him, our panic pounding into each other. Mine is terrified of whatever is happening with the crown; Leon's is fear for my safety as I race up the steps to get to Nueena, who clutches the jagged pieces in her trembling hands. Magic keeps rolling off her in waves. Every plant in this room is spilling over their pots.

The crown's endless magic rushes out of the room without anyone to control it.

Nueena looks between her mother and me. "The crown can't handle the magic it already had, plus my own magic and the Realm

Keeper's magic from the throne. We need to get it back together. I need that magic to restore Adreania!"

She and I stare at each other for just a moment. If we can return to my workshop, we can try to fix this. Alvina forged the crown there, so maybe I can put it back together. I know Nueena is thinking the same when we both bolt towards the small grove where the tree portals are, Tavien and Leon at our heels.

"Can you do it?" Nueena asks, running beside me. Hope in her words begs me to tell her yes.

I am a descendent of the Forger, but that doesn't mean I have the ability to fix such a powerful keyed item or even forge her a new crown, especially one that needs to hold such a vast amount of magic, but we have to try.

"Let's get to the forge. I will do whatever I can, everything within my power."

The bundle of tree portals are just outside the throne room, and the four of us sprint into the first tree we can reach. Nueena slams her hand onto the bark and when we stumble in, the portal magic launches us forward.

"Can you make a tree portal reach closer to my cottage?" I ask Nueena, Leon's arms wrapping around me for the journey.

"I can try but the trees are fickle when it comes to additional pathways. The Merawood Forest does not have the magic Ellova or the Verge does. I was able to form a connecting pathway to Kalvorn because it's full of magic."

Please let it work.

"Are you not Realm Keeper yet? Why would the forest not obey you?" Leon shouts over the whirling noise of the tree.

"The coronation has not been completed. We have one final part to the ceremony. The throne needs to accept me. The magic transfer was not completed."

The portal shakes, a sign that a new tree is being grown above us. Tendrils of hope rise up in Leon and me.

When it finally stops spinning, we step into the forest, and through the thick trees are the burnt remains of my cottage, my home.

My heart hurts all over again at the destruction, but I cannot let what has been lost distract me from what must be reborn.

I dash into the small stone workshop, stumbling inside.

"No!" I cry, burning with agony at the sight of the cold forge. I want to fall to my knees and scream.

The cerulean fire is gone. Remnants of the stained-glass windows are crushed under our feet.

I have never seen it not burning with its mighty blue flame. My mother always said that the forge fire would never die. That it had been burning for thousands of years and would do so for thousands more.

"It must have gone out the night I put on the crown. An explosion of magic blew out the windows too," Nueena explains, crestfallen.

Tavien steps forward. "Let me try to restart it. Nueena, take my hand."

I hold my breath as his powers light his hand, but it's a different type than I've ever seen him possess. The magic swirling around is a mix of his firefae abilities and Nueena's, their shared powers creating something new. He blasts his magic into the forge, blowing my hair back with its impact.

For a moment the forge remains lifeless, but then bright flames erupt within it, burning brightly, more powerful than ever before.

Now, it is my turn.

Nueena hands me the Realm Keeper's crown and the broken pieces of Inara's. "You can do this, Della. I know you can!"

I take it with trembling hands. Her trust in me is a beautiful thing. We will see if I deserve it.

"Everyone stand back," I demand, Leon reluctantly stepping away from me.

The fire's heat is a welcoming caress. The flames lap up my arms in greeting. My skin tingles as I stand so close to such magic within it.

I place Nyvenah's crown in the center of the forge and arrange the four broken pieces of Inara's, connecting it to each part of the Realm Keeper's.

My metal magic bursts through my fingertips, forging each of the shards of her future crown to Inara's. Both crowns melt and form a solid gold ball, merging together. I shift my hands, hollowing the gold into a hoop. I swirl up a high point in the center and two more on each side, slightly shorter as it goes down.

I think of all that is Nueena.

Her love for her garden flows through me and the gold swirls into flowers and leaves. I want to create a crown just for her. The glittering florals twine together. I leave a space open in the center.

"Give me your Zemra stone!"

She hands it to me, and I set the crystal. With the two crowns forged together, the vast well that is normally filled with magic is becoming barren. The new crown vibrates with irritation at the loss of its wearer, of its unending magic that is flooding out of it and into Ellova.

"Nueena, it's your turn. I need to key this to you. It needs your magic."

I have never keyed an item to a fae before, nor did my mother. It was too risky. It takes great magic and can have devastating consequences if done incorrectly, as keyed magic binds the item.

The weight of all presses down on me, but determination quickly rises, the metal eager for magic, greedy for it.

Any fear I cannot do this is smothered with Leon's belief in me, his awe in my abilities.

My jewelsmith powers sing in my veins, a sensation I've missed so very much.

I hold the crown deep into the forge, flames licking at my skin, and hold one hand out to Nueena. She places her hand in mine, Tavien at her side, holding her. I'm overwhelmed by the magic she has.

More power than any fae has had before.

My mortal body is a conduit for Nueena's magic as it blasts through me like lightning, down my arm, and into the waiting crown burning in the flames.

Stars blind my vision for a moment, my body swaying. It's too much for the mortal part of my body, burning me from the inside. Every part of me lights up in pain, but I focus on what I need to do.

Now it is time for my magic to do its part. A metallic taste fills my mouth. My power swirls around the crown, locking it in place with Nueena's power. She calls back all the magic the crown has lost. It builds and builds. The workshop trembles, the shattered colored glass rising around us as an ocean of magic floods into Nueena, through me, and into the crown.

I fear I might faint from the pain and the vastness of her lost magic I'm drowning in, about to become completely overwhelmed with it. The torrent of insurmountable magic blackens my vision.

I must finish this.

No matter the pain.

Strong arms and my Zemra's strawberry scent wrap around me, healing magic whirling through me, soothing me. Leon's healing powers restore all the damage being done to my body, our shared magic through our bond. The pain eases.

Nueena's magic pours into the crown, building and building.

The forge cannot take all the magic. The pressure within it crushes me. Too much magic is funneled in. The flames darken, rising higher and higher, but I need to keep it all contained for a few seconds longer. The well within the crown fills fast, siphoning in all it can.

The force of it all is about to explode!

"Leon, stay away!" I beg but he just tightens his hold on me. I let go of Nueena's hand and shove her with all my strength towards Tavien. "Take cover!"

He catches her, launching both of them to the floor, covering her with his own body and a protective shield right before the forge erupts in a fireball. The heat of it blasts me back, and I fight to stay upward as the last of the magic swirls into the crown.

The violet fire burns brightly one last time before shrinking down to those cheery blue flames I have always known. The enchantment to key the crown to Nueena vibrates through me before it snaps into place.

Shocked elation descends upon me. I did it! Oh, Ellova's grave.

The enchantment is complete.

Tavien rolls off Nueena, who pushes away his chest to once again be at my side. "Oh, Della! Are you all right?'"

I nod. The crown heats quickly, angry to find itself still in my care and not with the one it has been keyed to. I thrust it to her with my burning hands and turn to Leon.

I may be immune to fire, but Leon is not.

His shirt has been incinerated, every inch of exposed skin covered in angry red burns. I stare in horror at him, my panic flooding our bond, but he lets out a little laugh.

"Well, I guess we don't share every part of our magic with each other. Could have used that fire immunity."

My poor love.

I know he can heal himself, but I hate to see him harmed. He winces but waves his hand over his skin and handsome face. The scorched skin fades back to unblemished perfection.

He leans down and kisses me, before turning me around to face Nueena. "Did it work?" he asks her.

She gingerly places it on her head, swaying a little as the magic connects with her, but a wondrous smile spreads across her face. "Yeah, I believe it did, but there's only one way to find out. We have to go back to the throne room, but I think I have a way to test it."

Nueena steps away from Tavien and grabs my hand, pulling me into the soft sunlight of the forest and to the ruins of my childhood home.

"Oh, Nueena," I whisper.

Her eyes turn purple, that glow of power shining bright. She swirls her hand in the air and the burned bricks that built my home rise. Ash rises up, turning back into shards of wood that float together to make my door. The shattered glass of the window connects, sealing itself in.

Each piece of the cottage appears whole and new, her magic swirling around.

My heart locks in my chest, the air gone from my lungs.

Everything that had been lost has been restored. The little

cottage my ancestor survived her banishment in stands as it always has.

Sturdy and small and safe.

My home.

I open the door, and it is exactly as I left it, the morning I took Leon to Ellova. From the art on the walls and the copper pans that hang in the kitchen. Down to the slip of paper I had sketched out for the necklace I wear now. My happiest memories come flooding back.

My mother telling me fae stories by the brick fire.

My father slowly dancing with my mother in a kitchen soaked in moonlight.

Waking up next to Leon for the first time, never having rested so peacefully. Even that night, my soul knew who he was to be.

All that I thought I had lost, that Grayden had taken from me.

Quiet heeled boots trail after me and I spin around, launching myself at Nueena.

Appreciation for her swells, bringing with it tears of gratitude. I have my home back, my Zemra, my closest friends. I sob into her shoulder.

"T-thank you!"

"Anything for you, my Della," she whispers into my hair, making me cry harder.

We stay like that for a long moment before Tavien clears his throat.

"Ladies, I do not wish to ruin this moment, but we have a coronation to finish and a celebration to be had," he says with a wide grin.

* * *

It's late when we race towards the throne room.

The court Guardians and Nueena's family are still there when we enter, a flurry of voices, both concerned and angry as Nueena quickly ascends the dais to her mother. "It's all right. It's all right. We can continue."

I've never seen Nyvenah so vulnerable, her hand shaking as she pulls her daughter to her before Nueena addresses the crowd.

"Ellovians, I know tonight has been confusing. My magic combined with the throne's magic was too much. A new crown has been forged and keyed to me that has the abilities to hold the Realm Keeper's powers and my own." She holds out her hand to her mother. "Let's try this again."

A silent conversation passes between them, but Nueena gives a small nod to reassure her.

I silently pray to Ellova that the crown and throne will combine its magic, surrendering all power to Nueena.

Nyvenah holds Nueena's hand up to the crowd once more. "I release my title to my daughter as a new royal leadership will shepherd you. She now takes my place as Realm Keeper."

The room collectively holds their breath as Nueena sits down once again, magic swirling around her. Her eyes glow that same fantastical purple, glowing brightly for a moment before fading back to her golden brown. She closes her eyes and takes a deep breath, and we can feel the escaped magic gliding towards her, under her control once again.

Cheers and praise fill the room and pour into the night. Leon picks me up, twirling me around, the two of us laughing together. My relief loosens the tightness in my body, sweeping away my fears for my closest friend.

"I present to you, your new Realm Keeper, Nueena Verrelia. Long may she reign!" her mother declares.

The party continues well into the night. Drinks overflow and an endless dinner has been prepared. The joyous music is a siren call to the dance floor.

I sway in Leon's arms and my breath catches, overwhelmed to be here, celebrating my closest friend. A night we have dreamed about for so long.

To be here with Leon, my Zemra.

A gift from fate I never believed I would have. I was content with my life here before him, with my friends and family, but he has brought so much light and love into my world.

I was so close to losing all of this. Losing my life, losing Leon, losing my beautiful existence here. I cling to him a little tighter, knowing if a few things had been different, I would still be trapped in Adreania, Grayden as my husband, even if I wouldn't have survived long as his wife. Unknown tortures awaiting me. In that watery prison, desperate to escape, I thought the beautiful life I had here was truly taken from me.

I am safe. Cyanna is safe. A whole future awaits Leon and me. I may not know what it holds but I do know so much joy is ahead.

We can travel all over Ellova or spend time with his family, supporting Nueena however I can.

My jewelsmith magic swirls in my blood, ready and eager to create and mold. It has me wishing to make a sword or a necklace right here on the dance floor.

The bond is bright with his own gratefulness that I am here in his arms.

Wanting to show him my own appreciation for the life we will create together. A life of adventure and romance, friendship and hope, his hands slowly reaching further and further down my waist towards my backside, a tendril of lust turning into a burning need for me, for my body.

"Leon," I moan into his lips.

My heart pounds as his mouth leaves mine to trail down, whispering into my neck, "My Zemra, my love. Shall we find a dark corner so I can do unspeakable things to you?" His salacious words are soft as silk against my skin.

"I know the place for you to ruin me."

CHAPTER 49

LEON

*I*zadella giggles, pulling me down a dark hallway away from the crowded celebration.

Gods, I love her.

I don't care where we're going, only that I can have her all to myself for a little while. We reach an ornately carved door with long scrolls and stars etched into the wood.

A few crystal lights brighten as we enter the empty library, stars shining through the arched windows. She lets go of my hand and breaks into a run into the wooden rows of books and scrolls. My heart beats wildly as I take off after her. I could easily catch her. In my true fae form, speed is a natural gift, but her luscious ass bouncing as she dashes from me is too magnificent a sight to miss.

She weaves through the shelves and shadows, disappearing from my view, but I can hear her deep breaths, scent her need for me, the lemony-rose essences and her budding desire filling the air. Our bond lights up with her excitement at being chased.

I follow her soft breaths 'til I reach a door with thick velvet curtains. Above it is a painting of two lovers, dancing naked in a field. Below it is a gold tile that reads "Restricted: No dewlings allowed."

Where has my little mate taken me?

Her scent calls me, begging me to find my Zemra.

I pull back the fabric to find a smaller library, the tomes a variety of reds and golds, salacious titles that makes me wish to return here to find a few she would love. Reading them aloud to her while she bathes or before bed, filling her head with all the obscene ways I will treasure her.

Her back is against a tall shelf, her breasts shoved up by her bodice, which becomes tighter with each breath. I slow my pace, taking in her windswept hair, her body waiting for me to push her against the rows of books and show her exactly how much I love her.

I sink down to my knees onto the lavish carpet. Her lust bursts within us and my heated laugh fills the space. She's aching for me and I'm eager for every precious drop.

"I think you liked me chasing you through the tomes, on my knees before you, forever at your mercy, but do remember one thing." I raise up the skirts of her gown and slide down the soaking slip of lacy fabric that covers her needy center. I bring one of her legs over my shoulder and haul her lush hips towards me. Proof of her wanting glistens between her lush thighs, begging to be savored. "You are also at mine." I sink my tongue in her hot cunt.

My cock strains with each of her whimpers, desperate for its own release.

I long to touch every curve of her, kiss every inch of skin. To take between my lips every part that implores me to bring her pleasure. The type of rhapsodic satisfaction only I as her Zemra can give. Like a starved man at a bounty, I feast on her, licking and sucking.

Her moans of bliss, the pounding passion in the bond, builds and builds within us.

"More, Leon, More," Izadella gasps and I know she seeks the fullness of my length, but I won't fuck her until she comes. She is so close, her orgasm rising, and it feels so much like my own I worry I will come when she does. I sink one finger and then two into her slickness, earning a groan from her that turns into a whimper. I pump my fingers into her at a steady, swift rhythm, knowing exactly how fast she needs it.

My tongue swirls deep around her clit, keeping her on the edge. I want her to beg, plead with me, and that is exactly what she does.

"Please. *Please.* Let me come."

My Zemra, always so polite. I suck her in, her hips bucking. Her orgasm shoots through us. If I weren't already on my knees, she would have taken me there with the force of it. I wring every bit of pleasure out of her, licking away the proof of her desire as it cascades onto my waiting lips.

The taste of her will forever undo me, the sweet nectar of her need for me, now waiting for me to claim her body once more.

I stand, undoing the laces of my pants. Her eyes trail down my body, her cheeks pink from the pleasure of it all. She slides her fingers down her center, coating them in her desire, and she reaches for me, pumping my cock. I sigh deeply, lining myself up with her core, pushing into her in one motion. Her shock turns into elation with each movement, her head falling back to rest on the books as I thrust into her, the books behind us rattling.

We moan together, our lust a chorus of whispers and gasps.

Desperate to see more of my love, I pull down the front of her bodice, just enough for those perfect breasts to peek out, rosy-brown nipples begging to be sucked. She raises her arms above her head, clinging to the shelf, face twisted in beautiful euphoria. Every thrust of mine is met with a soft gasp or whimper.

Her kisses pepper my cheeks between my moans and brings me back to my body, clinging to her. Our lips find each other, and tongues meet. I could kiss her endlessly. Her time, her touch, it would never be enough. If she hadn't been in the forest that night, we would have missed this, missed everything.

She kisses me once, whispering in my ear, "Don't you dare hold back. You can heal me afterward, right?" And she bites my earlobe.

It unleashes me.

I slide out of her ethereal cunt. Her pouting face is the last thing I see before I spin, bend her over, and plunge back into her. She clings to the bookshelf with a laugh that quickly turns into an exhilarating moan.

I pound into her, my hips furiously snapping over and over again, fingers digging deep into her hips in a bruising touch. A surge of triumph that she is my Zemra rushes through our bond so swiftly she comes again, shattering while I keep burying myself deeper and deeper into her glorious heat.

She feels so damn good, perfection between her thighs, just for me.

Mine.

All mine.

Her shuddering breaths and our love in the bond steals the air from me. It is a symphony of lust and longing, our divine devotion to each other, for all time.

She gasps and groans with each slap of her ass against me, her fingerings slipping with the force of my attention, barely holding on to the shaking shelves, books falling at our feet.

I haul her against me. Her head rests on my chest as I reach around her to cup one of her breasts, teasing her nipple. My other hand rests securely around her throat, holding her in place, still roughly pumping.

The rush of pleasure in her is intoxicating in our bond.

Leaning down, I let the wild fae urge to bite take over, sinking my teeth into her neck. I would never break her skin, it's just enough to make her pulsate in my arms and mark her as mine.

Gracelessly groaning her name, I am lost in her.

Our orgasms come as one, our breaths heaving. My release pours out of me, blinding me with the force of it, stealing every thought. With each of her whimpers, my hips jolt forward uncontrollably. My pace slows to lazy pumps as I attempt to catch my breath, Izadella shaking in my arms, sated. I trail my nose up her jaw.

I glide out of her, my fingers replacing my cock. My healing magic floods her, the sharp ache and my desperate affections fading away. My other hand traces her hips where my demanding hands have left pink skin and blooming bruises, caressing them away.

Waving my hand to erase our mess and pull down her skirts, fanning them out so no one will suspect what we have been up to.

I take her in my arms once more. "Are you ready to return to our rooms or shall we dance 'til dawn?"

Izadella ignores my question. "Do you wish to be king?" Concerned eyes search mine, pulling me back to her.

Our chests are pressed together, our heartbeats fluttering as one.

Do I wish to be king?

That had always been the plan, the very dream I spent a century trying to bring to fruition.

I used to dream of my homecoming, sitting on my emerald throne with the crown on my head and endless power in my veins. After that fateful night I met Izadella, the dream had shifted to selfish desires of her husband falling ill or leaving. Any path for her to become *my* queen had replaced the dutiful desire to acquire the crown.

From the start, I'd imagined her beside me in the royal court of Kalvorn, dripping in diamonds, her children honored with royal titles, but that future faded away. After she'd taken the crown herself the night Jedrick died, my dreams merged, and I persuaded her to bring me to Ellova.

I just wanted, *needed*, to be beside her.

Whether that was on a bejeweled throne or in her tiny forest cottage with her fox at our feet, it didn't matter so long as we were together. The brighter she got in my world, what I used to want hardly seemed to matter anymore.

A vision of us as king and queen is so easy to conjure.

Matching thrones, side by side. Equals in power. A glittering crown she has chosen to wear, created by her own hands, rather than forced upon her by panicked necessity.

Allies with Ellova forever.

But do I want to be king because it's what I actually desire, or have I simply held on to the duty for so long that I never allowed myself to see another path? Callen has been caring for Kalvorn for decades. My country doesn't *need* me to be king, and my mother is no longer around to put her expectations upon us. My future with Izadella is as vast and open as the sea, and I could live centuries of bliss with her by my side. No crown or kingdom needed.

My Zemra was never meant for the pressures and demands of court, or the burdensome decisions of power. Izadella cherishes her quiet home and her craft, and she deserves the softest of lives. I wanted to give her comfort, space for her creativity, time for her friendships and family with afternoon teas in gardens, and late mornings in bed with me, her lush thighs wrapped around my head.

That is the only crown I'll ever need.

Ruling would never make her happy and I would be a poor Zemra if I let a duty I never questioned dictate our future. Her happiness is all I crave. I surrendered what my family had demanded of me, the compulsion to be king crumbling beneath my desire for an unburdened life with her.

I chose her.

Izadella must take my silence as a yes, and her disappointment spreads like an ink stain in our bond. She tries to shove the feeling away, adding a strained smile, but as her soulbonded, she cannot hide anymore.

"I wish to be with you," I say softly, tucking a fallen lock of hair behind her ear. "Nothing is more important to me."

"I did not ask you if you wanted to be with me. You *have* me. There is no going back on that." She lets out a little laugh. "Bonded forever and all. I have little interest in ruling. It's a far cry from the life I envisioned for us if we ever found a way to be together as a jewelry maker and a healer, but you would make a *great* king to Kalvorn. You were willing to give up everything for me. I can make swords and jewelry while you make decisions and laws. Ellova is my home, but it will always be here for me. I asked if you wanted to be king, and you promised you would never lie to me again."

Honesty is what I vowed to always give her.

"Once there was a time when all I wanted was to prove to my kingdom I was a king worth waiting for, even if they didn't know I was missing, but no, I do not want to be king. Callen is the ruler

Kalvorn needs, and he has been for a long time. You would be an extraordinary queen, but I would never put that burden upon you. You and I can be royal emissaries, but I only want to be your Zemra."

She lets out a noise that is pure delight, making me laugh. It's the most beautiful sound in the world. I pick her up, spinning her round and round, her hair twirling around us.

"Oh, Ellova's grave, thank you!" Our bond shines so brightly within us. Her trust and love for me, her willingness to give me such a gift, are more than I could have ever asked for. Her fingers comb in my hair and I close my eyes to the loving touch.

"Now let's go back to our rooms," she says with lust in her voice and desire in her eyes. "You can be king of our bedroom, and I can thank you under the covers."

CHAPTER 50

IZADELLA

After a three-day celebration, it is time to return to Adreania to visit with Queen Lyrora and discuss the union between our realms.

Early-morning sunbeams streak through the Merawood Forest. The flowers that pepper the lush ground bloom brightly in Nueena's presence and sweeten the air. Farren chases the rising and falling flora, hopping around us. Lula flies above us.

Nueena, Tavien, and Cyanna ride in front of us to Adreania. Leon holds Onyx's reins; his arms wrapped around me. Even with my family here and the honeyguards surrounding us, there is a pit at the bottom of my stomach at the thought of stepping foot there again. Despite Grayden's and Everett's deaths, my short time in that kingdom left wounds on my soul.

Leon sends a wave of loving concern down our bond, and he protectively pulls me a little closer. "We can turn around if you are not ready to return," he whispers in my ear, his lips so close I shiver and wish we were alone.

I shake my head. No, I will not allow myself to live in fear of a place that only holds the dark memories when new ones will be made, and ancient wrongs will be righted.

"I'll be all right." The sweet birdsong around us and Onyx's soft movements lure me to close my eyes, resting my head against Leon's shoulder as we make our journey. "So many nights I rode this path thinking of you, and here we are, Zemras."

"Hmmm," He kisses the top of my head. "My favorite word. Rest, my love."

"I wouldn't be so tired if someone had kept their hands to themselves last night," I tease him.

"Yes, you really should have. A fae needs his beauty rest."

I laugh, knowing we are each at fault. Neither of us could stop even if we wanted to; the need for new Zemras is too great. It's tempting, even now, to race to the cottage for a moment to fall apart with each other, but we have much to do in Adreania.

After a while the horses slow and Nueena gracefully descends off her horse.

We have reached the Divide.

The previously invisible line between Ellova and Adreania becomes visible in a swirl of her magic. With a wave of Nueena's hand and the swell of her power, the decaying Adreanian forest blooms to life. The darkness that had spread disappears with every step she takes, new flowers blossoming at her feet in greeting.

The sea of barren trees grows new leaves as life bursts around us.

She pushes back the darkness that creeps over the Divide, its wretched grasp on this place for so long. Bright clovers engulf the blackened soil, small buds of white flowers replacing the decay.

It's beautiful to witness the light driving out the darkness, and how much good she is doing so soon after taking power.

Once she is back on her horse, we ride, her magic renewing everything we pass. Now with no crown to steal and siphon the life force, winter no longer lingers here. Only a thriving forest remains after Nueena's touch.

Well, everything but the Airvell River. The dried bed is still empty of the healing waters, but I see her eyeing it and hope joins me. The water is behind a powerful enchantment meant to harm the mortals, but Nueena has more magic than Zarella ever had.

We make eye contact, and I nod. She lifts one shoulder to say *maybe,* but her smile is confident with a secretive twist. My wide grin makes her laugh, her crown glinting with the sunlight.

With that river, the mortals' lives would be completely changed.

Adreania's enormous black ironstone wall is a dreary sight among the rich green of the new forest. The kingdom has been sealed away for so long, the metal strips that form a grid are tarnished with a deep rust, the gate creaking loudly as it is slowly lifted, allowing us entrance to the back of the castle.

A tightness seizes my chest, a panic I could not hold back at the sight of such torment. Every painful moment rushes back to me of my time trapped in that castle.

Leon immediately reacts, his arm tightening around my waist, protectiveness surging in him. He twists Onyx's reins, turning us back towards the forest. "Nueena, we're leaving."

"No!" I say, my voice shaking as I take back the reins. "I will be all right."

Tendrils of Leon's displeasure at my insistence flicker within me, but I need to do this.

"Strawberries, if you are not ready to return, I'm taking you to our cottage."

Nueena rides to my side. "It's all right if you need more time before stepping foot in there."

Both of them stare at me with the same expression of concern and I take a deep breath. "I wish to be part of this meeting. I will not let the atrocities of vile men haunt me forever. I know it's only been a few days since I was trapped here, but they have ruined enough. I will not allow them to hold me back." At my direction, Onyx turns to the castle again, and I rub his neck lovingly.

They both nod and we head towards the castle.

Leon's pride overshadows my fear, wrapping me with the warmth of his love, and I know it will be all right.

Henrik, Lyrora's handsome guard, greets us all before facing me. "We are happy to have you back under much better circumstances, Princess Izadella."

Oh, right.

Callen and Lyrora must have already been in contact.

I suppose that is what I am but it's strange to hear.

Nueena giggles as if she can read my mind, giving me a teasing bow of her head that makes me roll my eyes as we dismount our horses. We follow Henrik inside so he can escort us to his queen.

Is it terribly impolite to ask him if anything will change between them now that she is in control? They were so tender and sweet; surely, they could be together now.

After a lifetime under her brother's cruelty, she deserves it.

The servants are smiling. Curtains are all drawn open, letting in the sunshine. Those horrible paintings of the royal family of Adreania are gone but new art has replaced them; all evidence of wicked families has been erased.

The new lightness to the castle calms me.

Someone has replaced all the gray-and-black Fasaile banners. Now white-and-blue ones hang with a new crest that shines brightly, embroidered with silver thread, of a castle with open doors, threaded stars around it.

CHAPTER 51

IZADELLA

She waits for us at a round table set for tea in a large library.

I should give a polite curtsy worthy of a royal, but I am overwhelmed with gratitude for her, so instead I hug her. If she hadn't sought out Leon, I would still be married and mistreated 'til death granted me an escape.

Leon is next to hug her. "It was a pleasure to murder your brother." He says with a sly smile.

She bursts out laughing. "It's by far the best gift you have ever given to me."

I introduce Nueena and Tavien to her. While they have seen each other, Cyanna and Lyrora officially meet.

"Thank you for coming," Lyrora says to us all as we take our seats. "I hope to have a great relationship with Ellova and Kalvorn. I know mortals and fae have had a great many conflicts in the past. It may take some time for my people to get used to the knowledge that the fae truly exists, but I would like us to be allies."

"That is what I desire as well," Nueena says. "Della said she was able to assist in some of your crops returning. I would like to offer further aid. Whatever you need 'til your kingdom is stable again."

"Kalvorn as well. My brother has ships on their way to you now." Leon adds.

Lyrora's shoulders sink in relief. "Thank you. Adreania is truly in disarray. Only a few guards returned to tell the tale of what happened in the woods. Once Grayden's body was retrieved, did his counsel concede. Thankfully, most of my citizens have given me their full support, but Grayden has many supporters who wish to challenge my birthright since I am a woman. There are whispers that the counsel wishes to seize control of the throne at my first misstep."

Nueena's answering smile is devious. "Well, we will have to teach them to keep their mouths shut on such matters. Let them know the support and friendship of both Ellova and Kalvorn is only offered to *you*. Those who threaten your rule will learn to understand that."

They share a smile, and I know a beautiful friendship has just begun.

Farren, who surprisingly followed us throughout our entire journey, hops onto Lyrora's lap, which delights her. She feeds him a few pieces of cured meat before he curls into a ball against her.

She wears the elegant sapphire tiara I made for her the night Leon and I met in the forest.

"May I make you a new crown while I am here?" I ask. "The one you wear now is beautiful for a princess, but you need a crown fitting of a queen." I hope she does not take offence.

Her eyes light up. "Oh yes, I would like that very much."

A honeyguard hands me the small wooden crate I brought. I unpack silver and gold bars, and open velvet pouches with gems and pearls.

"Gold or silver?"

She leans forward. "Silver, please."

The silver bar swirls in my hand into a circle and Lyrora lets out a little gasp, which amuses me.

"What would you like on it?"

"Stars," she says quickly.

I smile at that, touching the metal, my powers rushing forward, joyful about being used again. The wondrous sensation fills me with warmth as the silver spins around my fingertips. Soft points rise up around the whole crown with stars forming around them, smaller ones decorating the base. At my touch, every gem is placed in the center of each one, diamonds and light sapphires to match her blue-gray eyes.

It shines beautifully, and I walk over, presenting it to her. She takes it, awestruck, thanking me. A servant comes to take her tiara and Lyrora places her new crown on her head.

A perfect fit.

Now she looks like a true queen.

We dine together, happily enjoying the drinks and food.

Beggars' Row was condemned and all who remained were given new housing arrangements. Cyanna asks that the orphanage be relocated to the castle, an idea Lyrora loves, and plans are arranged to bring back all the children from Kalvorn.

Nueena shares the wisdom she has learned from four generations of rulers while Adreania's new queen listens intently.

Someone clears their throat, and we all turn to the source of the sound.

A terrified servant woman stands at the door, looking between all of us and then at Leon. "Excuse my interruption, but may I speak to Healer Leon? P-please."

CHAPTER 52

IZADELLA

*L*eon sets down his napkin, stands, and turns to me. "I believe my medical assistance is needed. Would you like to join me?" He offers me his hand, which I swiftly take, not willing to leave my Zemra's side while in this place.

"Thank you," the woman whispers as we approach.

"How can I help, Calliope?"

"My brother was in a stable accident two days ago. When we heard you returned, my family brought him to your workroom in hopes you may be able to help." She has tears in her eyes. Her gaze darts back and forth between his face and newly exposed fae ears.

Leon places a comforting hand on her shoulders. "Of course."

He leads me down long hallways, greeting every servant by name. Although some seem confused about his change in appearance, they are all genuinely happy to see him.

"I'm the only healer the castle had that never required any coin. Any ailments were secretly taken care of while Jedrick didn't need me. I had to find unique ways to heal and hide my magic," he tells me as we walk into what appears to be a large closet.

Water drips into a bucket on the floor from the ceiling, a few brooms in one corner, the metal door covered in rust. A long table is in the middle of the room, and a man lies on it, his face pale with pain.

This should have never been used as a healing room.

Leon must see the disbelief on my face. "It was the only option that would not arouse suspicion and was far away from the royal family or their guards so none of the servants would be spotted. I was only allowed to attend to Jedrick," he tells me before turning to the man, who explains what happened to him. A horse spooked in the stables, trampling him and breaking his leg.

I peruse the room while Leon talks with his patient. His desk is built into the stone on one side. Shelves line the wall above it, filled with glass vials and unique bottles of every color. Delicate labels mark their uses, but Leon does not need them anymore.

"The courtiers' doctor set the bone, but he charged three weeks of wages for it, and we do not think it was done properly," Calliope says, her brother nodding with a grimace.

Leon carefully unwraps the linen bandages, revealing wooden splints used to immobilize the leg. The man grips the side of the table. His leg is red and swollen, bone still pressing against the skin.

My stomach rolls with nausea. How could a healer be so incompetent?

"This will only hurt for a moment," Leon says, placing his hand on the injured leg.

The man finally takes notice of Leon's pointed ears and whispers, "Fae?" before trying to inch away from Leon.

It's too late for any escape out of misplaced fear. Leon's hand glows, magic seeping into the fracture. The bruising fades away, the bone righting itself, until the leg is healthy again, free of any evidence of ailment.

Calliope and her brother stare at Leon with open mouths.

"Stretch your leg out for me."

He slowly does as Leon asks, moving off the table to gently test out his leg on the stone floor. "It's…healed," he says, amazed. "Thank you. Thank you!"

"You are welcome. I will speak to Queen Lyrora about that healer. He will be removed from the castle immediately."

Calliope wipes away her tears, and they leave, repeating their gratitude as they go.

Leon's happiness at being able to freely use his magic is intoxicating, so much so I push him up against the stone wall, my greedy lips on his. His hands cup my face and our kiss is passionate. Leon's kindness and care for others is such a beautiful gift to witness.

My hands slide up his shirt, needy for him, but a knock on the door draws us away from each other.

Leon leans out the door, and his eyes widen.

I peer around him to find a line of people outside.

At the front, an elderly woman rubs her hands together. The joints of her fingers are swollen, and some are at odd angles. A pregnant woman stands in front of a man who throws up in a bucket next to another servant trying to clean honey off his hands, covered in bee stings. At least twenty people wait at the door, with more walking towards us.

Leon turns around to me. "This may take a while. I've been away for weeks, but I can finally use the extent of my magic now. Before, it would have been too suspicious if every illness was suddenly cured after they saw me. I had to use creams, tonics, and elixirs for the pain. Would you rather return to Nueena? I can escort you."

"And miss watching you care for these people? Never."

My sweet, caring Zemra, so eager to help.

His answering grin is wide with pride in his ability to finally use his powers to their full extent, and he ushers in the first woman.

Her voice is quiet and cracks when she speaks. "I'm so thankful you have returned." She holds up a small tin with a shaking hand. "Could you spare any salve?"

Leon's handsome face is lit with happiness. "Oh, I can do much more than that. May I see your hands?"

She is so small compared to him that his glowing hands engulf hers. Her face shifts from confusion and fear to awe as her fingers shift back into place, the swelling fading. It's beautiful to see how ecstatic she is, turning her hands over in amazement. "Thank you," she croaks before squeezing his waist in gratitude.

Leon gently pats her back and sends her on her way as she shows everyone in line her healing.

He is patient and kind with everyone. A few mortals fled when they found out who he is, believing the myths and stories on how evil the fae are, but most seem only to care that their diseases and ailments are gone, no matter the method.

We are gone so long, eventually Nueena and Tavien find us.

Nueena watches the last patient walk away. "Well done, Leon. I will gather with Lyrora every few weeks to discuss Adreania's progress. I hope you'll join us for those meetings."

"We would love that."

The five of us together for tea, forging our alliances.

Nueena links arms with me. "Wonderful! For now, though, it's time to return to Ellova. We have a river to see."

The sun is setting by the time we return to Ellova.

I expect Nueena to lead us back to the busy throne room to discuss our plans with Nyvenah, but she takes us up the steps to the palace's tree portals, ushering us inside.

The portal magic spins quickly only to stop again, and we step out onto a platform that bears the stone crest of the dam that alters the flow of the Airvell River.

Twin flames of hope light within me and Leon.

Nueena steps up the dam's crest, her magic swirling around her, power rising. "The crown has caused so much pain, for fae and mortals alike. Let us right that tonight," she says before a blast of magic radiates from her, the ground beneath us rumbles.

Elation quickly turns to confusion when someone steps out of one of the portals. Lightning flashes, the bolts striking down. Nueena, Tavien, and Leon all collapse to the stone floor when it hits them.

The fourth bolt misses me, but the electric strike that hit Leon lashes through me as if I was struck, and I stumble backward. A metallic taste coats my tongue and the bond itself feels charred, as whatever the lightning did has harmed Leon.

No, no, no.

Their crumpled bodies on the floor suffocate me in fear. Leon's bond is still within me, but I cannot tell if Nueena's and Tavien's chests rise and fall with life. I have to believe that if Leon is alive, they are too. I nearly faint with fear, but anger burns so much brighter within me.

If she has killed them…

Camarra's cloudkeeper magic sends dark storm clouds swirling in the sky to descend upon us, rain pouring down. She stalks towards me, her clothing torn, her dark blonde hair in tangles. Lightning strikes behind me, illuminating the wrath on her face. The floor cracks beneath me.

"WHERE IS MY SON?"

Her precious son took me to Adreania and handed me to a monster.

"He's *dead* and it is a gift to all of us! He murdered his own best friend! You knew of all his wicked plans, and you let him take me to Adreania to die. I heard you tell him not to get caught. You are as evil as he was."

She snarls at me, dark circles under her eyes, backing me towards a corner. "He could have controlled the crown! It was sucking the life from our fields. I did what needed to be done! Ellova would soon starve if someone didn't stop the crown. He would have made a great king!"

Her face contorts into rage and grief. Tears stream down her face. She waves her hand, and a bolt of lightning strikes me with a great boom.

Pure pain pulses in my bones like they're filled with molten fire. The force of the strike steals the breath from my lungs, knocking me into a wall. The magic I share with Leon shoots into me, healing and soothing.

Her hand lashes out, wrapping around my throat. I gasp for air as she lifts me off the floor.

Lightning flashes again, the light of it glinting off her necklace. I grab on to her wrist and the bracelets she has there. She narrows her eyes in anger, recognizing what I'm about to do. My jewelsmith magic erupts within me, slamming into her jewelry. She tries to let me go but I hold on. Her bracelets melt instantly and shoot up her arms just as fast as her lightning, swirling around her neck, nearly choking her.

She coughs and gasps for air. Her nails claw at the metal as it tightens and twists like a coiled snake, forcing her to drop to her knees.

"Your son did wear the crown." Camarra's eyes grow hopeful until I finish my sentence. "And the crown found him so unworthy it killed him the very moment he put it on. He was nothing but a pile of leaves at Nueena's feet."

"That's. Not. True!" She gasps out each word through her tears.

I stand over her. "It *is* true. We did not kill him. His own false belief he could control such powerful magic did. He thought he deserved it simply because he wanted it. Everett was never meant to rule *anything*. Now you will be the *only one* that mourns him."

She collapses to the ground, clawing at the stone floor, desperate for air but she doesn't get to die today. Being reunited with her son would be too good for her.

Camarra deserves to sit in a dungeon with only the memories of her son and the knowledge she betrayed her court for nothing.

I reach out and touch the gold still tightly wound around her, loosening it just enough to keep her alive. She sobs, taking in huge gulps of air.

A shaking Leon is the first to stand, pressing a hand to his chest. His entire body glows for a moment.

"Nueena!" I scream at him. He rushes to Nueena's side, the light in him fading. When he reaches her, he gently places his luminous touch on her shoulder, and I hold my breath.

Her eyes flash open, and oh, she is irate.

Leon quickly removes his hand. "You were struck by lightning. Give my magic a moment to heal any damage before handling Camarra. I'm going to help Tav now."

She nods. Her bottom lip wobbles and she reaches for Tavien, her eyes focusing on her Zemra's unconscious form nearby.

Leon slaps his hand into Tavien's chest, his back lifting off the floor as the healing magic wakes him up.

Rage floods me. Camarra just tried to kill me. Tried to kill all of us! After all Leon and I have gone through, how hard we have fought for our forever, and she tried to take that from me. What it would have done to Leon if she had succeeded in her revenge, if she had killed me with the bond so fresh.

Fuck her and her son.

A furious Nueena appears at my side, and her magic encircles Camarra like a rope, painfully tying her arms down. Leon pulls me back against his chest, enveloping me in his arms. His breaths coming in fast succession, hands digging into me, pulling me tighter to him. The distress in our bond overwhelms me, just as strong as my relief that we are all okay.

Nueena raises her hands, and red sparks rise high in the air. The light explodes, letting any honeyguards in the area know they are needed immediately.

Tavien steps up, glaring at Camarra. His protective flames become a sheer blue sphere.

"Della, are you all right?" Nueena calls over her shoulder.

"Yes. Pretty tired of this family trying to kill me, though."

"It won't happen again," Nueena says with a hiss, shoving at Camarra's shoulder with one boot. She rolls over, glaring up at Nueena with all the hate she has in her heart.

Unphased by Camarra's expression, Nueena smiles back, but her eyes are full of dark promises. "You will spend every last moment of your miserable life rotting in the same conditions your son gleefully put Della in. You will have centuries to relive your and your family's transgressions over and over again and I hope it eats you alive. It won't kill you, though. No. You see—" She points to Leon. "—we have a healer who can bring back the dead. So not even death will greet you and free you from your crimes." She stands. "May time haunt you forever."

Camarra glares at Nueena but more sobs follow once more.

Guards race up the stairs to assess the commotion, shocked to find their Realm Keeper has arrested the missing Guardian. Two of them roughly drag Camarra away after hearing she attempted to murder their new ruler.

"I will speak to the Court of Green leaders tomorrow. Now that their Guardian will need to stand trial, they will have to elect someone new."

The fight has left me, and I lean against Leon, shaking.

With Camarra caught, can we finally have some rest? This must be the end to all the pain; after this, the nightmare is over. Time for Leon and me to finally have some quiet time together. For Nueena to have a peaceful rule.

"Let's send this river to Adreania and have dinner in our chambers," Nueena says, walking back to the edge of the reservoir. "And then we will plan a visit to the Court of Shells. I think we could all do with some rest."

Tavien, Leon, and I agree, stepping up to the edge to witness what she is about to achieve.

Hope surges that Nueena can truly break the dam's enchantments, free the Airvell River, and send that lifesaving water to Adreania. All the mortals will know that it is a gift to Lyrora.

An alliance between the fae and mortals.

Who could threaten her reign when the river they have desperately needed is theirs once again, thanks to her?

As if Nueena can hear my thoughts, she says, "My mother never had enough power to break Zarella's protective wards around the river, though I'm sure she would have if she could. My magic alone wasn't strong enough either, but with the crown's magic, I can give Adreania a fresh start. The mortals can rebuild, and this will give them the best chance at that."

Livestock will be stronger, and crops will flourish. Now that they have a competent and compassionate queen, their needs met, and allies, Adreania will be a thriving kingdom once more.

Nueena rises above the water, her eyes glowing purple. Her magic swirls around her, so powerful I can feel it against my skin like a caress. She throws out her hands, a shock of power hitting the side of the dam. A wave of magic crushes the ancient enchantment, blinding us with light for a moment, as Zarella's punishment is broken.

If Zarella's vengeful soul still lingers here, I hope she is finally free.

A large crack appears, letting the healing river water pour through the side, the waterfall rushing downstream through the Merawood Forest. The water fills up the dusty riverbed Nueena and I spent years riding along on my journey to Adreania.

Leon pulls me close to him, and we all watch the river descend towards the mortals.

Nueena floats down next to her Zemra, taking his hand. Tavien kisses her knuckles before saying, "We will let Lyrora's adversaries know that if anything happens to her, the river will be taken back. Maybe the mortals will listen this time around."

She nods, wrapping her arms around him.

Leon turns his focus to me. His hand comes up to stroke my cheek, concern in his green eyes and in our bond. "Are you all right? The past two weeks have been unfairly difficult for you, and I fear today added another source of pain. Can I do anything for you?"

"Camarra got what she deserved and now she will face the consequences for her crimes. Attacking our Realm Keeper? She will never see the outside of a dungeon again."

Everything that has happened weighs heavily on me. I close my eyes but all I can see are my friends and Zemra on the reservoir's stone floor.

Leon presses his forehead to mine. "You were incredible, using your magic to defend yourself like that."

We stay like that for a moment, and I inhale his strong scent that makes me melt with each breath. We return to the palace and follow Nueena to the throne room, where her parents and court Guardians are dining, but Leon only grabs the wine off one of the tables, and then my hand.

"Nueena, it's been a long day, and I need some alone time with my Zemra. Enjoy your evening." He bows.

She laughs. "I will see you both later."

CHAPTER 53

IZADELLA

One month later

Sunlight streams through my cottage window.

I sit at my small vanity, my stomach fluttering with anticipation for the day. Viella pins back the last of my hair, ensuring that all of my copper curls stay out of my face for the ceremony. "Perfect," she says before the tears come flowing down again.

Oh, my sweet Viella.

Nueena, Hiliyah, and I can't help but softly laugh at our sweet friend's endearing burst of emotions for the third time this morning as they have all helped me prepare for today.

I stand up from my cushion to hug her.

"I just can't believe it, Izzy! You have a Zemra, and you are about to become a princess! I'm just so p-proud." She wails the last bit.

Lillian comes up behind us, holding out a handkerchief to her love. A knock on the door heralds the arrival of the palace attendant placed in charge of today's events. "We will be starting soon. May I ask you all to take your seats?"

My heart thunders wildly, a mix of excitement and apprehension. I just wish for today to be perfect.

Hiliyah moves towards the door but stops in front of me. "Spin."

I do, letting her assessing eye find any faults in my attire.

My gown is a creamy white, and the neckline has small round curves that remind me of a scallop's shell. My golden Zemra robes match the intricate gold detailing on the bodice. A chain of gold coins hangs down across my chest, attaching the robe. A Kalvorn tradition for good luck.

I wish for the crown I made to gather all the attention, so the only other jewelry I wear is the large teardrop-cut emerald necklace Leon had made for me.

My Zemra stone is tucked away in my pocket for the ceremony.

"Perfect," Hiliyah proclaims before following Lillian and Viella out and closing the door behind her.

"Are you nervous?" Nueena asks in a way that always draws out the truth from me. She holds my sheer veil in her hands.

"Yeah, a little. It's not every day that one has a wedding, a Zemra ceremony, and a gets crowned as a princess. I woke up a jewelry maker and will fall asleep as royalty."

Kalvornian princess. Emissary of Ellova to Adreania.

With Leon as my prince. Excitement takes flight in my chest. Leon's answering response is much more joyous, his steady presence amused by my elation.

"You will make a wonderful emissary," Nueena says with the deepest sincerity.

I laugh. "I plan on letting Leon do all the work."

"No, you won't." She sees right through me. "You spent years sneaking into a forbidden kingdom to bring food and coins to those who desperately needed it. As a Kalvornian royal, if there is a difference to be made, you will find it. You have a brother-in-law for a king who will listen to what you say."

I roll my eyes playfully. "Oh, I suppose I do have *some* ideas. What can I say? I wish every place could be just like Ellova."

I've already told Callen, Lyrora and Nueena all of my ideas. Ships can sail daily between Kalvorn and Adreania to trade goods and provide aid. We can build roads for passage through the Kalvorn Mountains to connect the peoples of Kalvorn, Adreania, and Ellova more easily. Perhaps an academy where Leon can assist in training new healers. While the people of Adreania recover and learn new skills, the artisans from the Gem Court could host more markets and introduce them to our fae wares. Maybe even a library, populated with books on fae history from the Ink Court to educate the mortals who have thought of us as myths for so long, and information about Adreania's history and former industries to educate them on their own home, as well.

Opening the Zemra temple to all fae mates from Kalvorn.

Before Leon, the end to my half-mortal life loomed and haunted, but now nothing but time is laid out before us.

An exquisitely long life with my Zemra.

We have time to make great changes and build a legacy for Leon to leave behind. After that? A whole world out there I will explore with him by my side.

I turn so Nueena can tuck the comb of my veil into my hair, flowing loosely behind me.

We loop our arms together to leave and she adds, "Your possessions may have been moved here but a place for you will always be in the palace."

"I know," I say, leaning my head against her shoulder.

We have lived together for so long, it's been strange not having her near, even if we have met for tea every day since I left and dined together twice.

Leon and Tavien are on the other side of the cottage door, waiting for us. My Zemra lets out a gasp, his eyes roaming all over me. He opens his mouth to speak and nothing comes out, but the bond bursts with affection and awe. His Zemra stone glows faintly, greeting mine from his robe's pocket.

Tavien slaps him on the back and offers his hand to Nu. "Let's give them a moment." Nueena slips her arm from mine and joins Tavien as they head to the garden. Leon's attire matches mine, the same chain of coins across his chest. His eyes shine with emotions I can feel pulsing through me.

In a shaking voice he says, "You are so beautiful."

My sweet Zemra. I step up, enveloped by his love, his arms

pulling me near. "Everything changes after today," I whisper into his chest, and I can feel him shake his head.

"Our titles may have changed, Princess, but you are every bit the wonder that captivated me. I am still the same male hopelessly in love with you, desperate to have you forever."

The garden is full of our loved ones waiting on us, but I just need a few more moments of this. When it still feels like we are just a healer and a jewelsmith.

Two liars in love.

His lips brush the top of my head, a reminder that a crown will be placed there soon. One completely void of magic, thank Ellova.

"We should go." I whisper.

Leon squeezes me tighter for a moment before he eases me away from him.

He runs his finger down the veil's trim, swallowing hard. "I know veils are not a fae tradition, but I spent so many nights imagining us married when you were mortal. Sliding a ring onto your finger as you vowed to be mine and I just—" He clears his throat. "Thank you for wearing this." Endless gratitude for us, for this day, lighting him up from the inside.

"Of course, my love."

"I have one last request. I know we have our Zemra stones, how powerful they are, and what they mean to us, but in a Kalvornian wedding ceremony, the groom would present the bride with gold, as a symbol he could take care of her..." Leon pulls out a golden nugget from his pocket. "Will you do me the honor of making us matching rings?" he asks sheepishly.

My heart sings and I happily complete his request. The gold melts in my palm and reforms itself. Each ring is made up of two bands that twirl together to symbolize our union.

He gently slips it over my left ring finger before bringing my hands up to his lips, pressing a kiss to each fingertip with such tenderness I could cry.

When he is done, I slide his ring on his finger, standing on my toes to seal this moment with a kiss.

"Ready?" he asks, eyes still half-closed.

"With you? I'm ready for anything."

We slowly walk hand in hand to the side of the cottage, where a new life awaits.

Nyvenah stands with a bouncing Kaylena, who holds a basket of soft pink rose petals, a few falling out with her excitement.

"You are a vision," Nyvenah says, kissing my cheek.

"Is it time?" Kaylena asks, hugging my legs. "Can I go?"

We laugh. "One moment. Let your mother take her seat first. Once you reach the end, Vaylin is waiting for you."

Nyvenah hugs me. "Your parents would be so proud of you."

I can only nod. Today holds so much joy, but it is not without the lingering pain of losing them.

She walks away, music floating around the forest. Vaylin and Alachite sit in the front row with Lillian, Hiliyah, Viella, and Cyanna.

Leon and I head down the stone walkway, letting Kaylena begin the evening's festivities. The musicians see our approach and change their tunes.

Everyone rises.

Our friends and family are seated in rows of wooden benches with soft pink pillows. Wisteria chandeliers dangle above them. Crystal lights are strung in every direction off tree branches; paired with the golden sunrays of late afternoon, the forest is illuminated.

At the end of each row is a large vase filled with pink and green blooms. A massive floral archway waits for us at the end.

Nervousness spikes as so many eyes fall on me, but Leon's bond is quick to quiet the fear. He holds my hand out to walk. Kaylena adorably throws the flower petals high in the air as she cascades down the aisle before us.

King Callen stands under the archway with two pedestals beside him. Deep green velvet cushions hold two identical crowns of gold leaves and emeralds, and a base of diamonds and peridot I made late last night in bed with Leon.

Across the aisle is Callen's family, sitting with a softly smiling Dowager Queen Erenia and Queen Lyrora. Henrik is dressed in fine clothing, free of his usual uniform. His hand entwines sweetly with Lyrora's.

Theodore and Clive are there too, richer than their wildest dreams now. When Leon found out they led the rebels into the castle to stop my wedding, a trove of treasures, and titles to land in Kalvorn was given to them.

Leon and I reach his brother, facing our friends and family. A public feast and celebration of our union will take place tomorrow for anyone in Kalvorn who wishes to attend, but Zemra ceremonies are an intimate event, and it was my one request to maintain that closeness today.

Callen loudly proclaims, "Thank you for coming to such a unique event to honor my brother and his Zemra, Izadella." He picks up the crown next to me and places it on my head. "I now crown Izadella Aranelle, daughter of Ambra and Nolan Aranelle, princess of Kalvorn." He turns to his brother. "Prince Leon-Zilas, son of Orion and Cordelia, here is your crown."

The look of pride on both brothers' faces spreads a smile on my face.

Callen places Leon's crown on his head. "Thank you for your sacrifices for our kingdom. Do you, Leon, take Izadella as your bride, princess, and Zemra?"

"I do."

My heart soars.

My new brother turns to me. "Do you take Leon to be your husband, prince, and Zemra?

"I do."

Love for me bursts through the bond.

Callen steps forward with two strands of soft leather cords. "Izadella, please present your Zemra stone to your soulbonded."

I pull out my precious stone wrapped in gold with an opening at the top and hold it up to Leon. He takes one of the cords and threads it through the hoop. I turn, lifting my hair so it's not in his way. His warm fingers brush my neck as he ties it, so my stone hangs over my chest.

Leon takes my hand, lifting it up to spin me towards him. I'm giddy as I take the final cord and he holds up his own stone so I can gently attach the leather. Leon bends down on one knee, making my heart skip several beats.

The sight of him on his knees before me sends lava into my veins and has me wishing we could skip our celebration feast entirely.

I tie the leather and gently place the necklace around his neck. He stands and we both hold our stones together. Bright green light flashes and the crowd lets out a thunderous cheer.

Zemras.

He pulls me close to spin and then dips me low. I grab my crown so it doesn't fall, laughing with pure delight.

"I love you, Izadella of the forge," he whispers just for me.

"I love you, too, Leon. My mate, my Zemra."

Leon kisses me with such passion, a promise of forever.

Our Zemra stones glow, but it is nothing compared to the luminous love within us. That union of our souls sings within us at our closeness, a melody of devotion I'm grateful to hear forever.

The end!

EPILOGUE

LEON

My last patient for the day heads down the stone path towards the cluster of tree portals that will take him home to Adreania, his broken arm healed. The cheerful night healers arrive to take over my duties for the evening, wishing me farewell.

I'm desperate to see Izadella after a long day of healing and teaching, and my need to be near my Zemra hums in my veins as the door shuts behind me. Her happiness at using her jewelsmith powers on whatever she is creating shimmers in the bond and it always pleases me.

The Healer's Hall Izadella and I had built stands near our cottage, surrounded by the tall trees of the Merawood Forest, alive with magic once more. It houses multiple birthing centers, healing chambers, kitchens, and lesson rooms for the medical academy I teach at. By the entrance the tree portals that connect to Ellova, Adreania, and Kalvorn are open, ready to receive patients.

It has become a sanctuary for fae and mortals alike for whatever medical need they may have.

The cottage has been expanded, giving my Zemra and me more space, growing to a sturdy three-story home. Nueena and Tavien even have their own room there.

We still spend many nights in Ellova and Kalvorn, but our home here among the trees is our favorite.

Farren watches me from a nearby bush and joins me on my walk to find Izadella. I pause and he brushes against my leg affectionately before we continue. He has a little more gray in his dark fur than when I met him, but my healing magic is keeping the feisty little fox with us as long as possible.

The door to the forge is open for my sake; when she keeps it shut all day, it's unbearably hot, and I'm always fascinated seeing her work. I could watch her for hours.

This was the place I lost her, the same place where I fought death to keep her.

Nothing can separate her from me now.

Farren picks up speed, dashing into the workshop. Izadella's delighted voice rings out and it sends warmth washing down my spine. I lean against the doorframe, watching the love of my life pick up her beloved pet and pepper his forehead with kisses. The jewelry she has created today is laid out on her workspace. Her desk is pushed up against the forge, the flames glinting off the precious metals she has scattered about.

She glances up at me, and she still steals the breath from my lungs after being away from her for most of the day.

She wears a loose, sleeveless yellow dress that brushes the tops of her thighs when she stands. The deep vee teases me with the swell of her breasts, just begging me to pull down the fabric for a taste.

"Hello," she says in the honeyed tone that lets me know she has missed me as much as I've missed her, our lust building in the bond.

"Strawberries."

Her smile widens, eyes heating. It may have been over a century since she became my beloved Zemra, but every day still feels new.

Farren struggles, demanding to be put down, and she gently places him on the floor. He runs out, probably spotting a firefly to chase, leaving her arms open for me.

Where I will always belong.

The fading light of the setting sun paints her front in golden hues. Behind her, the forge's flames roars. Its cerulean light haloes her, highlighting all the curves I've memorized. Skin I've kissed for countless hours during endless moonlit nights.

My own personal goddess.

Her warm hands have spent today commanding copper and guiding gold, but now she draws me to her. I step into her embrace and wrap my arms around her waist. Her hands ascend up the fabric on my chest, cupping my face with a happy sigh.

Our bond is filled with the contentment of reuniting, soft and serene.

My lips are on hers, gifting her with tender affection. My hips press up against her and gently push her towards her work desk. It rattles a bit from the force when her perfect ass hits it.

I need to show her all the ways I've missed her today. I haven't heard her moans of pleasure since this morning and that was far too long ago.

We break apart, just long enough for me to lift her up, gently placing her on her desk before I shower her with kiss after kiss.

"My love," I whisper into her ear before heading to her sensitive neck and suck deeply. She moans as I continue to lavish her with attention, marking her in a way that will last for days, before making my way back up her face, kissing her jaw and cheeks, anything I can get my lips on, all-consuming.

"You are wearing too much clothing, Leon," she sighs, hot on my skin.

"Well, we can't have that, now can we?" I say with a deep laugh.

I begin to unbutton my vest. I can feel her impatience in the bond. When I stumble on a button, too eager to get it off, she rips the fabric apart, buttons flying around us.

How greedy we are for each other.

"Arms up," I say and she obeys, letting me pull off the dress that separates us, tossing it to the stone floor.

I reach behind her to shove some of the jewelry to the side, clearing the space and gingerly help her to lie down on the desk. It's too short, so the top of her descends into the forge, glowing embers dancing beneath her. She looks up at me through the blue flames that kiss her skin as I do, swirling around her, lying among piles of gemstones and golden necklaces, looking like the fiery queen she will always be to me.

Our bond is pulsating with affection. I adore these moments with her, bare and ready for me.

I lean down to take one breast in my mouth, the other cupped in my palm, teasing each nipple with my tongue and fingers.

The heat of the forge is blistering, the fire scorching my skin, but my magic rushes to heal any burns.

Every lick and suck is worth it.

Through the bond I can sense the pressure of my body above her is a balm to her soul, making her feel feverish.

I reach down between us, finding her wet and wanting. I swirl my finger around her clit a few times before sliding two fingers into her, pumping slowly, captivated by her.

Her desire is burning between us and she will not be sated by a few leisurely touches.

My cock throbs, still retrained by my pants as I kiss down her stomach, hands grabbing her waist. I drag her ass to the edge of the desk and kneel before her.

She giggles, her legs open for me, and she places each one on my shoulders, wiggling her hips to taunt me with her taste.

This is exactly where I want her, open and desperate before me.

Fluttering my lips over her skin, I am slow to explore. My pleasure at her own rises with her panting begs as I playfully kiss the inside of her thighs. I know just how badly she wants me; her lust is blinding in the bond, but I enjoy drawing out the yearning.

"Please, Leon!"

I smile into her skin at her sweet supplication and give her what she aches for.

Anything for my Zemra.

I slide two fingers through her center, revealing her to me. She is spread before me. Her back arches at the first swipe of my tongue. "Mine."

That word shoots like lightning into her and she shudders.

"Yes, all yours, forever," she whimpers. "Please, don't deny me any longer."

I'm ravenous for her pleasure, delving into her, focusing on her clit, sucking and swirling around it, fingers returning to glide into her.

She gasps and moans, and the wanton sound is music to my ears.

Her fingers tangle in my hair before she grasps my hair at the root, moving my mouth to the exact rhythm she desires. Her hips move in time with my tongue, demanding her orgasm, taking what's hers.

She breaks apart so beautifully, lips in an exquisite O, my eyes nearly rolling back inside my head at the taste of her release.

I lick my lips, not willing to waste any of her, kissing my way back up her body.

Her hands grab for my pants and I chuckle, helping her to spring my cock free. She widens her bent knees, waiting for me.

I line up our hips, seating myself between her thighs. I slide myself up and down her, hitting her overly sensitive clit, gathering some of the wetness. I stroke myself a few times before pushing my length in slowly.

We have come together like this in countless ways, but each time, I have a renewed reverence at how perfect she is for me.

It's been well over a century since we almost lost each other, and I've never taken one day for granted. Every minute with her is precious, building a gentle life she loves.

I fill her with everything I have.

Each one of my thrusts slides her a little in and out of the forge, over and over again. Embers fly up like glittering stars, the flames cascading around her with the movement.

The sight is so magnificent I can easily forget the fire licks at my skin.

It's overwhelming that I have the honor of loving her, treasuring her. That after a day of healing and service to those in need, I get to come home to her.

Her moans echo around us. We cling to each other as I pound into her, pouring my love and obsession through the bond.

I could never have asked for a more perfect Zemra.

Our bond is burning with her budding orgasm, and I will be quick to follow. Her core tightens around me while she screams my name, writhing under me.

We fall over the edge together, lost in each other's pleasure.

I slowly rise off her, helping her up, and she kisses me, long and slow, our tongues meeting in the middle before we dress and leave the forge.

The sky is clear, and the stars shine above us as we walk hand in hand back to our cottage.

We will spend the evening reading, sipping on blackberry wine, and making grand plans for the future. She and I have traveled all over every kingdom, have friends in every realm. Some nights are slow and intimate here, some are lively and vibrant at the palace.

There never seems to be enough time with her, but I'm eternally grateful for each moment.

All we need is each other, those we love, and our fox.

The gift of a long, fae life with her.

My Zemra.

ART BY: IJWID.ART

ART BY: ACETALDIGITAL

ART BY: VAMORII_

ART BY: YUKSIIIS

AFTERWORD

Thank you so much for reading Captive Queen. This duology took half a decade to write and I'm so thankful for everyone who read the first one and supported me throughout this process. I still cannot believe it's over.

I feel like this is the place to say something profound but I'm at a rare loss for words. This book series changed my life. The friends I've made, the dreams that have come true, the places I've traveled to. It all started with a vision of a woman putting on a crown while I was doing laundry in 2020, and a single blank Google Doc.

I've always been a storyteller. Whether it was with Barbies I was too old to be playing with or poorly spelled fanfiction, characters have always been loud in my head. I was so honored I got to tell Leon and Izadella's story. They mean so much to me.

It's terrifying putting one's work out into the world, but I wanted to be brave for them. I'm so fucking grateful I was. This chapter of my author career is closing—new stories to tell, new worlds to build—but I will always love my kind healer and soft jewelry maker the most.

Writing this was somehow the hardest thing I've ever done, but at the same time, it was as easy as breathing. These books have been my sanctuary, a blissful escape from reality. Ellova has been my beautiful break from the real world, and I loved sharing it with you.

ACKNOWLEDGMENTS

I need to first thank my fantastic editing team. Having a dyslexic client is no easy feat. Sierra, my personal literary guardian and late night Zoom bestie, who after a long day of writing her own fantastic novels would spend months editing this with me on Zoom as we went chapter by chapter together. Thank you for bullying me into giving you the earliest draft. Thank you for making me kill my darlings and reminding me that characters, did in fact, need some internal thoughts alongside lengthy descriptions. Thank you for repeating the answers to questions I've already asked but my gold-fish ADHD memory forgot.

For pushing me to be a better writer.

For caring about these books as if they were your own.

When the crushing tide of doubt and fear comes crashing year after year, you never let me drown. Your help and feedback is as priceless as your friendship.

Alexia, thank you for wearing so many different hats during the process and helping at every stage of this book!

Ivy, I'm eternally grateful for all the editing you did for both books. There were so many errors and mistakes, I honestly don't know how you did it. You are the absolute best!

Kelly, thank you so much for your work on both books. You are a rock star!

My wonderful beta readers:

Stephanie, I adore you and your feedback. I'm so glad we got to work together on these books.

Justine, your passion for this duology makes my heart so happy.

Thank you for all your feedback and listening to me yap for years about these books.

Kassidy, thank you so much for your time and honest feedback.

Delani, you are amazing. I'm so glad we met.

Taylor, thank you so much for your help with both books. You saw all the things when I was blinded by the romance. I'm so sorry for all the times you had to read about Leon's dick.

My fantastic PA, Ivana. Thank you so much for helping me with EVERYTHING. I would have been so behind on everything without you. You took so much off my plate so I could focus on writing and I'm so grateful.

Fallon, thank you for the countless times you reminded me I could finish this book and for all the encouragement and laughs over Zoom. Writing a book is hard (there were quite a few crying voice memos) but you were always by my side, cheering me on.

Fallon and Sierra (as a unit, my Do It Ladies). Y'all are my rock. Publishing is so fucking hard and I'm so glad we have each other.

Nicole and Chris, your friendship is cliffside champagne at sunset.

Alisha, you have truly been a ride-or-die friend. Thank you for the countless check-ins and encouragement. You have been such a pillar of support for this book. You were sunlight when I had storm clouds in my head over making this book perfect. I cannot wait to scream just as loud for you.

Alexis, you are one of the funniest people I know. It's a treasure to be your friend.

Blair, thank you for your wonderful feedback on Reyna, sign language, and insights on Deaf culture.

Sandra, for your stunning covers that brought my vision to life! I'm forever obsessed with them.

My Smutty Sunday girls. Y'all keep me sane.

All my fellow writers at *Late Night Writes*, thank you for joining me for countless hours of writing sprints over the past 5 years.

The *Bad at Books* baddies, sorry I nearly died on our writing retreat.

My Friday morning library crew, thank you for the account-
ability.

Lastly, my family who always believed in me.

Thank you to my ARC team, my readers, and everyone who has
supported this dream.

BIBLIOGRAPHY

Sienna Harlow is a neurodivergent writer and digital artist from Southern California. She loves writing about fierce friendships, heroes with hearts of gold, and whimsical world-building.

As a storyteller with dyslexia, she is eternally grateful for spell check and compassionate editors.

When she is not daydreaming about romantasy, she runs two book clubs, a weekly writing group, and enjoys sending her friends an alarming amount of TikToks and voice memos.

SOCIAL MEDIA

Find Sienna yapping all over the internet.

TikTok:@SiennaHarlowAuthor
Instagram: @SiennaHarlowAuthor
Twitter:@Sienna_Harlow
Substack: @SiennaHarlow
Patreon: SiennaHarlow